Alice

I toss the coin to him and he whips it out of the air, quick as a seagull, and slaps it onto the back of his hand, then points left, leans over, flicks the turn signal.

"Let's wait a few exits to flip it again. Not much adventure in Stony Bay."

"So it's adventure you're looking for today, Alice?"

I shrug. Tim resettles his legs again, rubs the side of one thigh, makes a face.

"Leg cramp? Navy Seal workout getting to you?"

"Pain is weakness leaving the body," Tim says solemnly. "Also nicotine. The coin says take this right."

Right, and flip left, and finally we wind up at McNair Beach, three towns away, but still a destination beach because it's a lot less rocky than the ones close by.

"Just so you know," Tim says as I park in the empty lot, "I cheated. I wanted the beach. Shame not to get that bikini wet."

He grins at me, unabashedly checking me out. I straighten, pull my shoulders back, smile sideways at him. Then freeze. I've made those moves a thousand times and can translate them, even if Tim can't. *Go ahead. Look. I want you to.* What the hell am I thinking, pulling this with him? There should be sky-writing, a billboard, a Jumbotron: *You know better.* And I do. And still.

OTHER BOOKS YOU MAY ENJOY

THE BOY MOST LIKELY TO

by Huntley Fitzpatrick

speak

SPEAK
An imprint of Penguin Random House LLC
375 Hudson Street
New York, New York 10014

First published in the United States of America by Dial Books,
an imprint of Penguin Group (USA) LLC, 2015
Published by Speak, an imprint of Penguin Random House LLC, 2016

THE LIBRARY OF CONGRESS HAS CATALOGED THE DIAL BOOKS EDITION AS FOLLOWS:
Fitzpatrick, Huntley.
The boy most likely to / Huntley Fitzpatrick.
pages cm
Summary: "When Tim and Alice begin to fall in love, Tim thinks he is finally on the right track, until the
unexpected consequences of his drug-addicted and alcoholic past throw a wrench in his new life"
—Provided by publisher.
ISBN 9780803741423 (hardcover)
[1. Love—Fiction. 2. Alcoholism—Fiction. 3. Drug abuse—Fiction.]
PZ7.F578 Bo 2015   [FIC] 2015015536

Speak ISBN 9780147513076

Printed in the United States of America

1 3 5 7 9 10 8 6 4 2

• ○ • ○

To my mother, who knew how to love. And had a weakness for troublemakers with hearts of gold.

To my father, who has always loved and admired strong women.

And to Georgia Funsten and Patricia Young, the smartest and strongest women I know.

• ○ • ○

Chapter One

TIM

I've been summoned to see the Nowhere Man.

He's at his desk when I step inside the gray cave of his office, his back turned.

"Uh, Pop?"

He holds up his hand, keeps scribbling on a blue-lined pad. Standard operating procedure.

I flick my eyes around the room: the mantel, the carpet, the bookshelves, the window; try to find a comfortable place to land.

No dice.

Ma's fond of "cute"—teddy bears in seasonal outfits and pillows with little sayings and shit she gets on QVC. They're everywhere. Except here, a room spliced out of John Grisham, all leather-bound, only muted light through the shades. August heat outdoors, but no hint of that allowed here. I face the rear of Pop's neck, hunch further into the gray, granite-hard sofa, rub my eyes, sink back on my elbows.

On his desk, three pictures of Nan, my twin, at various ages—poofy red curls, missing teeth, then baring them in braces. Always worried eyes. Two more of her on the wall, straightened hair, expensive white smile, plus a framed newspaper clipping of her after delivering a speech at this summer's Stony Bay Fourth of July thing.

No pics of me.

Were there ever? Can't remember. In the bad old days, I always got high before a father/son office visit.

Clear my throat.

Crack my knuckles.

"Pop? You asked to see me?"

He actually startles. "Tim?"

"Yep."

Swiveling the chair, he looks at me. His eyes, like Nan's and my own, are gray. Match his hair. Match his office.

"So," he says.

I wait. Try not to scope out the bottle of Macallan on the . . . what do you call it. Sidebar? Sideboard? Generally, Ma brings in the ice in the little silver bucket thing ten minutes after he gets home from work, six p.m., synched up like those weird-ass cuckoo clock people who pop out of their tiny wooden doors, dead on schedule when the clock strikes, so Pop can have the first of his two scotches ready to go.

Today must be special. It's only three o'clock and there's the bucket, oozing cool sweat like I am. Even when I was little, I knew he'd leave the second drink half-finished. So I could slurp down the last of the scotchy ice water without him knowing while he was washing his hands before dinner. Can't remember when I started doing that, but it was well before my balls dropped.

"Ma said you wanted to talk."

He brushes some invisible whatever from his knee, like his attention's already gone. "Did she say why?"

I clear my throat again. "Because I'm moving out? Planning to do that. Today." Ten minutes ago, ideally.

His eyes return to mine. "Do you think this is the best choice for you?"

Classic Nowhere Man. Moving out was hardly my choice. His ultimatum, in fact. The only "best choice" I've made lately was to stop drinking. Etc.

But Pop likes to tack and turn, and no matter that this was his order, he can shove that rudder over without even looking and make me feel like shit.

"I asked you a question, Tim."

"It's fine. It's a good idea."

Pop steeples his fingers, sets his chin on them, my chin, cleft and all. "How long has it been since you got kicked out of Ellery Prep?"

"Uh. Eight months." Early December. Hadn't even unpacked my suitcase from Thanksgiving break.

"Since then you've had how many jobs?"

Maybe he doesn't remember. I fudge it. "Um. Three."

"Seven," Pop corrects.

Damn.

"How many of those were you fired from?"

"I still have the one at—"

He pivots in his chair, halfway back to his desk, frowns down at his cell phone. "How many?"

"Well, I quit the senator's office, so really only five."

Pop twists back around, lowers the phone, studies me over his reading glasses. "I'm very clear on the fact that you left that job. You say 'only' like it's something to brag about. Fired from five out of seven jobs since February. Kicked out of three schools . . . Do you know that I've never been let go from a job in my life? Never gotten a bad performance review? A grade lower than a B? Neither has your sister."

Right. Perfect old Nano. "My grades were always good," I say. My eyes stray again to the Macallan. Need something to do with my hands. Rolling a joint would be good.

"Exactly," Pop says. He jerks from the chair, nearly as angular and almost as tall as me, drops his glasses on the desk with a clatter, runs his hands quickly through his short hair, then focuses on scooping out ice and measuring scotch.

I catch a musky, iodine-y whiff of it, and man, it smells good.

"You're not stupid, Tim. But you sure act that way."

Yo-kay . . . He's barely spoken to me all summer. *Now* he's on my nuts? But I should try. I drag my eyes off the caramel-colored liquid in his glass and back to his face.

"Pop. Dad. I know I'm not the son you would have . . . special-ordered—"

"Would you like a drink?"

He sloshes more scotch into another glass, uncharacteristically careless, sets it out on the Columbia University coaster on the side table next to the couch, slides it toward me. He tips his own glass to his lips, then places it neatly on his coaster, almost completely chugged.

Well, this is fucked up.

"Uh, look." My throat's so tight, my voice comes out weird—husky, then high-pitched. "I haven't had a drink or anything like that since the end of June, so that's, uh, fifty-nine days, but who's counting. I'm doing my best. And I'll—"

Pop is scrutinizing the fish tank against the wall.

I'm boring him.

"And I'll keep doin' it . . ." I trail off.

There's a long pause. During which I have no idea what he's thinking. Only that my best friend is on his way over, and my Jetta in the driveway is seeming more and more like a getaway car.

"Four months," Pop says in this, like, flat voice, like he's reading it off a piece of paper. Since he's turned back to look down at his desk, it's possible.

"Um . . . yes . . . What?"

"I'm giving you four months from today to pull your life together. You'll be eighteen in December. A man. After that, unless I see you acting like one—in every way—I'm cutting off your allowance, I'll no longer pay your health and car insurance, and I'll transfer your college fund into your sister's."

Not as though there was ever a welcome mat under me, but whatever the fuck was there has been yanked out and I'm slammed down hard on my ass.

Wait . . . what?

A man by December. Like, *poof, snap, shazam.* Like there's some expiration date on . . . where I am now.

"But—" I start.

He checks his Seiko, hitting a button, maybe starting the countdown. "Today is August twenty-fourth. That gives you until just before Christmas."

"But—"

He holds up his hand, like he's slapping the off button on my words. It's ultimatum number two or nothing.

No clue what to say anyway, but it doesn't matter, because the conversation is over.

We're done here.

Unfold my legs, yank myself to my feet, and I head for the door on autopilot.

Can't get out of the room fast enough.

For either of us, apparently.

Ho, ho, ho to you too, Pop.

Chapter Two

TIM

"You're really doing this?"

I'm shoving the last of my clothes into a cardboard box when my ma comes in, without knocking, because she never does. Risky as hell when you have a horny seventeen-year-old son. She hovers in the doorway, wearing a pink shirt and this denim skirt with—what are those? Crabs?—sewn all over it.

"Just following orders, Ma." I cram flip-flops into the stuffed box, push down on them hard. "Pop's wish is my command."

She takes a step back like I've slapped her. I guess it's my tone. I've been sober nearly two months, but I have yet to go cold turkey on assholicism. Ha.

"You had so much I never had, Timothy . . ."

Away we go.

". . . private school, swimming lessons, tennis camp . . ."

Yep, I'm an alcoholic high school dropout, but check out my backhand!

She shakes out the wrinkles in a blue blazer, one quick motion, flapping it into the air with an abrasive crack. "What are you going to do—keep working at that hardware store? Going to those meetings?"

She says "hardware store" like "strip club" and "going to

those meetings" like "making those sex tapes."

"It's a good job. And I need those meetings."

Ma's hands start smoothing my stack of folded clothes. Blue veins stand out on her freckled, pale arms. "I don't see what strangers can do for you that your own family can't."

I open my mouth to say: "I know you don't. That's why I need the strangers." Or: "Uncle Sean sure could have used those strangers." But we don't talk about that, or him.

I shove a pair of possibly too-small loafers in the box and go over to give her a hug.

She pats my back, quick and sharp, and pulls away.

"Cheer up, Ma. Nan'll definitely get into Columbia. Only one of your children is a fuck-up."

"Language, Tim."

"Sorry. My bad. Cock-up."

"That," she says, "is even worse."

Okeydokey. Whatever.

My bedroom door flies open—*again* no knock.

"Some girl who sounds like she has laryngitis is on the phone for you, Tim," Nan says, eyeing my packing job. "God, everything's going to be all wrinkly."

"I don't care—" But she's already dumped the cardboard box onto my bed.

"Where's your suitcase?" She starts dividing stuff into piles. "The blue plaid one with your monogram?"

"No clue."

"I'll check the basement," Ma says, looking relieved to have a reason to head for the door. "This girl, Timothy? Should I bring you the phone?"

I can't think of any girl I have a thing to say to. Except Alice Garrett. Who definitely would not be calling me.

"Tell her I'm not home."

Permanently.

Nan's folding things rapidly, piling up my shirts in order of style. I reach out to still her hands. "Forget it. Not important."

She looks up. Shit, she's crying.

We Masons cry easily. Curse of the Irish (one of 'em). I loop one elbow around her neck, thump her on the back a little too hard. She starts coughing, chokes, gives a weak laugh.

"You can come visit me, Nano. Any time you need to . . . escape . . . or whatever."

"Please. It won't be the same," Nan says, then blows her nose on the hem of my shirt.

It won't. No more staying up till nearly dawn, watching old Steve McQueen movies because I think he's badass and Nan thinks he's hot. No Twizzlers and Twix and shit appearing in my room like magic because Nan knows massive sugar infusions are the only sure cure for drug addiction.

"Lucky for you. No more covering my lame ass when I stay out all night, no more getting creative with excuses when I don't show for something, no more me bumming money off you constantly."

Now she's wiping her eyes with my shirt. I haul it off, hand it to her. "Something to remember me by."

She actually folds *that*, then stares at the neat little square, all sad-faced. "Sometimes it's like I'm missing everyone I ever met. I actually even miss Daniel. I miss Samantha."

"Daniel was a pompous prickface and a crap boyfriend.

Samantha, your actual best friend, is ten blocks and ten minutes away—shorter if you text her."

She blows that off, hunkers down, pulling knobbly knees to her chest and lowering her forehead so her hair sweeps forward to cover her blotchy face. Nan and I are both ginger, but she got all the freckles, everywhere, while mine are only across my nose. She looks up at me with that face she does, all pathetic and quivery. I hate that face. It always wins.

"You'll be fine, Nan." I tap my temple. "You're just as smart as me. Much less messed up. At least as far as most people know."

Nan twitches back. We lock eyes. The elephant in the room lies bleeding out on the floor between us. Then she looks away, gets busy picking up another T-shirt to fold expertly, like the only thing that matters in the world is for the sleeves to align.

"Not really," she says in a subdued voice. Not taking the bait there either, I guess.

I grope around the quilt on my bed, locate my cigs, light one, and take a deep drag. I know it's all kinds of bad for me, but *God*, how does anyone get through the day without smoking? Setting the smoldering butt down in the ashtray, I tap her on the back again, gently this time.

"Hey now. Don't stress. You know Pop. He wants to add it up and get a positive bottom line. Job. High school diploma. College-bound. Check, check, check. It only has to *look* good. I can pull that off."

Don't know if this is cheering my sister up, but as I talk, the squirming fireball in my stomach cools and settles. Fake it. That I can do.

Mom pops her head into the room. "That Garrett boy's here. Heavens, put on a shirt, Tim." She digs in a bureau drawer and thrusts a Camp Wyoda T-shirt I thought I'd ditched years ago at me. Nan leaps up, knuckling away her tears, pulling at her own shirt, wiping her palms on her shorts. She has a zillion twitchy habits—biting her nails, twisting her hair, tapping her pencils. I could always get by on a fake ID, a calm face, and a smile. My sister could look guilty saying her prayers. Feet on the stairs, staccato knock on the door—the one person who knocks!—and Jase comes in, swipes back his damp hair with the heel of one hand.

"Shit, man. We haven't even started loading and you're already sweating?"

"Ran here," he says, hands planted hard on his kneecaps. He glances up. "Hey, Nan."

Nan, who has turned her back, gives a quick, jerky nod. When she twists around to tumble more neatly balled socks into my cardboard box, her eyes stray to Jase, up, slowly down. He's the guy girls always look at twice.

"You ran here? It's like five miles from your house! Are you nuts?"

"Three, and nah." Jase braces his forearm against the wall, bending his leg, holding his ankle, stretching out. "Seriously out of shape after sitting around the store all summer. Even after three weeks of training camp, I'm nowhere near up to speed."

"You don't *seem* out of shape," Nan says, then shakes her head so her hair slips forward over her face. "Don't leave without telling me, Tim." She scoots out the door.

"You set?" Jase looks around the room, oblivious to my sister's hormone spike.

"Uh . . . I guess." I look around too, frickin' blank. All I can think to take is my clamshell ashtray. "The clothes, anyway. I suck at packing."

"Toothbrush?" Jase suggests mildly. "Razor. Books, maybe? Sports stuff."

"My lacrosse stick from Ellery Prep? Don't think I'll need it." I tap out another cigarette.

"Bike? Skateboard? Swim gear?" Jase glances over at me, smile flashing in the flare of my lighter.

Mom barges back in so fast, the door knocks against the wall. An umbrella and a huge yellow slicker are draped over one arm, an iron in one hand. "You'll want these. Should I pack you blankets? What happened to that nice boy you were going to move in with, anyway?"

"Didn't work out." As in: That nice boy, my AA buddy Connell, relapsed on both booze and crack, called me all slurry and screwed up, full of blurry suck-ass excuses, so he's obviously out. The garage apartment is my best option.

"Is there even any heat in that ratty place?"

"Jesus God, Ma. You haven't even seen the frickin'—"

"It's pretty reliable," Jase says, not even wincing. "It was my brother's, and Joel likes his comforts."

"All right. I'll . . . leave you two boys to—carry on." She pauses, runs her hand through her hair, showing half an inch of gray roots beneath the red. "Don't forget to take the stenciled paper Aunt Nancy sent in case you need to write thank-you notes."

"Wouldn't dream of it, Ma. Uh, forgetting, I mean."

Jase bows his head, smiling, then shoulders the cardboard box.

"What about pillows?" she says. "You can tuck those right under the other arm, can't you, a big strapping boy like you?"

Christ.

He obediently raises an elbow and she rams two pillows into his armpit.

"I'll throw all this in the Jetta. Take your time, Tim."

I scan the room one last time. Tacked to the corkboard over my desk is a sheet of paper with the words *THE BOY MOST LIKELY TO* scrawled in red marker at the top. One of the few days last fall I remember clearly—hanging with a bunch of my (loser) friends at Ellery out by the boathouse, where they stowed the kayaks (and the stoners). We came up with our antidote to those stupid yearbook lists: *Most likely to be a millionaire by twenty-five. Most likely to star in her own reality show. Most likely to get an NFL contract.* Don't know why I kept the thing.

I pop the list off the wall, fold it carefully, jam it into my back pocket.

Nan emerges as soon as Jase, who's been waiting for me in the foyer, opens the creaky front door to head out.

"Tim," she whispers, cool hand wrapping around my forearm. "Don't vanish." As if when I leave our house I'll evaporate like fog rising off the river.

Maybe I will.

By the time we pull into the Garretts' driveway, I've burned through three cigarettes, hitting up the car lighter for the next before I've chucked the last. If I could have smoked all of them at once, I would've.

"You should kick those," Jase says, looking out the window, not pinning me with some accusatory face.

I make to hurl the final butt, then stop myself.

Yeah, toss it next to little Patsy's Cozy Coupe and four-year-old George's midget baby-blue bike with training wheels. Plus, George thinks I've quit.

"Can't," I tell him. "Tried. Besides, I've already given up drinking, drugs, and sex. Gotta have a few vices or I'd be too perfect."

Jase snorts. "Sex? Don't think you have to give *that* up." He opens the passenger-side door, starts to slide out.

"The way I did it, I do. Gotta stop messing with any chick with a pulse."

Now *Jase* looks uncomfortable. "That was an addiction too?" he asks, half in, half out the door, nudging the pile of old newspapers on the passenger side with the toe of one Converse.

"Not in the sense that I, like, had to have it, or whatever. It was just . . another way to blow stuff off. Numb out."

He nods like he gets it, but I'm pretty sure he doesn't. Gotta explain. "I'd get wasted at parties. Hook up with girls I didn't like or even know. It was never all that great."

"Guess not"—he slides out completely—"if you're with someone you don't even like or know. Might be different if you were sober and actually cared."

"Yeah, well." I light up one last cigarette. "Don't hold your breath."

Chapter Three

ALICE

"There is," I say through my teeth, "an owl in the freezer. Can any of you guys explain this to me?"

Three of my younger brothers stare back at me. Blank walls. My younger sister doesn't look up from texting.

I repeat the question.

"Harry put it there," Duff says.

"Duff told me to," Harry says.

George, my youngest brother, cranes his neck. "What kind of owl? Is it dead? Is it white like Hedwig?"

I poke at the rock-solid owl, which is wrapped in a frosty freezer bag. "Very dead. Not white. And someone ate all the frozen waffles and put the box back in empty again."

They all shrug, as if this is as much of an unsolvable mystery as the owl.

"Let's try again. *Why* is this owl in the freezer?"

"Harry's going to bring it in for show-and-tell when school starts," Duff says.

"Sanjay Sapati brought in a seal skull last year. This is way better. You can still see its eyeballs. They're only a little rotted." Harry stirs his oatmeal, frowning down at what I've tried to pass off as a fun "breakfast for lunch" occasion. He upturns the spoon, shakes it, but the glob of oatmeal sticks, thick as paste, stubborn as my brother. Harry holds the spoon out toward me, accusingly.

"You get what you get and you don't get upset," I say to him.

"But I do. I do get upset. This is nasty, Alice."

"Just eat it," I say, clinging to patience with all my fingernails. This is all temporary. Just until Dad gets a bit better, until Mom doesn't have to be in three places at once. "It's healthy," I add, but I have to agree with my seven-year-old brother. We're way overdue for a grocery run. The fridge has nothing but eggs, applesauce, and ketchup, the cabinet is bare of anything but Joel's protein-enhanced oatmeal. And the only thing in the freezer is . . . a dead bird.

"We can't have an owl in here, guys." I scramble for Mom's reasonable tone. "It'll make the ice cream taste bad."

"Can we have ice cream instead of this?" Harry pushes, sticking his spoon into the oatmeal, where it pokes out like a gravestone on a gray hill.

I try to sell it as "the kind of porridge the Three Bears ate," but George and Harry are skeptical, Duff, at eleven, is too old for all that, and Andy wrinkles her nose and says, "I'll eat later. I'm too nervous now anyway."

"It's lame to be nervous about Kyle Comstock," Duff says. "He's a boob."

"*Boooooob*," Patsy repeats from her high chair, the eighteen-month-old copycat.

"You don't understand anything," Andy says, leaving the kitchen, no doubt to try on yet another outfit before sailing camp awards. Six hours away from now.

"Who cares what she wears? It's the stupid sailing awards," Duff grumbles. "This stuff is vomitous, Alice. It's like gruel. Like what they make Oliver Twist eat."

"*He* wanted more," I point out.

"He was *starving*," Duff counters.

"Look, stop arguing and eat the damn stuff."

George's eyes go big. "Mommy doesn't say that word. Daddy says not to."

"Well, they aren't here, are they?"

George looks mournfully down at his oatmeal, poking at it with his spoon like he might find Mom and Dad in there.

"Sorry, Georgie," I say repentantly. "How about some eggs, guys?"

"No!" they all say at once. They've had my eggs before. Since Mom has been spending a lot of time at either doctors' appointments for herself or doctor and physical therapy consults for Dad, they've suffered through the full range of my limited culinary talents.

"I'll get rid of the owl if you give us money to eat breakfast in town," Duff says.

"Alice, look!" Andy says despairingly, "I knew this wouldn't fit." She hovers in the doorway in the sundress I lent her, the front sagging. "When do I get off the itty-bitty-titty committee? You did before you were even thirteen." She sounds accusatory, like I used up the last available bigger chest size in the family.

"Titty committee?" Duff starts laughing. "Who's on that? I bet Joel is. And Tim."

"You are *so* immature that listening to you actually makes *me* younger," Andy tells him. "Alice, help! I love this dress. You never lend it to me. I'm going to die if I can't wear it." She looks wildly around the kitchen. "Do I stuff it? With what?"

"Bread crumbs?" Duff is still cracking up. "Oatmeal? Owl feathers?"

I point the oatmeal spoon at her. "Never stuff. Own your size."

"I want to wear this dress." Andy scowls at me. "It's perfect. Except it doesn't fit. There. Do you have anything else? That's flatter?"

"Did you ask Samantha?" I glare at Duff, who is shoving several kitchen sponges down his shirt. Harry, who doesn't get what's going on—I hope—but is happy to join in on tormenting Andy, is wadding up some diapers from Patsy's clean stack and following suit. My brother's girlfriend has much more patience than I do. Maybe because Samantha only has one sibling to deal with.

"She's helping her mom take her sister to college—she probably won't be back till tonight. Alice! What do I do?"

My jaw clenches at the mere mention of Grace Reed, Sam's mom, the closest thing our family has to a nemesis. Or maybe it's the owl. *God. Get me out of here.*

"I'm hungry," Harry says. "I'm starving here. I'll be dead by night."

"It takes three weeks to starve," George tells him, his air of authority undermined by his hot cocoa mustache.

"Ughhh. No one cares!" Andy storms away.

"She's got the hormones going on," Duff confides to Harry. Ever since hearing it from my mother, my little brothers treat "hormones" like a contagious disease.

My cell phone vibrates on the cluttered counter. Brad again. I ignore it, start banging open cabinets. "Look, guys, we're out of everything, got it? We can't go shopping until we get this week's take-home from the store, and no one has time to go anyway. I'm not giving you money. So it's oatmeal or empty stomachs. Unless you want peanut butter on toast."

"Not again," Duff groans, shoving away from the table and stalking out of the kitchen.

"Gross," Harry says, doing the same, after accidentally knocking over his orange juice—and ignoring it.

How does Mom stand this? I pinch the muscles at the base of my neck, hard, close my eyes. Push away the most treacherous thought of all: *Why* does Mom stand this?

George is still doggedly trying to eat a spoonful of oatmeal, one rolled oat at a time.

"Don't bother, G. You still like peanut butter, right?"

Breathing out a long sigh, world-weary at four, George rests his freckled cheek against his hand, watching me with a focus that reminds me of Jase. "You can make diamonds out of peanut butter. I readed about it."

"Read," I say automatically, replenishing the raisins I'd sprinkled on the tray of Patsy's high chair.

"Yucks a dis," she says, picking each raisin up with a delicate pincer grip and dropping it off the side of the high chair.

"Do you think we could make diamonds out of this peanut butter?" George asks hopefully as I open the jar of Jif.

"I wish, Georgie," I say, looking at the empty cabinet over by the window, and then noticing a dark blue Jetta pull into our driveway, the door kick open, a tall figure climb out, the sun hitting his rusty hair, lighting it like a match.

Fabulous. Exactly what we need for the flammable family mix. Tim Mason. The human equivalent of C-4.

We walk up the creaky garage stairs and Jase hauls a key out of his pocket, unlocks the door, flips on the lights. I brush past him and drop my cardboard box on the ground. Joel's old apartment is low-ceilinged and decorated with milk crate bookcases, ugly couch, mini-fridge, microwave, denim bean-bag chair with Sox logo, walls covered in *Sports Illustrated* swimsuit issue and all that—tits everywhere—and a gigantic iron weight rack with a shit-ton of weights.

"*This* is where Joel took all those au pairs? I thought he had better game than this massive cliché."

Jase grimaces. "Welcome to Bootytown. Supposedly the nannies never minded because they expected it of *American boys*. Want me to help yank 'em down?"

"Nah, I can always count body parts if I have trouble sleeping."

After a brief scope-out of the apartment, during which he makes a face and empties a few trash cans, he asks, "This gonna work for you?"

"Absolutely." I reach into my pocket, pull out the lined paper list I snatched off my bulletin board, and slap it on the refrigerator, *adios*-ing a babe in hot-pink spandex.

Jase scans my sign, shakes his head. "Mase . . . you know you can come on over anytime."

"I've been to boarding school, Garrett. Not like I'm afraid of the dark."

"Don't be a dick," he says mildly. He points in the direction of the bathroom. "The plumbing backs up sometimes. If the plunger doesn't work, text; I can fix it. I repeat, you're always welcome to head to our house. Or join me on the predawn job. I gotta pick up Samantha now. She ended up not going to Vermont. Ride along?"

"With the perfect high school sweethearts? Nah. I think I'll stay and see if I can break the plunger. *Then* I'll text you."

He flips me off, grins, and leaves.

Time to get my ass to a meeting. Better that than alone with a ton of airbrushed boobs and my unfiltered thoughts.

Chapter Four

When I walk up the Garretts' overgrown lawn after the meeting—which only partially took the edge off—the first thing I see is Jase's older sister, Alice, tanning in the front yard.

In a bikini.

Shockwave scarlet.

Straps untied.

Olive skin.

Toenails painted the color of fireballs.

Can I say there are few things on earth that cheer me up more than Alice Garrett in a bikini?

Except Alice without a bikini. Which I've never seen, but I've a hell of an imagination.

She's almost asleep, in a tiny blue-and-green lawn chair, her head and her long, always-morphing hair (brown with blond streaks right now) flopping heavily to one side, curling shorter in the late-summer heat. Because I'm unscrupulous, I flop down on the grass next to her and take a good long look.

Oh, Alice.

After a few seconds, she opens her eyes, squints, flips her hand to her forehead to block the sun, stares at me.

"Now," I tell her, "would be an excellent time to avoid unsightly tan lines. I stand ready to assist."

"Now," she says, with that killer smile, "would be an even *better* time to avoid lame come-ons."

"Aw, Alice, I swear I'll be there to soothe your regret for wasting time once you realize I've been right for you all along."

"Tim, I'd chew you up and spit you out." She slants forward, yanks the straps of her bikini behind her neck, ties them, and settles back. *God.* I almost can't breathe.

But I can talk.

I can always talk.

"We could progress to that, Alice. But maybe we start with some gentle nibbling?"

Alice shuts her eyes, opens them again, and gives me an indecipherable look.

"Why don't I scare you?" she asks.

"You do. You're scary as hell," I assure her. "But that works for me. Completely."

She's about to say something, but the family van pulls in just then, even more battered than usual. The right front fender has flaking paint. They've tried to put some rust primer around the sliding back door. The side looks like it's been keyed. Both hubcap covers on this side are missing. Alice starts to get up, but I rest my hand on a smooth brown shoulder, press her down.

"On it."

She squints up at me, head cocked to the side, rubs her bottom lip with her finger. Then settles back in the chair. "Thanks."

Mrs. Garrett, wearing a bright blue beach cover-up-type thing and a wigged-out face, climbs out of the van.

"Everything okay?" I ask, sort of a joke since there's nothing but ear-melting screeching when I slide open the side door. Patsy, George, and Harry are all red-faced and sweaty. Patsy's mouth is open in a huge O and she's a sobbing mess. George also looks teary-eyed. Harry's more like pissed off.

"I'm not a baby," he announces to me.

"Clear on that, man." Though he's wearing bathing trunks with little red fire hats on them.

"*She*"—he jabs a sandy finger at his mom—"made us leave the beach."

"Patsy's naptime, Harry. You know this. You can swim in the big pool for a while. Maybe we can get a cone at Castle's after the sailing awards."

"Pools aren't cool," Harry moans. "We left before the ice-cream truck, Mommy. They have Spider-Man Bomb Pops." He stalks up the steps, his angry, scrawny back all hunched over his skinny, little-dude legs. The screen door slams behind him.

"Whoa," I say. "Child abuse."

Mrs. Garrett laughs. "I'm the meanest mom in the world. I have it on good authority." Then she glances at George and leans into me, smelling like coconut sunscreen. At first I think she's sniff-checking my breath, because that's why adults ever get this close. Instead she whispers, "Don't mention asteroids."

Not my go-to conversation starter, so all good there.

But George is clutching a copy of *Newsweek*, his shoulders heaving. Patsy's still shrieking. Mrs. Garrett looks back and forth between them, like, who to triage first.

"I'll take Screaming Mimi here," I offer. Mrs. Garrett shoots me a grateful smile and flicks open Patsy's car seat. Good thing, since I know dick about car seats.

As soon as she's freed, Patsy looks up at me and her sobs dry up, like that. She still does that *hic-hic-hic* thing, but reaches out both hands for me.

"Hon," she says. *Hic-hic-hic.*

I don't get why, but this kid loves me crazy much. I pick her up and her sweaty little hands settle on my cheeks, patting them gently, never mind the stubble.

"Oh Hon," she says, all loving and shit, giving me her cutescary grin with her pointy incisors, like a baby vampire.

Mrs. Garrett smiles, swinging George out of the car onto her hip. He snuggles his head into her neck, magazine still rumpled in his clammy fingers.

"You'll make a good dad, Tim. Someday in the far distant future."

To cover a sudden embarrassing rush of . . . whatever . . . from the consoling weight of her hand on my back, I answer, "You better believe it. No the hell way am I adding knocking up some girl to my list of crimes and misdemeanors."

The minute it's out of my mouth I get that I'm an ass. Mrs. Garrett still looks pretty frickin' young and her oldest kid is twenty-two. Could be *she* got knocked up and had to get married.

Also, probably? *Knocking up?* Not a phrase you should use with parents.

"Always good to have a plan," she answers, unfazed.

She carries George into the house, leaving me with Patsy,

who tips her teary, soft cheek against my own, nuzzling. Alice still has her eyes closed and is evidently removing herself from this scene every way but physically.

"Hon," Patsy says again, slanting back to plant a sloppy kiss on my shoulder, checking me out from under her dew-droppy eyelashes. "Boob?"

"Sorry, kid, can't help you there."

I avoid looking at Alice, who has again untied the top strings of her bikini. She yawns, stretches. The top edges down a little lower. No tan lines. I close my eyes for a second.

Patsy grabs my ear, as if that's a cool substitute for a boob. Could be. What do I know about babies? Or toddlers, or whatever you are when you're one and a half. Could be it's all about holding on to something and doesn't matter much what you grab. I, of all people, get that.

Chapter Five

ALICE

"Alice?"

"Dad?"

"Recognized your Gators," he says.

"Crocs, Dad."

"Those. Come on in."

I brush aside the stiff hospital curtain. Even nearly a month after the car accident, I still have to struggle to pull on the "all is well" nurse face I never dreamed I'd need with my own father. He looks a lot better. Fewer tubes, color better, bruises faded away. But Dad in a hospital bed still makes my stomach cramp and my lungs too heavy to pull in air. Before all this, I'd almost never seen him lying down, not in motion. Now the only thing that moves is one hand, stroking Mom's hair. She's asleep, nestled tight against him in the tiny, cramped bed.

"*Shh*," Dad says. "She's beat."

She's totally out, for sure. One arm hooked behind his neck, one wrapped around his waist.

"You too, hmm?" His voice is still faintly slurry, but gentle, the same steadying sound that got me through kid-nightmares, mean teachers, and Sophie McCade in eighth grade spreading rumors I'd had boob implants during the summer.

"I could ask you the same, Dad."

He makes a scoffing sound. "I lounge around all day."

"You have a broken pelvis. Not to mention lung damage from a pulmonary embolism. You're not exactly eating bonbons."

He peers at me, shifting aside Mom's hair so he can look me more clearly in the eye. "What *are* bonbons? I've heard it and I've never known."

"I have no idea, actually. But if I figure it out and bring you some, *will* you eat them?"

"I will if you will. We could make a contest of it. 'My boy says he can eat fifty eggs . . .'"

"No, God. No *Cool Hand Luke*. What is it with that movie? Every male I know has, like, a thing with it."

"We all like to believe we have a winning hand, Alice," he says, dragging up the pillow behind him one-handed and giving it a hard punch to fluff it up.

"Say no more." I reach for the cards in their familiar, worn box, next to the pink hospital-issue carafe of water, the kidney-shaped trough to spit into after tooth brushing, the clutter of empty, one-ounce pill cups, and the roll of medical tape to re-bandage his IV shunt. Nothing like home, his nightstand piled with wobbly, homemade, clay penholders and mugs, heaps of sci-fi books, the picture of him and Mom in high school—big curly hair on her, leather jacket on him.

"I haven't the heart to break your streak," he says with that grin that crinkles the corners of his eyes before overtaking his entire face. "The painkillers gave you an unfair advantage."

"I'm six for seven, Dad. Is it your painkillers or my raw talent?" I smile.

"Well, I'm off 'em now. So we'll see." He edges to one side a bit and his face goes sheet-white. He looks up at the ceiling, his lips moving, counting away the pain, taking deep breaths.

"Pant, pant, blow," I murmur. Labor breathing. Everyone in our family knows it.

"Whoo, who, hee." Dad's voice is tight. "God knows I should have that one down."

"And yet Mom says you still don't." I try for another smile but it slips a little, so I focus on the cards, shuffling them once, twice, three times. "Do you want me to call your nurse?"

He reaches out for the cards, takes them, and does his famous one-handed shuffle.

"Only if she's got bonbons. Look, they're kicking me out of here soon," he says abruptly. "Not enough beds, I've outstayed my welcome, I'm all fixed now. Not sure what the latest explanation is."

"And then—?"

"Home," he says on a sigh. "Or a rehab facility. They've left it up to us." He glances down at Mom, smiles, the same grin as in the SBH photo, tucks the hanging-out tag of her dress under the neckline. She nestles closer.

"Rehab's covered by our deal with the devil," I point out. Our devil may be a tall, blond, conservative state senator, but facts are facts.

"You can't think of it that way, Alice." He shakes his head, winces.

Still in pain, no matter how often he says it's not a problem. The last of his summer tan is fading, the line of his jaw cuts sharper, his shoulders locked in rigid lines. He looks at least four years older than he did four weeks ago and it's all that woman's fault. However often she sends fancy dinner salads and gourmet casseroles over with Samantha, I can't forget. I can't drive past reality without even stopping, the way she did.

"Grace Reed did this, Dad. She wrecked us. She—"

"Look at me," he says. I do, trying not to flinch at the shaved part of his scalp where they drilled the hole to relieve pressure from his head injury. Duff, Harry, and George just call it "Dad's weird haircut."

"A little battered maybe. But definitely not wrecked. Accepting rehab, on top of all the hospital bills—charity."

"Not charity, Dad. Justice."

"You know as well as I do that it's time to get on with things, Alice. Suck it up and get on home. I'm needed there."

I want him there. I want everything back the way it was. Coming in late at night from a date or whatever to find him watching random History Channel or National Geographic documentaries, baby after baby, Duff, Harry, then George, then Patsy conked out against his shoulder, clicker poised in his hand, nearly dozing himself, but awake enough to rouse and say, "Do you know the plane Lindbergh flew to Paris was only made of fabric? A little glue brushed over it. Amazing what people can do." But I'm enough of a professional to look at his vital signs and translate his medical chart by heart. No matter how amazing it is what people can do, bodies have their limits.

"You know better," I say, "about what's needed. What you have to do."

A muscle in Dad's jaw jumps.

How much pain is he in? He should still be on those pills.

I wipe my expression clean, rubbing the back of my neck with one hand. Game face.

The things Mom and I traded off doing, today alone. I did breakfast while she did morning sickness and talked on the phone setting up everyone's back to school doctor appointments. I drove Duff to the eye doctor, she took Andy to the orthodontist, then the little guys to the beach. Then we all went to the sailing awards. Mom cheered up Andy in the bathroom after Jade Whelan said something stupid to her, then took her to get frozen yogurt. I hauled the little kids to Castle's for hot dogs. Mom ferried the gang to Jase's practice, then dropped them off and came to visit Dad—and dozed off. I stayed home until everyone crashed except Andy, then came here, chugging a venti Starbucks on the way. And I'm only Mom's stunt double. I'm not Dad.

"If you leave here for home, you'll be picking up George and Patsy, toting them to the car. You'll be driving Harry and Duff to soccer. Taking Andy to middle school dances. Relieving Jase at the store. You'll be *on* all the time, Dad. You can't do that yet. It'll only set you back and make things worse. For all of us."

He scrubs his hand over his forehead. Sighs.

"Aren't you supposed to be the child I'm imparting all my hard-earned wisdom to, Alice?"

Mom shifts in her sleep, pulling her arm from his waist to rest on her stomach.

The new baby. Right. I almost always forget about that. Her. Him.

Dad reaches his good hand down to cover hers. *He* never forgets.

I rest against the windowsill, put my head down on my crossed arms. Cloudless night with, I don't know, crickets, locusts, whatever, making sounds in the high grass the Garretts wait too long to cut. You can even hear the river if you listen hard enough.

When my eyes adjust to the dark, I see her.

Alice is tipped back against the hood of the Bug, looking up. Not at me. At the sky. Full moon, a few clouds. Stars. She's darkly silhouetted against the white car, all curves, one foot on the bumper, moonlight shining off a knee.

Jesus.

A *knee*.

Oh, Alice.

Chapter Six

TIM

Early the next morning, I jolt out of bed so fast my brain practically sloshes against my skull. Where am I? The familiar feeling—the burning, dizzy *oh shit* of it—makes my temples crash and bang.

I got drunk last night.

Or something.

Because, if not, why am I so freaking disoriented?

Then I remember, assisted by the twelve girls in twelve different improbable contortions staring at me. I rub sweat off my forehead, fall back on the hard-as-hell couch I crashed on after too much quality time with the Xbox, and listen to the emptiness.

I never realized how freaking *quiet* it is when you're all alone in a building.

Then I'm up, yanking one poster off the wall, then the next, then the next, until the walls are bare and I'm breathing hard.

Running—isn't that what Jase does when he doesn't want to think? I rummage around in my cardboard box for gym shorts I can't find. Just lame gray slacks. Who packed those? And my Asics—nowhere to be found. I pull on the only workout option, a faded pair of swim trunks, and head for Stony Bay Beach. I read once that Navy Seals train by running on sand. Barefoot. It's harder, a better workout.

I'll jog to the pier. Gotta be like a mile or something. Good start, right?

It would be, except that a mile's a hell of a long way. The pier's still as distant as a mirage and I'm gasping for breath, wanting to collapse in the sand.

I'm seven-fuckin'-teen, for God's sake. The prime of my life. The height of my physical prowess. The golden age I look back on one day when I'm boring my own kids. But I can't run like the wind. I can't run like the *breeze*. Patsy could run faster, without needing an oxygen tank afterward. I slump down in the sand, falling first to my knees, then rolling to collapse onto my back, hand over my eyes against the early-morning light, sucking in air like it's filtered through nicotine.

Gotta lose the cigarettes.

"Need mouth to mouth?" asks a female voice.

Damn, I didn't know there was anyone on the beach, much less someone close . . . Alice. How long has she been watching me? I edge my hand away from my eyes.

Ah, another bikini. Thank you, Jesus. If I'm gonna die of shame, at least I'll die happy. This is one of those Bond-girl types, dark green with a lime green zipper down the front, a little belt cinching in the bottom, about three fingers below where her waist swoops in before her hips fan out. My fingers twitch, will of their own. I shove my fists in my pockets. "Definitely," I gasp. "I need mouth to mouth. Right now."

"If you can talk, I think you'll survive."

I lick my dry lips. "Don't think I'm ready for the triathlon, Alice."

She does an unexpected thing, lying down next to me on her side, tilting toward me, sudden smile, curvy as the rest of her.

"At least you've got your running shoes on." She looks down at my feet. "No, you don't even, do you? Who jogs barefoot?" Her toes tangle with mine for a second, then move away. She looks down at the sand, not at me, draws a squiggly line between us.

"It matters?"

"Traction, honey," Alice says.

"I thought that was only when you'd broken a leg. Navy Seals do it. So I've heard."

I wait for her to make fun of that, but instead she smiles a little more, almost undetectably, unless you're looking hard at her lips, which I may be doing—says, "Maybe put off the BUDs challenge until you've built up more . . . stamina."

There are so many ways I could answer that.

She moves closer; smells like I've always thought Hawaii would, green and sweet, earthy, sun and sea mixed together, smoky warm. Her greenish gray eyes, flecks of gold too—

"You've only got one dimple," she says.

"That a drawback? I had two, but I misplaced one after a particularly hard night."

She gives my shoulder a shove. "You joke about everything."

"Everything *is* pretty funny," I say, trying to sit up, but sinking down immediately, back groaning. "If you look at it the right way."

"How do you know you're looking at it the right way?" Alice's head's lowered, she's still circling an index finger in the sand, only inches from brushing her knuckles past my stomach. The morning air is still and calm—no sound of the waves, even.

"If it's funny," I wheeze, "you're looking at it the right way."

"Yo, Aleece!" I look up and there's that douche-canoe, her boyfriend, Brad, looming large, big shoulders muscling out the sun.

"Brad." She's up, brushing sand from her swimsuit. He pats her on the butt, looking at me in this *my territory* way.

Dick.

"You're late. Brad, Tim. Tim, Brad."

"Yo, Tim." Brad, man of few, and strictly one-syllable, words. One of those guys built like a linebacker but with a little kid face, all rosy cheeks and twinkly eyes. To compensate, I guess, he has a scruffy, barely there beard.

"So, Ally-pals," he says to Alice.

Ally-pals?

"Ready?"

"I've been ready for a while. You're the one who's late," Alice says, sharply.

Attagirl.

She turns to me, running her hands through her hair, flipping it back from her face. "I'm training for the five K—Brad's timing me."

"You're a runner? How did I not know that?"

She opens her mouth, like why on earth would I know anything whatsoever about her, but then looks down, tightens the notch on the belt of her bikini bottom. Which brings my attention back to her stomach, the belly ring, and I . . .

Roll over onto my stomach.

Brad clears his throat, arms folded, chin jutting. Got it, caveman.

"I won't hold you up," I add. Alice shoots Brad an unreadable look, drops down on her knees, bending over me again, her breath biting sweet as peppermint candy. "Sneakers next time, Tim."

ALICE

I'm panting, hands on knees, at the end of my first sprint. Sweat slides into my eyes, and I brush my hair back, try to corral what isn't in my ponytail behind my ears.

Brad uncaps the water bottle, hands it to me, stooping low to squint at my face. Then he says in a low voice, "You wanna tell me what that was about?" He jerks his thumb toward the distant figure of Tim, still collapsed on the sand, head on his folded arms.

"What? Tim? He's my kid brother's friend. We were talking."

He rubs his chin. "I dunno, Ally. That's all it was?"

Two more sips of water, then I pour some into my hand, rub it over my face.

Tim's standing up now, shielding his eyes, looking toward us—then the other way down the beach. Now he's sprinting in that direction, no stretching out, no slow jog to start, right into a flat-out run. Gah.

"Ally?"

"Of course that's all it was."

Chapter Seven

ALICE

Sam's Club is no stranger to Garrett family meltdowns. Harry always loses it in the toy aisle, George is extremely sensitive about our ice-cream choices, Patsy gets overtired and screeches. This time, though, the meltdown is all mine.

"I think you're taking this waaay too seriously," Joel says, holding up both palms in that *Whoa, you overemotional woman* way that makes me furious.

I shake the papers at him. "It says two red, one-inch binders. Red. One-inch. I send you off to do that one simple thing. These are blue. Two-inch."

"So what?" Joel scratches the back of his neck, checking out a girl who's smiling at him while daintily placing huge packs of glitter glue in her cart.

"*So*, the school list says red. We get red. That's what lists are for. So people get things right."

"Al, I don't think this is about school supplies. You're scaring Patsy. You're scaring *me*."

"Good," I snap.

Patsy points at me. "Bad." She's scowling from her perch in the shopping cart.

"Not you, honey. *You*, Joel. Maybe you *need* scaring, or some reminder of what's really going on. Because you're not around—not all the time. You don't see how close everything is to—to—"

"*That's* what this is about." My brother settles back against a wall of paper towels, tilts his chin. "Me not being around all the time. That you are."

"No," I say. "Not that at all. What do I care if you're moving in with your girlfriend and starting your training at the police academy when everything is up in the air? So what? Whatever."

Joel sighs, reaches over, and plucks a handful of chocolate chip cookies off a free sample tray. "Al, I'm twenty-two. Out of college. I need to get on with it. Gisele and I have been seeing each other for a while. I want to find out where that goes. I don't want to be living above our garage for the rest of my life. Not too functional."

"Since when has that mattered?" I say, moving away from Patsy, who's trying to yank down the top of my shirt, still scowling.

"Uh, since I spent my twenty-second birthday at the *hospital* the night Dad was hit. I love our family, Al. I'd do anything for any of us, even you. But everything—my life—it can't stop."

Everything has done anything but *stop*—as Joel should know. It's accelerated to warp speed. Before that, this summer, for me, there were a few classes, a few hours of work at the hospital rehab center, maybe covering at the store, but other than that it was the beach and Brad and my favorite time of year. Sand and salt and ice-cream cones.

Now it's almost Labor Day and things—classes, sports, after-school stuff—will be picking up—for everyone. Dad will be recovering for who knows how much longer, Mom pregnant,

Jase's football schedule, band for Andy and Duff—we'll need to figure out more babysitting and my actual own life is—

Deep breath. I lower my shoulders, which are practically grazing my earlobes.

Joel tosses a 500-pack box of Slim Jims into the cart. I snatch them out and shove them back on the shelf. "Do you even know what's *in* those?"

"Is this about you not liking Gisele?"

"I like Gisele fine," I say.

Can't stand Gisele.

Last time she came by, she had Joel pumping up her bicycle tires while she stood there looking all Parisian in a striped blue-and-white dress and a red scarf, fluttering her hands. But I know better than to say that. He's moving in with her. *That* should be the kiss of death for both of them.

"Sure you do. Brad's no prize, you know." Joel hands Patsy a chocolate chip cookie, which she immediately smooshes all over her face and into her hair, wiping the last of the chocolate across her pink shirt for good measure.

"Brad's on his way out," I say, leafing through the school supplies lists, mentally crossing things off. Harry—still needs twelve-count colored pencils, one "quality" pack of erasers, whatever that is. Duff—no, I am *not* getting materials for the solar system project yet—otherwise he's set. Andy can get her own supplies, for God's sake, she's fourteen. "Too time-consuming." As if to confirm this, my phone vibrates with what turns out to be another selfie of Brad at the gym.

"Alice," Joel says, giving yet another girl the once-over (Gisele, you are toast!). "That's what I mean. You're *supposed* to have your time consumed by that sort of thing." He flicks the school supplies list. "Not this."

"That baby is too young for chocolate," says a grouchy-looking woman who has her own baby in one of those weird sling things.

"Nobody asked you," I snap. Her brows draw together. Joel gives her his most charming smile, drawing me away by the elbow.

"But we're grateful for your advice. Who knew? Thank you."

She smooths her shirt and actually smiles back at him.

Honestly.

Here's Brad sitting on our steps when we get home, texting—probably me—with a frown. "Allykins," he says, coming to his feet for a hug.

Joel raises an eyebrow at me with a smirk, mutters, "I'm off to see Dad." And leaves.

Without carrying in any of the school supplies.

In the kitchen, Jase, obviously fresh from practice, sweaty and with grass stains on his jersey, is plowing through a huge bowl of chicken and brown rice. Tim's planted on our counter like he belongs there, scarfing down something with melted cheese all over it, hot enough to be steaming. Duff, Harry, and George are eating blueberry pie with melting vanilla ice cream. Dirty plates everywhere. The kitchen smells like boy and feet.

And . . . Tim again.

All relaxed and at home, wearing the swimsuit he was jogging in this morning and a Hodges Heroes baseball shirt that's slightly too tight even on him. He grins at me, lopsided dimple and all.

Hot mess inside and out, that boy, probably hasn't even showered. Certainly hasn't shaved carefully, since he's got a little cut near his chin. Yet another person who needs a mother, a maid, a manager—

I set Patsy down, grab her pink princess sippy cup, slosh milk into it, screw on the top, shove it at him. "Slow down. I'm not driving you to the hospital when you get second-degree tongue burn."

Tim takes a defiant bite of scalding cheese. Another. Then slowly raises the sippy cup, salutes me, and, watching me with serious eyes, gulps it down.

"Pie," Brad says happily. "I love pie." He pulls out a chair, flips it around, straddles it, and says, "Cut my slice *extra*-big, Allosaurus."

George cocks his head, wrinkling his nose. "Allosauruses were some of the biggest dinosaurs of all. They ate Stegosauruses. Alice isn't very big. And she's a vegetarian."

Brad can get his own damn pie.

"Get your own damn pie," Tim mumbles between more mouthfuls of volcanic cheese.

"Hey, Alice, Joel's completely out of the garage—he's not coming back for anything, right?" Jase slosh-pours himself a huge glass of milk, drains half of it, refills. Finally got groceries, and at this rate they'll be gone tomorrow.

"Thank God, yes," I say.

"Great," he says. "I told Tim he could take it. He moved in last night."

"No escaping me now," Tim tells me cheerfully.

"Boy, Alice. Your face is really red," George says after a second.

"Al—" Jase starts, then falters.

Tim takes one look at me and jolts off the counter, hand outstretched. "Whoa. What—hell—what did I—?"

I hold up my own hand. "Don't say another word . . . There are groceries and school supplies in the Bug. Deal with them." Then I practically drag Brad out by his hair.

TIM

"I screwed up again, yeah?" I say to Jase as the door slams behind Alice and ol' Brad.

Jase rubs a hand down his face. "I'll talk to her."

"What, was she, like, going to move in there—with *that* guy? 'I love pie'? What is he, five?"

"Alice never said a thing to me, Tim." Jase picks up a forkful of chicken, puts it back down.

George says philosophically, "Pie *is* good. Except the kind with four and twenty blackbirds baked in it, prolly. You know, like, sing a songofsixpence, pockafullarye?" he warbles in this high voice that sort of slays me. "That sounds yuck."

"No way would they sing when they opened it," Harry says, with his mouth full of crust. "Because they'd all be cooked and dead."

George's eyes get big. "Would they?" he asks, looking back and forth between me and Jase. "*Cooked?*"

"No way," Jase says firmly, "because . . ." He hesitates a second, and George's eyes start filling.

"Because, dude, it wouldn't be an *eating* pie," I say. "It would be a *performance* pie. Like something to make the king laugh because he was all stressed from—"

"Counting out his money," Jase finishes, nodding, all confident. "Right, G-man? Isn't that what he was doing—'in the countinghouse, counting out his money'?"

George nods soberly. "He'd be all upset like Daddy at work, so they'd make him a performance pie? Like, like a play?"

"Exactly," I say. "They'd make this, uh, fake pie—"

"To make him laugh. Like Mommy does." George is nodding, like the whole thing makes total sense now.

"But where would they get the *blackbirds*?" Harry asks. "Who has blackbirds lying around?"

"They'd probably have them in the barn or something," Duff says, all fake-casual. "Like, kind of tame ones. Maybe the king was, uh, into birds."

This story is getting away from us. But George is down with it. "We could look them up in my *Big Birds of the World* book. See if you can tame blackbirds." He slides off the kitchen chair and trots off, Harry at his heels.

"Nice job, Duffy," Jase says. "Thanks for chiming in."

"I was sort of lame," Duff admits, scraping up the last of his pie. "'The king was into birds'? But I tried. It's just hard sometimes to see what's gonna scare George."

"Dead, baked birds? It'd give *me* nightmares." I shudder.

That or that asskite Brad, and what Alice might be getting up to with him right this very minute.

ALICE

"Do we have to?"

Brad may be upward of 225 pounds and over six feet tall, but he sounds like my little brothers when I drag them shoe shopping. "Yup," I say.

He weaves hesitantly through traffic—he drives like he's in one of his video games on slo-mo, sudden spurts of speed and then well below the limit. Staring out the car window, I don't see the blur of the maple trees that line the turnpike but the garage apartment reinvented, the way *I* was going to do it.

All of Joel's heinous furniture piled into the attic. My great-aunt Alice's brass bed down from there. Along with her big wardrobe that Jase and I were always trying to find Narnia in. The walls painted a deep burnt-orange color, October Sky, a paint we got in at Garrett's Hardware last week—so not the dingy white that's in there now—far from the "bridal pink" in the room Andy and I share. I saw something in a magazine last month—this tulle canopy that goes over your bed, making it into your own cocoon. Splurge on those billion-thread-count sheets that are so soft you barely notice them at all. Stereo speakers for my iPod and a reading corner full of books that aren't textbooks, with big, puffy floor pillows and—

"C'mon, Ally-pally. Let's hit Pizza Palace and you can bash my butt at Slimin' Sumos." Brad elbows me, giving me his best smile.

"I don't feel like eating bad pizza while we play videogames, Brad."

Now I sound whiny too. I dig my fingernails into my palm and kick my feet up onto the dashboard. *Let it go. It's just an apartment.* Just a space of my own, for the first time ever, and for the last time for a while too, assuming I can still accept the transfer to Nightingale Nursing in the spring, assuming things at home are running smoothly, assuming I can get student housing and—

Sharp inhale. Another.

Brad squeezes the back of my neck. "Yowch, you're tense,

Allo. Don't do that funky breathing thing. It freaks me out. How 'bout we go back to my place? I'll send Wally out for decent pizza. Like all the way to Ilario's or something. That would give us at least half an hour. I could . . . relax you." Now he's rubbing my shoulder, giving me a sunny, hopeful grin. No stormy weather with Brad. All one mood, like the easy-listening music they play at the dentist.

"I see a smile, Als. You want to, don't you? C'mon. Let's book it home. I'll boot the Walster for the whole night if you want. Bummer for sure about the apartment—that would have been sweet—but it's not like I don't have my own place."

Brad's "place" is a three-story house in White Bay. His parents live on the first two floors, Brad and Wally in the basement, his grandmother, who I'm pretty sure refers to me as That Whore, on the top.

He reaches over and gives my knee a squeeze while passing a camper on the right and leaning on the horn.

I sigh.

"Is that a yes? C'mon, Aliwishous. We could take a shower or something. My dad fixed the hot water tank."

"Let's go to the batting cages. I need to hit something."

"Works for me. Whatever floats your boat."

He's nothing if not steady. Which is good when you're a little bit shipwrecked. He's now singing along to the radio—a commercial for river cruises. Steady is solid ground under your feet. Even if the planks are a little thick.

But the garage apartment? I'm not letting that go down without a fight.

Chapter Eight

TIM

"You're actually knocking, sis?" I open the door to find Nan, one arm balancing sheets and towels, the other extended to knock again.

"I always knock," she says, swatting my nose instead. "*I* respect your privacy, unlike you, reading my diary."

I kick the door open wider. "C'mon, get my towels out of the rain, assuming those are for me and you're not dropping off laundry. And really? The diary again? Jesus. It was once, it was four years ago, and I had insomnia. Your diary was like a sleeping pill. 'Dear Diary, I—'" I start, all sugary. But I cut myself off. I'm being a jackass.

You want the truth, that diary about broke my damn heart. It was full of these letters from Nan to God. I knew she'd gotten the idea from this Judy Blume book she loved crazy much, because I'd read part of it when I was ten and someone told me it was all about tits. It was, but not in the way I was hoping. Anyway, Nan's diary entries were just sad—like, she was begging God as if he was Santa, the jolly old elf who could give you good grades and parents who were always proud of you, and a brother who wasn't a fuck-up and get Mark Winthrop to love you forever and ever, amen.

Nan dumps the sheets and towels on the Sox beanbag chair and looks around, pulling off her windbreaker and wrinkling her nose. "Since when are you the big sports fan? What's with the weights? Where'd you get all this stuff, anyway?"

"I robbed Dick's. What do you care? What's with all that?"

"Mom wanted me to bring it and to—" She stops dead.

"Spy on me, right? Make sure I wasn't up to no good?"

"Are you?" Her voice is sharp. "Are you in trouble again or something?"

"Wha-at? No. Not more than usual. Why?"

"Some woman, or girl, or whatever—keeps calling, asking for you. Do you owe anyone money? I—know what Dad said to you. If you need money, I have—"

"Nan, kid, I'm fine. I don't owe anyone anything but a shitload of apologies. Don't stress. It'll affect your grade point average."

Her cheeks flame at that last and she says, "I . . . I've been doing my college applications. Starting them. So maybe I can be early-decision, I won't have to freak out all year. And—"

"Nano—"

"It comes easy to you, Tim, but it's really hard for me to concentrate—" Her voice breaks a little. She's blinking rapidly, shoulders hunched, giving me the face.

But I shake my head. "Just no, okay. No."

Her expression goes blank for a second, then she says, "That's that, then. So . . . so . . . where do you sleep?"

I point to the bedroom door. "Be my guest. The drunk, naked babes are all in the shower right now, so no worries."

"You're such a jerk. I thought I'd make the bed, because I doubt you have any idea whatsoever how to do that. You can come watch and—"

"What, you'll quiz me on it later? I'll pass. I'm gonna get in the shower."

"Fine," she says. "Watch out for the naked girls. Word is they're slippery when wet."

I start laughing. She's a pain in my ass, Nano. But I'm a dick to her ninety percent of the time and she loves me anyhow. She went all uptight right when I went all crazy and I wish to hell there was an AA for perfectionism, because I'd haul her ass there in a heartbeat.

She's smiling back at me now, because I laughed, and she was the one who made it happen, because, as she said in that goddamn diary, "Dear God, make me funny like Tim, because people like funny people and maybe then Mark Winthrop would . . ."

Love her.

"Nano—the school shit," I say, then swallow. "I can't help you that way anymore. You get that, right?"

She nods, staring fixedly at the beanbag chair. "Look, about the college money, Tim—Dad said I'd probably get it for Columbia because you—" She stops, and I can hear the gears turning as she tries to figure out how to put it. *Because you—*

Are the boy most likely to.

Fail.

Everyone and everything.

ALICE

There it is again, its silver top gleaming under the light of the Schmidts' fake streetlamp, glossy from the rain. The car pauses at the end of our block, as it has three times since Brad dropped me off. Then, as I watch, it signals the turn, though our street is completely deserted. I edge down the steps, arms folded against the wet, silty breeze blown over from the river.

Looking up at the shaded windows of the garage apartment, I see Tim's rangy figure pass by, then someone else, a girl, hair in a ponytail, gesturing with both hands.

As I'm watching this, the car pulls slowly into our driveway at a bad parking angle, sharply slanted behind my Bug and Tim's Jetta.

The headlights snap off.

Enough. Who's this weird about pulling into a driveway? Who cases the street beforehand? I can't see through the tinted windows.

Dealers?

Maybe the garage apartment's new tenant has brought his sketchy past with him.

Or hired a hooker to join the party.

I stalk down the steps to the car.

Rap sharply on the window.

Right as it occurs to me what a stupid thing this is to do.

No weapon. No Mace. Unless they're vulnerable to the power of Harry's authentic Nerfblaster Lightsaber with glow-in-the-dark detailing, lying in the grass nearby.

The car turns back on, window slowly rolling down, and I'm staring at a girl, my own age or younger, with long brown hair and huge, thickly lashed blue eyes, wide and unblinking in the throwback glow of her headlights.

"Looking for someone?"

She edges back at the sound of my voice. Her fingers, with chipped dark pink polish, clenched at the ten-and-two position on the wheel, tighten even more.

"Yes. No. I mean . . . I . . ." she stammers. "I . . . I—"

"Are you lost?"

She gives a quick, unsteady laugh, and then says, "You got that right. Sorry—don't worry about it. I'll find my way." Then she rolls the window up and backs out as slowly as she drove in.

Chapter Nine

ALICE

"I'm coming in, we need to talk," I say before the door's even half-open.

Tim blinks at me, takes a step back, then peers over my head as though expecting a lynch mob.

"The scariest phrase in the universe." He's wearing baggy striped pajama bottoms, with a toothbrush in one hand, Crest poised in the other.

"Let me in," I repeat, louder.

"Not by the hair on my chinny-chin-chin. You're looking predatory." He stares down at my shirt, slightly damp with rain. "And your—uh—chest is heaving. Is that you huffing and puffing?"

"Tim. Now." I'm not here to be disarmed.

Raising his hands holding the toothbrush and Crest, he steps aside. I brush past him, into the center of the room. My room. Which he's completely marked as his territory. Open Grape-Nuts cereal box and an empty carton of orange juice on the counter next to a worn leather wallet and a handful of crumpled bills. Socks and a sweatshirt balled up in a corner. More clothes piled on the couch. Dishes in the sink. An iPod with a tangled wad of chargers and an Xbox next to the TV.

A lavender windbreaker tossed on the beanbag chair.

"Look, for starters, where's the girl?"

Except when he's loaded, I've never seen Tim so slow on the uptake. Now he's blinking again. "Um—you mean . . . ? What girl?"

"You've got more than one? Look—you can't do this—I need to be here, and I'm sorry if you were planning to use this place for your hookups and booty calls or whatever. I don't care what you told Jase you'd pay, he had no right to go ahead and hand this over to you."

Tim tosses the toothbrush and toothpaste on the counter, grabs a pack of Marlboros, whips out a lighter, shakes out a cigarette, and lights up, all in about two seconds.

I scowl at him. Smoking in *my* apartment.

"Sorry—where are my manners? Want one?" he asks around the cigarette trapped between his lips.

The bedroom door opens and out comes . . .

Nan, Tim's nervous as a cat on a hot tin roof twin sister.

"So, yeah," she says, twisting a coil of hair around a finger and reaching back to flip off the light, "I'll reassure Mom I did my duty. Think she wanted me to tuck you in too? I forgot to bring Pierre the Bear, but I can . . ." She stumbles to a halt. "Oh—hi, Alice."

"Hey, Nan." I give her a brief, but actually genuine smile, which she returns hesitantly. This girl, she's like one of Jase's animals that was badly treated by its previous owner.

"We can skip the tucking in," Tim tells her. "Sending over sheets and towels, that was—uh, nice. Tell Ma thanks. Not when Pop's around, though. Pretty sure I'm supposed to be sleeping under some newspaper on a sidewalk grate somewhere."

Nan bites her pinkie nail, tearing at the cuticle so savagely, mine nearly bleeds in sympathy. Studying me with a vertical line between her eyebrows, identical to Tim's, she picks up the windbreaker, looks back and forth between us, then doesn't budge—until Tim sets his hand in the middle of her back, steering her toward the door.

"Good deed done, Two-Shoes. You'd better beat it. I don't think Alice here wants any witnesses to the homicide."

When the door closes behind her, he gestures at me, like, *bring it on*. Then, before I can say a word, "You want me to get lost, right, Alice? Spreading like a virus, that. Schools, jobs, my folks—should I start a running tally? We can put a list on the fridge."

No flirty flippancy. Hard, sarcastic—like a shove. I haven't heard him like this since he first stopped drinking. Then he studies me, eyes drifting from my face down to my clenched fists, back to my face again.

He turns away. "Shit, I'm sorry, Alice. I was gonna go to my friend Connell's, but he relapsed, so that was a no-go. Jase said . . . I didn't know this place was supposed to be yours. Shoulda guessed. No worries. I'm one hell of a fast packer." He tosses me the kind of smile one of my little brothers would after skinning his knee. *See, I'm fine. It doesn't hurt at all.*

Then he starts skimming the crumpled bills off the counter, shoving them in the wallet, concentrating harder on it than the job requires.

"Where will you go? Back home?"

"Not your problem, Hot Alice."

I examine his downturned face, but the parts I can see reveal nothing. He finishes with the wallet, tries to shove it in his back pocket, then seems to realize his pajama bottoms have no such thing.

"Wait. Why exactly *are* you here, Tim?"

Shrugging, he steps around me to pick up an empty cardboard box from the floor, tosses the wallet, then the sweatshirt and socks into it. Automatically assuming I'm kicking him to the curb right this second, late on a windy, rainy night.

Even I am not that cold.

Then I get it, sharp as a slap.

His parents were on that get-lost list. His own mom and dad kicked him out.

When Tim glances at me, he goes suddenly, stunningly red, wraps both arms around his middle. "What?"

"How . . ." I start; I'm not sure how to finish. I can't even imagine. "Never mind. I'm making you tea and you're going to tell me what happened," I say.

"Or what? I might like my other options better. Spanking? Water torture? I can get the shower going in no time."

Amazingly, there is tea. But of course no kettle. I fill a saucepan with water and cross my fingers that there are mugs. Ah yes, ugly black-and-yellow ones from Planet Fitness. Joel's such a class act. I turn to the fridge to see if there's actually milk too, and there, tacked to it, is a list. A long one, in various different colors of messy, boy-handwriting scrawls.

Tim Mason: The Boy Most Likely To . . .

Need a liver transplant

Find the liquor cabinet blindfolded

Drive his car into a house

I scan down the paper.

"Find the sugar," I say to him. "Then tell me the rest."

"I doubt there's sugar," he says, "but I see resistance is futile. Hey—it's not a big deal. Turns out . . . I guess . . . my parents, my pop . . . Quitting the senator gig? Final straw. Embarrassing, see—Grace Reed is a family friend, yada, yada—he's done with me. I'm out the door—no need to turn up for Sunday dinner. Small upside, that. And I've got four months to turn it all around until I'm out a college fund, and probably stricken from the family Bible. End of story."

Now I feel sick. "He couldn't have been serious—I mean . . . he's your dad."

Tim looks down at his fingers, raising his eyebrows as though surprised not to find the cigarette still there. "He's a serious guy, Pop." His voice deepens. "*Time to be a man, Tim.* Maybe I should have read the fine print on ditching ol' Gracie. That it meant"—he indicates the apartment—"this. But, I mean—he didn't repo my car and yank my allowance or anything." The smile that follows is tight, not his open, wicked one. "In his defense? He did offer me a scotch for the road."

I inhale sharply and he reddens again, rubs his hands through his hair so some parts are sticking straight up. I turn to the cabinet again, searching for sugar, but no such luck. "You're going to have to go without sugar."

He nods. "Here's where I tell you you're sweet enough, right?"

"It's definitely not. Move, so I can pour this without burning you." I slosh the boiling liquid into one cup, then the other, nod toward the couch. "Keep talking."

"While the Ilsa-the-She-Wolf-of-the-SS act is hot as hell, Alice, there's really nothing more to say. It's probably temporary anyway. If me not being office boy for Senator Grace is embarrassing for Pop, you can only imagine how he'd feel about me hanging around the steps of the building and loan with a tin cup." Tim collapses onto the couch anyway, without bringing the mug along. "Can we talk about something else? You? Your endless collection of bikinis? Your tan lines? I notice you don't have any. Wanna show and tell?"

I carry both mugs from the kitchen, set his down in front of him.

"Look. Stay. I mean . . . I can wait. It's only fair. Jase didn't know I wanted it anyway. Four months is nothing. You can be here for four months and then . . ." I trail off.

Then what?

Troubled gray eyes search my face for a long time. Finally, he sighs, shakes his head. "Nah. I'll find somewhere else. You deserve it. You've earned it."

Like a home's something you have to earn when you're seventeen.

He's a kid. Not a man, not on some deadline. But with his jaw set and raised—I know that face. The *I'm going to push on through, no problem, I'll deal. Moving right along. Nothing to see here* face. Know it as well as my own. It is my own. And I picture the rest of the lines on that paper.

Tim Mason: The Boy Most Likely To . . .

Forget his own name even before we do

Turn down the hottest girl in the world for the coldest beer

Be six feet under by our fifth reunion

Don't go that way, Tim. Such a stupid, stupid waste. "I mean it," I say aloud. "Stay."

Pause.

"I want you here," I add, my cheeks flaring. He shifts on the couch and I'm hyper-aware of him next to me, the smell of soap and shampoo, the heat of him, the alive of him.

"Please, stay."

My words fall into the silence, and something changes. Tim's shoulders straighten. He stills, but not frozen, more like . . . more like . . . alert.

"Yeah? Then . . . I'll be here," he says quietly. "Since you asked so . . . nicely."

"Look—if you stick around, there'll be rules."

"Always are," Tim says immediately. "Helps if they're clear."

Like, posted on the refrigerator? But I don't say it.

"Not that I'll necessarily follow them, but—"

"The cigarettes go," I say. "This place is not going to be a refuge if you burn it to the ground, and if I ever *do* get it to myself, I don't want it smelling like an old-man bar."

Unfolding himself from the couch, he brushes past me, wings the pack of Marlboros into the trash can under the sink, knots the bag tight, sets it next to the door. Collapses back down on the couch next to me, laces his hands behind his head, stretches.

"Sorry—again. Trying to kick 'em. I tossed a whole carton but . . . that pack was an impulse buy. Trying to control that, because my impulses suck."

His eyes flick to my face, my lips, lower, back to my eyes.

Outside, it's gone on raining, slashing sideways against the windows, the wind loud and constant. It's warm in here. Overheated, even.

Even though I'm laying out rules, Tim is not one of my brothers.

He glances at my lips again, and there's the sound of a sharp inhale. His or mine?

I jolt up. "I have to get home."

"I'm walking you out." Tim gets quickly to his feet, grabs the green plastic garbage bag, steps in front of me. "Dangerous neighborhood and all that. There's a raccoon under the woodshed the size of a puma."

We keep our trash cans in a low shed near the stairs. When we reach it, Tim bends over to jettison the bag. "Don't tell Jase about, about . . . the whole thing with my parents, 'kay?" His voice is muffled. "A man has his pride."

I'm walking backward up the driveway, forcing a light laugh. "Of course not. I never kiss and—"

"I *missed* the part where we kissed? Wait, let's rewind. I promise not to put up a fight." He dodges in front of me, smiling, holding up his hands in surrender. "You'd take me, anyway. And I'd let you."

I shake my head, laughing, then shield my eyes as headlights flare, backlighting Tim, and a car backs slowly out of our driveway.

Chapter Ten

ALICE

"I'm two seconds from utter and total collapse!" Andy calls from her handstand position, her legs kicked up against the fence by the side of our driveway, swaying wildly.

"You can do this," Samantha says, slightly breathless, in the same position. "It's really great for your form, trust me. If you can get the handstand down, you're golden—right, Alice?"

"It's the core gymnastics move," I call. Andy and I share a bedroom, a bathroom, and half my clothes. I love my sister. But I thank God Sam's helping her practice for gymnastics tryouts.

Jase is fiddling with his Mustang. Mom's supervising Duff and Harry, who are mostly spraying each other and throwing sponges and sometimes washing the van. George is drawing on the blacktop, standing back, then jumping on his drawing, over and over again. Patsy waves at me from the kiddie pool. "Ayiss! A me, Ayiss!"

As usual, our driveway and lawn are completely overpopulated. Perfect. Easier with a crowd.

Brad has pulled gingerly in next to the Mustang, glancing around with an anxious look. He's terrified of our driveway. I think he worries about running over one of my siblings, but it might also be the damage Patsy's Cozy Coupe could do to his beloved Taurus. I slide into the passenger seat and Brad gives me a damp cheek smack and a thigh squeeze.

Beyond my open window, Harry swings the hose toward Brad's car, but, quick as lightning, Mom swoops down and puts a kink in it. "No spraying people unless they say yes, Harry. George, lovie, I think that only works when Mary Poppins is there."

George leaps again onto a chalk painting of, I think, a palm tree and a turtle. "Text her, then, Mommy."

"Mary Poppins doesn't believe in cell phones."

"So, Ally. Want to come over? We can hang with Wally, you can cook us up some mac and cheese. I scored the last copy of *Annihilation 7: The Grizzlies' Revenge*. I'm going to whip Wally's ass at it and wipe the floor with him."

I pause, turn to him. "Here's the thing, Brad. I've been thinking . . ."

Jase's gaze lights on me for a moment, eyebrows lifting. He's seen these dominoes fall before.

"Mommy!" Harry bellows, "Patsy's getting bitey!"

"She walked on my island picture. It's wrecked now!" George adds, pointing accusingly at Patsy, who is chasing Harry, top-knot of hair bobbing, tiny teeth bared.

Mom scoops up Patsy, who squirms in her arms. "I tiger, Mama," then "Grrr" to Harry.

"You're a friendly tiger," Mom suggests. "George, actually, the wave part looks more watery now. It's good. Step back and take another look."

Patsy's still glaring at Harry. "I bite," she says ominously.

"Mom!"

"A sleepy tiger." Mom strokes Patsy's back. "All cozy. With

her jungle friends. Harry, you're the elephant. The hose is your trunk. You missed a spot on the back window."

Brad chuckles. "Your mom's awesome."

And then he says things like that, which make this harder. Tim's car eases in behind Jase's Mustang, hanging half out in the street so as not to cover George's drawings. Sam waves him over, but he calls distractedly, "Late for a meeting! Been running. Gotta shower and book it."

He heads past the Taurus, pauses. "Hey Alice."

"What did you have on your feet this time?" I ask.

"Toes," he replies easily, and grins at me, lifting one long foot to put it on the sill of the car, wiggling his toes for emphasis. There's a jagged open cut near his big toenail. "Well, toes and blood. Cut it on a shell. But I made it all the way to the pier this time. Very Navy Seal, huh? Ran right through the pain, because I am just that full of testosterone."

I try hard not to laugh, looking away, straight at Samantha, who's descended from her handstand position, watching us with a very slight smile. Jase, who has a smudge of dirt on his nose, is frowning over something to do with the windshield wipers. Or something.

"Clean that up," I say to Tim. "And put something on it to *keep* it clean. Toes are seriously prone to infection because the bacteria can get trapped in your shoes."

"I love it when you talk dirty," Tim says, then, seeming to notice him for the first time, "Hey, Brad."

"Yo bro, do you mind?" Brad asks. "We're talking here."

Tim backs away, raising his hands in exactly the same gesture he used in the rain the other night. This flicker of—something— licks up my spine.

As he's climbing the steps, Andy comes over and calls, "Tim! You're a guy, right?"

"Last time I checked."

"Can I ask you a question I can't ask my brothers?"

"No," Jase calls.

"Uh—Andy—sorry, I really have to get to a meeting," Tim says, glancing at Jase before the garage apartment door slams behind him.

"What were you saying, Ally-baba?"

Bite the bullet.

"Look, Brad."

Obediently, Brad looks me in the eye. He's taken a bite of one of the zillion protein bars overflowing his glove compartment, and he's chewing, cheeks bulging. Harry and George have started playing Limbo with the water from the hose, Mom's pulling out the back of Patsy's swim diaper to check its contents, Jase has jerked his head up quickly and banged it on the hood, so Samantha, who's come up beside him, is rubbing the spot, saying something under her breath. Andy's doing a back walkover—without having stretched out enough first.

With the usual chaos and color, my chilly tone is suddenly so off.

Cold, really.

"Your family is a riot," Brad says. "Crazy as anything, but ya know . . ." He trails off.

More than one boyfriend has said to me that breaking up meant breaking up with my family too, and that was the hardest.

But I have to push on here. No point dragging things out. Maybe *I'm* hard, the hardest.

Brad swallows, gnaws off another chunk, and says, mouth full, "What is it, Ally?"

"Brad. Here's the thing."

Jase winces. "Hey, Sam, can you hold the hood open for me? The prop rod keeps giving out."

"Let's all go inside, guys," Mom says. "Duff, Harry, George— time to wash up and get something to eat. Andy, you too." Everyone but George, who's now jumping into the puddles left by the hose, follows. Jase keeps working on his car.

"We've come to the end of the road," I say quickly. "We've gone as far as we can go."

Brad looks puzzled. "It's a driveway."

"I mean us. As a couple . . . It's not working out."

"What?" Brad says frowning. "That . . . that's not possible."

"Can you hand me that Sharpie while still holding the hood?" Jase calls to Sam.

"We always knew it was temporary." I've said these lines so many times. It's possible that I am a complete bitch.

"We did? Why?" Brad, forehead squinched, says in a faint voice. "What was missing, Ally-baby? We hung out, we made out, we worked out. All the good stuff. I don't get it."

His brown eyes are pleading. Jase frowns over something on the inside of the hood. Samantha is also apparently very absorbed in the whole process.

"Brad, we never *talked*. We didn't—" *laugh*. Tears are starting to run down his cheeks. Oh God.

"Talked?" he repeats, sounding confused. "About what?"

This is going nowhere. Wrap it up. I set my hand on his knee, squeeze. "You're a good guy."

"Oh, no," he says, suddenly loud. "Don't do that. Don't 'good guy' me. I'm better than that. I'm a great guy. I've stuck by you. I've been there for you."

He has. He's put up with my crazy hours, all the homework and housework and babysitting I've had to do. On the other hand, I've put up with his roommate—the missing link—his CrossFit obsession, the wicked Grandmother of the West, and all those nicknames.

"You have, Brad. Which is what makes this so hard." My voice is gentle, but it doesn't make any difference. Now he's actually sobbing, giant shoulders heaving, tears streaming down his face, his nose running. I flick my gaze to the garage apartment. "Brad . . ." I say helplessly. How can he have felt this deeply without me realizing it?

Now he's buried his face in his hands. I try to rub his shoulder but he shakes me off. "Just go. Go away, Alice."

More tears.

"Brad—" I say helplessly. "I feel—"

"You feel nothing," he says. "You don't even know how to feel. Get out of my car."

My feet have barely hit the driveway when he yanks the door shut, then peels out with a screech of tires, zooms down the road, totally unlike himself. He usually drives like a little old lady.

I'm staring after him, biting my thumbnail, which I haven't done in years. Jase slams the hood closed, wipes his greasy hands on some rag. After the roar of the car fades away, the silence is particularly loud.

"Well . . . that could have gone better," Jase says. "Don't you ever get tired of this, Al?"

"Do you want to talk about it?" Samantha asks at nearly the same time.

I shake my head. Should I have known how he felt? Where were the signs? "I didn't . . ." Wait. Is that the same silver car, idling across the road?

"He's wrong. About the feelings thing. He was just pissed. Guys are dicks when their pride gets hurt," Jase offers.

"My fault," I say absently. "He was never a dick before."

"Want me to beat him up for you?" he asks. "He's big, but I could hire henchmen. George would go for it if there was a cool uniform."

"Tim would help," adds Samantha.

The stalker car jerks into reverse, then forward, like a replay of Brad. One of Joel's castoffs? Tim's drug connection? Whatever. The least of my problems.

Speak of the devil. I turn at the sound of Tim's feet banging down the garage steps. He's whistling, head bent, counting change. "I'll be back around seven, guys, do you wanna—"

The tension in the air is practically solid. He looks back and forth between us. "Alice? Sam? What'd I do?"

After they all leave, I plop down on the steps next to George. He looks at me, head cocked. "He cried."

Sighing, I tug him onto my lap, resting my chin on the top of his head. His flyaway hair tickles my nose as I inhale his scent— chalk and grass and hose water. "Yup, I know."

"I've never seen someone so big cry like that. It was kind of like when the Cowardly Lion cries."

It sure was.

Guess that makes me Tin Alice.

Chapter Eleven

TIM

Today's meeting is at the hospital, the same one Mr. Garrett is at. I come late, and my AA sponsor, Dominic, scowls at me when I slouch into the chair next to him.

"Unavoidably delayed," I mutter.

"Avoid it next time," he mutters back.

This is how Dominic got to be my sponsor: He copped on to me fast. Almost as fast as Mr. Garrett, who had the advantage of being my Cub Scout troop leader long ago. It was Mr. G. who told me to go to AA, and Mr. G. I went with, at first. But some days he couldn't, was working or doing something with the kids. Those days I would still go, but I would sit—or stand—near the door. Then I'd leave early. Never when Mr. Garrett was there, but when he wasn't, every time. Earlier and earlier. After I did this four or five times, Dominic grabbed me by the side of my T-shirt as he was walking in the door, towed me over to the seat next to him, and pulled me down. We were way in the back of the room, as far from the door as could be. He's this boxy-shouldered guy, young, huge hands, skinny but strong, deep tan skin, one of those permanent five-o'clock-shadow types. When I started to get up ten minutes before the end of the meeting, he stuck his foot out in front of mine, like he was going to trip me. "What is this, kindergarten?" I hissed out of the corner of my mouth. He mouthed, "Later." The minute the meeting ended I said, "I didn't know there was assigned seating at these things. You want to see my ID now? You're an asshole."

He stared at me, no expression. "No. No. You found me out. Don't leave early. Asshole."

No messing around with Dom.

Later I found out other stuff. That he was twenty-two. That he got married right out of SBH because he got his girlfriend pregnant on prom night. "In the car, on the way there," he always adds. "I didn't even buy her a corsage." That his wife left and took the baby when they'd been married a year. That he spent the next six months so smashed, he still doesn't remember if he went to work or not. That now he's been clean for three years.

So, here we all are, at the end of the meeting, all holding hands like it really is kindergarten. A few months ago, that would have seemed lame as hell; something you do all the time when you're little, crossing the street with your mom and all that. But after you're, say, ten, who does it? But I actually kind of like it, here, sandwiched between Tough Guy Dominic and Mr. Smooth Jake, who I formerly knew as Coach Somers, my gym teacher from Hodges. He smiles at me, which, trust me, he never did when I was at Hodges on his team. He was more given, back then, to asking me to drop and give him fifty for my lousy attitude. Back then, I thought he was a bitter-ass old guy who didn't get teenagers. He's maybe in his late twenties.

Now, as I head out to get coffee with Dominic, Jake tosses me a salute. Feels good.

Dom and I are at Cuppa Joe and Piece-a Pie—sucky coffee, awesome pie—talking about whether he should buy this old junker truck with 100,000 miles on it—when he suddenly looks up, eyebrows raised, then smirks at me. "Some guy hates one of us. My bet's on you. Because if looks could incinerate, you'd be a smoking pile of ashes."

"It's usually the girls I piss off—my money's on you. Where is he?"

"Riiight, I forgot you were the big Casanova. Third table from the left. I'm pretty sure that one-fingered salute was all yours. He has good aim. If he had a gun—"

"No man detests me like that except my pop." I pretend to be cracking my neck to get a glimpse of the guy.

Yeah, he looks like he hates my ass, all right. It's Alice's Brad.

"Need to go make amends?" Dominic asks. "I'm sure he'd be happy to accept it. If not, he only outweighs you by, maybe, ninety to a hundred pounds. Might show some mercy and leave you *almost* dead instead of a bloody smear on the floor."

"You seem to like imagining different ways for me to bite it, Dom. Way to be supportive."

"What did you do, sleep with his girlfriend?"

"Uh—what? No!" My voice goes a little loud on that one. "No," I repeat more quietly.

"You blushing?" Dominic asks, amused.

"No. So . . . tell me more about this truck thing—how does it, uh, handle?"

Dominic looks down, lips compressing to hide his smile. "Yeah, like *that's* what you care about handling." He sips his coffee. "Speaking of, what happened with the GED thing?"

Turns out that in Connecticut, you can't apply for a GED unless you're at least nineteen, or if you get a letter from your school saying you "withdrew." Not precisely how it went down at Ellery.

I rub my thumb into a glob of cherry pie, lick it off. "Um, yeah. I took care of it. Not exactly sure it was . . . kosher, twelve-step-wise."

"You didn't forge anything, did you, Tim? Because—"

"No! I, um, relied on something I sort of maybe shouldn't have. With the school secretary."

Dominic cocks an eyebrow. "And that would be?"

"My charm."

Dom snorts. "Had that one fooled too, huh? She should have talked to Smiley over there."

Christ. Brad's still glaring at me like I stole his favorite pacifier.

"Ms. Iszkiewicz—she always"—I hunch a little lower in my seat—"thought I was cute or something. She said she'd type up a letter and get the headmaster to sign off on it. Dobson never paid attention to shit he was signing unless it was a donation check."

"Tim," Dominic says. "C'mon."

"Did I cross the line?"

Dom takes another sip of coffee. "What do you think?"

"But if I don't lie, how can I get what I need?"

"Did you just hear yourself?" He relaxes back in his chair, watching my face.

I curse.

"I know," Dom says. "But part of this whole thing is not being a manipulative bastard anymore, remember?"

Brad's leaving. As he walks by our table, he accidentally on purpose bangs into the back of my chair with his giant thigh.

What, no wedgie? What the hell does Alice get from this douchewit?

Chapter Twelve

TIM

Alice's hands are behind her back, her beat-up purse hanging off her elbow. Green scrubs, circles under her eyes, smells like antibacterial gel . . . and she still kicks my pulse into high gear.

"I've got something for you," she says, brushing past me.

"Is it kinky? Does it involve you, me, some body oil?"

She snorts. "In your dreams, junior."

"Just the really good ones. But we could totally make those a reality."

"Here." She holds out what she's had hidden behind her. A package wrapped in bright blue tissue. She shoves the box at me so fast, I have to snatch at it before it drops to the ground.

"You got me a housewarming present, Alice?"

"Unwrap it already." She walks over to the sink, full of two days' worth of dishes. Most with Grape-Nuts laminated to the sides.

I open it to find a box with the Nike swoosh on it.

"If I wear these, does it mean we're going steady?"

"If you wear these while you're running, it means you won't wind up in a cast."

I examine the sneakers. They'll fit. Perfectly.

"You know my size?" I check the tiny tag. Yup, thirteens.

"You've left your disgusting Sasquatch shoes by our pool often enough. Your feet are, like, freaks of nature."

"You know what they say about large feet."

"Uh-huh. Big smelly socks. Stop it, Tim. I just thought if you were even remotely interested in being healthy, you should have the right equipment."

"Trust me, Alice. I have the right equipment."

She starts to laugh. "Please. You're like one of those over-grown puppies who can't stop humping everything."

My smile fades. But Alice has turned away, hands on hips, to survey the room. "You're a bigger slob than Brad," she says. "Impressive."

This means that she's been in lame-ass Brad's room—quick one-two punch to the gut, even though, Christ, *of course*. I mean, she's nineteen.

She squints at the apartment some more, walks around. Which is, ya know, embarrassing in the daylight. It was pretty dim when she was last here. In addition to the sink pileup, I have a small mountain of used boxers and shorts in one corner and the sweatpants I slept in last night draped over the couch.

"Hey. Uh . . ." I indicate the box of Grape-Nuts before she can notice the raised toilet seat and wad of wet towels on the floor of the bathroom. "I'd offer you cereal, but I only have one spoon. I know how anal you are about germs."

"I'm *educated* about germ transfer. You drink out of the orange juice carton. I've *seen* you. Why do guys do that? Foul."

"Because when we want things, we want them now. We're thirsty, we need a drink—we take a drink. Finding a clean glass, washing out a dirty one and all that crap—nah. We're just basic. We want what we want right this minute . . . Or maybe that's just me."

"Tim, cut it out. Now. Please." Her face is as expressionless as her voice. But of course, I keep going.

"Like that old song: *Antici-pay-ay-shun is making me way-yay—yait.* That could only be written by a chick. Guys hate anticipation. That's why we all write about satisfaction. Why we never wrap presents. I notice you wrapped mine."

"I thought it was because you're all too cheap to buy wrapping paper. Or too clueless to find it in the store."

"There's that. But honestly, you go to the trouble of getting someone a present, something you think they'd like—why hide it and make them work for it? It's coy."

Alice laughs, shifting aside my sweatpants and dropping down on the couch. "It's not coy. It . . . it shows you care." She gathers her hair up in a knot, showing off her long neck.

"The *present* shows you care. The wrapping paper shows you aren't as concerned about the environment as you should be. Like showering alone. A needless waste of resources."

"Are we ever going to have a conversation without you coming on to me, Tim Mason?"

"I doubt it. We want what we want, right? Basic, babe."

"Please. No 'babe.' No 'chick.'"

"You prefer Allykins? Ally-o? Ally-ums? Noted."

"Tim. Don't." Her voice sounds a little funny. Damn. Is she that sold on Brad?

She roots through her purse, pulls something out. "I have another present for you, actually. I didn't wrap this one." Holding up a small clinical-looking square box, she wags it at me without looking at my face.

"Nicotine patches, Alice—seriously?"

"I told you you can't smoke here."

"And I told you I'm trying to kick it."

"I know." She waves me over, clasping the box between her knees, and flips it open with her other hand. When I plunk down next to her, she slides the rolled-up sleeve of my shirt higher, cool fingers on my skin. "You need to put these on parts of your body that aren't hairy. Not that you're very hairy. Only a bit on your chest." Her fingers freeze for a second before she continues. "Stick it on your shoulder or your back. Or your ribs. But rotate the spot, because the nicotine irritates your skin."

She's touching my upper arm, totally professional, like the nurse she's training to be, and hell if I'm not reacting like she's unzipping my jeans.

I edge away, scratch the back of my neck, which doesn't itch, a little dizzy.

She pulls my arm to her stomach, holds it steady, and plasters on the patch. "Change it once a day. Different location. Six to eight weeks."

"Did you have a secret vice, Alice? You sound so knowledgeable."

"I read directions. Another thing guys rarely do." Patting my arm, she flips my sleeve back down, hesitates a second before meeting my eyes. "What you're doing is tough, Tim. Not drinking, no drugs. Living on your own. Add quitting smoking. I admire you for it."

I stare at her. "For real?"

"Of course. I'm nineteen and still at home. This is no easy thing"—she reaches out and taps where the patch is under my shirtsleeve—"but you don't always *have* to take the hard way. Not when there are easier ways."

My throat tightens. Of all people I expected to . . . whatever, Alice might be dead last. I swallow. Her green-brown eyes are sincere. I lift my hand a few inches toward her cheek. Then drop it, shove it in my pocket as I stand, jingle the loose coins in there.

Alice inspects me sharply for a sec, school-marm-over-her-glasses-style, then licks her lips and looks away, wiping her palms on her scrubs. She stands up. "What's it with you and the Grape-Nuts? Besides pizza, it's almost all I ever see you eat."

"I like Grape-Nuts."

"You *live* on Grape-Nuts. That's more than liking. It's obsession."

"You sure are getting worked up about this." To keep my dangerous hands occupied, I pour myself a bowl, get milk out of the fridge, sniff at it.

"Well, it isn't rational."

Her tone is mad huffy. Why? What'd I miss?

"All this emotion over cereal? What do you care what I eat?"

"You're all thin and pale, Tim. You look like you're not sleeping. People worry about you." She lobs her droopy, too-big purse back over her shoulder. "I should get going. I'm on babysitting call tonight."

I move between her and the door before I can think. "Okay, Alice. I'll grant that worrying people has always been a talent of mine. But my family's pretty much given up. You're the one who came all the way over here to save my ankles and so on. Are we talking worrying *people* . . . or are we talking worrying *you?*" The words rush out, hover in the air. I'm noticing again how little Alice is, aside from those curves, barely coming up to my shoulders. Five two? Five four?

She yanks her purse onto her shoulder again, looks down. Her cheeks go pink.

"Well?" I ask, because I've pushed it this far already.

One finger after another, she ticks things off. "You're my little brother's best friend. Though sometimes I have no idea how or why he puts up with you. You're a minor. You're a potential, if not an ongoing, disaster. You—" Then she sighs, shuts her eyes. "Listen, I have a long day tomorrow. Three classes, a clinical. When I get through it"—her voice drops to a low mutter, like even she doesn't want to hear what she's saying—"could we just meet for dinner? Like a . . . sample date?"

This goes through me like an electric shock.

A date.

With Alice Garrett?

Wait.

A *sample* date?

"What would we be sampling?"

She looks like she might laugh. Doesn't. "Not *that*. I don't do hookups."

"I didn't mean that. I never thought that for a second."

She gives my shoulder a shove. "Of course not."

"Okay. But it was like a millisecond, a nanosecond. Then I remembered how much I respected you and that I would never—"

Alice puts her hand, her fingertips, over my mouth. "Tim. Stop talking now."

I snap my mouth shut.

"We'd be sampling *dinner*."

Then I remember a certain two-hundred-and-fifty-pound

boyfriend. Who apparently already hates my ass. "Wait. Is this a setup? Are you trying to get my ass kicked by ol' Brad?"

She shakes her head quickly, pulling her hand away from my face and burying it in the pocket of her scrubs. Her purse strap falls down again. My hand goes to slip it back up, but then no, I shove it back in my pocket.

Alice hesitates for a second, then: "This has nothing to do with Brad. He wouldn't mind, anyway."

"Then he's even more of a putz than I thought. Hard to believe."

Her eyes flick to mine, then away. "It's not like that."

It's not? Okay. So that makes me . . .

Dinner.

"Meet me at Gary's Grill in Barnet. Six thirty. Tomorrow night."

Barnet is three towns away. Apparently Alice isn't prepared to be seen in the immediate vicinity with her underage, recovering alcoholic sample date.

I say I'll meet her there. She nods, gives me a subdued version of her sexy, crooked smile, then her lips brush my cheek. That Hawaii smell. *Oh, Alice.*

"See you then."

I nod, speechless, and shy-Alice morphs back into take-charge-Alice, jabbing a finger at me. "Don't you dare be late. I hate it when guys pull that, like my time doesn't matter. Like they're all casual and time is a relative thing while I'm sitting there with the waiter pitying me."

"Should we synchronize our watches?"

"Just don't let me down."

Chapter Thirteen

TIM

Waiting out in front of Hodges, school number one of my three, is bizarre. I've been back for Nan's this-or-that achievement awards, but my neck still starts to itch as I stand there, like I'm stuck in the old uniform, gray flannel pants and stiff white shirt.

Here to pick up Samantha, offered to walk with her to the condo she and her mom moved into a week ago—ol' Gracie's brilliant plan to get her away from Jase and the Garretts next door, by relocating across town. Out of sight, etc.

She comes out of the big-ass oak doors, down the steps with the stone lions, spots me, waves, then halfway down the path, gets called over by this cluster of girls. They're laughing and gesturing, and in their matching outfits, long straight hair, prep-clean looks, Hodges could slap 'em right on the cover of the school catalog.

Sam's not like that, but she blends.

Then I see something else. My sister, walking with her head down, rooting through her bag like she'll find the Ark of the Covenant in there. She's so preoccupied, I think she's gonna crash right into the girls, but she makes a wide, careful path around them. So I get it. She sees them, but doesn't want them to see her.

Sam does, though, raises one hand, hello. But Nan keeps

walking, rummaging away, because that treasure in her bag must and shall be found.

She's not short, Nan, five seven or so, but from here she looks it. Text her: You okay?

I think she's gonna look around and spot me, propped against the magnolia tree only a few yards from the brick pathway, but she doesn't.

Nan: Why wouldn't I be?

Chew my lip, try to figure out whether to say I'm right here or not. Nan would be . . . not happy with the Sam pickup—I mean, she knows we're still friends. But . . .

I settle for: Just checking in.

Nan: That's out of character.

She's stopped on the path and is making this phony face like she's oh so excited about whoever's texting her. It's a "for the benefit of others" face.

Me: Yeah, well, I'm all about turning over the new leaf. So . . . you know where I am if you need me, K?

Nan: Who are you and what have you done with my brother?

Me: Ha.

Nan: Look, I've got a thing. Gotta go.

Right, the infamous "thing" we all have. Jesus, Nan.

As I'm trying to figure out whether to call her out on it in person, Sam strides up next to me, cups one of her ears, then the other with a few swift taps. "Water in my ear. Forgot my earplugs, and I'm going crazy trying to up my time before tryouts next week. So, you're actually asking me for advice, Tim? The apocalypse, much?"

Her tone is light, but the look she shoots me isn't.

"The apocalypse? Come on. I ask for stuff."

"Tim, I've known you since we were five. Cash, yes. Excuses, totally. But not this."

"Well, I'll take whatever you've got."

I haul her bag off her shoulder onto my own, hunting around for Nan, but she's blended somewhere into the girl herd.

We walk. "It's left up here." Sam points to the road up the hill, the summit of Stony Bay, fanciest, richest part of town. "So, this is an actual date you're going on."

"Just—just something I'd rather not screw up. So—hit me with your best. Like, for starters, what the hell do I even wear?"

Samantha grins.

"Don't," I say. "I know exactly how lame I sound."

"Start by passing the sniff test," she says, smelling the air exaggeratedly, like some crazy bloodhound or whatever. "Which that shirt doesn't, by the way. And"—she smacks me on the shoulder—"if she's older than you, like you said, no shirts with school insignias. No point in rubbing it in that she's a cougar."

"She's not a cougar. Jesus God."

We're a little over one year apart, me and Alice. It's nothing.

Samantha studies me for a sec, then continues lightly. "Shower. Take her someplace low-key. Listen when she talks. Ask questions but only if you actually care about the answers. Don't keep trying to interrupt with stories about the last time you got drunk."

"Believe me, I'm not gonna touch that."

Besides, Alice has been there. I puked all over her and she took off her shirt, calm as moon-low tide, *owning* this black lace bra with this tiny red ribbon and . . . it's the one thing I remember perfectly about that night.

"You'd be surprised at how many guys do."

Samantha's shoulders stoop a little as we hit a bend in the road, cut off by huge black iron gates, tacked all over with signs: PRIVATE COMMUNITY, NO TRESPASSING, you are not welcome here. "Here we go, home sweet home as of last week. The code is 1776."

"Sorry, kid. Should have given you a housewarming present. A casserole, at least."

"Believe me, nothing could warm this place up. The condo makes our old house look festive. We're right up by the clubhouse." She gestures to this low building with a Swiss-chalet-looking roof, surrounded by a golf course spattered with dudes in pastel, knocking away at tiny white balls. It all looks like a retirement village.

"Wow," I say. I got nothin' else.

"I know." Samantha shakes her head. "I haven't even let Jase see it yet. I mean, did you notice the streets? General Dwight D. Eisenhower Drive, Lady of the Lake Lane, Pettipaug Peak? The names aren't even consistent! And check out the houses. You could walk into the wrong one and suddenly find yourself living someone else's life." She waves her hand at row after row of identical houses.

"What time do all the handsome husbands pop out of their doors with their matching briefcases?"

"Leaving their blond wives to take their Valium, at the same second, elbows bent just so? Not sure. We've only been here a week. Give me time. It's over here, Wolverine Wood Road."

I squint. "Are there any actual woods? Or wolverines?" The landscape is green and grassy and flat, except for an unnatural-looking lake.

"Right? No, they took down all the trees to build this. I'll keep you posted on the wolverines. We're here." She points past a narrow row of hedges. "By the statue of the nonspecified Revolutionary War soldier."

"Do I need to lay a wreath?" I ask as we head past the scarily smiling iron statue. "Or salute?"

"Why couldn't we have stayed put?" She sighs.

Samantha knows the obvious answer to that, so all I say is, "Cheer up, kid. College next year."

Gracie, Sam's mom, is out on the porch of Clairemont Cottage, planting some brassy orange flowers in big stone urns. She jolts to her knees when we turn the corner, trowel in hand, then, seeing it's me with Sam, beams, waves, settles back down on her heels again. For reasons known only to her and God, Grace persists in thinking Jase is the delinquent and I'm the upstanding citizen.

Samantha studies me for a sec, then says, "One more thing. The most important. On this date? Just be, you know, smart and funny and sweet. Like you are."

"Pretty sure that's not actually me."

"It is." She flips her hair out of its braid, sliding her fingers through to shake it out. "If she's going on a date with you, she probably thinks so too. Do I know her?"

"Not really."

"Tim, c'mon."

"It's not a big deal. It's just a"—I have no idea what it is—"thing."

Not buying it. All over her face.

But Samantha smiles, tugs her bag off my shoulder, puts her hand in its place. "Two more things, actually—but they're crucial. Don't wear that stupid Axe stuff clueless guys think is sexy. It reeks of desperation."

I fake-scribble on an imaginary pad. "Noted."

"And don't let her break your heart, okay?"

"Sammy-Sam, I think that's already a given."

ALICE

"I get to ride on the feet!" George squeals.

"Bro. You can't ride on the wheelchair feet. I'd lose my job," Brad says, maneuvering Dad out of the hospital room, skillful and grounded in his transporter role. We're a parade to help move Dad to the rehab part of Maplewood. Joel's got the duffel full of the clothes we brought so Dad would feel semi-normal. Mom's arms are bundled full of his books. Andy's carrying a stack of artwork the little guys made, carefully detached from the Scotch tape on the wall. Duff has the Xbox and the video games. Harry, the old deck of cards, the pick-up sticks, the dominoes, the old-fashioned games we rediscovered to make time pass.

I have all the paperwork, most of which my parents don't know about.

It *would* be Brad they sent to do the transfer, of all the 'porters in all of Maplewood Memorial. He's ignoring me. I'm ignoring him. This is fun. At least he's been decent to the kids, even though George keeps giving him sidelong glances, no doubt worried the tears will start again.

I check my watch—plenty of time to do what I need to do, get home, and get ready to go out with Tim, as long as this all goes quickly.

Two and a half hours later—twice as long as it was supposed to take—Dad's in his room, everything (more or less) sorted out.

Mom leaves with the kids, Joel heads to cop class, I linger.

Sticking the pictures up on the wall, stacking the games in piles, making the bare room a little like home. Dad shut his eyes the instant they all left, "just for a moment." But he immediately dropped off to sleep.

I sit down on the side of the bed. Really, I want to lie down too, put my head on his shoulder. I was up late last night studying, and George had a wake-up-screaming nightmare, something about a supervolcano under Yellowstone Park. After I convinced him it was absolutely nothing to worry about and he finally fell asleep in my lap and I carried him back to bed, I googled it.

There is one.

Looking at my father's face, worry lines smoothed out, faint smile, his big hands brown against the white hospital sheet, air siphons out of my lungs for an instant. Black spots collect at the corners of my vision.

Deep breath.

Deep breath.

The spots scatter and fade.

On to the next thing, because what else can I do?

I brought a change of clothes for tonight along with me, just in case.

I mean, I'm not dressing up. Not for Tim, for God's sake. But, I've been wearing this black V-neck and skirt all day long, and Harry squeezed his juice box too hard and—

Anyway.

I shower in the bathroom off Dad's new room, crowded in by the walker, the quad cane, and the commode chair. Tiny hospital-issue soap and body wash and shampoo, because I forgot to bring my own. Hospital towels are rough and tiny, it takes two to dry off, and still my dark blue sundress clings in a few wet patches. No blow dryer, so my hair will dry curly. So be it. When I look in the mirror, I recognize myself again.

There's a sharp sound from the other room, like air through teeth.

Sweat stands out on his forehead, and his face is chalky white.

"Dad?"

"Al," Dad says gently, "come back a little later, okay?"

"Not happening. What do you need?"

My hand is poised over the call button. He sets his on top of it. "They'll only dope me up. Not what I want."

Dad shifts in the bed with a crackle of plastic hospital mattress pad. He sucks his breath in hard, again blows it out. My own breath snags.

"Scale of one to ten," I say, groping to find the professional in me.

"I'm not your patient, tiger," Dad says. "Luckily for both of us."

Without warning, my eyes fill. I don't cry. I never cry.

Which Dad knows. His hand shoots out, squeezes my shoulder. "You know I didn't mean it like that. You know that." Now he's batting at the box of tissues at the side of his bed, which is slightly out of reach, and something about that, my dad, who can do *anything*, who can fix everything—

"You look gorgeous, Alice," Dad says. "Hot date?"

"Just a thing," I say, my face going hot.

He studies me, saying nothing, waiting for information to come to him. Mom and Dad have that one down to an art.

"How's Tim these days?"

These two questions are not connected. He's making conversation. Distracting me from calling the nurse and another debate about pain medication. "How Mom and Dad Met" is a family fairy tale—Mom's told us the story so often, we can all fill in words when she pauses. But there's a part she leaves out when we're younger...that charming, perceptive Jack Garrett had a dark side back then. He was, as he tells it, "mad at the whole live world" because his mother had died the year before, and his little sister and brother, my aunt Caroline and my uncle Jason, had stayed behind in Virginia with their grandparents, while his father had taken my father, alone, since he was sixteen and old enough to bring in a paycheck, up to Connecticut. Dad had a drinking problem, which got worse until his twenties, when he realized he could go that route, or have a life with Mom, and turned his around.

I have never seen my father drink alcohol. He doesn't even have soda, although he'll be the first to tell you that entire coffee plantations are supported by his caffeine habit.

It could go that way for Tim. Or it could go the other way.

"Oh . . . you know. The usual."

Dad laughs. "That kid has no 'usual.'"

Out in the hallway again, I rub my neck, close my eyes, flip back my hair. I'm looking forward to Tim—Tim!—like a steaming hot bath after a long, cold day.

Still, I pull Dad's chart from the plastic holder outside the door, page through it. Standard entry, expected procedure, the usual blah, blah, blah.

But then . . .

Holy.

Holy Mother of God.

Chapter Fourteen

TIM

I'm doing push-ups as a healthier alternative to a pack of Marlboros, wondering when the hell the magic powers of the nic patch will kick in, when I hear the knock at my door—so faint, it's not really a knock, more like a scratch or a tap. I'm at that top-of-the-push-up, arms-shaking point, right before I exhale—

Collapse.

Wipe my arm across my sweaty forehead. I'm wearing Ellery gym shorts and a sweaty black polo. Not exactly poised to receive company. But I've still got time to get it together for Alice.

Whatever it is we're sampling on this date, the thought of it has me grinning as I open the door.

But when I do, the face I see is so out of context, it takes me a few seconds.

Big blue eyes, small pointed chin, tidy ponytail. One seat to the left of me in English Writers of the Western World. I used to borrow her perfectly sharpened pencils. Never gave 'em back.

"Tim?" she says, like I might be Tim's evil twin.

"Hi. Uh . . . Heather." How I scrounge that name from my subconscious, I have no idea.

"It's Hester. Can I come in?"

What? I think, at the same time I say, "Sure," and open the door wider for her. She brushes past me, sits down on the couch, and looks at her shoes. Hester was a Brain and a Good Girl. So we had nothing in common. What's she doing here? She smooths down her khaki skirt, readjusts her white shirt. Prep wear. *Clothing as birth control,* my douchey friends and I used to joke. All those fuckin' buttons. Little gold hoop earrings, neat part in her brown hair. Shit, is she, like, a Jehovah's Witness or something? I don't have time for this. But now she's weaving her fingers together, studying them. "So, Tim . . . you left Ellery early this year."

"Yeah, left, as in got booted."

I look at the clock on the stove right as it flips from 5:58 to 59. Less than half an hour to meet Alice, and it takes fifteen minutes to drive. If you don't run the lights or speed.

Hester lifts her face and looks at me squarely. "Before that, you went to Ward Akins's pool party."

I did? Geez, I was so messed up back then, worst of my worst. I can hardly remember those last months of school. Little flashes. Ward Akins? Asskite guy on my tennis team. Pool party? Would I have gone to one of those? Who'm I kidding? I would have gone to *anyone's* party.

But also? Who the eff cares what party I did or didn't go to.

"Uh. Look, can we catch up some other time? Sorry—I mean . . . not to be a dick, but . . . why are you here?"

"Ward is my godmother's stepson," Hester says, like family history answers the question. "Even though he's an abject loser, I went to this party because . . . Well, never mind." Her voice, which is husky, throaty, stalls out for a sec. Then she braids her fingers together even more tightly, swallows. "Big house—very modern, glass windows . . . the pool's indoors, heated. They have a tiki bar . . . Do you remember any of this?"

Not even the tiki bar. "No. Sorry. I got nothing."

Her face shuffles through a boatload of emotions in, like, seconds—there and gone. Then her features smooth, totally composed. She looks dead on at me, blue eyes crystal clear, focused, narrowing, like she's aiming a gun. "You don't have 'nothing.' You have a son."

Chapter Fifteen

TIM

I do the most wrong thing I could possibly do.

Laugh.

Looking Hester straight in the eye, I slump down on the couch next to her.

And laugh.

It's like I can't stop. I'm holding up one hand, holding the other to my stomach, and she's staring at me like I'm dog shit she's stepped in, except that her eyes are filling with tears.

So I try to get a hold of myself, say something.

And again, straight to the worst thing.

"You're fucking kidding me, right?"

She's standing up now, slowly, in this rickety way, like she's aged fifty years at my response.

Brushes her hands on her skirt again. Tucks some stray hair behind her ears.

"No joke. Sorry."

She's halfway to the door before I stop her, hand on her shoulder. "Hester. That's not possible . . . I'm not *that* stupid."

Yeah, hack off foot and shove it permanently in mouth.

Her eyes flash. "You were. Sorry again. You were a bit drunk. For a change. Never mind."

"Never *mind?*" I repeat incredulously.

Hester reaches into her purse, foraging around, all anxious. Then smacks her forehead with the heel of her hand, stuffs it into the front pocket of her skirt, pulls something out, and hands it to me. "It's an awful picture. I didn't know that hospital pictures are a scam. They get you while you're groggy and suddenly you have all these wallet-sized photos and a mouse pad for, like, eighty bucks . . . He looks better now." She hands me this little snapshot. Of this baby with his eyes squinted shut like he's pissed off. And a fluff of red hair. My hair. When I was little it always stuck straight up exactly like that.

"His name's Calvin."

Really? What a sucky name.

I stare at the picture, the closed eyes, the defiant face. Scrabble for something . . . anything . . . to say.

Fuck.

"Where is he now?"

"In my car." Hester takes the picture back, tucking it into her wallet, carefully closing the purse back up, all focused. "He was sleeping and I thought it'd be better if I—"

"You serious? It's eighty-five degrees!" I hurtle down the garage steps.

"The windows are all open!" Hester calls after me.

The windows may be open, but the baby in the car is soaked with sweat, dark red hair plastered to his forehead, hunched down in one of those backward bucket baby-type seats, boneless and kinda bowlegged. He's wearing a blue undershirt, a diaper, and a weird-ass sailor hat. His eyes, with these little spiky eyelashes, dark like mine, oh hell, are shut tight, his mouth puckered like he's dreaming about kissing.

I bend in, try to unlock the car seat, sweating like a mother myself. There are these two thick red buttons on either side and I press them hard, jiggle harder. Nothing happens. Hester moves forward. I think she's gonna unlatch things, but instead, she takes off his hat.

"Here he is," she says, like, *ta-da*. "This is Calvin."

"Yeah, can we save the introductions?" I'm punching and jiggling the buttons. "This kid really needs air."

Actually, I don't know this. Just guessing. If he were a dog in the car, he'd need air. I sure need air. I'm breathing so hard, I'm pretty much panting when I finally hear the click of the car seat disengage and drag it out. Look at the kid.

My kid.

Wait, wait. No. This isn't. This isn't real and I'll wake up and see that this is some crazy dream test. At least I'm not naked. Except that I feel it, more naked than actual naked because—

He stares at me, blue eyes, confused face, and I might as well be looking at one of the baby pics on our living room wall. The world is sucked silent, just a faint hum. I'm gonna puke.

Because—

At the same time that I'm thinking *no, no, no way,* some other part of me is not surprised. Not at all. Of course. Of course I would do this. Of course.

Through the buzzing in my ears, Hester's talking again. "I want to go to college next spring. Taking a gap now. Because of Calvin. Obviously. I'm already in at Bryn Mawr. It's where my favorite teacher went, where I've always wanted to go. I took this time off so I could . . . deal."

I'm still looking at the kid, whose little dark eyelashes are fluttering, sinking closed again.

"My grandfather—I live with him—said you deserved to be told," she adds, in a voice so low, it's almost a whisper. "He said you deserved a chance to be a man."

A man. Shit. Not again. I don't want to be a man. I'm not even good at being a boy.

His eyes open again—blue as . . . blue stuff.

He stares, unfocused, for a second, then waves a fist at me.

"Hold out one finger," Hester says, and I do. Calvin knocks his fist against it, prizefighter-style, then opens up his little starfish hand and clenches onto my index finger. His clutch is hot and sticky. He stares at me, eyes crossing.

"Do you want to . . ." Hester clears her throat. "Hold him?"

Hell no. He looks completely breakable. But I *should* want to, right? "Uh, sure. Yeah. I do. Absolutely."

Hester peers at me. Like she's wondering if she can trust me not to break her baby. She shouldn't. I break everything.

She unlatches the little belt, scoops her hand behind Calvin's head and under his butt, straightens up and passes him to me.

My hand covers his entire backside. He's wet with—I hope—sweat, and has this weird milky smell.

I wait for him to start screaming because, Christ knows, *I* want to, but he doesn't. He simply gazes, all fathomless navy blue eyes.

"Serious little guy," I say, finally, because I should say *something*.

I'm holding the kid, my kid, for the first time and no natural instincts are kicking in. Except the "flee" one.

"They don't smile when they're this little," Hester says softly as I focus on pulling up the sock that's about to slide off Calvin's midget foot, the size of my goddamn thumb. "They learn in a month or two."

Hope so. On the other hand, this kid might not have much to smile about.

We stand there for a second next to the car—me awkwardly balancing the baby, Hester flicking her gaze between us. All I can think is, *What now? What does she really want?*

"What, uh . . . what can I do for you, Hes?" I'm startled to hear that abbreviation coming from my lips, like they know her better than the rest of me. She looks down at the tar of the driveway. The silent stillness is halted by a gentle rumbling noise. Her stomach.

Her fair skin flushes and she puts her hand there, like she can hush it that way. Or like there's still something—someone—in there.

"Can I start by giving you a sandwich?" I vaguely remember that you're supposed to eat a lot after you have a baby. Or is that before? Is she, like, nursing this kid?

Yikes. I steal a look at her tits. They look pretty much as I dimly recall. Small.

"I'd love that," she says, apparently not noticing the direction of my gaze. "He's probably hungry too."

I check Calvin's face, still waiting for the screaming to begin, but he's watching me, hanging tightly on to my finger.

Hester grabs what looks like a small suitcase—*Oh God*—from the backseat of the car and walks up the steps, leaving me to follow. With Calvin. And what may be the lead-up to a coronary squeezing my chest.

Is she here to—uh—stay? Please tell me I don't have to *marry* this girl. The bag doesn't look big enough to hold her stuff *and* his. But his things are probably pretty tiny. Maybe she's a really efficient packer. She *looks* like an efficient packer.

She holds the door open, as if she's inviting me into her own home. But, given that my hands are occupied with the kid, it's possible she's just being helpful.

As soon as we get in, I give him back to her, after carefully unpeeling his clingy, sweaty little paw from my finger.

Which is when the crying I've been waiting for gets going.

Hester hoists the small but solid weight of the baby against her shoulder, tipping her chin to hold him more firmly against her, and rummages the suitcase, pulling something out.

A bottle.

That answers the breastfeeding question. Thank Christ. I don't think I could deal with her exposed boob at the moment.

Then a can of formula, which she unseals with a *shhhzz*. Which sounds eerily like the beer I wish I were cracking open. "Just pour it in this and zap it for thirty seconds." She gestures at the microwave.

"Uh. Right. Sure." I take the bottle and the can, fill the bottle, then stare as it revolves in the microwave.

A wave of dizziness crashes over my head and I clutch the side of the counter.

An hour ago I was worrying about practice dating.

Now I'm heating formula for my baby. Alice is . . . *fuck* . . .

I glance over at Hester, her pink lip stuff and her neat, if slightly rumpled and a size too tight, white shirt. *She's not even my type, for God's sake.* Delicate. Fragile. These big

Bambi eyes. Someone I could do serious damage to.

Make *that* mission accomplished.

The microwave beeps. My hand is actually shaking as I crack it open. The kid's still wailing, cranking it up a notch or two every second.

When I hand the bottle to Hester, she whips me a quick look of gratitude, and then stuffs the nipple in Calvin's wide-open mouth. He hesitates, catching his breath, as if considering whether to continue with the misery or go for liquid comfort. He picks comfort.

Of course he does. My kid, after all.

My kid.

I shut my eyes, and, because I might possibly black out right now, I crouch next to Hester, putting a hand on her knee.

She looks down at it, and I get a sharp shock of weird. Wrong. Although I've clearly done a lot more than casually touch this girl. How is that even possible? I remember her from class. From *class*. Eyes forward, neat little notes, never even catching my eye, even when she lent me pencils. Now that I'm up close, I see there are dark smudges under her eyes, and that her hair in its ponytail is sorta messy. The Hester I recall (vaguely) was one of those chicks who always looked perfect. At the moment her stomach is kind of puffy, squishy. The shoulder of her white shirt has some yellowish stain on it.

I did that. I, like, *marked* this girl, changed her. And I don't even remember holding her hand.

Clawing for air in my own personal mineshaft now.

Okay.

She's here.

With this baby.

Why *now* and, Christ, what next?

"Hester." My voice cracks a little, like I'm still thirteen. "Look, I've got some leftover pizza. Orange juice. Milk. Some cheese that's not that old. Grape-Nuts. You can have any or all of that. But you gotta tell me why exactly you're here. What are you looking for from me?"

She looks up at me, her eyes vast, blue, and totally unreadable.

"Aside from the life-changing complication I've already provided," I add.

To my surprise, she gives a quick huff of laughter. "Poor Tim. You look terrified."

Now I'm ashamed, at least more familiar and comfortable than flat-out panic.

"Sorry," I say, approximately nine months too late. Calvin is glugging away again, his clenched fists waving in the air like he's fighting some invisible but formidable opponent.

"I'd love some pizza," Hester tells me, with a little smile.

Sudden surge of liking for her. She does seem to be able to handle this whole hundred-shades-of-awkward meeting practically, without, say, sobbing uncontrollably or pointing an accusing finger at me. Jesus. What a year she must have had. Ellery would not have been an easy place to be a pregnant teenager. Anorexic, sure. Addicted to cocaine—totally. But pregnant? Hell, no—that's for public school girls.

I stand up slowly, check out Calvin's face. His eyelids are so thin, you can see little blue veins. On his temples too, near the tips of his ears.

"Yeah, sure. Pizza. Coming up."

The pizza's several days old and pretty disgusting. I have to peel it off the bottom of the cardboard box. I slap two rubbery, congealed pieces into the microwave and pour orange juice into one of Joel's Fitness Galaxy coffee mugs.

No napkins. No paper towels, even. Offering her toilet paper would not be okay, right?

Hester somehow interprets my frantic hunt around the kitchen.

"I have baby wipes," she calls.

I go rigid. Somehow this just drives home the whole *I have a baby* thing.

I set the plate down in front of her. The kid's urgent gulping has emptied most of the bottle. He's bending his skinny, half-triangle legs up and down in time to his swallowing. Every time I look at him, I get a cold shock wave, like I have the flu. I know dick about babies. Patsy's cool, but she's a real person already, not, like, an amoeba.

"Hey, I know this is a surprise," Hester says, after swallowing a tiny bite of sucky pizza. "I've had months to take it in. You've had twenty minutes. I appreciate you"—she pauses, then finally continues—"not yelling or saying he's not yours or any of that."

I look at his wavy hair, dry now and as rusty red as my own. "I'm not that guy."

As I say it I realize that this is the first time in years, maybe in my whole life, that I've said what I was and had it mean anything good. Hester nods. "I know. I mean—I hoped not. That's . . . um . . . why I'm here." She tilts the bottle so Calvin has better access to the last bit.

I rest my hands on the countertop, try to beat back visions of this future where I'm suddenly married to her—this girl I don't know—with a child I have no memory of making, and we're living in the Garretts' garage apartment. Forever. I'm this old man hobbling out to my job at, I dunno, Hot Dog Haven again or Gas and Go, trying to convince myself my life hasn't been a complete waste.

As if she's reading my thoughts, Hester glances around the room. "So . . . do you have a roommate? A . . . girlfriend?"

"Why?" My voice comes out like a bark. Hester flinches. Calvin pauses for a second in his glugging but then speeds up again, his eyes practically lolling back in his head in ecstasy.

She shifts the baby so she can wave her hand around the apartment. "Just wondering why this is where you live now. You left Ellery and . . . you're . . . here?"

"It belongs to friends of mine. I, uh, needed a place away from home, so I . . ."

Can't even finish a sentence.

Hester nods, sharp dip of her chin. "It's"—she looks around at the bare white walls with their thumbtack holes, the milk-crate bookcase, the dead plant next to the bathroom door, the basketball hoop above the trash can in the corner of the living room—"roomy." I get this sense that Hester's a nice girl who's used to saying nice things about things that aren't nice.

"Look . . . *please*. I gotta know. What *do* you want from me?"

She squirms in her seat, chips a hardened piece of pepper-oni off the crappy pizza. "After Calvin was born, when I first saw his face—his hair—I knew I had to talk to you. So, as soon as I was, you know—"

"Back on your feet?"

"They put you on your feet right after you give birth, Tim," she says. "Practically as soon as the umbilical cord gets cut."

Gross. I flinch, yeah, I'm a dick. She had a baby, labor and all that, which probably involved some serious mess, and I can't even handle vaguely hearing about the minor details.

"So. When I saw his . . . when I knew, I was trying to figure out how to find you. I asked around and . . . heard that you were, well, better—"

"Sober," I clarify.

Hester turns pink again. "Yes. Like I said, Grand told me that you deserved a chance. So . . . here I am."

My temples are throbbing.

I need a smoke. Or a drink. Or a handy firing squad to end me.

"Right. Sure. What does 'a chance' look like to you?"

Her voice drops low and she adjusts Calvin's little sweaty shirt. "I'm hoping—I want—to go back to work next week. This school-slash-camp place where I've worked summers and vacations for the last few years. They know me, and they were happy to have me back. Even before he was born. But the day care doesn't have a space for him yet. Like I said, I put off college, but I can't just . . . tread water. This baby . . . derailed me. Grand could watch him some. He said he would, just so I know about the choices I'm making. But—" Her eyes are pleading, big and blue.

Fucketty fuck.

"He can't do it all the time, he has to be with my grand-mother—she's got Alzheimer's, she's at a home, but she needs him—and he's got his hospital work, and I *have* to get back to normal. I thought if you knew and all, you might want to take him for an afternoon or a day or, even, more than that. Get to know your son. See if you're all fine with him. I mean, obviously I'm planning on giving him away."

Christ. Wait? What? To me? I *can't* do this.

"You mean, like, getting adopted?" Please almighty God, mean that.

"Of course," Hester says in that calm, smart-girl voice I dimly remember from class, like there's only one right answer and she's got it. She's concentrating on detaching another bit of pepperoni from her slice, not even eating any of it, just making a dried-out stack on one side of the plate. Something about the tidy little pile just pisses me off.

"Why am I in here, Hes, if that's the choice you've already made?" The kid's turned his head to the side, eyelids drooping, but still looking as if he's watching me. I lower my voice, like he already knows how to listen to things he should never hear. "Are you some kind of sadist? Why should I even have to know about this if it's all decided?"

"My grandfather told me you should," she repeats again. "That it's the right thing to do."

Right. *Be a man.* "Sure. No problem. I'll do it." Accept the things you cannot change, right? Damn it.

She grins suddenly, and I get what I hadn't seen before. Rumpled, stained clothes, extra ten pounds, milk-pale skin aside, she's really pretty when she smiles.

"You will? That's great, Tim." She holds her hand out, bargain-style, and I reach out over the kid, grab hold, and shake it. "I was thinking—maybe—we could meet—for lunch tomorrow? That way you'll have time to let this—sink in."

Sure, I'll absolutely have my head wrapped around it by then.

"Okay. That'd be . . . . good. Fine. Yeah. Fine."

She looks grateful, the way she's been thankful for the crappy pizza and the fact that I didn't yell at her.

"Is there any place you'd like to go?" she asks, as if this is a date.

I try to think of a good meeting place. I never took girls anywhere, other than, say, whatever room was unoccupied at whichever party. Sweat beads on my forehead.

"There's this restaurant, Chez Nous, in Riverton," Hester continues. "It's really little and nice. They have great tarte Tatin. We can meet there and go over all the details."

Details? I can't even wrap myself around the big picture.

I swallow, nod.

Then, total autopilot, I open the door, gesture for her to go out first, lock up, trail her down to the car, watch Hester strap Calvin into the car seat, shove the diaper bag into the front passenger seat, smile and nod and knock once against the top of the car to say good-bye, because my voice has completely failed me.

I climb the steps, collapse on the top one, dig the heels of my hands into my eye sockets, like it'll relieve the pressure detonating in my brain.

Through the fog of panic and nausea, two things are crystal clear. I've found my way into a nightmare.

Also?

I've just stood up my dream girl.

Chapter Sixteen

ALICE

First thing I see when I pull in is Tim leaning in the driver's-side window of a little silver sedan. So much for my theory/excuse/delusion that he didn't meet me because he was run over by a truck or called away to the zombie apocalypse or some awful, urgent, no-way-around-it disaster.

I could strangle the part of me that's relieved he's here, with his baggy school shorts and hair that needs cutting, flopping over his ears and forehead. But apparently just fine. The asshole.

He straightens up to give the top of the car a fist-knock, all calm, pulled together, holding up a hand in a casual farewell as it backs down the driveway.

That same car. That same girl.

The moment the car jerks back onto the main road, he folds down on the steps, pats his chest where a pocket would be if his shirt had one. Then he rubs the shoulder where I put the nic patch, drops his head, and spreads one palm across his forehead as if he's taking his own temperature.

I slam the door of the Bug hard, and it pops right back open, because it's ancient and doesn't latch unless you prop it while closing. Slam again, louder this time.

Tim doesn't react at all, just keeps rubbing the patch.

"Just rip it off," I say, walking close, jangling my car keys in one palm. "Might as well admit it's no use."

Now he looks up, but almost through me, his eyes hazy and confused. Sighs. Doesn't say anything for a second, then, "Huh?"

"Tim. Where were you?"

He shudders like he has a fever, and he's staring into the distance, two streaks of color high on his cheekbones, the rest of his face pale.

"Tim."

Nothing.

As if he doesn't even know I'm here.

"You're drunk? Perfect. Good job, Tim."

He shakes his head, hunches his shoulders, doesn't look at me. Unbelievable.

I stand over him, for once taller. "Or is it weed? Or pills? God. Who was the girl? Your dealer? She was essential enough to blow me off? Fine."

I start to leave, brush past him, but he puts his hand on my leg, right above my knee. "It—it's not like that. I swear."

Clench my thumbs inside my curled fingers. "How many times have you 'sworn' about that one?"

"I didn't . . . bag on you on purpose, I mean. Something . . . came up."

I stare pointedly down at his hand until he curses under his breath, tucks it under him, then pulls it back out, picking at a hole in his shorts instead.

"So what made you do it? What was *that* bad? You were doing better!"

"Yeah, well, now I've done worse." He has the hoarse, smothered voice boys get when they're trying not to be emotional, eyes fixed unblinking on the end of the driveway, like if he looks any nearer, he'll cry. He looks younger than usual, keeps picking at that tear near his pocket, and I find myself wrapping my hand around his wrist, giving it a little shake.

"Just as expected, right, Alice? I wanted to be better than that." He glances at me for a moment. "You look incredible. God."

Obviously something serious has happened, but I'm not getting what it is, and he's not giving it to me.

But I've got my whole family. He has a lot less than that.

Ugh, the little guys have left the sidewalk chalk all over the grass near the steps for the millionth time. I start scooping them up and shoving them into the bucket. "Look. Relapses happen. People come back from them. You can get back from this."

His laugh doesn't sound like a laugh at all. "That's what you think."

"It's true. Ask Dad. He never relapsed, but he knows plenty of people who have. It happens."

"Alice. I'm not hammered. I'm stone-cold sober, though I wish to hell I—" He reaches into his pocket and pulls out car keys, flips them at me. "Here. Take these. Don't give them back until tomorrow. Even if I beg."

I snag the keys, move closer. He smells like sweat, but nothing criminal. Reaching up, I take his chin in my hand, turn his face to mine. The whites of his eyes are clear, his pupils look normal, his eyes aren't glassy. He's pale, not so flushed anymore.

But as I look, his eyebrows draw together. "Gonna breathalyze me now, Alice? Have me walk a straight line? Frisk me?"

I drop my hand. "You do *not* get to be sarcastic with me. You lost that right while I was waiting forever for you."

"I lost a lot of things, then," Tim mutters.

I open my mouth to ask, but he sets his hands on my shoulders, looks me full in the face.

"Alice. Please."

"Okay. Okay. I believe you. But I'm keeping your keys for now."

"Swell," Tim says, standing up in one swift fluid motion. No swaying.

"You're in trouble somehow, then?"

"You could sure as hell say that. Or you could just say I'm wicked good at getting other people into it."

"Tell me."

"I can't, Alice. I can't now. I just—" He waves his hand. "I'm sorry. Leave it at that. And keep the goddamn keys for all I care. I'm going nowhere. Trust me."

Chapter Seventeen

TIM

It's been in my wallet like a dirty little secret all this time.

You're only as sick as your secrets—that's the word in AA, and I've held on to this one.

My fake ID, a fifteenth-birthday present from my dealer's big brother. He was good at his job. I've never even gotten a suspicious glance when I handed it over. It helps that I'm so tall.

No car keys. Good. That's good.

Start to walk to a meeting, then don't trust my feet. Dominic didn't pick up on his shitty-service cell phone, so I end up hanging a left to town, down to the marina, looking for his battered old motorboat. I find the Cuddy, sure enough, tied up, bumping hard against the worn wooden dock. No sign of Dom, though. Although I do find his cell tossed on the yellow slicker that I bunch up to rest my head on.

He'll come.

I'll wait.

Simple.

I fall asleep so fast and hard, it's more like a pass-out. When I open my sandy eyes, sticky from the river mist, it's after ten. The liquor stores are closed. I'm safe.

But this feeling, this jangling itch to tear out of my own skin—it doesn't want to be safe, not anywhere near it.

I let Alice down, gave her my keys—and I am so pissed with her for thinking I'd go get spun—but at the same time I'm nearly dying for exactly that.

That blue dress. She was gorgeous.

Here's what I should do: Go to an online meeting since there aren't any this late. Go find safe people to be with. Mr. Garrett, for God's sake. It's after visiting hours at the hospital, but I could talk my way in somehow. Steal scrubs or something.

Here's what I actually do: Shuffle through my wallet for my fake ID, get forty bucks at the ATM of Dad's bank, head uptown to the Dark and Stormy, the only bar on the main drag. Stand staring at the ugly-ass wooden figurehead of a female pirate jutting out over the door of the bar.

It's late, but the D & S is hopping. Tourists love this place and Stony Bay gets 'em by the boatload, end of summer, Stony Bay sidewalk sale season and all that. The bartenders are all female and dressed like buccaneers with a lot of cleavage, and the poor bastards who happen to be waiters dress like French sailors in striped shirts and berets. Guess who gets more tips.

Stride on in.

Two minutes later, I've shoved my way through a crowd of yacht guys still wearing their goddamn captain hats, propped myself up against the thick-planked, dark pine wall, am staring at all the colors on the well-lit glass shelves—the deep amber of whiskey and the sunny yellow of white wine and the Hawaiian surf blue of curacao. Pretty. All that trouble wrapped up in beauty. Inhaling the must of sawdust, the musk of closely packed bodies, the sharp chemical scent of all that booze. I tell myself this is all I'll do and then I'll go. That'll work. Or maybe I'll have to sit at the bar and order something . . . I won't drink it . . . only get a whiff of it. Then I'll go. Safe and sound.

Simple.

Because—because the fact that I am a goddamn *father* does not mean I'm stupid enough to blow more than two months of sobriety, piss away my thirty-day chip, my two-month-er, the single solitary smart thing I've done this year.

Heaving myself off the wall, I sink onto one of the bar stools.

"Ahoy there, hottie," says a cheerful voice, and a waitress plunks the fake pirate's map that's the drinks menu down on the counter and gives me a jolly smile.

Jesus. The waitress is Ms. Sobieski, who was my sixth-grade math teacher. Also my Sunday school teacher. Now wearing a puffy white top that makes the most of the reasons I remember her so well.

Open my mouth to blurt out some excuse, tell her I'm waiting for a friend—*like, say, Jack Daniels?*

"Want the fancy stuff or something straight up?" She slides a wicker basket of unshelled peanuts in front of me, and gives a cheerful wink, and I get it. She has no clue who I am. Or used to be.

Still, she's gotta know I'm underage. But no ID request. Maybe she just figures I'll order a Coke or something.

Maybe I will do only that.

The responsible thing.

But the part of me that wants and needs to do the right thing has been avalanched and I can't dig far enough down to reach it.

Wet my lips. "I—" Before I can say more, she comes forward, giving me an up-close-and-personal with her great rack, and asks, "You've been away at school, right? I see your mom and dad at church. Surprised to see *you* here, though."

Me too.

Pop wouldn't be.

Wouldn't even raise an eyebrow if he walked in right now and saw me.

I edge off the stool. "Be right back."

Walking quickly—walking at all—toward the exit is not easy. I stall out at the ancient cigarette machine. Then I do more than that, put in a ton of change and pull the lever. But there aren't any Marlboros left; just Kool Menthol and I hate menthol even more than I crave nicotine. So I get outside, stumbling like I actually *had* taken a few drinks, prop myself against the brick wall, gasping, almost gagging, black spots flicking in front of my eyes.

Get some air. Don't, for Chrissake, go back in.

No sense of how long I stand there.

"Mase?" calls a voice, like it's been calling for a while, and there's Jase climbing off Joel's motorcycle. "You okay?" He walks closer, eyes moving from the door of the D & S and then back to me.

"Kinda," I say, still breathing hard, like I'm trying to outrun something.

He settles in next to me, stretches back against the wall like I am. Like this is no big deal. For a few minutes he's quiet. My raspy inhales and exhales are the only sound in the night air, except the clattering and laughter, the rumble of loud conversation from inside.

"You okay?" he asks again.

I nod but don't move. "What the hell are *you* doing out so late?"

He looks at his watch. "It's only ten thirty-seven." Jase has a digital watch and always tells the time to the exact minute. "I went for a run on the beach."

"Are you nuts? In the dark? Haven't you seen what happened to the chick in the opener of *Jaws*?"

"She swam. I was on the sand. The big mechanical shark can't jump that far," Jase says. "C'mon, Tim." He reaches for the extra helmet, looped around that steel thing at the end of the seat, unbuckles it, and tosses it at me.

I catch it automatically. "You kidding? I can't ride on that."

"I ride. You're the passenger," he says patiently, like he's explaining to George.

"No the hell way, man. I'll walk."

"Will you?" Jase asks. His tone gives nothing away, but his eyes steal back to the lit windows of the D & S.

"I didn't do anything," I say. "I didn't." I put my hands in my hair and pull, like I can tear out my thoughts.

"No? Good. Let's get out of here."

"On that? With you?"

"Jesus, Tim. Yeah. You need to leave this place. I have a fast exit. Put the helmet on. Get on the bike. You can hold on to the handle in back."

"You bet I will. You can save the reach-around for Samantha."

"Bite me," Jase says, knocking back the kickstand.

Chapter Eighteen

ALICE

Jase comes slamming in the kitchen door, bringing with him a whiff of the night air in town, silt of the river, wet grass, mud from his sneakers. He stomps a few times, leaving diamond-shaped pieces of dirt on the tile floor, then looks up. "Al—wow."

"Samantha did it for me. What do you think?"

He studies my newly re-dyed hair, the first time in years it's been nothing but plain brown, my real color. "Job interview?" he asks finally. "That supervisor at work giving you attitude?"

I ruffle my hands through the still-damp waves. "Just seemed pointless to keep doing something I started to do to bug Mom when I was fifteen. Does it look bad?"

He shakes his head. "Where's Sam?"

"Curfew." I point to the clock. "Everything all right there?"

Samantha was quiet and a little edgy, I thought. Only really relaxed with my siblings, where she's always in her element. The things that throw me, make me want to run screaming, never bother her. Not Harry insisting on sleeping with his soccer guards on, not Patsy calling Sam back to her crib twenty times in the usual way, by running her sippy cup back and forth across the crib slats like a prisoner summoning the jail warden, nothing. Except a call from her mother, which had her tossing on her hoodie and leaving almost without a word, nothing but a quick, embarrassed glance in my direction.

"Mmm," Jase says, opening the refrigerator and staring into it in that guy way. Like all the answers to any question I'd ask him are in the crisper or pasted onto the label of the orange juice.

"J., talk," I say, looking down at the ledger I'm balancing, my phone set to calculator, the red pen I'm using much more often than the black one. "You and Sam on the outs?"

"Mmm. What? No. Far from it, I think. Did you see Tim today?"

"God. Boys. Why do you have to be so inscrutable all the time? What do you mean 'I think'? Aren't you in this relationship? Wouldn't you actually know what's going on?"

Jase finally shuts the refrigerator door with a thunk, frowns at it, opens it again, reshuts it. "I think the seal is going here. But I can probably fix it."

"Forget the fridge. Did you and Samantha fight or something?"

He pulls out the orange juice, sloshes some into a cup. "No. It's just . . ."

"Does Tim have something to do with it?"

"What? No. Why?" Jase takes a long swallow of orange juice, his mouth twisting as though it's gone bad.

"You just asked about him," I prompt.

"Did I?" He's pulled his cell phone out of his pocket now and is studying it.

I angle my hip on the counter, reach over and give his chest a little shove. "You're being spacey and weird. Tim was—off— tonight. What gives?"

"Nothing," my brother says absently. He's dropped his phone now and is staring at the figures on the ledger. He swears under his breath. "Mom and Dad know?"

I swallow. "I've been doing the books. Said I'd do it for a little while. They know that, but not how bad it is. It keeps getting funkier and—I—but—Dad gets headaches every time he tries to look at numbers."

"Since when?"

"Since the accident. Apparently. He's got double vision. Periodically."

"The hell? No one told me that."

"No one told me either. I read it on his chart this afternoon. Mom knows. They didn't want to worry us."

Jase curses again, a long, creative string. He never swears, and some of these I've barely ever heard, which makes it extra jarring. God, everything is off today.

"Temporary, right?" he asks.

"They hope. It's from the head injury. Some weakness in an eye muscle. Probably temporary. There might need to be surgery, though. They just called in a specialist this week."

He turns his back, walks over to the sink, braces his hands on either side, stares out the window into the dark. Then he's kicking at the baseboard below the sink, swearing again. "How's Dad going to get back to the store if he can't see straight? Drive? How's he even going to get through rehab?"

"He can do physical therapy without having to see perfectly. As for the store—looking at the numbers? That may not be a concern anyway."

Jase curses again, polishes off the orange juice, drops the plastic carton to the ground and steps on it harder than necessary. "We can't just let it die, Alice. What then? Goddammit."

I swallow. I know what I have to say, to do. The math all those columns add up to. "I have to leave school. It's the only way. Until Dad's better. Mom can't do it. Which was a huge battle to convince her of in the first place. She has to be the one handling all the hands-on stuff with him."

He argues, of course. "I'll do it."

"And lose your scholarship shot? You've never been in better shape in your life. You can't."

"Joel—" he starts, talking over me. Then we both fall silent. Not Joel. He's given his summers and plenty of nights and weekends to Garrett's Hardware. He's finally finding his feet in the police academy. We can't let—we can't allow—Grace Reed to plow us *all* down. And I'm the expendable one here. It's not like I'm at some turning point. I've already delayed my transfer. What's a little more time?

"It's got to be me, J."

"I won't let you do it. Why should it be you? Because you're the girl? That's just stupid," he says. "There's got to be someone else who can pinch-hit. Someone it won't derail."

The door kicks open and Tim's standing there, river breeze ruffling his hair. "Came for my car keys."

"Get them tomorrow," Jase says, a slice of a hard edge in his voice.

"You said not even if you begged," I remind him.

"My apartment keys are on the chain too. I locked up—wasn't thinking. You want me on my knees, Alice?"

"Jesus, shut up, Tim." My brother's voice turns steely. Tim takes a step back.

"You're pissed at me now? How did our relationship status change in five minutes when I wasn't even here to eff it up?"

"Hon!" says a cheerful voice behind me. Tim glances over at the doorway to the living room. His eyes widen.

"A me! Hon!" Patsy is at her most imperious, her baby voice nearly a growl, stomping into the room, all proud for being the Houdini of crib breaks.

She wavers her way across the kitchen, surer of her purpose than her feet, arms raised to Tim. "Upsi. Now."

Not only has the baby escaped her crib, she's also peeled off her clothes, and her diaper. She must have gone looking for me in my room, opened my closet to find the overflowing wicker basket I keep there. Stark naked, except for one of my black thongs dangling from her neck, a flowered push-up bra draped across her pale little chest like a Miss America sash, and a bright red lacy garter belt perched in her fluffy hair like a tiara, hanging across one big brown eye.

Both Jase and Tim are openly laughing, like a relief valve has opened.

Tim scoops her up. "You, Patricia Garrett, are my kind of girl."

TIM

"I'll let Tim back in. You deal with Pats," Alice says.

Jase hesitates.

"You're better at getting her down, J.," Alice adds. "She gets all ornery with me."

Still the hesitation. Then, after one swift look at me, Jase hooks his hand around Patsy's waist, lifts her out of my arms, and sets her on his hip. She smooshes his cheeks between her hands, rubs her nose against his.

Alice gives me a tight smile, opens the screen door, strides out in front of me.

She always does that, walks ahead, like she expects people to fall in line after her like ducklings or something. She's wearing these yoga pants with a bleach stain on the back of the knee, another near the waistband. Probably supposed to be some comfortable, *I don't give a damn* outfit. But I spend the whole too-short walk up the steps trying to locate the thong lines under them.

Shoves the key in the lock, bumps open the door with her hip. Then she looks at me and everything goes quiet except for a car swishing by.

Crazy long eyelashes on this girl. Sparkling eye stuff on her lids, partially worn off—a little glint of it near the corner of her eye. Silver hoop earrings with these little bells hanging from them, which explains the faint jingling I hear when she tosses her hair back to look me in the eye. Then the clink of keys as her fingers tighten on them.

"You gonna hand those over or do I really have to beg?" I ask.

She doesn't say anything. Reaches out and takes my hand, flips it palm up. "I can rely on you with these, right?"

Her dark green-brown eyes probe mine, like they could zero in and lock on to any lie I'd tell.

"I'm reliable."

Even after the keys, warm from her hand, drop into my

palm, she keeps looking. If there's still darkness closing in on me, like earlier, she's sure to spot it.

"Scout's honor," I say, finally.

"That won't work," Alice says. "My father was your Cub master. I know all about your scouting career."

"What, you picked *that* as a bedtime story, Alice?"

"We have a picture. You're in the back row. You're holding the tie of the guy standing next to you and flicking a lighter underneath it. You were, what, nine? Ten? Worth a thousand words."

No defense there.

The breeze blows in through the maple trees, one hard gust up from the river, smelling like mud and sea grass. Alice's hair blows across her face, her mouth.

"That's your real hair color, huh?" Without the distraction of the extra chunks of different colors in her hair, she looks younger, eyes duskier, lips redder.

"Yes, dark brown. More like Joel than Jase and Andy. My dark secret."

"One of many, I'm sure." But not as dark as mine.

Alice shrugs, looking down at her bare feet. When she glances up, she's smiling unexpectedly. That crooked smile of hers. "No secrets about my lingerie anymore, though."

"And that was the best one." For a second, "back to normal" hovers between us . . . whatever our normal was.

But she's still watching me, seeing me a bit too well, even in the dark. "I want to believe you, Tim. That you're trustworthy right now. But you have to admit, this hasn't been your most reliable day."

Nope.

"Do you want to keep the keys, Alice?" I ask, and I can hear the completely illegitimate anger in my voice.

"Not exactly the point, Tim. Is there anything you want to tell me?"

Delay the inevitable, a tried and true habit that I thought I'd left in the rearview mirror.

Pull out my old smart-ass smile. "Only that you're more than welcome to store your lingerie collection here at my apartment. How extensive is it, anyway?"

Her lips flatten out and she shrugs, already turning away. "Guess you'll never know."

I watch her dark figure, only bright with the bleach stains, disappear into the night.

Chapter Nineteen

TIM

When Hester walks into the restaurant the next day and sees me, she does that thing where about six different emotions cross her face. Pissed, sad, relieved that I actually showed, hormonal, who the hell knows. I hop up to pull out her chair. I might have done a hump and dump, but what a gentleman, yeah?

"Wait a minute," she says. "I left something in the car. I wanted to make sure you were here first."

"Something" turns out to be the sleeping baby, huddled in his car seat—so frickin' puny—wearing this frilly bonnet-type thing.

"Hester—you gotta stop ditching the kid in the car," I say, watching her rest the car seat precariously on one of the chairs. It tips to one side. "Wouldn't he be better off on the floor?"

Listen to me, acting like I know anything at all.

Probably thinking the same thing, Hester says, "He's fine. This way we can keep an eye on him."

Like she was doing when she left him in the backseat? Jesus.

I pull out her chair again, and she settles in, spreading her napkin in her lap. "Have you looked at the menu?"

I bite my lip so I won't snarl, *This is not a freakin' date.*

Instead: "I need to understand more about how"—Calvin's eyelashes flutter and I lower my voice—"uh, how all this happened."

She nods, looking worried now. What'd she think we were going to talk about? The specials on the menu?

The waiter interrupts to plunk down bread, pour water, light the candle, and hover around until Hester sends him trotting off to get her a ginger ale.

"I just need . . ." What I need more than anything at the moment is something to do with my hands, so I pick up one of the books of matches with the restaurant logo from the little crystal bowl on the table, start methodically tearing them out one by one. "I need to know how we hooked up." *Why* too, but asking that? Dickish.

Hester blinks at me. "You honestly don't remember making love?"

"Nope." Wow, way to be an asshole. Apparently it's like riding a bicycle.

Her eyes well with tears. Jesus, no.

"Sorry, I . . . just don't get why you'd have anything to do with my drunken ass."

The waiter, who returned with the ginger ale just in time to hear "drunken ass" backs away, the glass still poised.

Her hand shoots out, rests on mine for an instant as I continue to mutilate the matchbook. Any time she touches me, or I touch her, it feels off, so . . . wrong. She's freaking *pure*-looking. A horrible thought occurs to me. "That wasn't, uh, it wasn't your, um, you'd had, um—"

Hester somehow makes sense of this.

"No. Oh no." She pats my hand reassuringly. "I'd had this boyfriend, Alex. Alex Robinson. Remember him?"

Total void there too.

"Head of the school newspaper? Tall? Student council? Class secretary?

I fumble through my unreliable memory bank. Alex Robinson . . . Dark-haired officious-type dude? Yeah . . . On my tennis team, major tool. Senior when I was a sophomore. And Hester was a junior.

"Riiiight," I say.

"The night before the party, Alex . . ." Hester pauses, clears her throat. Not that it makes any difference. She has one of those throaty, raspy voices that *should* be sexy. "He's doing a post-grad year at Choate. He called up and said we should admit the long-distance thing was hopeless." The waiter's crept back, sets down the ginger ale, then flees as though it might detonate. "I mean—come on!—it's still in the same state! Not even an hour away! We'd been going out since freshman spring! He was my first—" She stops dead. "Anyway. That's why I went to that party. I didn't want to think or remember; I wanted to have fun."

Having torn all the matches out of two different packs, I go to work on the bread basket, ripping off pieces, tearing them into smaller pieces, shoveling them in my mouth. Calvin—I freaking hate that name—stirs a little, frowns, but dozes on.

"Anyway . . . you were there and . . . kind of sad too."

I plunge another chunk of bread into the butter, ignoring the butter knife, take a bite, and then pause. "Please tell me this wasn't a mercy f— I mean, that you didn't have sex with me out of some kind of *pity,* Hester. Tell me you didn't screw up your life—and mine—and frickin' create his—because you *felt sorry* for me."

She twists at this little ring on her pinkie. "No. It wasn't like that. We talked. A lot. We went to Ward's room and we talked for, like, hours. You were charming and goofy and, yes, sad, but that's not why I . . . why we . . ."

Again with the waiter, who recites a long list of incomprehensible appetizers. Hester orders and I mutter, "I'll have what she's having."

"I didn't really notice how much you'd had to drink. You acted . . . great. I was upset. I wanted to be—not me. I just . . . kissed you. It went from there. It was stupid. I was stupid."

This little tear slides out of her eye, snakes down the side of her nose. She swats at it, hard enough to make a little *slap* sound. I wince.

"But, I mean, Hester. Didn't I even use anything? I can't believe I was that out of it." However badly I've generally messed up, this is a new low. I thought I'd stuck to being Thoughtless Bastard, rather than Complete Sack of Shit. I mean—I have a sister, after all.

"Oh, you did. You were very insistent on it. Made sure I got your . . . your wallet and all that," she assures me, turning red. "It's just that, afterward, you sort of, well, fell asleep without—" She makes this indecipherable waving gesture with her hand.

I decipher it well enough, though. I passed out without . . . removing, disposing of the condom. Which obviously leaked. Or broke. I'm a prince.

"I'm a catastrophe, Hester," I point out glumly. "You're too smart for that."

"Guess not, right?" She takes a gulp of soda like she's slinging back a shot of tequila. Now the glitter in her eyes comes off more like anger than tears. "I wasn't smart and you weren't sober. We made love . . ." She trails off as I cringe.

We made Calvin, not love.

"Then you got kicked out." She spreads her hands helplessly. "And here we all are."

"Not quite. Why the hell didn't you . . . find me, or contact me before things—when you first figured out what was doing. Or why didn't you ever once—*once*, Hester—think, maybe you should tell *the father?* Like, right away?" The waiter, who is approaching with more Perrier, once again scuttles off to a less emotionally volatile table.

"I didn't know how to get in touch with you."

"You found me now. You could have found me then. Instead you just went on ahead and had this baby on your own. Decided to keep him long enough to show him to me so now I'm guilty for the rest of my life." The words are spewing out. "You didn't give me any choices here." I almost can't see Hester; it's like the whole world is red and swirling, tight and hot as the feeling in my gut.

"Well, I didn't have a whole lot myself, Tim." She's definitely angry now. "You were a mess, like you said. Was I supposed to hunt you down and say, hey, mind putting down that liter of rum and the joint so we can have a rational discussion about *our baby?*"

I try to imagine what I would have done if she had. Got no

clue. The Tim Mason I was back then is like some loser roommate I had years ago. Except that that guy came over last night and nearly moved back in. The waiter plops down our appetizers, flees without a backward glance.

"Besides," Hester adds. "I . . ." She circles her index finger around the rim of her water glass. "I—"

I look down at the appetizers. Uh . . . what are they? Never mind.

"What?" I ask, poking with my fork.

"It's kind of personal."

I just stare at her. Though I barely know her, we are way past personal.

"I know. Silly, at this point. I have these irregular periods, and I didn't have any, well, morning sickness, so it took me a long time to figure out."

"How long?" She can't have been one of those chicks you hear about who thinks she's maybe gotten kinda chubby and then gets a stomachache and pops out a baby.

"Ten weeks. Then I went and had a sonogram. He was sucking his thumb . . . he was . . . I couldn't make any choice except to have him."

"Oh, Hester. Jesus Christ." My appetite is gone, but I eat a bite of whatever just to do something other than puke or say *I'm sorry I'm sorry I'm sorry* over and over and over again.

"This tastes better with lemon." She hands me a dish of lemons. Like what I'm really concerned about here is the right seasoning. "It wasn't that bad. Really."

"You can't tell me it didn't suck ass being a pregnant senior at Ellery."

"Well, good news." She raises her glass of ginger ale as if she's toasting me. "It took a long time to be obvious. Of course, a ton of *Scarlet Letter* jokes after that, but . . . my real friends, they stuck by me. So did Grand, of course."

"Yeah, and I've heard actually delivering a baby is a blast," I mutter.

"I went for drugs." Hester actually smiles. "Too bad you never got into epidurals recreationally. They're the best."

"I can't believe you're joking about this."

"Well . . . here we are, Tim. Things could be a lot worse."

How? Searching . . . searching . . .

The waiter comes back, practically on tiptoe. I decide to change the subject for a while.

"So, uh, how, uh, old is the kid?" The words sound twisted, bizarre, like I'm some stranger in a checkout line inquiring about a random baby, instead of the one plopped right in front of us, ours, fidgeting slightly in his sleep. "I mean, him, Calvin."

"He was three weeks early, I think, so now he's almost five and a half weeks. Beyond his birth weight by two whole pounds."

"Oh. That's nice. Uh . . ." I eat more whatever these round things are. They taste chewy and weird. The waiter advances with the wine list. Can't he tell we're frickin' underage? I wave him away with a scowl. Hester toys with her fork.

"So," she continues in nearly a whisper, "he was born and . . . I ended up finding your address in the yearbook."

"Wait—did you go to my parents' house first? With the kid, I mean?"

"No! I called, and I got this girl? She gave me your new address." The waiter whisks away our appetizer plates, replacing them with yet another plateful of unidentifiable stuff.

I sniff at it suspiciously. *This girl.* Nan, obviously. She could have given me a heads-up. But then, even though my twin usually fears the worst, how could she guess that some random girl on the other end of the phone would chuck my life into a wood chipper like this?

"So," Hester says, all businesslike suddenly. "We should talk about the details." She swishes whatever the hell she's eating around in whatever that gloppy white sauce is, takes a tiny nibble, sets it back down.

"Yeah, that . . . how exactly do we work this?" *And how long do we have to?* I gulp more water, draining the glass. At this point, the waiter is totally MIA, avoiding eye contact, standing with his arms folded, eyes cast to the ceiling. "I mean, I'm pretty booked—I have a job, and I'm getting my GED . . . and . . ."

Don't have time for you, kid. Calvin gives this little flicker of a frown.

Hester looks down at her plate. "We can figure it out. We can get the adoption thing rolling right away," she says quickly. "But before that's taken care of, it's not all on you. I mean, I'll help, and Grand can too. He wants to meet you, by the way."

Yeah, I'll bet.

Wait, did she say she'd *help?* Am I supposed to be the primary parent here? Hell, no. The baby stirs again, kicking a foot, and then quiets down. Fuck. He's so small. His hand is, like, the size of one of the cherry tomatoes in my salad.

"Don't think I'm a bad person," Hester warns. "But I can't just drop my whole life till I fix things."

"Obvious who the bad guy is here, Hester. Hey, I'll work around my schedule. I mean, I'll babysit, of course, because, because"—I swallow, set my jaw—"he's my son, after all."

She nods, blinking rapidly. "He is. Yours."

Undeniable. I might not get the fatherly bond, but the facts are the facts: I was wasted. I didn't use a condom right. There's a baby. Health class 101.

Suddenly, her shoulders start quivering and there's a complete tsunami of tears, ragged sobs that get louder and louder with each one. Her voice rises and she points a finger at me, jabbing in the air. "I know you don't want this. But you can't possibly know what it's like for me . . . He's tiny—he was born early and he's eating all the time to catch up and . . . and . . . he never ever sleeps. He's always pooping and crying and I have no idea why, what's wrong. Why can't he just be quiet? Isn't it all enough without that? For *days* after he was born my breasts were swollen and leaking, and I had to have stitches because of vaginal tearing. I'm eighteen years old . . . It's just *wrong*."

Jesus God. Kill me fast. All these other people are staring at us.

"All *you* did was get your rocks off! You don't even re-remember it. And I'm fat now—aren't I?"

This seems the slightest of her problems, but at least I know the answer to that one. "No! No. Of course not. Not at all. You look just the same."

As the girl I can't remember.

Sweat rolling down my forehead. "Better! You look better!"

She gulps, looks around for her napkin, which she must have dropped. I start to hand her mine, and then remember that I spat one of the scallops out into it.

"Better . . . really?"

"Totally." The waiter is in the corner, examining the ceiling some more. The bunch of women drinking cosmos at the next table look like they want to shoot me in the nuts, chop me up with dull knives, and throw my body in a sinkhole. Go right ahead, ladies, please.

I shove my chair back, come around next to her, pat her on the shoulders. "*Shh*, Hes. It's no problem. I got this. I don't sleep all that well myself, so that's probably my fault too. I'll just . . . I'll just deal. I mean, uh, do you want me to take him— uh—tonight?"

What am I saying? I can't have a baby at the garage apartment. Overnight? Next to the Garretts? To Alice? This is like a car pileup that keeps rolling on and on, like some replay Satan shows on a panoramic screen when you get to hell.

"I'll make sure he has everything he needs, don't worry," Hester assures me, her voice even lower and raspier than normal.

That kid is entire universes away from having everything he needs.

Somehow Calvin has managed to sleep through all of this. He stays conked out when we head to Hester's car, me lugging the car seat, Hester paving the way, somehow having recovered from total breakdown. If these are hormones, they suck.

The entire backseat of Hester's car, and her whole trunk, are jammed with baby stuff. How can he need so much? He's the size of a tennis racket.

First she hands me that big-ass diaper bag. Then this straw-basket-looking thing that looks like a supersized version of something Goldilocks would use.

Am I supposed to . . . take the kid on a picnic or something?

"I just washed the sheepskin," she adds.

"Uh?"

Hester rustles in the backseat, and comes out with an actual sheepskin, some blankets, and this sock monkey. The kind with the red butt. I'm still standing there with the picnic basket and the diaper bag, which is getting heavier by the second. My heart is cramping, squeezing tighter and tighter like my hand that's fisted around the handle of the basket.

"So you put this in the bottom, and then make sure Calvin's always on his back." She slides the sheepskin into the basket, then sets the monkey on top. He seems to be glaring at me with these evil little eyes. Those things have always creeped me the hell out. "Only a few more things, and then the baby and you can get going on your day together."

Yay.

Now she's back with a blanket, this little mirror, and what looks like a parachute pack.

The basket is a bed, then, but apparently I'm taking Calvin skydiving.

"I should have had this better organized. It's hard to get it together."

Having trouble getting *myself* together, so I head out to my own car, flip the hatch, shove aside my sleeping bag, a container of tennis balls, a jumbo pack of Dr Pepper, and a pillowcase full of laundry and put it all in the back. I leave the hatch open, because there may be more to come. Like a pup tent and a croquet set.

Starting to think she's giving me the kid permanently. She's here now, with him in her arms, bonnet on.

"Want me to help you with the car seat?"

"Nah. I'm good," I say. "No problem."

It takes an insane amount of time to get it in. I can't reach my fingers far enough under it to snag it, and when I do, the belt keeps snapping back out from the bottom, hitting my knuckles. Ow.

I pull back, sucking my knuckles; hit my head on the top of the open door.

"Here he is. You put that mirror right at his feet so you can see him while you're driving." Holding Calvin, she hands me the bucket part of the car seat. Awake now, he stares at me. I stare back. I have to watch him *while* I'm driving? How's that going to work?

"Uh. Hi there, Calvin." My voice starts out squeaky, then goes game-show-host-hearty. He gets that worried pucker between his eyes again, screws up his mouth a little, and his lower lip trembles.

Hester scoops him into my arms so quickly. No warning. Just boom, I'm holding this warm squirming thing. Wearing a bonnet. The back of his undershirt is damp. *He's* sweating too.

I pat him on his midget shoulder. "We're good," I tell him. Serious eyes, anxious expression. It's the Nan face, version 2.0.

Once he's all buckled in, Hester hands me this thick bunch of papers covered with round, loopy writing, torn from a loose-leaf notebook, stapled together. Like the first draft of an English paper in 1986. "Just because I'm anal, I wrote everything down." Then she keeps talking and talking and talking: *Make sure you do this and never do that, and I know you'd probably figure all this out, but just in case . . .*

Hell, no, I would not have figured it all out. How could I? Sure, I would have magically guessed which side of the diaper was the front and how to put him in that parachute thing, which turns out to be this weird little kangaroo pouch that you wear him in like a fanny pack for your chest, and that you need to hold his head at all times since it'll, like, snap off otherwise, because all that jazz is just instinctive, right?

Simple.

Finally, ten fucking thousand years later, we're on the road. I almost have an accident because when we hit the first stoplight, I worry that I braked too hard, reach back to check him, and this anger-management asshole with a beer gut and an attitude nearly hits us with a motorcycle, giving me the bird, and calling, "Go screw yourself, kid."

Done, dude.

Calvin starts making little squeaky sounds as we head onto Route 7, and I realize I've left the window open and he's probably getting a blast of exhaust in his face. The first exit leads to Brinkley Bay, a private beach area with those huge signs that make it sound like you'll be shot by a firing squad if you go anywhere close to the water.

I pull into the parking lot anyway.

Open the back door and crouch next to the car, reach under

his chin, tuck my fingers into this fold of skin, so soft, it's not even like skin. Like . . . like silk. Only drooly. Untie the bonnet thing, and toss it to the car floor. His lips give a little twitch, not a full-on smile, but better than that worried trembly jazz.

"Yeah, you won't be wearing ruffles. No son of mine, and all that shit—sorry, stuff—right? *That* goes." The wrinkle's back between his eyebrows. Automatically, I stick my fingertip there, smoothing it away the way Ma always used to do with me when she saw me do the same, back when I was a kid. *You'll give yourself wrinkles before you're nine!*

Ma. She's gonna kill me.

But first she'll cry.

Pop—

Shit.

Calvin can't even focus, really; his eyes keep looking like they're almost crossing. Is that normal? Is *he* normal? I hadn't even thought of that. I've done a hell of a lot of everything bad. God knows what funky stuff there could have been in anything that came from me. Maybe I've already messed him up without even knowing I made him.

I reach out a finger, bump it against his small soft fist, clamped so tightly shut. Probably a bit young to get the whole fist bump thing, so I uncurl his damp fingers, slide my index finger into his sweaty starfish hand. So small it curls around the top joint of my finger with room to spare.

"It'll be okay, Cal. You're okay," I say, patting his stomach under the straps, in what I hope is a reassuring way. Because that's what parents do, right? Lie their asses off.

Chapter Twenty

ALICE

A corner of something peeks out of the mailbox, some bright flyer. Harry must have forgotten his mail-boy duties yesterday. I scoop out the envelopes, flip through: some letter with lipstick kisses on it for Joel—really? *Justine* magazine for Andy, a box from Mustard of the Month Club for Mom (Christmas gift from Mr. Methuan from down the street—Mom drives him to doctors' appointments sometimes), electric bill, flyer about the SBH homecoming dance, letter from the bank. Shove the others under my armpit, flip that one open.

Read once.

Read twice.

My lungs lock shut, like a window slamming.

Who took all the oxygen out of the bright September air?

"I don't like this place," George says. "It makes my stomach hurt."

"Just a few minutes, G. Then we'll go to the bookstore. A book and a magazine." Bribery: My new middle name.

Patsy's silent, fingering the Pooh Bear Band-Aid from her polio vaccine. She fixes me with an unforgiving glare. I hold up my index finger, where she bit me during the shot, and glare back.

Yes, I am nineteen years old, but waiting on the hard bench

at Stony Bay Building and Loan makes my stomach hurt too. It doesn't help that I'm wearing a button-down shirt and my navy-blue interview skirt, control-top tights digging into my waist.

"How many more minutes?" George asks.

"Not sure, Georgie." I try to distract him with I Spy, but there's very little to see in the bank's main room, which looks like the "after" photo of a Suck the Personality Out of a Room challenge. Beige carpet. Beige walls. One of those white-noise machines whirring. Hushed voices.

"How many more minutes now?"

"Not long."

"Ice cream after?"

"It's not even noon, G."

Six more "How many more minutes?" before the door to the bank manager's office opens at last.

There's only one chair and George immediately claims it, sliding his butt back, his legs swinging high, kicking the metal chair legs. The man behind the desk doesn't look up despite the loud clanging.

"Hey!" George says loudly.

The man glances up briefly, raises a warning finger, keeps writing something, then, finally, sets down his pen with a heavy sigh. I expect him to look me in the eye at this point, but his gaze is fastened just beyond my shoulder.

"There was an urgent matter?"

"Yes. This." I set the letter from the bank on his desk. "We've been receiving money from a trust here. This says that won't be continuing. That's impossible, Mr."—I check out the brown placard with his name—"Mason."

Holy . . .

Tim's dad?

Yes, it's obvious somehow, although he looks like part of the Vacuum Out the Personality contest. Same thick hair with a slight wave as Tim's—but ash-gray instead of flame—same high cheekbones, but less prominent without a smile—same long, thin body, but it comes off gaunt instead of lean.

He's holding the paper up, reading through it. "Yes, I sent this, as instructed by the donor of the trust account. All further transactions are to cease."

"Did you kill that deer?" George asks, staring in horrified fascination at a moth-eaten deer head mounted on the wall.

Mr. Mason is wearing a similar expression, looking back at George. "It was here when I inherited the office."

"They can't *cease*," I say. "There was an agreement. As long as bills come in, they're supposed to be paid."

My voice is rising. George chews his lip. Patsy shoves her sturdy body closer to mine, hard enough to knock my breath out.

"I sent the letter as instructed by my client," Mr. Mason says. "I don't know the details, except that, as you say, the expenses sent to this address were to be covered as some sort of scholarship donation—political in nature, perhaps? Perhaps the monetary cap for such donations has been reached and so . . ."

He's still not meeting my eyes. It's weirdly disorienting, especially since his eyes are the same color as Tim's. But Tim's tilt up slightly at the corners, perpetual smile almost always lurking. Nothing like that going on here. Mr. Mason doesn't look mad or sad. Just . . . gone.

"No cap. There was no limit. The bills were just supposed to be—"

My voice is full-on loud, and now there's a flicker of expression, but indecipherable. Alarm, annoyance—I can't tell. He glances at the screen of his cell phone, as though he might have an app to summon some armed guards to escort the crazy girl from the room.

"If you'll just give me the legal document stating the terms of the agreement, I'm sure we can settle this. It's notarized, of course."

It's nonexistent, of course. My parents would never have thought to get the arrangement with Grace Reed in writing. Half the agreements Dad does with suppliers at Garrett's are handshake deals—and I'm sure Senator Grace would have flat-out refused to put this in writing anyway. What if it leaked to the press? No. There was no notarized anything. But we should've at least gotten a damn lawyer.

I put my head in my hands, look up. "It was a debt of honor. There isn't any—"

Honor here.

"Proof," Mr. Mason says, sounding faintly—very faintly— sympathetic. "I'm afraid I have no authorization to do anything without documentation."

"You have to—we're depending on this—we can't do without it. It pays my father's hospital bills and—"

He shakes his head. "My hands are tied, Ms."—he glances down at the paper—"Garrett. I'm sympathetic, of course, but I'm afraid the bank requires more than that."

I open my mouth to argue again, but there's no point. For the first time, I can translate the expression in his eyes. Dead end.

Chapter Twenty-one

TIM

When I set the car seat down on the church basement floor with a semi-defiant clunk, the conversations going on all around me shut right down. Dominic, who I finally got on the phone last night—he'd been out night-fishing on some friend's boat and left it behind—mutters a quick, "Whoa," before turning away and keeping on talking to my old coach Jake. But before another minute passes, everyone is crowding up, jostling, freaking out over Cal.

They're all flipping out and all I can think is—*You take him. Or you. Or you. Please.*

I've had him for half an hour. Already I'm wiped out. I've got this kid for hell knows how long, and it's only 3:00 and what do you *do* with babies, for God's sake? Take 'em to the playground? Obviously I'm not going to whip him down the slide or put him on a swing. He can't even hold up his head. He's like one of those bobblehead dolls. When I went to pull him out of the car seat, he just stared at me, like, *Oh hey. Yeah, I'm trusting you with this dad stuff, because, face it, I'm completely at your mercy. Please don't screw up. I'm gonna fall asleep again now.*

He makes it about halfway through the hour before starting to twist from side to side, opening and closing his mouth. I drag myself outside, pop the top of a can of formula, offer him the bottle. He receives it with tremendous enthusiasm. Occasionally he turns his head toward me, in what I can tell is a gesture of Supreme Will. *Look. Although all I want is to keep drinking, I'm acknowledging your existence. Get it? Good. 'Cause I'm really, really thirsty.*

I'm sitting, bending over him, watching his face carefully, when a hand descends lightly on my back, someone slides into place next to me.

Coach Somers—Jake—dark blond hair all rumpled, Hodges Soccer sweatshirt with the sleeves cut off. He reaches out to straighten the kid's wrinkled undershirt, brushes his hair back from his forehead.

"No one thought for a second I was just babysitting, did they?"

"Well, he's a really cute kid," he tells me, "who looks a lot like you, newborn-style."

"I've only got one chin," I point out.

"True—but look—his top one has a little cleft, just like yours." Jake puts his index finger in the appropriate spot on Cal's midget face.

"I'm not denying paternity," I say, though that sounds awesome right about now. Jake rests back on his elbows and grins at me. I catch a faint whiff of cigarette smoke. One sharp inhale and I'm dying to bum one off him. But what am I gonna do, blow smoke in this baby's face while he chows down? No. I'm no textbook dad, but still. I balance him carefully on my knees, touch the nic patch Alice gave me.

There's the snick of the big wooden door closing, and

Dominic's standing behind us. Looking down at Cal. His thick brows pulled together. Can't tell what he's thinking. Sometimes he cries in meetings when he talks about his daughter. This tough-skinned guy, all angles and attitude, sobbing.

Jake himself has gotten emotional lately because he and his partner have been trying to have a baby through a surrogate and things keep falling through. He's trying to quit smoking for the sake of the baby and then can't keep it going because there *is* no baby—shit's fallen through twice in the three months I've been around. I'm surrounded by men who want to be in my shoes.

Fuck, welcome to 'em.

I'm cradling the kid's head in one hand and tilting the bottle into his mouth. Little milky dribbles of formula keep escaping out the corners, running down his chin, and he suddenly stops, sneezes. Then looks really upset, brow all squinchy, like, *Fix me, Dad.* "Dad" is hard enough to wrap my head around, let alone *do something about it.*

"Try burping him," Dom suggests.

"How?"

Hester's printed instructions are crumpled in my glove compartment, but I don't remember her covering burping. Yeah, I skimmed.

"Pat him on the back—real soft," Dominic says. "They like that." Amazing he's not grabbing the baby out of my hands and doing it himself.

I tip Cal cautiously forward and tap him between his little sharp shoulder blades with three fingers of my hand, then with my whole palm. So freakin' fragile.

And . . . nothing. Now he's whimpering, and I have no tools whatsoever to solve this.

I shoot a pleading look at Dom, my own version of *Fix me*, but he just smiles.

"Sometimes you have to do it a few times."

More tapping. More whimpering and squirming.

"Try putting him on your shoulder," Jake says. "Up high."

I hoist him there, so his head is dangling over my shoulder and give a few more taps. Then he lets out this huge belch, like someone's fat old uncle. This warm spurt of liquid dribbles down the back of my shirt.

"Holy shit," I say. "That is . . ."

Gross. Surreal. Everything I'm thinking is wrong.

"Real. Right?" Jake pulls a crumpled Kleenex out of his pocket, tosses it my way as I settle the kid back down on my legs. Cal looks at me urgently, smacking his lips, then making a feeble swipe at the bottle, fingers splayed.

"I think he's still thirsty," I tell them, settling the bottle back into his mouth.

"Who isn't?" Dominic asks with a short laugh.

"Don't drink over this, Tim," Jake adds.

I know, I know, I know.

The bottle slips out for a sec and the kid gives this high-pitched, desperate squeak, like a baby mouse. That sound, helpless and mine to fix—it's like someone heated up a knife and jabbed it hard in my stomach, then twisted. I actually put my hand there, where it grips and burns. Goddamn Jake and his surrogates and Dominic, who misses his kid like a lost leg, and Hester and her effin' endless-care essay and this guy I see walking by just now with a kid on his shoulders, knobbly kid-knees kicking out, heels back against his dad's chest, giggling. Goddamn everyone else in the world who had kids or wants kids and knows what the eff to do with them. I try to cram this fury far down or take it out somewhere safe and contained, kicking my loafer against the wrought iron fence, but that jiggles Cal. His half-closed eyes fly open and he looks at me in alarm, like, *Are you having a tantrum, Dad?*

After the meeting, I shove the baby in his backpack and just walk on the beach, on and on and on, like some endless Bataan march. Then he needs a new diaper, which I don't have on me, and I've walked from Stony Creek past the breakwater practically to Maplecrest. When I look at my watch it's nearing six. So I turn around, slog back to my car, and change the kid. Four hours with him and he's not dead yet. But now I have to go home.

The Garretts.

Alice.

When there are no cars in the Garretts' driveway as I pull in, I'm not sure whether I've dodged a bullet or my parachute hasn't opened.

Between the baby, the car seat, and the shit-ton of stuff Hester unloaded all over me, I need a Sherpa trailing behind to get all this in at once. Obviously, since I've been über-self-righteous to Hester about leaving him in the car, the first thing to do is to move him in. But the moment we get in the door, he starts screaming like a mother. He's turning purple, his fists are clenched, his knees are pulled up to his stomach, he's a banshee. I try to jam the bottle in his mouth and he pretty much punts it away. I consider the burping thing again but I'm afraid to pick him up. He's frickin' possessed. No wonder Hester was losing it after five and a half weeks of this. Screw adoption. Can we just do the leaving-on-the-doorstep thing?

I left the trunk open with all the incriminating baby crap inside, visible to every Garrett eye. But it's not as if I can leave this kid behind to close it. He's obviously about to pop an aneurysm. How come he was so Zen at the restaurant?

There's nothing to do but carry him with me and lug the stuff in piece by piece. Any minute the van or the Bug or the Mustang will pull in and the jig will be up.

The pauses between eardrum-exploding shrieks are getting longer and longer. The kid probably has no air left in his lungs. I'm the same, worse off than the other day when I ran all the way to the pier and had to lie on my back in the sand for half an hour before slogging back. Now he's limp over my shoulder, asleep. I stagger back upstairs, put him back in the car seat, lock him in, and trudge back down to the car.

I'm just about done carrying up way more than I packed even for my own move, am shouldering the heavy suitcase, aka diaper bag, when someone taps me on the back.

"Tim?"

It's Andy. She's dragging off her bike helmet, pitching it next to her bike, which is already cast aside in the grass, whisking back her wavy light brown hair.

She studies me, silent.

Uh-oh.

Quick scan of the exterior of the diaper bag reveals no obvious "baby" signs—it's not, like, covered with yellow ducks or anything. Just navy blue. Butch enough. Except for the spare bottle peeking out of one side. I shove it farther down.

"'S up, Ands?"

"Remember I said I had a question for you? That I really needed to ask *you*?"

"Andy, if this is about hooking you up with drugs or something, I don't—"

She starts giggling, mouth full of braces, and pretty soon I'm smiling too.

"Seriously, Tim. Please?"

"Uh, whatever it is, just say no?"

She tilts her head, shakes back her hair, then stills, squinting a little.

Is that Cal cranking up again? "Hit me, Andy. I'm kinda in a hurry."

"Okay." Then she says in a rush, "Whenyouarekissingsome- onelikereallykissingthemwheredoyouputyourhands?"

Christ.

"Uh. Well. Uh." She nods, encouraging me, all hopeful hazel eyes. "Shoulders are a good start." That seems safe. Nothing Jase is going to whale on me for.

"What about after that?"

"Stick with shoulders for at least a year."

"C'mon, Tim."

That's definitely Cal.

"Waist. I guess. Or back. I don't know. Don't ask me, Andy. Whatever I'd tell you, do the goddamn opposite. Take it slow, is all I can say."

She takes a step back, shaking her head. "You're so mean to yourself. It makes me sad. What's that sound?"

"Uh—teakettle." I start to book it up the stairs, then remember something, stop. Andy's heading toward the house, her shoulders sort of drooping

"Andrea! Wait. Who's the dude?"

"Kyle Comstock."

"You mean the putz who ditched you by Post-it note?" Squalling's getting louder.

"He said he wanted to go with Jade Whelan because I was a bad kisser. I thought—"

"Stay miles away from that douchewit. I mean it, Andy. Like, frickin' oceans away. Or I'll tell Jase, Joel, *and* Alice."

"Not Alice!" She gives a shiver, smiles at me, and says, "That's kind of what I thought. I just wanted to ask someone who might . . ." Her voice gets all quiet, so I bend closer to hear her. Or maybe it's the kid's roar amping up even louder.

"Know how a sleazehead thinks?"

Swift, embarrassed, smile.

"'S all good, Andy. I'm glad my shady, manipulative past is of use to someone."

"Hey, Tim? Tim!"

I'm leaning back on the couch with Cal on my shoulder. He finally fell asleep and I'm just lying there, staring into space, dying for a smoke, running the whole thing in my head, the crackle of plastic, the light, smooth weight of the cigarette between my fingers, the molasses-y smell of unburnt tobacco, the first drag, inhale, brain unclogged. Why am I so freaking tired? It's not like Cal's all physically demanding. He can barely do a thing. Thank Christ we won't have to worry about him when he's Patsy's age and trying to eat rocks and drink shit from under the sink.

"Mase!" I hear again. It's been noisy out my window on the Garretts' lawn, but this is nothing new, so I've ignored it, trying to get Cal to crash. Now I open the casement and peer out, easing Cal onto his back, flush against the couch cushion. There's a crew of people in the driveway, a bunch of Jase's football buddies, Mac Johnson and Ben Rylance, kids from Samantha's swim team, maybe, that prepster Hodges crowd. Jase and Sam are standing at the bottom of the garage apartment steps.

"We're going to Sandy Claw Beach for a bonfire," Samantha calls up. She's in a blue sarong thing, towel around her neck, arm around Jase's waist. "Come with?"

Jase jerks his head in the direction of the Mustang. "Yeah, come on."

Everyone's already crowding into various vehicles, laughing and shoving, little squeals from girls climbing on guys' laps, low laughter from the dudes.

It looks like fun. The kind of fun I haven't had in a while.

"Can't." It's not like I can drag the kid along to a beach party. *Toss me a Coke without braining the infant?* Besides, he's already asleep . . . for a while.

"C'mon, Tim. You can't just lurk in there like a troll under a bridge," Sam calls. "Throw on your trunks. We're going to have a swim to the breakwater challenge. We need your speed."

Cal stirs, makes this strange face, and I hear a gurgling sound.

Crap. Literally.

"I can't, got it? Not right now."

Sam starts to protest and Jase puts his hand on her arm. He shoots me a look. "Hey, we can blow this off, snag a pizza and hang out."

He thinks it's about getting spun. And I let him. "Nah. I'm just gonna study"—maybe Hester's baby instructions—"and crash. I'm good."

Samantha shields her eyes. "We'll stay." She puts her hand on the railing, all set to climb the steps and charge into the middle of my current nightmare.

Cal's squirming around and kicking off to cry.

"No!" I say. "Take no for an answer, will you?"

"Oh!" she says. "Got it. Okay."

She obviously thinks I've got some chick up here. Jase thinks I'm stressing about booze.

I'm lying to both of them.

Thought I was done with that garbage.

Feels as shitty as Cal's diaper.

Well, almost.

Chapter Twenty-two

ALICE

"You're not taking the Mustang? Reliving your lost youth on the school bus, J.?"

"Ha-ha. My youth isn't lost, Al. Still around here somewhere. But nah. Too much hassle for parking spots on the first day. Just ends in aggravation and dings on the 5.0."

"You certainly wouldn't want dings on perfection," I say, eyeing Jase's battered car, which he spent half the summer rehabbing and tinkering over, after buying it with a chunk of his college savings.

He grins, sliding his palm along the side. He's repainted only the hood so far, a deep, rich, sparkling dark green. The rest of the paint job is a jumble of dark red-orange primer and the original color, a metallic '70s-style lime. "Some respect. She's a work in progress."

He's been up for hours now—for his paper route, the second job he insists on having, despite the fact that he's either too old or way too young to be delivering *The Stony Bay Sentinel* before dawn's early light. Then for a run on the beach. Now it's barely six thirty and he's showered and plowed his way through a virtual coop full of eggs and is already waiting at our mailbox, the bus stop. In a decent mood.

I can't bring myself to drag him into the hospital bill mess, the bank—he was already offering to quit school over Garrett's—let alone tell Mom and Dad. I picture Mr. Mason at his desk, feel my breath come short, my throat shrink. I close my eyes. Open them. Deep breath. I'll figure something out. I just need a little time.

"Andeeeee," I call back to the house. First day of ninth grade and she's, of course, running late.

"You'd be better off texting her," Jase advises. "She's been in the upstairs bathroom for nearly an hour."

On cue, Andy comes hurtling down the front steps, heels in one hand, hair straightened, tank top and bright red mini on.

"Go change," I say flatly. "You look like the poster girl for freshman fresh meat."

"No time," Andy says breathlessly. "Besides, you're one to talk. This is *your* skirt. It's in your first-day-of-high-school picture. I can't believe Mom's not awake to take one for us today."

It's my skirt. Of course it is. Though Mom and I had plenty of debates about my clothing choices, I don't sound like her now; I sound like some bitchy Puritan. Some days I don't even recognize myself anymore.

"She's exhausted, Ands. And trust me, those pics are hard to live down if the bus comes while she's still lining up the shot," Jase says. "But Alice is right about the outfit."

"Again, let me repeat: You guys are *not* Mom and Dad," Andy says. "I have a hoodie, anyway." She wags her backpack in our direction with one hand, tugging a shoe on with the other.

"I need evidence." I reach for the backpack.

"Al-ice. God. It's like you two have been replaced by pod people."

Of course there's no hoodie in there ("I swear I put it in"), so

I'm about to head for the house to get some Amish cover-up when Jase pulls a T-shirt out of his backpack.

"Wear this." He tosses it to her. It's one of our Garrett's Hardware WE NAIL IT shirts, which we just had done up for the Fourth of July sale. God, how much did those set us back? "Promotion and protection in one handy package."

Andy regards him dubiously. I can read her thoughts. *A T-shirt? Big-brother-sized? On the first day of high school? Might as well just commit social hari-kari during first assembly.*

"Okaaaay," she says finally, dragging it on over the tank top. Andy is a nicer person than I am. Or more devious. As she stretches to pull it over her head, I realize my little sister is taller than me. No wonder that skirt looks so short.

"Twenty bucks says that lives in her locker all day. Maybe all year."

Jase shrugs. "Not taking that one, Alice. You were young once too."

"Of course, I also have my period," Andy adds, looking back and forth between us as though we both, definitely, need to hear this. "Naturally. Because why *wouldn't* I be breaking out on the first day of school? Does being on the Pill really help with that, or is that just something people say because they need to use it for other reasons?"

"Don't look at *me*," Jase says.

"Why not? Sam's on it, right? And she never has pimples— ever."

"Andy. None of your business."

"Alice? Come on, *you* know, right?"

"Talk to Mom," I mutter. Wait—I've been taking mine, right?

I can't remember punching the little vacuum pack, holding the pink tablet in my hand, washing it down. But I wouldn't forget. I never forget. Besides, Brad's gone.

Or not. My cell phone dings. Brad. Early-morning at the gym probably. It's a picture of a puppy begging, "I may not be Red Rover, but can I come over?"

What happened to *we're* over?

I put my head in my hands.

"Alice!" shouts Duff from the house steps. "I can't find my glasses anywhere! Or my summer reading book."

"Alice!" yells Harry from the screen door. "Whatja do with my owl? Someone moved it!"

"Alice!" George calls from Jase's window upstairs. "That lady who lived in the shoe—what kind of shoe was it? I hafta draw a picture."

"Alice," Jase says, bending to pick up his backpack, "go for a long run on the beach as soon as we get on the bus. I grabbed a three-pack of spearmint Mentos for you at Gas and Go this morning—it's hidden behind the box of that oatmeal stuff so no one else gets to it first. There's an everything bagel too."

The school bus screeches, hitting the top of the hill. As it comes down the street, the brakes shrill out a long, groaning sigh, almost exactly like the sound I'm trying hard to repress.

I'm a hundred and ten.

I'm the old woman who lives in the shoe.

"Hang in there," Jase calls, turning back with one foot on the bus stairs. "You're only temping as Mom."

"Thank God for that," I call. "I'm selling these kids on eBay and never having any of my own."

Andy scrambles up the steps, the door slams shut, there's more squealing from the brakes, a puff of gray exhaust rising into the bright blue sky.

A whistle and an "Al-eece!" from some guy in the back of the bus. Jimmy Pieretti. Dated his brother Tom three years ago. Under normal circumstances, the whistle would make me roll my eyes. Jim's, what, Jase's age?

Oh.

Right.

So's Tim.

But Tom was fun, Jim's a sweetheart, and I'm grateful for any evidence that I'm not as ancient as I feel, so I shoot a smile at the window.

Scattered whistles.

There's almost a spring in my step as I turn away from the bus.

TIM

Total blur. All of it.

Cal's sleeping, he's crying, he's drinking, he's lying on my stomach while I lie on the floor of the apartment or the grass at Dominic's waiting for the fever to break or the buzz to go away so everything goes back to normal.

But it doesn't, because neither of those things is real. Cal is real. When he sleeps for a while, I jolt up sweaty because I'm afraid he's dead. When he only sleeps for a short time, I walk around sweaty because I'm so bushed and what's *wrong* with this kid anyway? He doesn't have any rhythm or I can't find one. He drinks the whole bottle and then screams for an hour like he's starving. He drinks nothing and falls asleep fast. I don't know if this is because he's a baby or because he's mine and therefore terminally unreliable. Either way, it blows. I can't believe I ever felt sorry for myself about anything ever before because I should have saved it all up for this. This tops anything Pop could have devised—I mean, he could have sectioned me, for Chrissake, locked me away to recover in rehab for as long as he wanted. Because *this*? It's been three whole days and it's honestly lasted longer than the entire seventeen years of my life.

Not to mention:

It was cake to pull crap over on my parents because *they didn't want to know*, so sucky excuses and lame explanations played fine.

But with the Garretts, I don't have that home-field advantage. Too many sharp eyes, too many working brains. Not to mention the fact that I'm not trying to smuggle Bacardi into a movie theater in an antibacterial gel container, but an actual human in and out of my apartment and their yard with his diaper bag and all his other crap. I actually do drive-bys to make sure there are no cars in the driveway or the lights are off or whatever before I skulk into or out of the apartment. Then I haul ass faster than Christmas. So Cal and I are spending a lot of time hanging at Dominic's, since he's in between fishing gigs. I sit on his steps, throw sticks for Dom's massive German shepherd Sarge, and hold the kid while Cal sleeps or drinks or stares, and Dom power-washes the hull of his boat or chops firewood or repaves the driveway.

"Could you maybe, like, bake cupcakes or sew an apron or something?" I ask, after watching him clean out the storm drains.

"You have messed-up ideas about manhood. I bake awesome cakes, by the way. What's losing you *cojones* points is that you're holing up here."

I know, I know, I know.

Me on the phone with Hester, way the eff early in the morning on day three: "Look, I've got—stuff—to do. I've got an econ class online that I'm behind in and a civics test and a physics one I need to get in by the end of the week. Not to mention a couple days on at the hardware store." With Alice there too, during at least one of them. God. "When can I drop off Cal?"

Hester: (long pause) "This morning. We need to talk anyway."

Do we hafta? The thought does not fill me with joyous anticipation.

First off, I smuggle Cal into the car as the school bus pulls away and the screen door flaps shut behind Alice. Hester and I have set up a Cal swap in Willoughby Park, where I used to buy weed. She didn't want me to come to her house, but all she'd say when I pushed for an explanation was, "It's not a good time."

When I get to the park, I try to give back all the baby crap, but about all Hester'll take is the actual child. I half expect her to hand me a dime bag in exchange.

Right away she's rooting through the big-ass diaper bag, like she's counting stuff in there, like maybe I stole some of the formula and fenced it on the street or something, and my jaw clenches so tight, my neck muscles start throbbing. I never used to get angry, and now it's like I'm a goddamn volcano set on "continuous erupt."

I look away, kicking the dust with the toe of my flip-flops. Willoughby is not one of those nice parks with tons of green grass and leafy trees and all that jazz. It's more on the scraggly, sad side. The better to do the drug deals. In fact, I see one going on as we speak. Over in the far corner, near the stone wall that marks the end of the park, there's Troy Rhodes, the guy every school has at least one of, the guy who can set you up with whatever you want or need, any day, any night, any second, as long as you can pay.

My dealer, in other words.

Until a few months ago, probably the person I knew best in town.

He's doing the old hand-shake pass-off with some middle-school type. The guy's little-kid skinny, his chest practically concave, pants hanging low, wearing a Pokémon shirt that he probably doesn't know yet is uncool.

When I refocus, Hester's passing her hand back and forth in front of my face. I grab her wrist and she does this cringe thing like I'm going to snap it.

Christ, I was annoyed, but I'm not a psychopath.

"I know you're not, Tim."

Whoops, said that out loud.

"You looked glazed. I know what that can mean. But you're just tired, right? And trust me, you look way better than I usually do after time with him. It's like your worst nightmare ever, isn't it? Like hell."

I've spent the past days thinking that 345,678,900 times,

but when she says it, it sounds almost criminal, like there's something really wrong with *her*.

Seeing me blink, she focuses on packing things back into the bag. "I don't have any brothers or sisters, and I do the older kids at camp and I just"—she shrugs—"thought they were like babies in commercials, somehow."

"Like, as long as you gave 'em"—I pull out my Moviefone voice—"Sleepy Hollow Brand Formula, your little one will sleep like Rip Van Winkle."

She laughs, the first one I've heard from her since that first day, then covers her mouth like she's let something shameful escape. When her fingers move away, there's still a smile.

"That," she says, "is how Calvin happened." Her voice is accusing.

"Uh—"

"You made me laugh."

"Luckily, I don't need a rubber for that. When do I have to get him back again?" That sounds even worse than what she said, so I'm not surprised that she looks like she wants to deck me with the diaper bag. "I mean—"

"You don't. Never mind. Here's the thing, Tim. I thought about what you said—that I was being a sadist by bringing you into the picture at all."

I can barely remember using those words, even though *of course* I did. I'm such an asshole. "Forget about it, I shouldn't—"

"No, I can't. It makes sense. I was the one who got in trouble."

"Fuck that, Hester. This is not actually *The Scarlet Letter*. I don't have a problem with babysitting."

She purses her lips, looks down at Cal, away into the distance, narrowing her eyes in the bright sunlight.

"It's not babysitting if it's your own child. What I'm saying is that you don't have to be involved. It can just end here."

Cal's punted off a sock. He loves to do that, like it's some personal baby challenge. I bend over and pick it up, pulling it up his squirmy pink foot. He watches me somberly. Probably can hardly see me at this distance yet, according to the baby facts I've googled. I could be gone before he can. Say *yeah, sure, I'm done*, and putting his sock on could be the last thing I ever do for him, other than, presumably, sign off on some paperwork. *A baby? Right, I had one for a day or two. It didn't work out. End of story.* He'd never remember I existed and I could try to forget he ever had. I can see the tape rewinding, me walking backward through the past few days, up the steps to the apartment, lying back down after push-ups, the only thing on my mind meeting Alice in forty-five minutes. Poof. Erased.

But.

Hester's still staring out at the river, so I turn her chin toward me. She sort of freezes at my touch, wash of pink under her pale skin. "Hes. He happened. You let me know. We can't time-travel and un-happen it any more than I can go further back and unscrew you."

That was beautiful, I hear Dominic say in my head.

She looks like I've smacked her. Of course. "You—I—" Tears come to her eyes.

Can't go back and unsay it either, so I bumble onward:

"What I mean is—I'm in this. He's not, like, a movie I checked out the preview of and decided not to watch. He's my kid. So, let's just get on with it. What happens next?"

She blinks, her face smooths. Totally back to prissy-tone: "I'm doing a follow-up with the adoption agency this morning—that should help us figure out the timetable."

She looks even more rumpled today than the first time I saw her. Her dark hair's in this twisted-knot-thing that looks like a squirrel's nest: she's got khakis on, but they're tight—and not in a good way—and her shirt is buttoned wrong. She's going somewhere like this?

"So when's your appointment?"

She brushes some flyaway hair out of her eyes. "It doesn't matter. You don't need to come. I wasn't asking you to. Your name isn't on the birth certificate anyway."

I hadn't given one second of thought to the birth certificate, but, "Uh, shouldn't it be?"

Hester explains, in this elaborately patient tone, that she wasn't sure I would "acknowledge paternity."

"And yet here I am, acknowledging," I say, my voice, like hers, sounding like someone is chopping each word off from the one next to it. She pulls out her phone and scrolls through it, the text-check blow-off move. Usually I have to know someone better for them to piss me off this much.

The kid who was over in the bushes buying is now riding down the street toward us on his bike. He's got the backward-hat thing going on and kind of a freak-out face—because he sees us, or because he hasn't done this before, or because he somehow knows he's taken a giant step down the Road to Stupid.

He can't be more than twelve.

Almost as much of a baby as Cal.

He speeds on by, his eyes dead ahead, jaw set, legs a blur.

Takes just about all I have not to step out into the street in front of him like the goddamn Ghost of Christmas Future.

ALICE

I come into the kitchen after the school bus trundles away to find Duff and Harry dueling with Popsicles. It's seven o'clock in the morning.

"I am not left-handed," Duff says triumphantly as I walk in, swapping his Popsicle to the other hand and smashing it into Harry's, shattering sugary purple shards of ice all over the floor.

Harry leaps onto Duff's back, all ready for hand-to-hand combat. I grab both the backs of their pajamas, twist, and pull them apart. "Knock it off or you're both going to the fire swamp."

I serve breakfast, helped by the presence of actual food in our cabinets and fridge.

I even find both Duff's glasses and his summer reading book hidden in and under Harry's LEGO castle, as part of a complicated revenge plot, the details of which I'd rather not know. "You have a lot to learn about revenge," I say, drowning out Harry's outraged "No fair no fair no fair." "Never hide things in the most obvious place, for starters."

"Don't give him *tips*, Alice!" Duff says. "Whose side are you on?"

"Whichever pays better. Get dressed."

I have this down. I can hear water running, so Mom's up, but the least I can do is give her time for a shower. Assuming Andy left any hot water.

Patsy has escaped from her crib, of course, but she's no match for me. Although my diapering while she's trying to run away skills really aren't up to Dad's.

I tell George to draw eight kids for the Old Woman's shoe, and negotiate a discussion of what kind of shoe it would be, which turns ugly.

"It wouldn't be a high heel, duh," Duff says. "They'd all escape."

Or she would. But I don't even say that out loud. I'm a goddess.

Except I forgot about the owl.

"Where is it?" Harry asks, tears streaming down his freckled cheeks, searching frantically through our kitchen junk drawer, scattering pizza delivery menus and pencils all over the floor.

"Do you have something to do with this?" I ask Duff.

He gives me an actually innocent look, instead of the super-wide-eyed one that is always suspect. "I was the one who found it for him in the first place!"

Text Jase: Where is effin owl?

But he doesn't answer because no cell phones at school, duh.

Harry's now on his hands and knees, rummaging through the drawer where all the Tupperware is, tossing it all out on the floor, sobbing. His skinny little shoulders . . . he sounds so lost— and I could be right there on the floor with him in a heartbeat, kicking and screaming. I put my arms around him, try to pull him onto my lap, the way I would George (who is hunting for the owl in the broom closet, judging by the crashes) but he looks at me like I'm a demon from the pits of hell. "You took him. I know you did, Alice. You never wanted me to have him in the first place. I hate you."

"Jesus God," I say loudly, sounding like Tim. "Shut up."

Beat of silence.

"We're not supposed to say that," Duff says righteously.

Patsy is now crunching something that looks a lot like it came from the cat dish.

I can't do this. I don't want to do this. I never, ever signed on for this.

Now my chest is seizing up and I really can't breathe, and . . .

Mom comes in, slightly green, and solves it all. She might as well have a wand. The owl turns out to have mysteriously disappeared, but there are many photographs of it, from every disgusting angle. "This is better," she tells Harry firmly. "I'm fairly sure Mrs. Costa is allergic to feathers. Besides, it would've been hard to carry in your backpack."

"I could have put him in my lunch box," Harry says sulkily, but the fight's gone out of him, even as he still has almost as many tears on his face as freckles.

She admires George's picture, while scooping the cat food (yes, it was) out of Patsy's mouth, saying, "Jase needs to keep this in his own room."

Sends Duff off to reorganize the broom closet, because he loves to do stuff like that, and I'm glad someone does.

Then Mom looks up at me, shielding her eyes from the light streaming in from the window over the sink. "Go for a run, Alice. I'm on this."

I practically beat my best time just getting to the hallway, then turn back. "Mom . . ." *Why the hell would you ever do this? Why?* "How do you do this?"

"I have access to the Dark Arts. Run, Alice."

So I do.

Chapter Twenty-three

TIM

From hell to heaven, the minute I get back to the Garretts'.

Alice is in the driveway, washing the Bug. White halter bikini top, cutoffs. Man, will it suck when the cold weather comes. Right now, this can make up for everything—GEDs, global warming, even the last few days of my life.

Alice swipes her forehead with the back of her hand, which aims the hose directly at me.

"Hey!"

She jumps, whips around. Sees me soaking. Smiles so wide, I think I might die right there. Happy. She covers the end of the hose with her thumb and slowly flicks the spray up and down, so now I'm drenched. I look around for another weapon—tossing the entire water bucket over her seems brutal. But before I can seize the Super Soaker from the lawn, she lifts her hands in surrender, which, since she's still holding the hose, does the job for me, getting her totally wet.

"Always asking for trouble, Tim."

"You started it. Trouble pretty much finds me without having to ask directions."

We stand there dripping. Droplets on her long eyelashes and this fine mist in her hair.

It's crazy quiet, except for the *shhh* of the water still draining from the hose.

"Where the hell is everyone?"

"First day of school," Alice says.

The bus earlier. Right. *First day of school.*

I swallow. Not for me. For the first September since I turned five, I'm not walking through any school doors.

"So, you're saying that as of today, I'm *officially* a high school dropout."

Alice wipes her wet hands on a towel, hoops it around her neck, scans me over, lingering on my eyes. She pulls her lower lip between her teeth, and squints at me, then nods like she's come to some decision. "Change clothes and meet me here in five, okay?"

When I do, she's now in a yellow bikini top and this orange skirt that technically covers her ass. But I can trace the outline of the rest of the bikini through it. As if she's reading those thoughts, she almost touches the nic patch, now on my side, a square bump under my T-shirt. "How're you doing with everything, Tim?"

Yeah, about that everything. Got some news. I open my mouth, but only a slice of the truth comes out. "Well, shitty. Basically."

She studies me for a sec, then turns and walks toward the Bug. "Come on. Let's just . . . go."

Anywhere.

I slide into the passenger seat. Those cars? Your legs are, like, right there. So I accidentally brush against Alice's smooth, tanned thigh with the back of my knuckles as I'm fastening the seat belt. Drum my fingers on my knee. Close my eyes. Deep gulp of air. Salt, sea, sun, sand.

Alice.

ALICE

The Bug has shrunk. Tim seems to be taking up more space—more air—than his fair share. He adjusts his long legs, knees bumping the dash, hand grazing my leg. I grind the gears as I shift into reverse. Look over quickly to see if he's giving me that annoying cocky smile, but he's tipped his head partly out the window, resting his chin on the heel of the hand propped on the sill, eyes closed, hair whipping around like a dark red hurricane.

The only other time we've been in this car together he was passed out cold in the backseat after a suicidal joyride with Samantha and his jumpy sister. We had to carry him into his house, he was so wasted. That was barely three months ago.

No time at all, really.

I open my mouth to say *Let's go back, not a good idea*, but then the breeze shifts, I smell the tarry open road and the sparkling clean air and Tim's shampoo.

We've passed the Reeds' old house, wind through downtown, past the building and loan, away from everything.

Just for right now. This once.

We hit the intersection of Old Town Road and Route 17. I smooth my thumbs against the worn plastic of the steering wheel, hesitate over the turn signal.

Tim angles his hip, pulls something out of his pocket. "Let's play Flip It," he says, and hands me a quarter. "Every time we get to an intersection, we flip the coin. Heads are right, tails are left."

I toss the coin to him and he whips it out of the air, quick as a seagull, and slaps it onto the back of his hand, then points left, leans over, flicks the turn signal.

"Let's wait a few exits to flip it again. Not much adventure in Stony Bay."

"So it's adventure you're looking for today, Alice?"

I shrug. Tim resettles his legs again, rubs the side of one thigh, makes a face.

"Leg cramp? Navy Seal workout getting to you?"

"Pain is weakness leaving the body," Tim says solemnly. "Also nicotine. The coin says take this right."

Right, and flip left, and finally we wind up at McNair Beach, three towns away, but still a destination beach because it's a lot less rocky than the ones close by.

"Just so you know," Tim says as I park in the empty lot, "I cheated. I wanted the beach. Shame not to get that bikini wet."

He grins at me, unabashedly checking me out. I straighten, pull my shoulders back, smile sideways at him. Then freeze. I've made those moves a thousand times and can translate them, even if Tim can't. *Go ahead. Look. I want you to.* What the hell am I thinking, pulling this with him? There should be sky-writing, a billboard, a Jumbotron: *You know better.* And I do. And still.

TIM

Alice flicks off her flip-flops, tosses them into the backseat without saying a word. Then strides off like she's leading a charge. I trail after her, hands crammed in my pockets.

Still without talking, we walk down the path lined with sea grass, onto the wide beach, the ragged, stony breakwater, toward the boarded-up hot dog and burger stand. She's still a length ahead and it occurs to me that I'm trailing after her like Brad or any of her lame-ass boytoys.

I catch up to her easy—longer legs and all that. "I'm not some lapdog, like your Cro-Magnons," I tell her. "You don't get to call all the shots."

She stops, shading her eyes to look up at me. "No, you're not a lapdog, Tim. I know that."

"Just so we're clear," I say, my eyes straying to her belly ring, which is winking in the late-morning sun.

"You're too big to be a lapdog. An Irish setter maybe." Then she turns and starts to run down the beach.

I laugh. So I'm, like, the sample workout buddy in this scenario? Cramping quad muscle and all, it takes me a minute to catch up to her this time. At least I'm not gasping like a landed trout. I tag her on the shoulder.

She whips around but doesn't realize how near I am, so she winds up smack against me. Smile fading, she steps back, folds her arms tight against the bare brown skin of her stomach, exactly where I want to reach out and set my fingers, nudge my thumb against that little silver belly ring.

"Let's . . . let's . . ."

"Yeah?" I say, and step closer. Because Alice, fierce Alice, who always meets my eyes square on, doesn't seem to know where to look.

"Let's just . . ."

I close my eyes, blood pounding in my ears.

Let's just lie down in the sand.

Please.

Let me just . . .

Have this.

She looks up at me through her lashes for a second, lips parted just a little.

Then . . . "God." She shields her eyes, staring out at the tossing waves, then down the beach. "It's really over. Summer. So fast."

"Naaah." I point. "The Shore Shack cart's still here. Always summer in the land of frozen dairy products in colors not seen in nature. C'mon. I'll buy you something." I shove my hand back into my pocket, jingle the change and crumpled bills I stuffed in there on my way out the door. "As long as it doesn't cost me more than four bucks and twenty-seven cents."

"Big spender."

"Hey, eternal youth doesn't come cheap." I start to set my hand on her back to steer her toward the cart but can't because there's no end to what I want to touch when it comes to Alice. I'm almost as wheredoyouputyourhands as Andy.

We have a brief argument over which flavors are the most immature. "Neapolitan," Alice insists. "Vanilla, chocolate, strawberry. The basics. It's the first ice cream babies get to eat."

Cal.

Don't think about it. I want to pull this day out of time and space the way a magician snatches a quarter from thin air.

"That's just a sneaky way of using up all that strawberry," I argue, "because who the hell likes that shit?"

"You're overthinking this."

"I specialize in that."

"Live in the moment, Tim." Her tone's cheerful, even a little goofy, and hell yeah.

In the end she gets Cake Batter, which is pink and has little strips of frosting mixed into it. I get electric-blue Bubble Gum, complete with waxy little gum balls. Watching Alice lick her cone makes me happy in all sorts of non-little-kid ways. I bite the bottom of my cone off.

"I *knew* you'd be that guy," she says, polishing off her own.

"What guy?" I slurp down the last bits of ice cream, discarding one of the hard, stale-tasting gumballs, a perfect basket into the rusting iron trash barrel.

"The one who just has to do it the wrong way."

The fact of Calvin, successfully shoved out of my head for a good two minutes, smacks me in the face again like a cold wave.

But.

I take a breath.

Live in the moment.

Cal's not here at *this* moment, and I am, and Alice is.

ALICE

Nobody looks mature eating ice cream, and Tim, with a streak of blue on his right cheekbone, is no exception.

He would be in *high school* right now if he hadn't taken the wrong exit.

I'm only one year out, it's true, but it feels longer. So much longer. Field hockey and band and Spirit Day and dances . . . some other girl's life.

Tim lobs the last of his cone toward the trash, grabs the back of his shirt and pulls it off, wipes his face.

There's suddenly a lot of bare skin in front of me.

I point at the sand. "Lie down."

His mouth drops open for a second. "Uh . . . what?"

"Lie down," I repeat.

"Do I get a biscuit if I obey?" But he does, he lies down, falling on his back in the sand as I drop to my knees next to his hip. I start scooping sand onto him, beginning with his chest.

"Only if you're very good. Stop moving, Tim, I can't cover you up if you keep moving."

His hand shoots out, grabs my wrist. "You'll leave a hole for oxygen, right?"

"I—I—" His thumb presses in a little harder, right where my pulse jumps. I yank my hand away, keep piling on the sand. "When I did this to Andy, I always sculpted a mermaid tail out of sand over her legs."

"Yeah, and you won't be doing that this time."

I'm just starting to smooth down around his thighs when he erupts out, scattering sand, in my hair, down my suit, everywhere.

He shakes his head, whipping more sand onto me. Then crouches, hands on his knees, breathing like he's been sprinting—barefoot—instead of lying flat under my moving hands.

TIM

Cold water.

Now.

"Now we *have* to swim," Alice says to me, like she's reading my mind. Or, you know, body.

"Race you to the buoy line?"

"*Pffft*," I say. "Kids' stuff. Gotta head for the breakwater, if you're going for a challenge."

"Isn't kid's stuff what we're doing? Besides, the breakwater is out of bounds for swimmers."

I point to the empty lifeguard chairs. "Come on. Take a chance, Alice."

"Stretch out that right leg first," she advises.

"You forgot to say 'Simon says.'"

She flushes, looks down and readjusts her halter strap. "What's that supposed to mean?"

"Just that you don't get to be the boss of me."

She shakes her head. Like she wants my words and this weird push-pull between us to flip away with the breeze.

"I wasn't saying that. I wasn't doing that."

"No?"

"No." All brisk and practical now. "You're still favoring one leg when you run. That's probably why the other one is cramping up. I do that when I don't pay attention, because of this broken ankle I had a few years ago. Ever break anything?"

"Other than curfew and the speed limit? A few hearts here and there."

Total bullshit, the last. I wait for her to call me on it, to know that no one ever got that close. Instead she squares her shoulders, widens her stance, hands on hips. Like a dare.

"No worries. I'm pretty heartless."

That's bullshit too, but I don't say so. "So how do I fix it? The favoring-the-leg thing?"

"Try a few lunges." She demonstrates, one toned, tanned

thigh balanced, bending smoothly at the knee, jaw fixed, looking out over the water, strong chin, full lips, these two little dimples inset neatly at the base of her spine.

Oh Alice.

Trying *not* to lunge, thank you very much.

ALICE

No sign of Tim anywhere. I'm bobbing in the cool water beyond the slimy swim line that connects the buoys and he was *right there*, yards ahead of me, and now there's nothing. No splash, no streak of arms against the waves, nothing but a seagull shrilling and plunging in the air overhead.

Nothing at all.

Panic flickers at the edge of my vision, almost visibly, like someone flipping white lights on and off in a dark room. A wave slaps me in the face. I can't catch my breath.

Not one of these.

Not here.

Not now.

And not him. *Where is he?*

I shield my eyes, sweep a look one direction, the other. A head, rusty hair nearly the same color as the buoys, bobs up.

Laughing, damn it.

"Where the hell were you?"

"To the breakwater—and back. Underwater. I win."

"I thought you'd drowned."

He cocks his head at me. "Seriously? I was on the swim team."

"How would I know that? I thought you'd gone under." My voice is trembling. "Which is the last thing I need, I mean, we need—I mean, what would happen if you drowned? If you got hurt or *died* while I was watching you?"

"*Watching* me? You're not *babysitting* me," he says, then flushes.

"I didn't mean that. I just meant—you could have hit your head on a rock or come across a riptide or—"

"The really bad riptide is at Stony Bay Beach," he interrupts. "Not here. Besides, I know how to get out of it. I'm a big boy, Alice. And not your problem."

"I didn't mean that. But you—" I stop, not even sure what I'm so angry about.

He purses his lips, studying me, moving up and down in the waves, so close, his feet whirl the water around me as he treads, red hair dark and glinting. "I don't fuck up *everything*, Alice."

The sound is that clear, sea-glass green it often turns in the fall, though it's still summer-warm. His eyes are also a clear grayish blue, nothing shielded.

"I know that." Some things you say automatically and then, inside, feel a quiet little nod. The hitch in my breath, the knot in my chest, they untangle and wash away as I look back at him, waves slapping around us.

TIM

"Hot fake leather! Hot fake leather! I forgot to leave a towel on the seat," Alice says after sliding into the driver's side. "Holy! I never forget to do that."

"You were probably distracted by my hard, manly body." I stretch into the backseat for a towel and toss it to her. She misses the catch, fumbles for it, crams it beneath her. Then turns to face me. Presses her lips together, sets her jaw, bracing herself. I wait for her to blast me for something—scaring her in the water, that she already knows about the kid, that she can read my mind and knows every little nook and cranny it's gone to in the last two hours.

"What?"

Pucker between her brows now. Her eyes move over my face.

"What?" I ask again, reaching up to rub my chin self-consciously. I haven't shaved.

Still frowning, she rests her index finger between my eyebrows, brushes away the worry lines.

Then she wraps one arm around my waist, sets her fingers at the back of my neck to pull my head down. She touches her tongue to my bottom lip, and then opens her mouth. Tastes like salty ocean and sweet birthday cake and everything I've ever blown out candles and wished for.

I kiss her back, skim one thumb slowly down her spine, the other hand hesitating at her waist for only one inhale before I press my palm hard against her soft skin, turn her to face me more fully, pull her all the way into my lap, bend all I have into all of her.

We're in a Volkswagen and I'm six three. The fine German engineering of the People's Car was *not* engineered for this. Still, there's no freaking way I'm gonna stop and request a more comfortable situation. Even if my legs are wedged under the glove compartment and my rib cage is about to be cracked by the gearshift.

"What am I doing with you?" Alice whispers, sliding her hands up my back. "This is crazy," she says, shifting her hips to accommodate me. "You're a kid."

"I'm no kid. And you know it." I move my lips behind her ear, along her throat, her neck, lower. Then slip one hand very slowly, tips of my fingers, edge of my thumb under the triangle of her suit.

God, God, God.

There we are in a tiny car with the windows down in a public parking lot and you'd think sanity would stop us, but nothing does.

I pluck the strap of her halter top to the side.

Drop my mouth to her collarbone where the strap has left a small red indentation.

Her hands on me, my lips on her, her fingers tightening, my breath catching.

Hers coming in these little puffs of air, hot against me.

I edge one hand down to touch the lever to recline the seat back and instead it folds around this thing, this loop of plastic and squish of rubber that I don't immediately identify until I get it—a pacifier. For a baby.

In this case, Patsy, but . . .

Alice will hate herself, and me. Why did this have to happen now?

"This is . . . probably not a good idea."

"Hmm?" She's kissing my collarbone, her palm flat against my chest, over my heart.

"Alice."

She looks up.

"We need to cool off here," I tell her. *Now* I have to discover my inner maturity?

Her eyes are hazy. "We do?"

No. "Yeah."

"Right, you're right," she says, sliding off my lap back into the driver's seat. I'm abruptly cold without her heat. Her head's bowed and I bend over to kiss her forehead.

"In case it wasn't obvious, I didn't want to stop."

"Uh-huh," she says, still looking down.

"Alice. Look at me."

She slowly raises her head and swallows. All shimmery eyes and wild hair and every kind of gorgeous. Then holds up a hand, stopping anything I might say.

"Give me a second."

Reaches into the back of the car for a sweatshirt, pulls it on like armor, rests the flat of her hand over her eyes for a beat of my heart. Then another.

Then she turns her keys in the ignition, looks over her shoulder, and peels out of the parking lot so fast, rubber would burn if the drive weren't made of broken clamshells. As it is, shells fly.

ALICE

We don't say a word the entire ride back. Tim opens his window all the way, tips his head out, drums his fingers on the dashboard. I can only see his profile, and not much of that.

My legs are shaking, like I've run miles, breath hard to scrape out of my lungs, my toes tingling as if coming back from numbness. Probably true, they were so tightly curled before. When I reach over to shift gears, my hand trembles a little. I stop to get gas and he pulls up the parking brake, his thumb slipping along my calf as he does so.

He looks down at my leg for a moment, swallows, his Adam's apple visibly bobbing.

"There's something I think—I know—I should tell you. But first, I've got to know. What *was* that?" he asks in a low voice.

"What was what?" I scribble my name on the receipt and hand the card back to the gas station guy, turn the car out onto the main road.

Tim jerks his thumb over his shoulder, indicating the beach we've driven away from. "You know. Are you, like, toying with me, Alice? Just be straight up, if that's what this is."

I hate that he's so much taller than I am, the top of his head brushing the roof of the car.

"I'm not toying with you," I say, pulling up to a red light. "God. Like I do that."

Tim meets my eyes.

"Fine. I do that. But I'm not doing that now. At least"—I put my head in my hands—"I don't know what I'm doing. But it's not toying, like a cat with a mouse. Or whatever."

"So this is . . . what? Sample dating? Even though I screwed up our first? Temporary insanity? I don't know what this *is*."

"I don't know either," I say, looking at him. "Besides . . . you're the one who got smart and put the brakes on." My voice sounds hurt, and I hate that.

"I didn't want to. You had to know that. It couldn't have been more obvious. But . . ."

I wave one hand at him, brushing it off, him away. "Whatever. It doesn't matter."

"Alice."

I flick my hand at him again, trying to regain myself, shift back into Tin Alice, the girl with no heart.

"Alice. Don't *whatever* me. It matters. Could you look at me, for Chrissake?"

"I'm driving. Have to focus."

He sighs.

I drive down the main street of Stony Bay, around the roundabout shaped like a lighthouse, then out onto the straightaway without looking at him again. But, just as we get to our road, I reach out my hand, palm up, and after a pause, he slides his big warm hand into mine, squeezes. Holds on.

When I pull into the driveway and finally sneak a look, he's drumming on the other leg with one thumb. I turn to him.

"Look, Tim. What if we just try—"

"Alice. There's something important I've got to tell you—"

He breaks off, stares over at the garage apartment.

"Oh, fuck me."

"What?" I follow the direction of his gaze. A girl is sitting on the steps. Silver-car girl. With a huge bag slung over her shoulder. And a baby in a car seat beside her.

Chapter Twenty-four

TIM

Hester waves, all welcoming and chipper, like I've popped by to see her at *her* house with some flowers and a meat loaf.

"My car was acting crazy—making all these strange noises, like *Eeeeeeee*," she calls, walking over, leaving the baby behind, "so I left it at that garage on North Street. They gave me a lift over here. It's good you're back. Cal's all fussy, and he probably shouldn't be out in the sun too long."

Alice is a statue, hand frozen on the gearshift. Hester's smiling. Cal's asleep. I, at this moment, would sell my soul for any number of things, but first and foremost that stupid sailor hat. Or the lame-ass bonnet. Because there's nothing covering Cal's head but his shiny, incriminating red hair.

Hester processes the fact that I'm in the car with this dazzling girl in a bikini at exactly the same second that Alice takes in the whole picture. Hester's smile dims. Alice squares her shoulders. "Sounds like the fan belt needs replacing," she says flatly. "Yeah, you should probably get that baby out of the sun."

"Alice . . ." I say. "It's not . . ." *What, not what it looks like? It's exactly what it looks like.* "I can . . ." *Explain? Not really.* "I—"

"It's most likely a good idea if you don't say anything right now," she says, kicking open the car door.

"But—" I slide out of my seat, start to circle around the Bug.

"Don't. Talk." She slams the door, then shoves it shut after it pops open again. Cal startles and begins to cry. Alice casts one incredulous look at me, then strides toward the house.

"I thought you said you didn't have a girlfriend." Hester's voice lifts over the baby's shrill wails. She's scooped him into her arms and is jiggling him up and down. His eyes are saucers.

"I don't."

She stares after Alice's fine retreating ass. I punch the side of the Bug, hard, and then boot the tire for good measure.

"So who was that?"

"Hester." I'm gritting my teeth so hard, I expect shards of molars to fly out onto the tar of the driveway. "None of your business."

"If it would help to talk about it—" Her voice is all soothing, and where the hell does she get off with that? The baby, who has paused with the screeching, cranks it up again.

"No offense, but you don't know me at all."

More shrieking from Cal.

"Hell, give him to me, Hes."

Gnawing her lip with her teeth, she passes him over. "My car should be done soon. You could drop me off in town. Or . . ." Her shoulders slump. "I guess I could walk. How far do you think it is?"

Nail yourself to the freakin' cross, already. I hoist the baby on my shoulder, bury my nose in his neck. He makes this little wiggling movement, snuggling in safe. I don't feel safe, my gut tight, my intestines squirming like snakes, so I shut my eyes; try to recite the Serenity Prayer or something in my head. The best I can do is take my mind back to the beach, cool water glistening silver on Alice's tanned shoulders, the flash of her ring in the sunlight, her smile.

"Sure she's not your girlfriend?" Hester asks. "Because she's looking out the window at us."

"It doesn't matter. Let's get Cal inside."

"His name is Calvin."

I'm spoiling for a fight, and I'll take one anywhere, on any grounds, no matter how much of an asshole that makes me.

"I'm calling him Cal. Calvin is a pussy name."

Hester flinches, blue eyes, pale face. I've sucker-punched a kitten. Muttering an apology, I head up the stairs, Hester following. Only one quick backward glance to see if Alice actually is watching.

She's not.

Inside, I fill a glass of water from the tap, guzzle it down, then set the glass on the counter and stick my face right under the faucet. Gulping, trying to cool down.

Hester's got Cal now, patting his back. She keeps trying to talk to me, going on and on, something about the adoption intake interview and my medical history and ethnic background and paperwork, paperwork, paperwork.

My temples are pounding and I'm hot, then cold, then hot again. "How long is your car going to take? I can't do this now," I say. "Call the garage and tell them it's the fan belt. Better yet, let's just go over there."

"It may not be the fan belt. Unless that girl is a car mechanic. She didn't look like a car mechanic. Is she—"

"Leave it alone," I say, picking my cell up off the counter. "Which garage is it?"

"Oh, no. This diaper is leaking. Here." She shoves the baby at me in this offhand way, like he's a pile of towels, then heads to the sink to wash her hands, adding over her shoulder, "Can you get this one? As I said, they need a medical history. Do you have any chronic diseases?"

"Nope," I snap, resting Cal against my chest, head on my shoulder, with one hand and bending over to rummage through all the crap in the bag for one of his postage-stamp-sized diapers.

"Unless you count my slight touch of alcoholism." And horniness. And douchebaggery.

Cal's little scratchy fingernails are digging into my chest like Jase's cat's paws do, like milk's going to come spilling right on out. "Hang on," I mutter to him. "Cleanup first."

Something's warm and sticky on the hand that's holding him and I know before looking what it is.

"Jesus God, Hes. Why is it this color? What is *wrong* with this kid?"

"Nothing! He's just fine. Fine. Why would you even ask that?"

Shifting Calvin to the other side, I hold out my hand, the hand that was on Alice's back, her neck, her waist, less than an hour ago. "It's green. That can't be right."

"He's fine," she repeats, handing me a box of baby wipes and this folded plastic thing and, for some reason, a little woolly hat with a pompom. "Sorry about that. Change him on that so he doesn't leak on the couch."

"Do you think I give a damn about the couch? God knows what could be in those genes or chromosomes or whatever was my contribution to the party. I'm surprised my sperm could even swim straight, if you want the truth."

"He's perfectly healthy. Calm down. You're making him upset." She pauses. "Look, Tim." Her voice softens. "I know this is hard. For both of us. But we need to get along for the sake of the baby."

My hand jerks as I'm undoing the tape thing on the side of the diaper, and the plastic shreds, so more crap spills out, on the couch, on me. "We do not need to get along for the sake of the baby. We are not married. He's, like, an amoeba." And he'll be gone as soon as I can possibly make that happen.

I drive her to Reynold's Garage, all but change the fan belt myself (yes, it's the fan belt). Guilty for comparing my son to a one-celled organism, and a major pussy, I agree to take Cal for another night. When I ditch her in town, it's like I'm scraping her off my shoe.

ALICE

The house is dead quiet when I come storming in, sandy, and suit still damp with seawater. I chuck my wet towel in the corner of the kitchen, like I'm one of my messier brothers. Then I kick one of the stools near the island, which crashes to the ground. My repaired ankle is already killing me from my assault on the car door while making my mature exit.

I'm glad Mom's not here.

I wish Mom were here.

Just Mom, alone. Nobody else she had to pay attention to.

My throat feels as though I've swallowed clamshells from the beach parking lot. My eyes are hot sand.

I pick up my cell to call her, and then drop it with a clatter on the counter. What would I say? *Guess what, we'll need to be picking up a Father's Day card for Tim Mason next year. In other news, I kissed him and I didn't want to stop and now I have to because, well, obviously. And also, great news! Grace Reed stopped paying Dad's bills, so there's that to celebrate too.* The thought brings a crush of guilt, heavy, like someone sitting on my chest, because my dad, my family, is screwed if I don't figure this out, and here I am thinking about *Tim Mason.*

I kick the stool again, harder, so it smashes into the trash can, which someone must have pulled out to empty and then forgot about. The can tips over, spilling orange rinds and a coffee can and some of Patsy's diapers out on the floor, which was already getting grimy.

I'll just let myself cry. Blast some music. Shower off. Shake it off.

He and that girl made a baby. Whatever.

That's his type?

God, I hate it when people even say there *are* types, like people come in flavors.

Was *that* why his parents kicked him out? He's been here for three weeks. That baby seems older than that. Was that why he got kicked out of prep school? Who *is* that girl? Is she going to move into my apartment with him? Sleep in his bed and eat Grape-Nuts with him and go to the beach and—

She's very pale. I bet she sunburns.

I am the worst person in the world.

I start to drag myself upstairs to my room, throw myself down on the bed, and cry myself to sleep. Trash the room. Something.

But I share my room with Andy, who, because she's now in high school, as of today, is already home. She's lying on her back on my bed (because hers is covered with clean laundry she hasn't taken the time to put away yet), painting her fingernails, periodically pausing to eat a Nilla Wafer from the jumbo box propped against my Tardis pillow.

When I come in the door, she jolts up guiltily. "I didn't get any crumbs on— What's wrong? Is it Dad? Mom? Oh, God, Alice, don't look like that." She's jumping up and putting her arms around me, getting pink nail polish in my hair as she brushes it back. "Oh honey," she says, in a quite good imitation of our mother.

"Everyone's fine," I choke out. Tears would be a relief at this point, my eyes sting so badly.

"But not you. You aren't fine," Andy says, pulling me over to my own bed and tapping the comforter (also getting nail polish on that, but what the hell at this point). "Talk to me. Alice, please."

"And what, you'll braid my hair and do *my* nails?"

She blinks for a moment. I'm Tin Alice once again. My little sister with her open heart and her open arms.

"If you want," she says after a minute. "I was thinking of just listening."

I swallow, can barely swallow. "It's . . ."

I can't. I can't get the words out, because then . . . then they'll be true. That he's a dad, and that I'm a mess. That he lied to me. With what he did, if not actually what he said, since I didn't happen to ask him if, by any chance, he'd recently fathered any children.

I was thinking . . . for just a moment, I was thinking we could—nothing serious—but we could—

Well, no we can't.

"It's a guy," my sister says. "Brad? No, it would never be Brad."

"Why not?" I ask immediately. It would be a natural assumption. I just broke up with Brad. Andy was a wreck for a month after Kyle Comstock broke up with her, the faithless twit.

"Flip?" she guesses again. "I liked Flip. He took me wakeboarding."

"That was two years ago. Not Flip. Why wouldn't it be Brad?"

"Brad couldn't get to you. Not the real you. He didn't have the—"

"Balls?"

"Gag." Andy makes a face. "No. The . . . I don't know, the strength or whatever . . . the depth. You didn't *need* Brad."

I'm brushing at my eyes, even though they're dry as driftwood. "What I don't need is *this*."

"No. You don't," Andy says with absolute certainty. "To hell with this. Whatever this is. You're too great and tough to let anything or anyone get to you."

Yeah, except unpaid bills and Dad and school and redheaded ex-junkie alcoholics with infants and my entire life.

Don't panic. Don't go there. I take a minute, focus on drawing a slow, invisible circle on my thigh. Chase away all that. Andy would freak out.

"I'm not all that tough, Andy," I say on a slow exhalation. "Just so you know. I mean, don't do that to yourself. Think I'm the tough one so you have to be the not-tough one. It's just—I just—"

"Alice, c'mon. You can have a bad day. Without it being your period or you being a ballbuster—see, I said it—or a wimp or calling yourself names. Although, if it would help, we can call this guy names. I know a lot. Dip-twit. Tool. Douchemonkey. Eejit. Wenis. Sludgeball. Asskite. Showerfunk. Dirtbag. Ratfink. And those are just the nice ones. I've been collecting them."

She's still got her skinny arms around me, and my head is tipped against her shoulder. She smells like vanilla and nail polish remover and my gardenia perfume.

I'm laughing a little, and she does too, bumping her shoulder against mine. "Tim taught me most of them. Along with how to knee a guy in the crotch. He taught me lots more, but they might shock you."

"Not much can at this point," I say sadly. But that's not true. I am shocked. Well down the road beyond that, even—all the way to flabbergasted. Floored. But why? Isn't this the kind of thing everyone would expect to happen? The Boy Most Likely To strikes again?

Oh, Tim.

Just as expected, right, Alice? I wanted to be better than that.

I flop down on the bed, fold my arms, rest my head in them.

"Tim also taught me to hit someone in the nose, upward, with the heel of your hand"—Andy pulls on a lock of my hair, raising my face so she can demonstrate—"to break it."

"You're going to pull this move on some poor fourteen-year-old idiot?"

"Only if absolutely necessary. He gave me a whole lecture about that. Not to bust it out on some poor sucker who was just trying to cop a—anyway. He was awesome. Like a brother."

"You've already got more than your share of those, Ands."

"Joel and Jase would want to go beat the guy up *for* me. They're not going to teach me swears or kickass moves. I'd love to have Tim as a brother."

"I wouldn't," I say, which comes out a little louder than I'd like.

"You probably don't know him as well as I do," Andy points out. "Speaking of shock, would it shock you if I told you I needed a ride to Megan's? Or that you're late to pick up Jase from practice? And I could use some money for Starbucks."

"No. That wouldn't shock me at all."

"Alice. We all love you. If this guy doesn't, he's a rhino-skinned, horse-faced baboon-butt."

"Tim again?"

"Duff and Harry," Andy says, smiling full-on, braces shining. "I have multiple sources."

TIM

Holy crap. Literally. On the short car ride back from the garage, despite the fact that you'd think there'd be nothing left in that tiny-ass body, Cal's managed to fill his diaper and the entire back of his shirt and part of his *hat*! How is this even possible?

I'm squatting in front of him as he stretches out on a blanket on the living room floor. I knew things were bad when I ejected him from the car seat, but . . . He looks back at me anxiously, little tears crystalized on his eyelashes.

"Don't worry. I'm on this. We'll handle it," I say in a manly, deeper-than-my-own-voice way, when in fact I'm not sure there are enough wipes to handle this. In all of Target. In all the Targets in all the world.

He keeps staring at my face. *So sorry, Dad. I seem to have lost control here.*

"No big deal, Cal. These things happen," I tell him, although I'm not sure they do. His hat?! Maybe my genes really did completely screw him over. All this can't have come from a body so small. There are only two thin wipes left. And no paper towels or anything like that.

The shower is the only answer. His clothes are already off, in a hellish pile on the floor that I'll have to deal with later, so I shuck my own off quickly, kicking my loafers across the room, and carry him into the shower stall. He goes rigid with shock at the blast of water.

Please don't scream again, Cal.

"'S fine. It's a shower. Us guys like 'em. Give it a chance."

He's clinging to my chest like a spider monkey. A messy redheaded spider monkey. I rub down his back under the water. His face crumples—yikes, the water *is* a little hot. I turn it down to nearly cold. Cal looks even more freaked out.

I scrub up and down his back with the soap again, then lift him up so we're face-to-face. "You're fine, Cal. It's all good," I say firmly. His round blue eyes stare into mine. He bobs his head forward, puts his mouth on my nose . . .

Begins to suck on it.

I can't help it, I start laughing. He keeps sucking away.

"You're not going to get what you need from my nose, kid," I tell him.

Probably not from the rest of me either. But here in the cold-as-hell shower, him slippery as a bar of Ivory soap, and both of us barely recovered from the diaper of doom, I'm happy. For the moment anyway, I can be what this baby needs.

Or at least my nose can.

Ten minutes later, I'm knocking on the Garretts' screen door with my big secret in one arm.

"MOMMMMMY. Tim's brought us a baby. Can we keep him?"

Mrs. Garrett's washing dishes at the sink. She turns around, looks at me, Cal, back at me. "Oh . . . wow."

"George, this is Cal." I bend down to George's level. "He's, uh, mine. So you can't keep him."

Neither can I.

"Geez," says George. "He's got a lot of fur."

I laugh. It's true. Even damp, Cal's fluff of red hair sticks up like a rooster comb.

Mrs. Garrett has come over, kneeling next to me. "Oh my," she says, even more softly.

I can't tell what she's thinking, so I say, "Oops. Sorry, Mrs. G. You did say I'd make a good dad. My timing got a little screwed up. Alice home?"

She stands. "She went to pick up Jase. I'm sure there's quite a story here, Tim. Why don't you let me hold your baby, get yourself something to eat, and tell me about it."

I run through the story between bites as I engage in a feeding frenzy of epic proportions. No old pizza here. I eat three turkey sandwiches, two containers of lemon Greek yogurt, a bag of pretzels, and guzzle practically a gallon of chocolate milk.

Explaining Hester's part in the whole thing? Awkward. Especially with George (and soon Harry and Patsy too) sitting right there, round-eyed.

"So . . . I went to this party, last winter; there was this girl—I didn't know her very well—and, um, she got an extra prize in her goody bag, but I didn't hear until a few days ago that this prize was, uh, handed out."

Mrs. Garrett nods in comprehension.

"That must have been some party." George sighs. "All I ever get to take home is a bunch of gum and Super Balls and squirt guns and stuff."

"Tim might have been happy with that, George," Mrs. Garrett says.

She cradles Cal expertly over the small bump of her own stomach and reaches out to ruffle my hair. "You know you could have come straight to us. This is a lot to handle on your own."

"He's pretty teeny," George says. "*I* could handle him. He could sleep in my bed. I bet *he* pees too. Then I'd for sure have a baby brother, in case the new baby is another dopey girl."

"Hon!" Patsy commands, and stretches her arms up to me, elbowing my knee insistently, making it known she's my *real* baby. And no dopey girl.

I pick her up, put my face in her hair and without warning my eyes sear like they've taken a hit of Tabasco. *Fuck, no*.

Mrs. Garrett sighs. "He's a lovely baby, which of course you know. Looks healthy too."

I nod without looking up.

"But your plate was already full. I'm sorry, Tim."

"'S okay," I say hastily, since sympathy is making it harder to ditch the dampness in my eyes. "I can handle full plates. Just power through 'em. You know that—I eat here all the time."

When I glance up, Mrs. Garrett looks unfooled by my bullshit.

"This girl," she asks carefully. "What's she like?"

"Is she hot?" asks Harry.

"Harry!"

"What?! Joel asks that all the time. So does Duff."

Mrs. Garrett rolls her eyes. "Duff too, now?" Joel has always been a walking hormone, but Duff's only eleven.

Patsy is stroking my arm lovingly, sighing "Hon" periodically.

"I don't even *know* what she's like. She's very, uh, clean. Got straight A's in the classes we were in together. Always did the extra credit work too. She writes her baby-care notes in outline form."

"Doesn't *sound* hot," Harry mutters.

"Harry, be still. Eat something." Mrs. Garrett reaches into the fruit bowl, hands him an apple. "So . . . you'll be getting to know her at the same time you get to know your son."

"Yup. Like I say, my timing has always su—" I glance at George and Patsy. "Stunk."

Mrs. Garrett's eyes are sad, but her voice is brisk and practical. "I bet you need supplies—clothes and things. Joel's *Animal House* bachelor pad doesn't come equipped with baby gear. We have lots. Let's go look in the basement."

Downstairs, Mrs. Garrett is opening up big plastic bins marked BOY and GIRL and GEAR and making little stacks of stuff.

Because none of the kids have followed us down here, wanting to stay upstairs and make faces at Cal, I can say what I couldn't before.

"I don't need much. She gave me a ton of crap. It's all temporary anyway; Hester's plan is to get him adopted quickly." By this morning would have been perfect.

She pauses in the act of folding some fluffy blue blanket, face neutral, and then starts folding it again, without looking at me. "How do you feel about that?"

"I got nothin', Mrs. G." Then I flinch, remembering the last time I used that phrase.

She reaches out for a second and rubs my cheek with the back of her hand. Doesn't say a thing. Then she hands me a stack of blankets, little undershirts folded on top. One of the blankets has DUFFY sewn onto it in wobbly red yarn letters.

"Won't you need this shit yourself? Stuff, I mean."

"I'm not going to wash your mouth out with soap, Tim. I've heard the word. Used it, even. Recently. And, not for another six months or so. By that time your Cal will be bigger, or he'll be gone. Take it for now."

"But, the thing is, for now?" I add. "Don't know my ass from my elbow here." I explain about the in-the-hat thing. And the green thing.

She laughs. "Normal. As long as you have a handle on which is Cal's elbow, you'll be fine. None of us knows what to do, to start, Tim. You and the baby will figure it out together."

I trudge upstairs with a ton of things—including a baby gym, whatever the fuck that is (*Oh good, I've noticed that my abs lack definition, Dad*) and a windup stuffed bear that plays

"Twinkle, Twinkle Little Star," and a stack of what looks like fuzzy long underwear.

When I get to the top, there, standing in the kitchen, is Alice, still in her yellow bikini and cover-up, hair ruffled, face flushed, eyes boring into mine. With Jase and Sam right next to her. And my kid in her arms.

Shit? Meet Fan.

Chapter Twenty-five

ALICE

Tim peers at me around a huge pile of baby supplies, then drops it all at his feet, cocks his head at me, complete with smirk. "I see you've met Calvin. Guess the cat's out of the bag that I'm no virgin."

"Tim—" Samantha starts.

"What's a virgin?" Harry asks loudly.

"Something about a forest," George whisper-yells back.

"This"—I joggle the baby, and Mom, who's come up the stairs behind Tim, makes a concerned sound—"is no joke. This could only happen to you!"

"Technically," he drawls, sloping back against the wall, "it could happen to any guy with a working—"

"What the hell is wrong with you? You're seventeen years old!"

Tim pats the pocket of his shirt, looks down at his feet. "Eighteen in December. You're fuckin' nineteen, in case you've forgotten. Not nearly old enough to be my mom, babe, so you can ditch *that* line of bullshit right now. Besides, you didn't mind—"

The kitchen is dead quiet.

Jase was bending over to unlace his Converse, and his fingers go motionless.

Sam has her hand to her mouth.

Even the baby looks stunned.

Then Harry says cheerfully, "Tim swore. Twice. The bad ones."

Tim looks over at George, who's watching us with a scared expression, nearly in tears. Tim brushes his hand over his face, lets out a short, shaky laugh. "Uh. Sorry, guys."

I cradle the baby's head in my hand, look from him to Tim, back again. "Even though I saw . . . I knew . . . it had to be . . . Unbelievable."

"And yet true. Exactly why are you so ballistic? It doesn't eff up *your* life. You don't have to babysit. That one's on me, babe."

"How about you reserve the 'babe' for your actual *baby*? And, newsflash, it's not called babysitting when it's your own child."

Jase and Samantha are exchanging glances like crazy. Jase clears his throat. "Guys . . ."

"George, Harry," Mom cuts in, gathering up Patsy, who kicks her feet ferociously, twisting and reaching out for Tim. "Let's go get some of your stuffed animals to lend the baby. Something soft you don't play with anymore."

The boys trail toward the stairs. "He can't have Happy," George says belligerently.

"Who is that girl? Apparently *not* your dealer. That's one whopper of a secret you've been keeping for nine months. Not to mention—"

"I didn't know! I just found out, like, days ago. I didn't know," Tim repeats. "I don't even remember doing her. Like, total blank."

"Jesus," Jase mutters.

"Is that supposed to make it better? You ruined her life, but that's all good, *babe*, it was in a blackout? *That's* your get-out-of-jail-free card?" The baby starts to fuss and I rest him against my shoulder, rub his back, sway from side to side automatically. Baby on board, activate Garrett instincts.

"Let me have him," Samantha suggests, when the whimpering continues.

"Nah, he's probably hungry. Again," Tim mutters. "My job. Hand him over." He reaches for the baby, lifting him out of my arms, setting his palm against the soft folds at the back of the baby's neck. "I'll come back for that stuff later." He heads for the screen door, kicks it open with his bare foot, and lets it slam behind him.

Jase gives a long, low whistle under his breath.

Samantha bends to scoop up the clothes and blankets. "Wow," she says. "His parents must— I can't even imagine."

Yup. The Boy Most Likely To has really outdone himself this time. If the Masons kicked him out of the house for job stuff, what now? Get him deported?

"It is honestly like the guy makes a profession of messing up. As if he wakes up and the first thing he does, before he even showers—*if* he even showers—is write a punch list of all the many creative and moronic ways he can be more of a disaster."

I'm yanking open the screen door as I speak, and when Jase puts his hand on my shoulder, saying, "Al, this is not your fight," I just yank away.

"Let me talk to him," Samantha says, almost, but not quite, blocking my path. "He—"

"No way. You'll both be too nice."

• ○ • ○

"What now?" Tim says when I catch up to him at the threshold of the apartment, which he's pushing open with his elbow. "A little busy here, Alice. Hands full and all that."

"In." I shove the door open, set my hand on his back, and follow him. The room now has an open diaper bag, a bouncy seat, a few bottles soaking in the sink, and a Moses basket, in addition to the usual piles of dirty clothes and Grape-Nuts–encrusted bowls.

Tim looks back at me, straightening his spine like *hit me*. Waiting for it, like all the ugly things I want to say are already out there, hanging in the air like toxic smoke. I press my lips together as if that will keep the words sealed up.

He brushes past me, taking up more space than he needs to, cracks open a formula can, sloshes a bottle full to the top and puts it in the microwave, whistling under his breath. Cal's head bobs up and down over his shoulder, round blue eyes staring at me.

"How is it that all you do is screw up?"

He caps the bottle, shakes it, collapses back down on the couch, kicking his legs out onto the scarred coffee table, resting the baby's head on his thigh. "Sometimes I screw around. Clearly."

"Don't you dare do that." The baby sneezes and formula sprays. Tim cleans his little face with the bottom of his T-shirt. "Don't pull your *la-la-la, everything's funny if you look at it the right way* act."

"What else am I supposed to do?" he asks, suddenly heated.

"Gosh, I don't know, Tim. What's your plan?"

"I don't have a fucking plan, Alice. It's been less than a week."

"You're going to have to do better than that. I can't fix this for you."

"Sorry—did I forget when I even *asked* you to?"

I'm pacing. Cal sneezes again, this time gushing Tim's face.

"Could be—sounds like you have a talent for forgetting key moments in your—"

"What's with the sneezing?" he interrupts, wiping his face. "D'you think he's sick?"

"No, I think you have him too flat. You've got to prop up his head more."

Tim edges his knee up a little.

"Like this." I take his arm and move it so Cal's resting in the crook of his elbow. "And tilt the bottle like this or he gets too much air."

"You're good at this." His voice is resigned.

"I would be, wouldn't I?" I step back. The baby wriggles, and one hand smacks Tim in the eye. He raises his hand to cup it and Calvin—Calvin, right?—evidently thinks Tim is letting go of him, because he does that startle-reflex motion, neck stiffening, hands flying out to his sides, eyes wide and shocked.

"Let me have him," I say, practically dragging him out of Tim's arms.

His face has gone whiter. "What the hell was that? Why'd he do that? Was that, like, a fit or something? Did I hurt him?"

I'm pulling a blanket from the side of the couch, a red one with scary sock monkey heads all over it, turning it, folding the bottom, one arm down, fold, the other arm up, wrap around. Basic baby burrito. A life skill, by now.

"You wrap him like this," I say wearily. "Makes him feel safe. And, for God's sake, wash your hands."

I survey the apartment. "When was the last time you did laundry? I'll bring you over two baskets—one for him and one for you and—do you have a pad of paper? I'll make a list. You can probably get everything at Target, but—"

Tim's studying me. "I hate this," he says quietly.

"Too bad," I say shortly. "He's all yours. Congratulations."

He does look all Tim's. The red hair, the stormy eyes, bluer than Tim's, the long string-bean skinny body. I don't see much of that girl in him, but he's a baby, still a blank canvas. Besides, I barely looked at her.

"Not him," Tim says. "This. I don't want this."

"Sorry, stud. You don't wrap it before you tap it"—air quotes—"*this* is what you get."

He winces, opens his mouth as if to argue, then says quietly, "I don't need baby tips from you, Alice." He swallows and then looks at me squarely. "That's not what I want. With us."

"Us?" I say, and sigh. "There isn't an us. There's a you and a me."

"And baby makes three?" he suggests.

"You're hilarious. I'll take your laundry back for now and throw it in with ours, but I'll be damned if I'm folding it for you."

"Cut it out. I'm not one of your brothers. No way are you washing my boxers."

I continue as if he hadn't spoken. "Have you worked out a schedule with this—"

"Can you keep holding him for a sec? I gotta hit the head. Or puke. Something."

He unfolds himself from the couch, slowly, as if the movement hurts his stomach.

Calvin stares at me, his barely there reddish eyebrows pulling together, half worried, half cross. All Tim. I pull one minuscule hand out of the blanket, set my finger in his palm.

"Boy. The stork really dropped *you* off on the wrong doorstep," I tell him.

In six months, I'll have another sister. Or brother. Nine of us. Patsy's not even two. Where's the new baby even going to sleep? Patsy's still in Mom and Dad's room. Do Andy and I get him or her bunking with us, while Tim and Calvin occupy the apartment that was going to be my getaway?

Damn it.

"The last thing we need around here is another kid to worry about," I say out loud.

I don't notice that Tim has returned until I hear his quiet question. "Are you talking about Cal, or me?"

I hand over the baby.

"Figure it out. Babe."

Chapter Twenty-six

TIM

Can't face Jase, my best friend. Can't face Samantha, my oldest friend. Can't face me.

Tell Nan? My folks? Right.

Can barely look at Cal. Do all the tending-to-him stuff without meeting his eyes. It helps that he can't focus his.

Dom's out on his ten-day shtick with the fishing fleet, so I call Jake. He's at work, staying late at Hodges with the soccer team. First day of school. First day of practice. He lets me in the back door of the gym. A door I used to walk through all the time, two schools ago. Before I snuck a joint in the music closet, left in a panic, didn't notice the spark that had jumped from my sputtering lighter to the cheap-ass choir robe fabric—and nearly burned down Hodges, crenellated buttresses and all.

"Signed you in for backboard time," he says. "You can use my racquet."

He doesn't even wait for me to say anything, just takes the handle of the car seat out of my hands and winks at me. "I'll handle this guy. Go get your head on straight. Head to my office when you've blown off enough steam. I *know* you know the way there. Right near detention."

ALICE

Text from Brad: Ally-baby. Got carried away the other week. No hard feelings? Come for a run? I can at least train you. I will talk! LOL.

Attached is a shot of him doing burpees at CrossFit.

Dad has this saying: "Sometimes the best solution is no solution."

He means: Don't rush into decisions you're not ready to make.

Not: Decide not to decide.

I text back. Nice shirt.

My phone dings. It looks better on the floor. :)

Brad. No big surprises. No dark corners.

Another of Dad's sayings: Less drama, more dishes.

My fingers move before I think. Brad doesn't care if I think. *What* I think. Will you be too beat for the beach?

He answers with a picture of a Scottie begging.

I'm not some lapdog, like your Cro-Magnons.

My thumb freezes over the phone for only an instant. Then I send him a thumbs-up emoji.

When I reach Brad on the beach, his face breaks into a big smile, then he shuffles his feet in the sand. "I didn't think you'd really show. I was a moron the other day, right?"

"You were." I flop on my back, start stretching out my hamstring. Brad wraps his hand around my ankle, inclines in a little, lengthening the stretch.

"I thought," he starts, then shakes his head, "you were ditching me for some other guy. Like that bud of your brother's who's always around now. Jealous, y'know? But I thought about it, talked to the Wall-man. Realized that wasn't it. I mean, you barely have time for me. When would you be hanging with anyone else?"

It's a windy day, whitecaps curling on the water, distant buoys rocking wildly, rose hip bushes blowing in the dunes. The ocean is dark green gray. The sky dull. A puff of wind gusts sand into my face, into my mouth, and I cough.

Brad uncaps a bottle of orange-flavored Gatorade and hands it to me with the swift efficiency of a nurse passing a scalpel.

After a few deep swallows, I look him in the eye. "I meant it. We can't date anymore. We are not on a break, or whatever. We're done, that way."

"I heard you," he says, after a second. "But I think you'll change your mind."

"I won't."

"You're stubborn, Alice." He takes a swig of Gatorade. "But you're wrong here. I can wait until you figure it out."

"Look, I'm not going to lead you on—"

"We'll just see who's doing the leading. I'm gonna give you a head start on the run, 'kay?"

I squint at him, my jaw tight. "Don't baby me."

Babe. Baby.

I shake my head to let everything—boys and babies—blow out to sea in the cold, sandy wind.

"I don't need a head start." I skip the rest of the stretching, use pure annoyance to power my steps and am a good distance away before I realize he gave me a head start anyhow.

Because he thinks he knows what I need better than I do.

Chapter Twenty-seven

TIM

Knock. Knock. Knockknockknockknock.

Barely light out. Before I even open the door, I know it's Jase. Who else is up this early but enterprising teen dads like me and guys with a crazy-ass training schedule—and/or a paper route. When I whip open the door, he's resting his forearm against the jamb, rubbing his hip.

I'm holding a kid against my shoulder.

One of those moments that *has* to be a dream because this is *not* my life and I want a rewind and a refund. Then Cal squirms and Jase reaches out to steady him, hand on back, eyes meeting mine.

"Ride along?"

This is how he knows I'm probably awake. After his dad had the accident, when Samantha broke things off for a while, we got into a habit. Once or twice a week, he'd show up early outside my parents' house and I'd do the paper route thing with him. Toss the papers that were on my side. Half the time we didn't even talk. When we did, it was about George's fear of tsunamis, or the new shipment of paint at the hardware store, or how to get rid of athlete's foot.

He has the car seat out of my car, buckled into his in nothing flat. Pulls into Gas and Go and orders two large black coffees for me without having to ask what I want. Tosses me a sleeve of Drake's cakes and an apple.

"Mom worries you're not eating enough."

"Yeah, gotta keep my energy up now that I'm breastfeeding."

He grins, turning right out of the gas station. "Jesus, Tim. Were you planning on mentioning this any time before I—or the baby—went to college?"

We pull onto Caldicott Street and he inclines his head toward my window—my turn to throw. I wing the paper at the stoop and it skids and nearly falls off the side.

"I was working up to it. Not because I thought you'd ream me, just—" So tired of being the fuckup.

He's squinting, lining up the perfect shot out the other side, a much farther toss than mine. And yes, *smack*, centered on the mat.

"I could do that if you'd let me use a tennis racket, you know."

I hit against the backboard at Hodges last night until my arm ached so bad, the racquet was too heavy to lift. Trailed after Jake to a meeting, then went to his house and ate about ten bowls of pasta and meatballs while Jake and his partner traded Cal back and forth between them like the world's most coveted baseball card (a 1909 Honus Wagner, apparently—Jake is a baseball fanatic).

"No doubt." Jase pulls the car forward to the next house, which is one Samantha, Nan, and I used to call The White Witch's House when we were little because the whole front yard is cluttered with statues of lions and rearing horses and dudes on horseback and this fountain with a kid peeing water into it.

We're quiet for the next four houses. He pops some cinnamon gum. I pound the first cup of coffee in three scalding gulps, scarf one of the coffee cakes, fiddle with the radio, flipping channels until he reaches over and punches the off button. Our little ritual.

Jase doesn't have a lot of nervous habits. But now he's biting his lip, edging around in his seat like the peeling leather's stuffed with barbed wire and hot rocks.

"What's doing?" I ask, staring straight ahead.

"Wishing life were more like football." He tosses another paper.

"But then *I'd* suck at it even worse."

"Yeah, but . . . you know, the rules are defined." He lets out an unconvincing laugh. "Chaos, but controlled chaos. You have some discipline, you use your head, you put the team first—it works." He sighs. "Everything's such a mess since Dad got hurt."

I grope for something wise to say.

"Yeah, it blows."

Fail miserably.

"But," I add, "still seems like it's working. I mean—you're training, in the game, still showing up for stuff. The rest of the family—it's working. Right?"

Christ, now *I'm* asking *him* to tell *me* stuff is okay.

"Dad and Mom say just to keep doing what we're all doing. Every day I wake up and try to figure out what matters most." He's pushed the gas pedal a little too hard and we've gone past the right house. Jase reverses, moves back, and lobs the paper onto the stoop.

Another genius throw.

"Getting a scholarship? Samantha? The store? Grades? Trying to help keep things sane at home? What about next year—assuming I can go to college—are things gonna be on an even keel with my family by then? And if not, can I really just take off?"

"Have you talked to your dad about this?"

Jase hands me two copies of the paper and indicates the house nearest me. "They fight over the newspaper, the couple who lives there. Used to stand on the stoop and practically engage in hand-to-hand combat. Now I just give 'em an extra for free. Dad and Mom say to focus on school and ball. But the store is . . ."

Out it comes in a rush—Garrett's Hardware is circling the drain, fast. Bank loans coming due. Not enough income. Not enough to hire anyone to cover. Where Joel is. Mr. Garrett's medical crap. Jase's football stuff. Alice, what Alice plans to do.

I hold up a hand halfway through this last, halting part, which Jase doesn't even see, because he's pulled over, talking with his head tipped back against the seat, eyes shut, like saying this all is shitty-tasting medicine he has to force down his throat.

"I got this, Jase. I can cover the store. No problem. I mean—what the hell else do I have going on?"

He starts laughing. "Sure. Life's just one big party for you. Except for, oh, him." He points a thumb toward the backseat.

"Well, isn't there a 'take your kid to work' day? He's portable. Weighs less than your gym bag. Besides—it's only a few weeks with him. A month, maybe. Then he's history." As I say this, I hear this little snuffle from the back, Cal moving around, making himself known.

Jase studies me for a second. "A month, huh? Why wait that long? Doorsteps all over the place around here."

I laugh. "You'd have to do the toss—no way would I get the landing right."

Glance to the backseat myself. Kid's kicked that blanket off his feet. Doesn't like the covered-up thing. The socks will be next.

Jase ticks off the other things I'm supposed to be doing too, meetings, GED, and I shoot them down like we're playing that video game Andy and Duff are so crazy about, *Allied Aces* or whatever the hell it's called. "And you don't need to pay me. I've still got my allowance, and I've cut waaaaaay down on expenses, if you know what I mean."

Got my allowance through December, anyway. Well before the new year, Cal'll be gone and I can forget this whole chapter. Maybe Pop will be impressed with my initiative here anyway. Singlehandedly Saved Struggling Store—that's got to look better to him than Stayed Sober. Or Sired Son.

"What about the other night?" Jase asks, bending down to my feet, where another stack of papers is tied up, pulling a Swiss Army knife to cut the rope.

Yeah. That.

"I fucked up," I say. "But not all the way."

He presses his lips together, looks weirdly like Alice for a second, puts the car into gear, and rolls forward a few houses.

I try to read his profile, but get served a helping of Jase Blank Face, his bland, *I'm just a jock* look. He throws yet another newspaper, another flawless-without-even-trying toss and, hell knows why but there's that rage, white-bright as lightning.

I slouch down in my seat and mutter, "Hard to explain this crap to someone who never makes mistakes. The guy who fixes everything. *Text me if the plunger breaks.*"

Jase balls up one hand on the steering wheel, sets his jaw. Stares straight ahead for a second, and then finally starts in on me, his voice low and furious. "Stop it. I can't even talk to you when you pull *this* crap. It's like you climb into a time-out corner, with the *I'm some poor, misbegotten creature you can't possibly understand* garbage. You know me better than that. Like everything I touch turns to gold? Jesus, Tim, I wish."

My face heats. "I'm sorry, I—"

"Don't be sorry. Be—here. Instead of in some swamp in your head." He rubs a hand over his face. "You want mistakes? I got plenty." Turns to me, props his elbow next to the headrest. "Apparently I should have made a collage video of my game highlights and uploaded it to YouTube *months* ago, so coaches could review it for the scholarship thing. Didn't. No one told me to, and I was too dumb or preoccupied or whatever to think ahead and come up with it myself. I mean, all the colleges that might work for me aren't going to be sending scouts to Stony Bay, Connecticut. But I didn't plan ahead. Speaking of which, Sam and I nearly—um—" His face turns this deep, dull red color. "We were at the bonfire and—I didn't have—"

"Oh," I say. "Yikes, man."

"Sam's mom would love that, right? If I couldn't get to college and the baby in the car seat was mine next time? Just what she expects from me. To stupidly blow away my future and Samantha's too." His voice is bitter.

Exactly what she probably expects. He's one of "those Garretts" to Samantha's mom, like I'm "What now Tim" with my folks.

Silence while I try to figure out how to say I'm sorry in a way that actually means something and Jase rolls up about ten more newspapers, snapping rubber bands around them.

"I'm right, aren't I?" he says finally. "I mean, you know her better than I do, but—"

"You're right. It's prolly what she expects," I admit. "My advice: If you're going to mess up, score points for creativity. Do it in a way ol' Gracie would never imagine. Don't give her the satisfaction."

He grins, anger gone like it was never there. How does he *do* that?

"This *was* bad. I feel guilty, Sam feels guilty. It's been a lousy week. Plus her mom's doing something, putting pressure on her, and I don't know how or where or why. Every time I ask, she just changes the subject."

"I'm sure you have ways of getting her to talk," I say mildly.

Jase jiggles his leg, and then winces. "I haven't even told her what I've told you. She's got swim tryouts this week—"

"Garrett, the spare-the-girlfriend-spare-the-boyfriend junk never works out for you two. Come on."

He passes me a paper and I toss it haphazardly, so it lands in a bush. I have to get out and retrieve it. The slamming car door wakes up Cal, who starts bawling.

Jase pulls over and I drag the kid out and do the patting-the-back thing. He'd better not be hungry, because I forgot to bring a bottle or the diaper bag or anything. I put my knuckle in his mouth and he sucks on it, loud slurpy sounds.

"All that with Dad was probably what was going on when Alice jumped all over you the other day," Jase says, slanting me a look. Cal's clenching and unclenching his fists in my shirt, and I concentrate on unbending his little fingers and freeing myself, heat rushing to my face so fast, my ears burn.

"Uh—what?" Alice wouldn't have said anything about the beach to Jase—would she?

Fuck, should *I*? But there's nothing to say. Me and Alice = nowhere now.

I get Cal buckled back in and slide into the passanger seat.

"Getting on your back about Cal." Jase shifts gears as we head onto Shore Road, looping around by the river. "It's not like her to play the blame game like that. Things are getting under her skin these days."

Not the moment to think about Alice's skin. Anything of hers.

He's focused hard on the road, even though it's pin-straight and we're clocking two miles an hour. He clears his throat. "Maybe not the best time to—uh—start something with Alice."

"What, you don't think my plan to sex it up with your sister, make another baby, and move us all into the garage apartment is flawless?"

"Dial down the default-dick mode, Mase. I know Al well enough to know no one gets close without permission. It's just— Forget it. I don't know why I brought it up."

"Hey, not a big deal. But Jase, Jesus, tell Samantha what's up.

Saying nothing about real shit—that's the Mason family way, which, trust me, is a one-way ticket through the Looking Glass to the land of up is down, wrong is right."

And like a show-and-tell of what I just said, I spot a figure standing on the sidewalk three houses away from us, windbreaker hood up, shoulders hunched against the river breeze, one hand twisting a lock of her hair, just a little lighter, but unmistakably similar to Cal's. Nano. Right in front of her, slouched casually against the bed of a beat-up old dune buggy, longish hair blowing back, good old Troy Rhodes.

I watch him tap her on the back with the hand nearer me, and I can't see—is he slipping something into her windbreaker pocket with the other hand? Fuckketty fuck fuck.

I duck down.

Jase looks at me quizzically. "You planning on lying on the floorboards and asking me to gun the car? What happened to getting things out in the open?"

"Do as I say, not as I do. Now drive."

Chapter Twenty-eight

TIM

For the next week, I manage to avoid Alice, except in the most extreme, strangers-passing-in-the-night way, like when my car has hers blocked in, or I come out to help her unload groceries, which I do even though she tells me she can do it all herself. On one of my non-Cal days, I'm jogging on the beach, and there she is in the distance, cooling down. I play through this whole lame-ass movie in my head where she hurts herself and I have to carry her to her car and—there my imagination stalls out because the minute I make it to the Bug in my mind, I rewind and replay that day at the beach and think of all the things I might have done—or even said—if I'd known for sure that was my one shot.

ALICE

For the next week, I almost never bump into Tim. Evasive maneuvers—my new favorite pastime. Forget schoolwork, and rotation at the hospital, the forty-thousand pounds of paperwork that go with moving Dad to the rehab, the unpaid hospital bills piling up. There's running as though I'm being chased by cheetahs, going to the batting cage with the baffled Brad as though I'm training for the majors, and taking care of my brothers and sisters like Mary

Poppins on amphetamines. I keep waiting for Tim to show up with Cal and ask for help, but he doesn't. I keep waiting to get used to seeing him climbing the steps of the garage apartment with the car seat, but I don't. When I look out the kitchen window while I'm doing dishes, I think I see him on the steps, but he never snaps the outdoor light on, and without the glow of a cigarette to place him in space, he could be only a shadow. It's a rainy, cloudy September too, cool for Connecticut, and there are times when I think the last time the sun shone was with him on McNair Beach.

"Al," Andy says, her voice drifting through the dark in our bedroom, scantily lit by the blue lava lamp night-light, one of the few things we agreed on when we redid the room two years ago.

"Mmm."

"When I see Kyle in the hallway—"

"Ugh, Ands, not Kyle again."

"When I see Kyle in the hallway," she perseveres, "should I ignore him? Like, obviously? Look away or make a face or glare at him?"

I honestly can't remember where the Kyle saga left off—just that he's either playing games or is oblivious. Either way, he's no good for Andy.

"Just live your life. Don't glare, because then he'll think it matters too much to you."

Sigh from my sister. "It kind of does matter."

"Don't give him that power. Really. It won't be worth it."

And what, exactly, am I doing with Tim, while handing out this sage advice to my sister?

It kind of does matter.

"Honey, I'm home."

I've wanted it, dreaded it, known it can't be avoided, and here it is: Tim and me, working together at Garrett's Hardware.

Here *he* is, striding into the back office, carrying a large cup of coffee with a blueberry muffin balanced precariously on top, assorted baby paraphernalia, including Cal in his car seat, and a greasy-looking brown paper bag. He hands me the last, drops everything else down on the counter. (Except Cal.)

And I make no sense because the moment I see him, a wave of sheer happiness rolls in, swamps me completely. His hair's shorter, freshly trimmed. He's wearing an olive-green T-shirt that brings out the fire in his hair, and worn-in jeans. Somehow, he looks less lost; there's something competent and confident in the way he sets Cal in the car seat down.

I fumble for Dad's reading glasses, which I've been using as I sit at his desk, crunching numbers, making lists. When I shove them onto my nose, Tim goes blurry, except for his wicked smile.

"Hullo, Alice."

The wave rolls on, snatching my breath too, because I don't, can't, say anything. I look down. Scribble *Make appt. at eye doctor* on the to-do list unfurling in front of me.

"Vegan breakfast burrito from Doane's. I had no idea they made those. They acted kinda surprised too."

I write the date at the top of the list. Don't look up because I'm just so busy.

"Here I am to save the day. You're free to go." He studies me, head tilted, grin broadening as he takes in the glasses. "Ah, the librarian look. A classic for a reason."

Now the wave sucks right back out, leaves behind a jumble of anger and sadness—because once again, one small turn of events—a car crash, a baby—and the whole landscape has changed. I keep tripping over things that just aren't where I expect them to be.

I look at him over the glasses. "We're playing it this way, are we?"

He passes me the coffee, which turns out to be an extra-large cinnamon mocha cappuccino, my favorite. "The Doane's barista guy knew this about you, for some reason. I assumed you'd want the biggest size."

"Don't pull the evasive maneuver. I'm immune." Hypocritical to the max. But I can't seem to stop it. I ball my hands into fists under the desk.

Tim sighs, wedges his hip against the edge of the desk, then says in an overly patient voice, "Playing it what way, Alice?"

"Like everything's carrying on the way it was before. Like—Calvin—didn't exist."

"That would be hard, even with my well-honed denial skills, since Cal is right here in front of us. Got a better plan? Hit me."

The truth comes crashing out. "I'd love to."

"Yeah, got that down last time we actually spoke. I'm sure you would. Get in fucking line." Still the relaxed lean against the desk, but his voice has roughened.

I take off the glasses, rub my eyes, stare down at the list in front of me like that's the only thing that matters in my world.

"I'm not disappearing in a puff of smoke if you shut your eyes, Alice, if that's what you're hoping. I'm here. He's here. But you don't need to be here. Go—study. Administer CPR. Stick pins in a voodoo doll of me. Whatever you need to do. You're free. I'm on for today."

"So am I."

"Alice," he says. "It doesn't have to be both of us."

"But here we are. So let's just keep this civilized, shall we?" I thrust the glasses onto my nose again, tilt my chin up so they don't slide right off.

He bursts out laughing. Then salutes me. "Whatever you say, Professor."

I ignore that, even though my cheeks heat, even though my hand is suddenly tingling with the urge to slap him. Something I've never done to anyone. Not even Joel.

"You're right, though," I manage. "At this point, the store really doesn't need two people manning it. So from here on we should come up with a schedule, some rules."

"Again with the rules. You're so rule-based. Is that a nurse thing or an oldest-daughter thing?"

"It's a practical thing," I say. "I'm assuming you've worked out some kind of a schedule with Hester?"

"Does 'you get the baby when I'm about to lose my mind' count as a schedule?"

"If that's all you've got."

He spreads his hands.

I outline a plan, working around classes and clinicals—maybe I can have someone take notes for me—I can keep it all going if I do that. Then we sketch out his work days. "So basically, four days a week, alternating mornings and afternoons," I finish. "Stock delivery is Monday and Friday, so if you can manage not to have Cal with you then—"

"No overlap with me and you, Alice?"

"Not much need for it, is there?"

"That would depend on what need we're talking about." He does that stupid smirk thing.

"Professional. You asshole."

"Alice said a bad word." Singsong.

I drop my pen, bend forward, planting my hands flat on the desk—the better not to slap him. "Tell me something, Boy Most Likely To. Why is it you are the biggest sarcastic idiot when you are entirely and deeply in the wrong?"

The second the words are out, I know I've gone too far.

Tim opens his mouth, shuts it, looks up at the ceiling, turns to go. Stops, comes back, bends over the desk, landing hard on his elbows. "I did something I'm not proud of. Yep. But you are not my judge or my sponsor or my pop. You want to keep things professional? Fine. I'm not even sure what that means in your dictionary, but in mine, it doesn't mean making judgey personal jabs. I did not do this to you. I did not even do it to me. I did it to Hester and this kid. Especially to him. So my penance, or punishment—if that's what you're looking for—is to take care of him. Which I am now going to do. Out front. Where you will find me if you want to continue our *professional* discussion about when stock deliveries are. Which I already know, because I've been working here all summer long—and I only black things out when I'm wasted. Which I do not happen to be at the moment. Although, if you'd like to take my car keys, be my guest."

He scoops up the car seat and stalks to the door.

"You *gave* me your car keys!" I call after him.

• ○ • ○

Three hours later, the store's still dead. As is the air between us. You wouldn't think you could completely avoid each other in an eight-hundred-square-foot space, but we succeed. I rip open the boxes full of new deliveries out back, wielding the box cutter, waving Tim off.

He backs away, stone-faced.

As I restock, he sits behind the counter, studying trigonometry, feeding Cal, drumming the callused fingers of one hand on his thigh, changing Cal's diaper, biting his thumbnail, rocking the car seat with one foot—in the shoes I gave him—while frowning over a textbook, jumping up every once in a while to refill his coffee cup.

I arrange and rearrange a short and simple string of words in my head, but they never make it all the way to my lips. Five words. "I was wrong. I'm sorry." Every time I head toward Tim, he busies himself with something else. There's just not that much to do around here, trust me.

Coming back from a totally unnecessary mail run, I find him trying to wedge open the bottom of our broken cash register with a screwdriver—pointless. "Don't bother with that."

He mutters under his breath, "At least I can fix this."

In goes the screwdriver once again. He's trying. Cal squawks a little and Tim again rocks the seat distractedly, still wrestling with the cash register.

He's trying.

"Look," I start. "I was—"

He looks up at me, then away, doing the whole muscle-twitching-in-jaw thing so beloved of angry boys. Then turns his back—actually physically turns his back—on me and keeps on jamming the screwdriver into the bottom of the register. At least it's not into my head.

"Tim," I start again.

More screwdriver action. Back turned.

"Never mind."

Brad stops in for last-minute tips on his way to an interview for a part-time training job at the gym. Tim scowls at him over the top of his civics textbook, highlighting away in multiple colors, while I hand Brad a comb, get a stain off his sleeve, etc. Tim's hunched so far down in the seat, feet kicked up on the counter, that Brad doesn't even notice him. "Kiss for luck, Liss?" he says, popping the collar of his shirt.

I fold it back down. "Remember to call your boss by his name, not 'Big Mac' during the interview."

"You forgot to put a note with a smiley face in his lunch box," Tim says without looking up from his civics book as the door closes behind Brad.

TIM

"Nans, I need you," I mutter into my cell, on break out behind Garrett's, slouching on the back stoop.

My twin's voice goes instantly high-pitched. "Why? Do you need bail money?"

"Jesus Christ, Nan. When have I ever needed *bail* money?"

"Well, I don't know. You've been gone for weeks and I've hardly heard anything from you. I just thought . . . I don't know." She sighs.

"Well, I've missed you too. Jesus. Can I see you—" Uh,

where? *Not* ready to spring *Mason Family: A New Generation* on the parents. So I say, "What are Ma and Pop up to these days?"

"Who knows? She's doing all that Garden Club fall planting stuff. He's . . . just busy all the time. Till six when he heads for the 'home office,' then goes comatose in his recliner. So it's safe to come here, unless you want to meet in an underground garage or something."

I laugh. "Not only do I not need bail money, kid, but I haven't become a government mole. Can I come over in a little while, during lunch?"

"Why? I've got Key Club this afternoon, and I was going to go to the library and—" The twin-psychic-connection thing is bullshit, but her voice is high-pitched again, nervous. Guilty conscience much?

"Blow off Key Club. This is important."

"I'm home," she says simply after this pause where I can hear her breathing a little fast. "Come anytime."

ALICE

I don't even hear the bell ring when Tim's Hester comes in, as though she materialized in the room, hovering near the garden tools.

When I do look up and see her, she's watching me, her dark eyebrows drawn together.

"Oh. It's you. I didn't recognize you without your bikini."

We're studying each other like there's going to be a midterm. She's tall with longish, straight brown hair, wearing sort of plain, old-fashioned clothes, blue skirt, white long-sleeved T-shirt, pale blue sweater. Almost like a uniform. She has one of those old-fashioned faces, too, heart-shaped, sweet, like something you'd see inside a locket. I try to picture her with Tim and I can't bring that into focus at all and *why* am I even doing that.

Stranger still is that she's chewing her lip and looking me up and down and maybe sort of doing the same thing.

Pause.

"Where's Tim? Where's the baby?" She looks around a little wildly, like I've maybe done away with both of them.

"Cal's right here."

"It's Calvin," she corrects. "That's the name I gave him. After Calvin O'Keefe."

"*A Wrinkle in Time*," I say. "My first book boyfriend."

"I loved him too," Hester says. "Obviously. He was so smart. And he liked the awkward girl. And—"

"He had red hair," I finish.

Oh God. Is she in love with Tim?

Her hand moves to her neckline, and she pulls on her necklace, a plain gold chain with a single pearl. "Are you—you and Tim—"

"I'm a friend of his." Not sure if that's strictly true at the moment. "That's all."

"I'm—" She falters. Understandably. "Calvin's mother. Obviously. I mean, of course you know that. I thought Tim was expecting me. I'm only half an hour late."

We both check the clock, which at least breaks up our staring contest.

"He's late himself, actually." A lash of worry whips up my spine. It doesn't seem like Tim, who is apparently making a mission out of not asking for baby help, to abandon Cal for long.

Or at all. I had to kind of insist on him leaving the sleeping Cal behind when he went to get lunch.

Even then, he started to tell me what to do if he wakes up, more talkative than he'd been all day. "Look, I'll be fast with the pickup. I've got an errand to run afterward, but it won't take me long. And Hester should be here any minute. He always gets a little freaked out when he first opens his eyes, if he doesn't see anyone there, you have to pick him up right away, or he gets cranking and—" He stopped himself. "I'm sure you've got this."

Do I tell Hester to wake Cal up and get going? Pour her a cup of coffee and talk books with her?

"So—have you known Tim a long time?" She's toying with her necklace again.

Now, as Hester pauses mid-sentence, there's a gasping, indrawn breath from behind the counter, then a piercing scream. She practically rockets to the ceiling and back.

I hurry to scoop up Cal, already blotchy, teary, legs rigid. "*Shh. Shh.* Got you," I whisper into his ear. He snuffles, bumping his head into my cheek for a second, then resting against it, fisting a hand in my hair. I'm holding him, swaying back and forth, and he's giving those shivery little baby sobs. Hester stares at us for a moment. "It's so constant. He cries *all the time.*"

He seems pretty mellow to me, but I'm not with him 24/7.

She takes him, with a sigh, and is fumbling in the diaper bag one-handed when Tim returns, whistling, with a white cardboard box of takeout from Esquidero's, splotched with grease, the peppery-spice smell of their signature curly fries heavy in the air.

Hester hands me Cal.

I'm holding him reflexively, stunned, to tell the truth. She just passed him on over, like he was Hot Potato and her turn was up.

Now she's pouring out the words on Tim.

"Thank you so much for holding on to him for so long. You honestly saved my life. My sanity, anyway."

Tim nods, without saying anything, looks over at me, face unreadable.

"Have you ever had any STDs? I forgot to ask the other day," Hester continues.

My eyebrows hit my hairline. Tim, who has scarfed a french fry out of the bag, coughs.

"Um. No?" Then he clears his throat and repeats, not as a question this time, "No."

"Did you finish filling out the medical history? We need to get that in as soon as possible."

"E-mailed it to you last night. That's everything from me, so we should be able to really get a move on this, right?"

"Oh. Good. That's good. Yes."

They sound like polite strangers on an elevator. But here's Cal, with his Mason hair and his wide, innocent Hester eyes.

"Put him in the basket. Thanks, Alice," she says briskly. She has a raspy voice, almost as though she's been a pack-a-day smoker for a long time, which I somehow doubt is the case.

Then there's a weird pass-off thing, where Tim, with an exasperated glance from Hester to me, takes Cal out of my arms, hands him to Hester, and she puts him in the Moses basket, straightens up, looks back and forth between us, then focuses on Tim again.

"My grandfather really wants to meet you. Do you want to

come over for dinner—tomorrow night? Or the night after? Or do you . . . have plans with . . . someone?" Her voice goes higher on the last part, the words running together fast.

"I've got nothing going on. Nothing at all."

"That's good. My grandfather's a great cook. So . . ." She hesitates, as though she's waiting for Tim to fill in, make this any less awkward.

But he only adjusts the blanket around Cal, skims a tear away from the baby's cheek, nudges it with a knuckle, gives him a little smile.

Hester half waves to me, scoots toward the door, bending to pick up the car seat. Then she tries to open the door with her foot, with the basket in one hand and the seat in the other, bumps both against the wall. Cal lets out a thin wail that gets louder.

"Oh for Chrissake," Tim mutters, striding over to take the basket, open the door with his hip, and usher her out.

TIM

The outside of my parents' house is "cheery." Not a word I usually use, but there really is no other. Ma's got yellow flowers blooming along the walkway. There's this little statue of a girl in a polka-dotted dress bending over with a watering can, and then another kid, in overalls, flopped back against our lamppost, blowing a horn for some weird-ass reason. They've been there as long as I can remember, but their paint's still shiny. Does Ma repaint them? Freakin' depressing thought.

I push open the front door. "Kid?"

My sister bursts out of the living room.

Unlike the house, Nan is totally different from just a few

days ago. She never even wears makeup, and now she's got dark eyeliner, bloodred lipstick, a black T-shirt, and white jeans. Her hair is chopped short just below her chin.

"Nans. You look different."

"Different, like, better, right? As in incredibly chic and urbane and not like I'm from some dinky Connecticut town?"

"Right. Like that. You look . . ." Guilty, honestly. But it's Nan's curse that she constantly looks that way. The girl could tell the stone-cold truth and come off guilty as hell. The house smells the same, like musty stuff covered by Tropical Breeze Febreze. Same old Thomas Kinkade crap paintings lining the wall. She leads me into the living room, like I'm a guest.

Here it's all Tim and Nan Are Twins shots, each one worse than the last.

"Because that's the idea—New Nan, new leaf, moving on." She's chattering. Also plumping the pillows and straightening coasters and all busy-busy-busy.

I'm barely listening, because what I'm mostly thinking is that I'm a stranger in my own home. Like my life has already left all this behind, and it's some museum I'm visiting, trying not to disturb the velvet ropes, the Hummel stuff everywhere, the window seat with a tiny village on it and a mirror that's supposed to be a lake, and a bunch of houses with windows Ma plugs in so they light up at night. She puts cotton on the roofs in the winter to look like snow. Now there's some miniature pumpkins scattered around and a tiny bale or two of hay. It's possible that my ma, like me, like Nano, does not have enough to do with her hands.

"What's wrong?" Nan asks.

I collapse onto the couch, plop my feet on the coffee table, knocking to the ground a pile of books like *Chicken Soup for the Whatever* and *Who Moved My Cheese?*

"Well, yeah, here's the deal." As I give her the details, quick and dirty, she methodically chomps her fingernails down. When I wind up, Nan gusts a long, exhausted sigh, like she's been doing all the talking and is just. So. Tired.

"Say something. What? You'd rather you had to post bail than find out you're an aunt to a son of mine?"

She steeples her fingers, lowers her forehead onto them.

Shades of Pop.

When she finally says something, it's the last thing I expect.

"How are you sure he's yours?"

Chapter Twenty-nine

TIM

"Wha-at?"

"Tim," Nan says, all exasperated. "You can't possibly have been the only ginger guy at Ellery Prep. What about that Mike McClasky guy you roomed with fall semester? The one with the pierced eyebrow? Why not him? How do you know this Hester is telling the truth?"

"What . . . you think she's come up with some con because I'm, like, such a great candidate for fatherhood? Ha."

"Well, I don't know." Nan plunks down on the sofa and reaches for the cut glass bowl Ma always keeps full of gumdrops and Swedish fish and begins pulling out a school of the suckers, holding up one after another as she counts off. "You have no recall of the party. You only remember seeing her in classes. You didn't hear anything about this pregnancy, which had to have been major gossip."

"I was booted. How the hell would I hear?"

"You're not in touch with *anyone?* Not one single, solitary person passing on the latest Ellery drama?"

"Nah. The crowd I hung with? I barely remember them, and I'm sure likewise. It's not like we're all pals-y online."

Nan's troubled expression lasts only a second before it's traded for deep suspicion.

"I'm trying to protect you here, Tim. This girl . . . I don't know what she's up to, but it doesn't sound right to me."

She scarfs down a few fish, then offers me the candy bowl.

I shake my head, shuddering. Gummy crap—give me stale Peeps or Pixy Stix any day.

"How can you be sure?" she presses. "That this girl wasn't involved with some other guy who wouldn't take responsibility, and then decided to use you?"

"Because she's not that kind of girl? Because that's freakin' psychotic? Because I'm hardly known for taking responsibility?" I look around the room like one of the Hummel figurines has the key to convincing my surprisingly cynical sister that I'm Cal's dad. Even though by all rights I should be jumping at the idea that I might not be.

My eyes light on the bookshelf by the mantel where, sure enough, there's a baby picture of Nan and me—our first Christmas—propped against each other in a puffy pink armchair with a stuffed Rudolph at our feet. I'm dressed in a Santa suit, Nan as Mrs. Santa (nice, Ma—incestuous baby outfits). Of course, I've got the Santa hat on so no hair's visible, but still, there's that little chin cleft Dominic pointed out on Cal.

"He looks like me," I say finally.

I still don't have this "blood bond" thing with the kid, but after you've slept next to someone (me on the couch, Cal in the basket, my hand on his stomach half the night) and cleaned up after them and fed them and frickin' *worn* them, you're kinda tight with them.

"All babies pretty much look alike, Timmy."

All Patient Tone.

Patient gives me a rash. Subtext: *I know what's really going on here while you're wandering around in the dark.*

"Since when do you know shit about babies? *Babies pretty much look alike, Tim,*" I say, high and squeaky. "Right, Captain Infant Expert. The last time you were around one for any amount of time was *me.*"

I expect her to get pissed and yell back. I *want* her to get as angry as I am, chuck it right back in my face. Instead, she hooks an arm around my waist. The sharp point of her chin digs into my collarbone. Nan never eats enough. That *I'm too fat* crap girls do.

Or is it actually drugs now?

I sigh. Release my fingers from fists. "He's my kid. I mean . . . it's not like I want this. Since when did you get all cynical? That's supposed to be my deal, Nano."

"You were always faking that," Nan says.

"BullSHIT," I say on a startled laugh.

She picks up the Easter picture of us posed next to a chick the size of Godzilla in comparison. She's screaming in it; I look zoned out. Now Nan wrinkles her freckled nose as she traces a finger over our bunny-ear hats, first mine, then hers. "How old were we when Mommy stopped with the dress-ups?"

"Fifteen or so. Kid, you're not four. Lay off the 'Mommy' jazz. That's not going to play with the sophisticated set. Makes you sound ridiculous, trust me."

She starts to laugh, tightens her arm around my waist. "You have no idea how much of a difference it makes not having you home." She lifts her face and, hell, I should've guessed it from the sound of her voice. She's crying.

"Hey." I tap her back awkwardly, drumming my fingers. "I know I'm a ray of happy sunshine, but how different can it really be?"

"There's no one to make me laugh. No spare change to scrounge out of the swear box without you being a supplier. There's no one to rearrange the Hummels in compromising positions." She sniffs and wipes her face with a swat of her wrist.

"Well, I grant you that was an important service I provided."

She looks up at me, all gray eyes spilling over, cheeks wet, lower lip quivering. The Fix Me face. Doesn't work as well as it used to, not since Cal. Who has no one else to fix him and honestly can't do it himself.

"Speaking of services, wanna itemize the ones ol' Troy Rhodes is providing for you?"

Nan jerks away like I'm a downed wire.

"Who told you? Samantha?"

"Nooo. Why would she know? I was under the impression you two weren't speaking."

Nan grabs a handful of Swedish fish and shovels them into her mouth. "Then who?"

"I spied you with my own little eye. What gives, Nan?"

She's still chewing the fish, points to her mouth like "I can't talk."

Once she finishes, and swallows, she folds her arms and stares me down. "So, when do I get to meet Cal?"

"Don't pull this crap with me, Nan. You don't get to change the subject here."

That angry, hard voice? Dead ringer for Pop's.

"Why are we talking about me? You're the one with a *baby!*"

"What's going on in here?" asks an even voice from the door.

I don't have time to arrange my face, so Nan and I probably both look equally guilty as we turn to face Pop.

Hell, I forgot the time—nearly six. His tie's loosened, jacket still on. Thank God no scotch yet. But then, Ma isn't home to bring him the ice bucket. Don't think I've ever seen him get it himself.

"Hi, Daddy. Dad," Nan says, flicking me a glance.

"What's doin', Pop?"

He looks back and forth between us the way he did when we were little and up to no good.

"We haven't seen you lately, Tim. In some kind of trouble?"

"Nope, all good. Just, you know, don't live here anymore. Checking in with Nano."

"Asking her for money?"

"No, Dad," from Nan, just as I say, "Nah, Pop." Then add, "The drug-running gig is really working out for me. Add in the pimping and I'm golden."

"Is that a joke? Is he joking?" Pop addresses Nan, who's fidgeting and turning red at the drug reference. Then to me: "Not seeing the humor."

"Not all that funny," I say. "Look, I'd better beat it. I have a— thing." I jerk my chin at my sister. "We'll talk about this new little project of yours later. Count on it."

Nan starts twisting at a hunk of her hair. I notice that she's twirled one on the other side so much that she's got this Rasta thing going on. Not the best look with the new do. She doesn't answer.

Pop claps me on the back, gives me a very small shove in the direction of the door. I'm half expecting him to pick me up by the collar and toss me out on the lawn. Instead he says, "I'll walk you to your car."

"What, to make sure I really leave?"

He actually steers me down the driveway. It's half prison march and half one of those scenes in some old flick where the dad dispenses fatherly advice. But ten will get you twenty he's not slipping me some cash so I can take Mary Lou to the soda fountain for a milkshake.

We reach the Jetta. He stands there for a sec, his eyes darting around the street. I kinda expect cops to leap out of the Crosbys' bushes, clap cuffs on me, and shove me into the backseat of my own car.

Nothing but silence.

Pop, looking anywhere but at me.

Me, waiting for whatever he has to say.

We're not in his office, though, and I'm not under his roof. I prop my back against the car, cross my arms. If he can wait, I can wait.

And wait.

Pop edges his cell phone out of his pocket, glances at it, shoves it back in, more like a reflex than like he's actually checking. I scrape at a callus on my hand with a thumbnail. Some dry leaves blow across the street. The grass grows. Somewhere, a star is born.

Again with the cell phone check. How many important calls

can the manager of the Stony Bay Building and Loan get?

"Pop. I've gotta head back to work. I took an hour off to come see Nan. Time's up now. Are we done?"

His lips compress and he looks at me but doesn't say anything. Then, finally, "I've never understood you, Tim. Not one single day of your life."

What is there to say to that? *Ever try?*

"We're done," I say, and get into the driver's seat, shift into first, and pull away.

ALICE

"So—just friends," Andy says, leaning her elbows on the counter next to the scattered pieces of the cash register. "Does that mean *anything*? Or is it some kind of code? Does it ever mean what it says?"

"I need context," I say, looking up from reorganizing the paint chips.

"It's a kiss-off." Tim flips a page in his chem book, without looking up.

"Really? Like, not even a second-place-ribbon thing? An actual 'get lost'?" Andy sounds crushed. Tim looks up, checks her face, and says, "Wait. No. Not always. Uh—context is right. Need that. Could have it all wrong."

"Suppose there's this guy—" Andy says.

"Kyle. Ditch him," I interrupt.

"Whoever. That's not the point. When he's around his friends, he doesn't even talk to me. But whenever he sees me on my own, he's all nice and talky and jokey and says he wants to be friends."

"Loser. Ditch him," I repeat. "He's just hoping for benefits."

"We weren't doing that," Andy says. "We were nowhere near that. We were just barely beyond hanging out. Like at—hanging out with potential. And some kissing. With definite potential."

Tim's all about the cash register once again, trying to re-attach the type transfer wheel to the spindle, brow furrowed. He flashes me a quick look midway through Andy's explanation, then hunkers back down, wipes grease off on his jeans, refocuses on the scattered parts.

"If he acts differently in front of his friends, forget him. Hypo-crite *and* player. Ditch him."

"He's not mine to ditch," Andy says. "We aren't dating and we weren't even friends before we went out. Up till then, we'd said, maybe, three sentences to each other? Or, actually, he'd said them all to me, because I was always speechless. He has this really great smile—you just want to lick his cheek when he does it. And the first month of sailing camp three years ago, he said, 'Will you untie the jib sheet?' and then last year, he told me to haul down the clew lines while slacking away on the hal-yard and—"

"So, you weren't friends," I sum up. "Before the potential kicked in."

"Exactly. We were basically strangers. With magnetism. Or not. I mean, I thought there was. And obviously he did for at least a moment or two—because he asked me on a date. And, you know, kissed me? Some. But then that didn't work out. Although I thought it was working, but obviously I was wrong, which is why I doubt my own instincts now."

"Bottom line," I translate, "you didn't know each other."

"Yes. So there's no context . . . to translate him. Which is why

I need you guys. Together you've probably dated, like, fifty people, right?"

"I didn't date," Tim says flatly.

"Far fewer than fifty," I tell her.

Andy rolls her eyes. "You're missing the point. I need experienced perspective. Because I. Know. Nothing. Does he want us to be something we weren't before—like now that we aren't . . . possible . . . now that there's no potential, does he want to get to know me?"

"Probably not," I say.

Andy's lip quivers a little. "So it's all bullshit?"

"Not necessarily," Tim says.

"Oh come on. Give me a break, Tim."

"Give *someone* a break, Alice. Maybe he's genuinely sorry. Maybe he really thinks he blew it. Maybe he's one of those poor bastards who doesn't know what he has until it's gone. Maybe he sees what a great girl Andy is and wants to honestly, actually get to know her. Everyone who makes a mistake isn't doomed to be an asshole forever." He waves one hand for emphasis, and the counting arm, which he'd been trying to reattach, goes flying, tinkling on the tile floor and disappearing somewhere near a tub of asphalt sealant.

"This guy is," I say. "He's just playing games."

"So, basically, *let's be friends* is at best an insult and at worst completely meaningless," Andy says. "Great. That's wonderful. Thanks, you two have been a huge help. Self-esteem at an all-time high now."

"It isn't you," I say. "Some guy being a loser takes nothing away from you."

"It takes away potential," Andy says, raising her eyebrows, widening her eyes as if the answer's so completely obvious. "Which is another word for *hope*."

"Ands—" both Tim and I say at the same time, each of us starting forward. He reaches her first, circling around the counter, arm around her shoulders.

"Maybe we're wrong, maybe—"

Tim should be trying to fix the bell over the door because, again, it makes no sound as the door swings open, but Tim's dad's footsteps are loud enough to stop Tim mid-sentence.

"I'll cut to the chase," he says abruptly, his face thunderous. "Your sister spoke with me. We have a few things to talk about."

"We were just headed out back," I say, motioning urgently to Andy, who mouths *Why?* at me, then takes one look at Mr. Mason's face and follows me out.

TIM

Pop barely registers that two people have fled the room. His eyes are, for once, locked on mine, not on his desk or his phone.

"As I said, Nan and I talked. I've heard about your latest—"

Ah, Nano. Always so forthcoming with my sins.

"Escapade?"

Long sigh from Pop. "Issue. I know about this girl, and this child. I'm not happy, but that's beside the point."

So used to having my hands full of the kid. Pull on my ear, weave them through my hair, thrust 'em in my pockets. Look down the long back hall to the open office door. Alice has her legs propped up on Mr. Garrett's desk. Tour my gaze slowly from her crossed ankles to the fall of her skirt above her knees, the long line of her body, her face, with those crazy glasses on. With luck not overhearing any of this crap. The back door slammed a minute or two ago, so Andy's gone, at least.

"This is the last thing you should be tangled up in," Pop continues, pointing his cell at me like he can Tase me with it.

"Obviously too late for that, Pop."

"I'd appreciate it if you could try not to automatically make a smart-ass response so we can have a reasonable conversation."

"I'm not expecting you to fix this for me." Alice crosses and recrosses her ankles, fidgeting. Listening?

"I won't. But that's also beside the point." He drops the phone back into his pocket. "You have enough going on without this added complication."

"And yet it exists. Whoops."

"Goddamnit, Timothy." My head snaps up. Not a cusser, Pop. Not with me, anyway.

"What I'm saying is that this is not something you should waste time on."

"He's my son. What happened to manning up?"

Again with the cell phone. He should get a holster.

"You need to focus on getting yourself and your own life together. That's the bottom line. Unless your plan is to marry the girl, which—"

Jesus. He doesn't *want* me to do that, does he? Talk about the ultimate ultimatum.

"No. We're—he's going to be adopted as soon as Hester and I figure that out."

"That's the first smart plan you've had in years. The girl is on board?"

Hate that corporate-speak shit. "Yeah, the girl and I are looking at the big picture, thinking outside the box, we're going to do some team-building, deliverable by leveraging—" But he's talking over me.

". . . extricate yourself," he finishes, annoyed.

"It's all on me. My problem to solve. Understood. Anything else I need to know?"

My hands in my pockets, jingling my keys.

Pop digs in his jacket pocket, pulls out his wallet, where the bills are crisp and tidy, no doubt lined up correctly. He edges out a fifty. "Get out of this mess. Here."

"Thanks, but no thanks. Buy Ma a milkshake."

He studies me for a sec, then turns to go. Stops at the door. "Tim."

Christ. Enough already.

"This changes nothing about December."

ALICE

"Hey," I say quietly, coming up behind Tim.

He's pouring himself another cup of coffee, doesn't turn around. The only way I know he's heard me is the slight stiffening of his shoulders. He's looking down, and something about the back of his neck, slumped, a little defeated-looking, makes me almost reach out to hug him. But we're barely even on speaking terms. I wrap my arms tight around my own ribs instead.

His *father*. This is the man he grew up knowing best. At the bank, he came off sort of awkward and bureaucratic. But this?

"Tim."

"If you've come to point out that you were right about my chances of fixing the cash register—"

"'This changes nothing about December'? What the hell, Tim?"

"Yeah, I know." He finally turns around with a smile that doesn't reach his eyes. "I'm shocked too. I was *sure* this would totally wipe me off the naughty list."

"I'm sorry—"

"Don't," he cuts in. "I don't want—that. The pity thing. Which I—" He runs his hand through the hair at the nape of his neck. When he speaks again, it's in an embarrassed voice. "Which I've been known to go for, I think. I mean, I see how my sister kinda makes a play for it. Hester too. It's . . . I don't know. I just don't— want that. Okay? So if that's all you've got? Don't bother." He turns his back again, gathers up the guts of the cash register and dumps them into the trash can.

There is some perfect thing to say or do here, and I can't get a hold of it.

"Where's the extra garage apartment key again, Mom?" I ask, wiping my feet and pulling off my raincoat.

Mom, who's sitting at the kitchen table with Duff, Harry, and a large assortment of balls of various sizes, barely looks up. "Should be right on the hook."

"It's not there. Are there any others?"

"Duff, I don't think you can sew the fishing line on the foam. Andy tried that and it broke off really easily."

"God, Mom, not the solar system project again. Duffy, try

wrapping Saran Wrap around the ball. Then you can sew through that. Where could the key be? Do you think Jase has it?"

"Try Patsy's purse."

"The old crib is still in the basement, right?"

"Yes, over against the far wall. Duff, tie the fishing line to the hanger *after* you put the planet on it. Harry, you have three more spelling-word sentences to write. Then you can help make the rings for Saturn."

"I hate this stupid project," Duff says savagely. "Why can't *we* decide what we want to make a scale model of? Why does our project have to be just exactly like everyone else's in the class?"

"And the class the year before and the class the year before that, and on and on into the distant mists of history. We should have just saved Joel's," Mom says wearily.

The missing keys are indeed in Patsy's Elmo purse. Opening it is like cutting open the stomach of a great white shark, except instead of seal bones and partially digested life rafts, Patsy's purse has Matchbox cars, LEGOS, credit cards, spoons, crumbled graham crackers, etc.

Mom watches, bemused, as I clunk up from the basement with the various crib parts, the bag full of nuts and bolts, sheets under my arm.

"I'm assuming that's for Calvin. Tim going to help you put it together?"

"This one's on me," I grunt, moving one of the crib's unassembled sides out the door. Move them across to the garage apartment. Looking back through the screen, I can see Duff hold up the biggest planet. It all looks near normal, the typical chaos.

The little things that once were a big deal. For the first time in a while, we're maybe, finally, putting the shipwreck behind us.

Except that I'm totally ignoring a looming iceberg.

The bills.

It takes me forty-five minutes to put together the crib . . . a job that still defeats Dad, in spite of all his experience. After snapping the fitted bottom sheet into place, I go to the kitchen to wash my hands, passing the refrigerator. The list on the door—

The Boy Most Likely To . . . self-destruct in various ways.

I used that against him. Those very words. Tin Alice.

I pick up a pen. Stare at the paper. Not quite brave enough to cross it all out, I scrawl on the bottom:

. . . have more formula than food in his fridge

. . . keep trying to fix things

I chew my lip, then scribble the last.

. . . deserve a . . . My pen wavers. Second chance? As many chances as it takes? Different dad? Apology?

TIM

I let myself in just as the dark clouds overhead break and the rain comes sheeting down.

The garage apartment has a tin roof and the sound is pure music. Which I'm too wiped out to appreciate. I kick off my pants, toss 'em with my T-shirt to the side of the room.

In serious need of oblivion. Too beat to shower, my legs nearly boneless as I tug off my boxers and dive onto the bed.

Crash right into a warm, soft, very female form.

"What the hell?" she snaps, rocketing upright so fast and

hard that her forehead smacks into mine and I see flashes of light even in the darkness just as her knee comes in hard right where it counts.

Feel no pain.

No pain.

But I know this freaking pause and then . . .

"Ow." I hunch to my side on the end of the bed, eyes watering.

"What are you doing here?" Alice asks, bewildered but feisty-sounding.

"Nothing for a long, long time, that's for sure. Where's a pillow? Gimme a pillow."

"Oh. God. I'm sorry. Let me turn on the light." Alice is evidently swinging her arm at the bedside table, because I hear a pile of books cascade to the floor.

"No! Just get me a pillow. And an ice pack. And . . . last rites or something."

She shoves several pillows in my direction, then starts giggling.

"Yeah, yeah. Hilarious," I mutter, trying not to whimper. Or puke. "Maybe now you can take my appendix out with a fork or something."

"Ice pack?" she asks. "Does that actually help?"

I groan. "Let me die in peace. After you tell me what you were doing between my sheets. And maybe if you're wearing anything, 'cause that might give me something to live for."

She flips over on her stomach, I guess, because her face is suddenly right against mine. "Fully clothed. Sorry. I was just closing my eyes for a sec. I didn't mean to sleep."

I try to answer, but it's sort of a moan. The bed shakes with her suppressed laughter. I swat at her feebly, jam the pillow more firmly in front of me.

Ow.

"I'm truly, truly sorry," Alice says. "It was instinct. Well, that and self-defense classes."

"Can you get me a—" I'm buck-naked here, but I can't stand the thought of any cloth brushing over me. Not that I have a robe or anything. I shift the other pillow over my bare ass. Just that movement makes me grit my teeth.

"Be right back."

I hear the door outside open, the louder whoosh of rain and wind, and then it slams shut. Commando-crawl slowly up to the top of my bed, lie down on my stomach, swear. Try my back, which is no better. Roll over. Rest my weight on my knees and elbows, head on pillow. No improvement. Collapse. Pull up the sheets, which feel like roof tiles weighed down with lead. Everything is throbbing, honestly.

Since I'm alone, I can swear out loud, and I do, but then time passes and there's nothing but the sound of the wind and the too-quiet of the apartment.

Would she leave me like this?

Door slamming again. Alice, carrying the rain smell with her. "I have ice," she whispers. "And Motrin. Still alive? Can I turn on the light now?"

The dark, her figure-eight shadow against the dim light from the living room, the sense of Alice bringing all the out-side world, its damp-leaf smells and its whooshing-wind and river sounds, with her into this stuffy silent bedroom.

"No. Let's just . . . keep it like this."

The mattress dips as she settles down next to me. I suppress any sound of agony by grabbing the pillow and biting it.

"Here," she says, reaching out for my hand, flipping it palm up and dropping tablets into it, then placing a cool bottle of water next to me. I swallow and chug, let my head fall back again.

"Can I—" I bite down on my lip. The pain seems to be moving off. Sort of.

She leans closer. Nope, still hurts like a mother.

"Am I allowed to ask what you were doing in my apartment, much less my bed, Goldilocks?"

Silence. A sigh. Then:

"I was . . . wrong. You were right to call me on it, Tim. I don't—apologize often. Or well. So . . . So . . . I thought . . . deeds speak louder than words and all that." Hers are coming out in a rush and she's so close I can feel her breath on my cheek. "I put together a crib. For Cal. It took forever. You'd think I could do it in the dark with my eyes closed, but no. I had class tonight and—it was a long, emotional day at the store—and I thought I'd take a power nap."

"You definitely regained your power. No worries there."

"No, listen. Don't joke. Listen. Really. I'm sorry."

"You're forgiven. Don't do it again. Either thing."

"I promise," she says, her voice solemn and serious in the darkness, so near that if I turned, I'd be brushing right up against the length of her.

Except that rolling to my side might kill me.

"This is so not how I imagined getting you into my bed."

"So not how I imagined being in it."

"You've—" I start to sit up. *Ow.*

"Shh," Alice says, and lies down next to me, on her back, on top of the sheet I'm under. Wrapping her fingers around mine, she edges my hand over to the ice pack.

"Hush," she says again, but somehow it's not like she's calming down some fussy kid. It's more like the dark makes things clearer. Cleaner. Sharper. No blurry lines.

She turns her nose to my shoulder, breathes in. Her hair's wet. She shivers a little. The rain is pinging against the roof, and suddenly the wind gusts loud, spattering drops hard against the window, like someone throwing pebbles to get attention. I start to sidle my arm around Alice, but that simple movement jars me and aches like holy hell. So I don't move, Alice doesn't either, except to burrow closer, as her shivers die down.

Her fingers are still laced in mine, warm against the melting ice. The tension in my muscles—everywhere—is slowly easing too, undone by her small, solid weight against me.

"Tim?"

"Mmmm."

She props herself up on an elbow, barely visible except the glimmer of her wide eyes, the slight sheen of her hair in the distant light from the streetlamp.

"When I was twelve . . ." She stops.

"Go on," I whisper.

"I came back after the summer and I had"—she looks down at her chest, then sweeps her hands across—"this." She moves the hand that's holding mine, presses it against her chest, so her breast . . . God . . . fills my palm, no doubt freezing cold from the ice pack. My fingers tighten. Then I pull my hand away—sheer force of will.

"I was basically the first girl in my class with boobs. It was like—overnight—and suddenly all these people—these kids I'd known forever were calling me names. Some of these girls hated me—again, overnight. Guys were always asking stuff about whether I'd gotten implants, and whether Dad had to take a loan out to pay for them." She looks up at me again. "Joel had just moved on to high school, so he didn't know about the teasing. Jase was still in elementary. I didn't want to tell my parents, because Mom was pregnant with Harry, and Dad's dad was really sick. I have no idea why I'm telling you this," she says.

Alice's eyes meet mine, searching for something. Even in the dim light, she must find whatever it is, because she continues. "So I just decided to flip it. If people were going to take how I looked and figure out how I was, I was going to . . . I don't know . . . take charge of it. So I wore things that showed off my body, and I picked boys I was stronger than, and . . . that's the way I handled it."

I have to admit I've never thought of Alice as "managing her image," as the politicians would call it. I've always thought she knew she had a great body and felt fine about showing it off. I pull her even tighter against me, bury my lips near the pale gleam of the part in her hair. Her body goes rigid, then relaxes against me. She mutters something, too soft for me to hear.

"That's what you do. With your father. You flip it. Just sort of own whatever it is. Not just with him. You do it a lot. 'Everything's funny if you look at it the right way.'"

"Um." I squint against the prickle of dampness in my eyes. "Right? It is."

Her only answer is to press closer. "You can get under the covers, you know," I whisper.

"Better not." Her voice is low.

I smile. "You've never been safer with me than you are now."

Her quiet laugh shakes the bed, but not painfully anymore. Alice shifts, her wavy hair tickling my cheek. Warm skin, soap, damp hair that smells like rain and leaves.

The branch of the tree outside scratches against the window, moving with the wind. All the rain sheeting down . . . it's like we're in a cocoon, wrapped up, falling into sleep.

ALICE

"Mmmm," Tim murmurs, then yawns into the pillow, stretches his arms over his head, then yawns again.

"I've got to go. Will you be able to crash again?"

"Incredibly."

I tug the sheet and the blanket up to his neck. Pat him quickly on the back, bend to put my lips there, just where his hair curls down, before I even think, then pull back before I make contact.

"I'll lock the door."

I scribble one more note. *The Boy Most Likely To . . . need a little recovery time.* Call "Sweet dreams." But there's no answer.

He's already asleep.

I could have kissed him after all.

TIM

I'd have said there was no way in hell I could sleep with Alice sitting there beside me, one hand on my back and the other brushing my hair away from my forehead. But when I wake up, it's morning—the rain long gone and the sun slanting through the window, so I must have done just exactly that.

ALICE

It's only later, when I'm in the kitchen, slurping coffee, unknotting George's shoelaces, Krazy Gluing the broken nose pad back onto Duff's glasses, quizzing Harry on his spelling words, and I stand up to stretch, sore from Tim's hard mattress, that I know what happened here.

Lying next to him, breathing in the rhythm of his breaths. Watching dreams chase across his no-defenses face. Having him tuck me closer, head under his chin, anchored against his heart and heat . . .

Out the kitchen window, I watch Tim plunge down the garage steps, long legs, hands shoved in pockets. He hits the grass, headed for his car, washed clean and sparkling by last night's rain, windshield plastered with stuck-on leaves, then shields his eyes and looks toward our house. His face blazes, happiness purer and more unfiltered than I've ever seen from him.

Like the whole wide world is dazzling with potential.

Another word for *hope*.

Chapter Thirty

TIM

The guy who opens the door at Hester's three days later looks like a skinny Jerry Garcia. He wears a faded, tie-dyed T-shirt and baggy corduroy cargo pants. He's barefoot, balding, and bearded.

"You must be Tim," he says.

You can't *be Hester's grandfather,* I think. Lousy casting. They'd never even be in the same movie.

"Yep," I say. "That's me."

"Waldo Connolly. Come on in. Like Thai food?"

I haul in Cal and all his crap, looking around. *Not* what I expected for Hester's backdrop. Shitloads of big, bright abstract oil paintings, one glass wall that juts out back, turning into a greenhouse-type room, plants everywhere, big braided rugs, loads of furniture that looks like it's been carved out of trees, sometimes with the bark still on. A hobbit would be right at home.

I'm definitely not.

Waldo Connolly's just standing there, smiling at me, thumbs hooked into his belt loops. I finally remember that he asked me a question. "Oh, uh, yes, uh, sir. Thai food. Love it. Probably. I've never had it."

"Hester, he's here," he calls up the stairs.

I guess no court-martial.

I look around at the tables and bookcases. Lots of pictures of Hester with friends, Hester alone, Hester with Waldo, Hester with Waldo and some old lady—her grandmother, maybe. No pictures of the kid.

Speaking of, he's chomping on my finger ferociously with his gummy little mouth. I scrounge out his bottle.

"Come on into the kitchen. You can heat it up in there," Waldo says, walking through a brick-lined archway into another room.

The kitchen too is decorated in early Middle Earth. Copper kettle, huge black iron stove, lots of woven rug things on the walls and glass witch's balls hanging in front of the windows, big puffy red armchair, big table that looks like it was hewn from a hundred-year-old redwood by John Henry or whatever.

"Microwave's right there." Waldo waves to a corner of the counter.

I'm actually surprised there's a microwave and not a huge iron kettle over the fireplace.

The air smells spicy and thick. Waldo picks up a gigantic machete-type knife and stands looking at me as Cal's bottle revolves. I resist the urge to protect my privates. But then Waldo pivots and starts whacking away at some big green vegetable-type thing on the counter.

"You like green papaya salad?" he calls over his shoulder.

"Love it." I push the nipple into Cal's mouth, and his head immediately lolls back against my forearm, eyelids half-lowered in ecstasy. This kid sure does love to drink. Can only hope he's equally stoked about the solid stuff.

"That's what we got going for dinner tonight. That and tom yum goong."

"Great." Whatever.

"Take a load off. Tell me about yourself." Waldo aims the machete toward the big red armchair.

"I'm Tim and I'm an alcoholic" would not be the appropriate response. *I'm a Sagittarius? I'm generally much more reliable with birth control than you might think? Not that I've had sex in a while. Like forever. Like since I had it with your granddaughter. Not that I remember that.*

"Hi Tim. Hi Grand." Hester bounces into the room at this point, wearing a surprisingly clingy blue dress—with cleave, even. Her hair's wet and not in a ponytail, just down. Lipstick, eye stuff, the works.

"You look good," I say, rising to my feet.

"Thanks. Um, thanks, Tim. Grand, did you give him a drink?"

I glance at Waldo, who's looking a hell of a lot less friendly than he was a second ago. Oh, right, dumbass. He'll think you just want in her pants again.

Screw being charming. I'm not good at that anyway when I'm not buzzed.

"Sir, I know what you must think of me . . . well, no, I don't really, but I want to apologize. The year must have sucked for you too. I mean, that is, it must not have been easy for you either. So—" I cross the kitchen and extend the hand that's not cradling Cal, which means I let go of his bottle. Cal lets out an angry squawk. I check on Hester, figuring she'll reach for him, but she doesn't.

Her fingers don't even twitch like she's restraining herself. Instead, she keeps her eyes steady on me.

"That's mature of you, Tim," Waldo says, pointedly not taking my hand. "I think Hester's the one who deserves the apology. All *I* had to do was watch her suffer."

Oh, just use the damn machete.

"He did. He did apologize to me, Grand. I told you that," she says quickly.

Cal wriggles around in my arm, trying to latch back onto the bottle.

Dad? Dad! Help me. It's right there. Dad!

I drop my hand and reposition the thing. At least I can make *him* happy.

"Would you like some nam dang-mu pan?" Waldo asks pleasantly, as though he hadn't just left me hanging and made me feel like shit. Which is, I know, appropriate under the circumstances.

Still.

"It's like a watermelon cooler," Hester translates for me. "You'll like it. Really delicious. Grand was a chaplain in Vietnam during the war, then he and Gran lived in Thailand for a few years after that."

A chaplain. Like a minister. That explains the lack of soldja vibe.

"I'll have that, then. Sir." I'm standing straight and stiff in front of him, practically saluting. Or genuflecting.

"Tim, relax!" Hester pulls this big rocking chair that's over in the corner of the room toward me, tips it so it rocks a little, pats the seat. Her grandfather gives her a sharp look over his granny glasses, then goes back to mashing something up in a big wooden bowl with this mallet-type thing.

Cal's nearly fast asleep, his lips still twitching.

Waldo plunks a large hand-blown glassful of orange-red liquid next to me. "Here's your drink."

"It's not alcoholic, is it?" I eye the glass, praying for a "no," because right now I'm not sure I wouldn't pound it even if it is.

"Just watermelon and ice. I know you're in the program now. I respect that."

Hester, who I didn't notice had left the room, returns with a picture. "That's my gran," she tells me, her raggedly trimmed index finger tapping the face of a gorgeous brunette laughing, her head thrown back. "There's Waldo. And here's my mom."

Ah. Hester's missing mother. I've wondered what her story was, how she died, all that. I squint at the photo. Uh, she looks quite a lot like Madonna in her *Like a Virgin* phase. Fake pearls, crazy hair, shiny bustier displaying a shit-ton of tit. This is Hester's mom?

"When did your mom, uh"—not *croak* . . .—"pass away?" I ask.

Hester and Waldo both laugh.

"She's alive and well," Hester assures me.

"Lives in Vegas. She can still kick it as a showgirl," Waldo says with a trace of pride. "Got her mother's legs and her sense of rhythm. Not a damn thing of mine, lucky girl."

Not the background I would have pictured, if I even imagined one for Hester. More like the double strand of pearls and the blue blazers. No showgirls. No Vegas. I glance at Hester for a sec. She's so orderly, controlled-looking. Well, no wonder, I guess. Her grandfather is the lead guitarist of the Grateful Dead, her mother, Madonna. How else could she rebel but to be Nancy Drew?

I sip the watermelon thing cautiously, trying not to jiggle Cal awake. "I should probably put him to bed."

"It's this way." Hester stands up and leads me upstairs . . . to her room.

Which kinda breaks my heart.

It's a kid's room, that's all I can say. Pink flowy curtains, flow-ered bedspread, concert stubs and movie stubs and those pics in vertical rows of four you get at booths in the mall—Hester and some girls—all shoved into the corners of a mirror. Worn, well-loved-looking teddy bear on the yellow pillow. Lots of chick-type books—*Jane Eyre* and *Twilight*—all that.

"Calvin's crib's in here."

Not in her room. *Through* her room in a hallway. Plus it's one of those port-a-crib type things, not like some ancestral cra-dle carved from ancient oak. Plain sheet, plain blue blanket, no stuffed animals—not even a sock monkey. I mean, it's not like Cal lives the life of luxury at the garage apartment. But, ya know, he's got his plastic keys, and this stuffed duck I found, and the weird blanket with bears Mrs. G. lent me that he likes best—he always sucks on a corner of it. This is like the baby equivalent of a Motel 6. It screams "just passing through." I ease Cal onto his back. He waves his arms, screws up his face like he's ready to blast us, but gives in to sleep faster than I could snap my fingers.

We tiptoe out, back through Hester's room. She's walking in front of me. I touch her on the shoulder.

"I know I apologized before. But I am sorry. I'm so fucking sorry I screwed up your life."

Hester drops down on her bed. "Tim." She blows out a long sigh. "I don't know how different forgiving you would be from now. I don't blame you for what happened. It was just as much my fault."

"I was the one who was plastered, Hes."

Her eyes fill with tears.

"Oh shit. Don't do that." I look wildly around the room for tissues or whatever. "Don't cry on me. Hes . . . stop it. Please stop it."

"It's just weird. That's what you called me that night. You kept calling me 'Hes.'" Her chin wobbles. "I liked it. Hester's so formal. It's odd to me that you don't remember anything else, but that nickname keeps slipping out. I keep thinking maybe you're lying and you do remember."

Not even a sliver of light in that blackout. Sometimes I get little flares of lost days or nights, but that one—tiki bar, her—

"There's nothing there," I say, as gently as possible.

She sniffs and wipes her eyes with the back of her hand briskly, then sniffs again. "Not one thing? Not even the color of my bra? You didn't have any trouble getting it off. Do you remember that at least?"

"Uh . . . pink?"

"It. Was. Navy blue." She pounds the heel of her hand against her forehead.

I rub my own through the hair at the back of my neck, look out the window at my car.

"I don't know why it matters to me. It's just . . . right before we, you know . . ."

There's a pause, and I feel like a bastard, and also totally pissed off. *You know?* Can't you even say *sex*, Hester? You have a baby. We all know how it got here.

"I kind of realized how drunk you were, and I said we shouldn't . . . because you wouldn't remember. And you said, you said"—she stops to grab a Kleenex by the side of the bed and blow her nose—" 'Of course I'll remember. Why wouldn't I? How couldn't I?' Like I was so special, I'd be unforgettable. And . . . I believed you. And . . . and . . . you just *didn't*."

Now she's sobbing away, and it's starting to get loud and either she'll wake up Cal, or Waldo will come charging up with his handy-dandy machete. No idea what else to do but sink down on the flowery bedspread next to her. Not too close.

"It had nothing to do with you, Hester. That's just . . . not the way it works. I'm an alcoholic and I was an active one then and I just blacked the fuck out because of how I am—was—not because of anything about you. You could have been . . . Marilyn Monroe . . . and it wouldn't have made one bit of difference."

Her sobs quiet down. She looks up at me through her damp lashes, and then lowers her eyes. Edges a little closer. Flips back the dark hair that's fallen over one side of her face.

Her eyes shift to my mouth.

I've kissed a ton of girls. They didn't matter to me. I didn't matter to them. *I* didn't even matter to me.

I know what Hester's going for here . . . some way to think of what happened with us as not just random. Believe there was actual feeling going on, not just biology. And Bacardi. But . . . I can't. I'm a dick, but not that much of a dick. Not anymore, anyway.

I jerk my hand away from her back, shove it through my hair, jolt to my feet. "Man, I'm starving. Is your grandfather as good a cook as it smells?"

Hester's head remains lowered, her hair parting to show the nape of her pale neck. I suddenly remember George Garrett telling me that showing your neck or your stomach were "the most vun-rable thing" animals could do, their softest, most easily destroyed parts exposed. I hate myself more than usual.

"Hester!" Waldo shouts up the stairs. "You two come on down. Dinner!"

"He's great. A great cook."

Waldo looks at us from under bristly brows as we enter the room. "Baby take a while settling down?"

"Not at all," Hester says, just as I say, "Uh, yeah. Sort of."

"Hmmph." He pulls this wooden tray over and starts whacking at the round pieces of bread on it. *Thwack.* "About Calvin." *Thwack.* "How much nuts-and-bolts talking have you two done?" He points the knife at me, then Hester.

"We've talked . . ." she says slowly.

"More about how he got here than what to do with him now that he is," I blurt. Waldo's face darkens. Hester turns red.

He ladles out a stew thing that includes shrimp with their tails still on, poking freakishly out of the broth, slides the wooden bowl toward me. "You two are on the threshold. This is the space between the questions. How are you going to walk through and come out enlightened?" He gives both me and Hester this hardcore stare, like he can pull the enlightenment out of us and slap it on the table next to the stew.

Uh . . . I dip a spoonful of steaming rice into the bowl and slurp it down, buying time. Hester sighs, shoulders slumping.

Minutes pass and we're all staring down at our plates. Waldo starts eating, and then looks up through that forest of eyebrows at each of us again. "Well?"

"I just want to get back on track," Hester says.

"I'm just hoping to come out of this sober," I add.

"On track. Sober." Waldo takes a mouthful of stew. "Those are destinations, for sure. But for now, there are doors known and unknown."

Hester drops her spoon with a clatter. "Grand. So help me God, if you quote Jim Morrison at me one more time—I don't want to hear it. He was as big a mess as Tim."

Her voice is low, shaking. Waldo's eyes widen for a second and he stops chewing.

"Bigger, even," I say. "I wouldn't be caught dead in leather pants."

Waldo chuckles. Hester picks up her soup spoon again.

"Sooo. Where are we with the adoption agency?" I ask.

She's right back to straight-A student, like her outburst never happened. "Obviously we're not going to have any trouble placing him. The adoptive parents have to prove themselves to us more than we ever do to them—home studies, health tests, all that. That's their job." She's scooping up broth with her bread. It's hot as hell. I took one sip, my eyes watered, and I pounded back my entire glass of watermelon stuff. She doesn't even blink. Waldo has actually picked up his bowl now and is drinking from it.

"So the question is the next step," Waldo says. "The way through the woods."

"We're taking our time," Hester assures him.

We are? There's a "we"? My temples are starting to pulse.

"I'm all for doing this fast, like right away," I say. "I mean, take the bull by the horns, bite the bullet."

I have never used either of those expressions in my life.

"This is why it's good that Tim's involved," Hester tells Waldo. "We're on the same page here, as a couple."

Waldo looks at me; back at her. "You're both very young for this, Hester. And you two are not exactly a couple." He smiles at me, but it's a little like baring his teeth.

"Exactly," I say. "We're not."

"You're his father," Hester says, looking down at her bowl like she's reading tea leaves. "I'm his mother."

"Yeah, but—"

"Our baby. Our decision. Do you understand, Grand?" Again, she's looking at him, not me. "It has to be between Tim and me."

He nods, weaves his fingers behind his neck, tilts it to one side, then the other, cracking it. "Which is why I thought you should bring him in in the first place."

"And here he is," Hester tells him.

Sometimes I really think I broke my brain, messing with it the way I did. I'm hearing what they're saying, but it's like I can't make sense of it. What *are* they saying? I may be here, but am I really? Because I *feel* like the sperm donor. Which, I guess, is pretty close to the truth.

"We'll figure it out. Together. Right, Tim?"

"Sure," I say, staring at the clock. There's a quiet wail getting louder and louder.

Thanks, Cal. I half rise from my chair. Hester heaves a heavy sigh. "No . . . I've got this. My turn, after all." She straightens her back like she's facing enemy gunfire and not a seven-week-old baby. Takes a slug of watermelon drink. Squares her shoulders.

For God's sake. "Lemme see what's going on," I say, moving in front of her toward the stairs. Not hard, since she's walking like her feet are encased in lead boots. "I'll take him again tonight," I tell her. "No big deal. What's another night?" *Of no sleep.* And probably no late-night visit from Alice. Man—my own place, no parents, no house-parents, no hall monitors, but now I have a baby monitor.

Cal's soggy and has leaked onto his long-underwear-type thing.

"I have a fresh sleeper he can wear," Hester says from behind me. I nearly jump out of my skin. She has this ultra-silent way of moving—like her feet make no impression on the ground. She'd be an awesome assassin.

"Thanks," I say, swabbing at him. I'm fumbling the diaper back on, clumsier than usual because Hester's watching, then he pees. In my eye.

Blech. He's my kid and by now I actually think he's, you know, semi-cute and all that, but he frickin' *peed* in my *eye.*

Hester starts laughing.

"Not funny," I snap, swabbing my face with a baby wipe. Which makes my eye sting and water. She's giggling more, laughing outright now, practically holding her stomach.

"Sorry. Sorry. I'll be serious." She makes an elaborate attempt to keep a straight face and hands me this fuzzy thing that looks like a pillowcase with arms.

"What's that?"

"It's a sleeper. You just zip him into it."

I zip up Cal, who has stopped bawling and is looking at me nervously. Then I put him against my shoulder and pick up the diaper bag. Just a few weeks ago, I never needed to carry anything, just shove my license and my ATM card in my back pocket. Now I'm a pack mule.

After a shit-ton of *that dinner was awesome* and *thank you so much*, I stick one hand out to Waldo, ready to say good-bye. He clasps it between both of his hairy hands and kind of wags our hands back and forth while staring me in the eye like he's reading my aura or seeing through to my soul or making sure my pupils aren't dilated.

My voice, which has been going on and on with the *this was great*'s, falters and grinds to a halt.

"You're connected to Calvin," he says, not like it's a question.

"Uh," I say. "Not really." Cal wriggles, and I boost him back up, hand on his butt. He smells like diaper rash cream and laundry detergent. "I don't know what that means," I add. "Sir."

"That's the question, isn't it?" Waldo says, lowering his chin and looking at me over his granny glasses, bushy gray brows drawn together. He finally gives me back my hand and says, "Anon, then, Timothy."

"Right on," I say, fisting and unfisting my hand. He'd held on to it kind of tight.

Right on? Jesus.

Just as I'm about to shift into drive, Hester taps on the window. When I open it, she rests her elbows on the sill. "Have you done that with anyone else?" she whispers.

"Uh, you mean sex?" *How bad* was *I?*

"No—the forgetting. All of it."

"What do you want me to say, Hester?"

Yep, you're the only one I totally forgot. Nope, you're one of many. The truth is the first, as far as I know. Then the thought sinks in. The gear knob slips through my fingers as I imagine a tangle of girls I've left behind in guest bedrooms, backseats, empty class-rooms, hair rumpled, shirts askew, faces accusing, all trooping my way with redheaded babies in their extended arms.

Takes me three more tries to get my shaky hands to shift from park.

"Never mind," she says.

Waldo's watching me, a thick-set statue in the doorframe, when I surge forward out of his driveway.

"See," I say, crashing on my back on the couch with Cal on my chest, "this is why you never hook up with some random person for some random reason at some random place. Sure, she could have an STD, she could get pregnant. No picnic. But really, you find yourself *in* the life of someone you don't know and don't get and they're in yours too and there's no fucking way out."

Cal bobs his head against my collarbone.

My phone vibrates with a text. Hester again. If she asks me what color the nail polish on her toes was, I am going to lose my mind.

Again, don't know how to thank you.

Thank me by getting the adoption ball rolling ASAP, I am dead serious, I text back, holding the phone up over Cal's back. Vaguely guilty typing this, with his fluffy hair brushing my chin. But he *has* to be a blip in the rearview mirror before Dad does my year-end performance review.

Sleep well, she responds.

Ironically, I have to assume.

A car wheels into the Garretts' driveway and, after a second, I peer out my window to see Sam and Jase standing by Jase's Mustang, which I know he's been giving her driving lessons in. He's got his hands in her hair and she has her arms around his waist, her head on his chest, and I just want that.

I'm like some weird voyeur, but . . . it's all quiet, peaceful. No big rush to make the moves, just easy, natural. As much of a creep as I am for watching, for not making any noise, not clearing my throat to let them know I'm there, I'm even worse for this, like, *wanting*. Like a vise grip on my shoulder, I feel it harder than any craving for booze or that kind of oblivion. It's something that actually . . . aches . . . instead of nagging like a mosquito I can't manage to swat. Jase says something, and Samantha laughs, buries her head against him, fits right into him even though she's almost as short as Alice and he's almost as tall as me.

I'm a douche wanting what my best friend has. He loves

her, she loves him . . . the rest can wait. There are no crazy complications, no classmate you can't imagine screwing, no baby you don't remember making.

I want the best for Jase—and Sam—who deserve all that. But at the same time, I wish my missteps could be canceled out by the times I did the right thing. Which I can probably count on one hand.

Finger?

Less than a week ago I had Alice here in my bed, and now I've got the baby from the pits of hell.

Blue eyes so red, he looks like he needs an exorcism, deep painful breaths, knees yanked hard up to his chest. It's bum-crack of morning, Cal's miserable, and I have no clue how to fix him. He wants nothing to do with my nose, but whenever I put him down to try to get a bottle or something, he screams even louder. My ears hurt so bad and I want so damn much to put him down and go into another room, shut the door. Go outside, onto the lawn, down the street, to the beach. I mean—no one's ever died from crying, right? Maybe he'll just wear himself out?

So. I don't leave. The least I can do. I just keep on holding him while he thrashes around like a hammerhead on a line.

And cries. Endless. And wicked loud.

"Cal. I don't know what the f— I don't get what you want. What you need. I wanna help you here, kid. Help me understand." He pauses for a second, like he's thinking my words over, then starts screeching yet again, desperate.

I'm asking for direction from someone who has had less time on the planet than I've had in recovery. Pick him up and put him on my stomach, hold tight to his tense, flailing body. He collapses, sweaty, all his damp red waves flopped down, instead of sticking straight up as usual. After a long while, as though it's taken time to collect his strength, he raises his big heavy head back up and looks me straight in the eyes.

Smiles.

This goofy, toothless smile, his head bobbling back and forth like it weighs extra to show emotion. It completely changes his whole face—from worried crinkle dude to jolly Buddha guy. *Hi, Cal. Hey, kid.* I grin back at him.

Dad. Hi, Dad.

That whatever, that blood bond, that "Luke, I am your father" thing . . . I don't know, but maybe I get it. A little.

Then, like his smile has taken all his energy, he slumps his head to the side, grabs a handful of my chest hair, snorts loudly, and tumbles off to sleep.

My left hand still covers his whole butt. The other hand is bigger than the side of Cal's head. I can hardly breathe, but I'm damn sure not gonna move and wake him up. So I just stay there, listening to his snuffly breaths, almost counting them, breathing in that same slow rhythm. He's partly me. Because of me. I did this.

For the first time, that idea doesn't make me sick, or guilty, or wrong. For the first time, I really know he's mine.

Chapter Thirty-one

TIM

"Mom always lets me sit in the front," Harry tells me, wedging his skinny, seven-year-old ass into that very seat as I sweat to install Cal's car seat in the middle of the Garretts' van. Cal's wiggling and trying to whack me with his stuffed duck. George is cracking up over it.

I smell Alice's salt-air scent before I see her standing next to me like a mirage. All the craziness around me and in me shuts down. Catch a whiff of peppermint—minty soap, or candy she's sucked on just now.

"Better?" she asks. "No permanent side effects?"

"Mom does not *ever* let you sit in front," Duff says from the way back. "That's bull, Harry."

"Tim, tell him he can't say that. It's bad," George says.

"Watch your mouth," I call over my shoulder. *Hypocrites are us.* I expect Duff to call me on this, but instead he just kicks his shoes against the back of George's seat.

"Completely recovered," I answer Alice. "All systems go." I concentrate on polishing off my water bottle. Alice doesn't need to know she was in the shower with me this morning.

But she flashes her killer grin and says nothing.

"Do you have class tonight?" I ask as Andy hurtles out of the house.

"Whew, thanks for waiting, Tim! Can you speed? I'm late for band and I swore to Alyssa I'd bring her Munchkins before the game—you don't mind stopping at Dunkin', do you? Do you have any cash? Is my hair a mess? Did I put on too much mascara?"

"You're fine," Alice says firmly. "Tim is not your ATM." She turns back to me. "No—I had night duty, but that's done for now. Come by after the game?"

I cough, nearly spitting out the water. "Um. Do we have a plan?" Why am I asking? Who cares?

She stretches. Air's crisp. Sun's out. She sweeps her hair off her neck. "We can improvise."

"Can we get going, plleeeease?" Andy groans from the front seat. Harry's now in back.

"Harry burped in my face on purpose!" Duff says. "That's rank."

"After the game? You'll be here? I'll . . . be here too."

Christ.

"Sounds good." Alice looks down, pushes her toe into the soft tar of the driveway.

"Tim! Come *on*! I know you two are all busy, but have some mercy here."

Check the rearview mirror of the van, because this thing is humongous.

Cal, who had zonked out, now pops his eyes open, so wide-awake in the back-facing mirror thing. He goggles at Alice, and then gives his biggest, goofiest smile.

"Wow," she says. "Look at that." She sets her finger in the corner of Cal's mouth. They look at each other for a second, as if they're adding each other up. Then his smile gets wider.

"Yeah, he just started doing it."

She bends closer, brushes his hair back. "There you go, Tim."

"Huh?"

"There's your missing dimple. Cal's got the other one." She touches her finger into the little crease on his cheek.

God, I hadn't noticed, but it's true.

Alice backs off, drags her heavy purse up her arm, and heads toward the house, giving me one quick grin over her shoulder.

"Fi-nal-ly," Andy says as I climb in.

"*Buuull*," Patsy yells now, experimentally. I shake my head at her. She leans back, looking like I've offended her deeply.

"Why don't guys ever put emojis in their texts? How are we supposed to have any idea how they're feeling!"

"Most of the time we have no clue ourselves, Andy," I mutter.

I love the Garrett kids, but my mind is definitely in another place now. Plus, they're all fighting like fisher cats the entire drive. By the time we get to the crowded SBH parking lot, vans and SUVs parked everywhere, I have a headache like a frickin' ice pick, sharp between my eyes.

HESTER—PLS. NEED YOU TO TAKE HIM TONIGHT. PICK HIM UP FROM SB HIGH. TEXT IF NEED DIRECTIONS.—YOUR SO-CALLED COPARENT.

The last was dick mode, I know, but c'mon. Alice aside, I could fall asleep right here. The twenty-four-ouncer with an espresso shot didn't make a dent.

"Whassup," asks a familiar voice as the little guys and I are wedging our asses into the second row of bleachers. "Long time no see, Tim Mason."

"What are you doing with my sister?" I ask immediately.

Troy cups a hand behind his ear, shrugging helplessly. Word is his hearing's shot on one side because his dad whaled on him a bit too hard a bit too often.

Then he moves in, arms outstretched, lurching in for an actual hug, not noticing that I have a person strapped to my chest. When he encounters the front pack and the feathery back of Cal's head, he edges back, then just readjusts his reach and loops his arms around my neck. "Missed you, man! What the hell? You're a manny now?"

"What? No," I say, before I realize that I sort of am.

"Hi!" George says cheerfully. "You're Tim's friend?" He sticks out a hand. "Name of George. That's me."

Troy fist-bumps George's outstretched palm, which is just messed up, then checks out Harry and Patsy, who are watching this exchange curiously. Cal's sucking his hand with these loud slurpy sounds.

"Don't talk to him. He's a stranger," Harry stage-whispers to George, suddenly Mr. Play By the Rules despite his totally illegit bid for the front seat.

"Naaah. Tim here, he and I go way back," Troy says easily, flipping his too-long hair out of his eyes. He looks, as always, like Hollywood's idea of a teenage drug dealer. I've never been able to figure out if this is irony on his part or pure stupidity. I'm thinking Door Number Two.

"Need anything to take the edge off, Mason? You look tense

as hell," Troy says. "No wonder, am I right? Hear you're home for the duration now."

"I'm fine," I snap. Troy backs up, palms extended.

"No big," he assures me. " 'S all cool. Priorities change and all that."

"This is Tim's baby," George tells him chattily. "Name of Cal. He got him at a party."

"Geez," Troy says profoundly, shifting his glance between Cal's head with its telltale red hair, and me. "I heard rumors, but whoa. Talk about your misspent youth coming back to haunt you."

"My misspent youth funded yours, Rhodes."

"True," Troy says, looking unaccountably stung. "But I get to go to college baggage free. Sucks to be you, I guess."

"Wait here, guys," I tell the Garretts, then give Troy's forearm a shove in the direction of the back of the bleachers.

"Ha. I knew you'd go for it, Mason," he says smugly. "Phonying up for the kiddos, huh? What can I getcha?"

"The truth. What are you selling my sister? She's screwed up enough."

"Your sister?" he says thoughtfully, with the wide-eyed, *I'm so wrongly accused* look that hasn't gotten him out of detention since middle school. "You mean Nan?"

"Cut the bullshit, Troy. Yes. Her. What's going on?"

His slow, faux-surfer voice goes hard as physics. "I don't mess with family drama. You want to know what's going down with the girl, ask her."

George scoots around from the front of the bleachers, extending Cal's bottle and then yanking on my sleeve. "Hurry up! The team's coming out now! Hurry!" He pulls on Troy's army jacket. "You can come too. Are you a soldier?"

"Kind of," Troy answers cheerfully.

"A freedom fighter against the war on drugs?" I ask, and he laughs, pointing his finger at me like a gun.

"Ex-act-ly. Lead on, midget."

"More civilians than soldiers get killded during any war," George tells him. "Look—there's the team!"

At this point, the Stony Bay and Maplecrest teams jog, two by three, onto the field, round into a circle.

"*Raah!*" Cal says, shifting angrily in the front pack. "*Raah. Raah. Raahaaah.*"

"He cwying, Hon. Do somfin. Cal cwying." Patsy sounds like a pissed-off truck driver, at odds with her little sprouty ponytails.

"There's my brother!" George says to Troy. "He's number twenty-two. Right over there. The one who just stopped that big running guy in the orange shirt."

George, Harry, and Duff all have their eyes riveted to the field.

"Nice tackle for a loss," Duff calls. "Take that, Maplecrest High—you stink."

"Duff said another bad word," George singsongs.

I'm thinking of a few that would put him to shame.

Patsy watches me try to feed Cal, and then looks at me with this betrayed expression, lower lip trembling. "Hon . . ." she says, like it's my funeral.

"Maybe I could, like, walk her around," Troy suggests. "I've got this half sister. She's an infant. I mean, being on the move helps, man, I know that."

"Are you jacked?" I ask.

His face twitches, miffed. "I, like, deal it, man. I don't, like, do it."

Yep, you're a real man of principle, Troy. I assess his clear eyes, his healthy color. Messed up that I never asked or wondered about this before. But then, first things first. "Back and forth, then, in front of the bleachers where I can see you," I order.

So here, in Surrealland, my friendly neighborhood drug dealer soothes a kid I'm babysitting, while I try to change my own kid's diaper on my lap—not a brilliant idea, that—and Harry, Duff, and George cheer Jase on like this is all totally normal and fine.

"Hoo boy," Duff says under his breath. "Jase got burned deep on that pass."

Cal yanks his mouth away from the bottle like this knowledge personally pains him. I shove it back in. "Just chug it, kid."

Troy has Patsy up on his shoulders and is hovering near us, pointing out Jase on the field. "Check it out, little babe. See how he was smart and stayed in his lane on the punt return so the returner couldn't get outside of him?"

"No," George says solemnly, edging closer to Troy. "But is that good?"

"It rocks, little dude. It, like, so rules."

The game's winding down when Hester taps me on the shoulder. I unsnap the BabyBjörn thing and haul Cal out, pushing him unceremoniously into her arms so fast, she nearly drops him. He looks back at me, lower lip wobbly, gives this tentative version of his smile. *Dad?*

I take him back, hold him against my shoulder. "Sorry, sorry, sorry, kid." Low in his ear.

She's studying me, squinting, hand to her mouth, chewing a thumbnail. "Ready to let him go now?"

I stand still for a minute, put my hand on the back of his head, the little folds of skin there, like extra skin he's waiting to grow into. Kills me a little bit.

"Keep him safe, 'kay?"

Chapter Thirty-two

TIM

I'm up to the door, in what, three steps, standing there in the shoes Alice gave me, hand upraised to rattle the screen, when she opens it before I can.

My brain freezes, because she's in nothing but a short dark green towel, hair dripping, fresh out of the shower. She smells like baby shampoo and damp skin. Tanned and clean and wet.

As the silence lengthens, she stares back at me, eyebrows slowly climbing.

A trickle of water slides slowly down from her collarbone, disappearing into the cleavage just barely covered by the green terry cloth, which she adjusts, pulling the towel higher in the front but making it dip on the side.

Having trouble thinking in words.

"I just . . ."

"Happened to be in the neighborhood?"

"That's it."

"Come in."

ALICE

In our kitchen now, dark except for the electric light above the stove and what spills in from the street. Quiet except for my music from the other room and a semi-insistent complaint from Jase's cat, Mazda, because something must be done about that empty food dish.

Tim bends down to pet her and she batters herself against his calf, gets up immediately on her hind legs and begins kneading his thigh, butting against it. His hand looks big against her fur, and Mazda is not a small cat.

She attempts to clamber into his lap, but she's too fat, so she does the disdainful-tail, *you're beneath me anyway* cat thing and wanders off.

Tim looks up and smiles at me.

That same dazzled smile from the other day.

The glow from the streetlamp far down our driveway throws everything in the room into sharp relief, lighting Tim's red hair and bringing out deeper, warmer tones.

He rubs a hand over his face. Yawns, says "Sorry," blinks, smiles again.

"Look . . . do you want to . . . take a walk? I'll throw on some clothes."

Not go out in this towel, in case you were assuming that.

"Damn," Tim says, but it sounds almost automatic, a reflex, like that's what he thinks he'll say, all I expect from him.

"I'll just . . . get dressed."

He nods, standing up. Walking to the table aimlessly. Picking up my tea mug, a smudge of red on the side, turning it around in his hands, setting it down. Selecting one of Joel's left-behind drumsticks, tapping it against the corner of the table, setting it down.

When he opens the refrigerator, stares into it, shuts it

again, I repeat, "I'll put some clothes on . . . my body."

"Sounds like a plan," Tim says absently.

When I come back, having thrown on my favorite jeans and Jase's football jersey, he's at the kitchen table with his head down on his folded arms.

I touch his back and he startles, rubs his eyes, blinks up at me.

"I wasn't gone that long," I say, amused. "Sure you're up for—anything?"

"Yeah. Hold on." He turns on the tap, splashes water on his face, frowns at the coffeemaker, which still has about two inches of cold coffee in it from this morning, then actually tips the carafe to his lips and downs about half of it.

"No mug?"

"We want what we want when we want it, Alice, remember?" He wipes his lips with the back of his hand, smiles a little, the one dimple making a brief appearance. "So, where to?"

His car has mine boxed in, so we take that, drive along some bumpy unpaved roads in Maplewood to the Hollister Fairgrounds, all set up for the annual Fall Fair this weekend, but for now dark except for the parking lot floodlights.

The Ferris wheel is a ghostly-looking hoop against the sky, the Funhouse and the Balloon Burst and the Tilt-A-Whirl and Teacup still and mute.

"I haven't been to this thing in years," Tim says, sliding out of the car and peering up at the Ferris wheel. "Ma always does that jam contest. Ol' Gracie Reed wins it every time. Drives Ma ballistic."

"Grace probably pays off the judges."

But not the bills. Tomorrow, I promise myself. Tomorrow I will find a way to fix this. Her. Two more fat bills in the mail today, stamped all over with TIME SENSITIVE and URGENT.

Tim shoots me a sharp look, but says a noncommittal, "Mmm." I know he's known Samantha's mom all his life, but can he really have any sympathy for her now?

We've gotten close to the Ferris wheel, and one of the passenger cars is docked right next to the metal platform. I climb in. "C'mon."

Tim reaches for my hand, his grip tightening as he slips into the car beside me. Then he doesn't let go, looking down, his thumb pressing over my knuckles.

The night air wraps around us, dry leaves, someone's smoky wood fire.

I break the silence. Poetically.

"Andy throws up on this thing. Every time. It's a tradition."

"Nan too," he says. "Scared of heights. I used to bribe the operator to stop it when she was at the top, just to make it extra-humiliating for her. Of course, I usually barfed too, but that was too much beer or whatever."

I kick my feet against the footrest and the car rocks slightly, a creak of metal.

"Since you were how old?"

He shrugs. "Twelve?"

A year older than Duff—whose idea of getting high is, literally, hitting the top of the Ferris wheel.

"Hey, Tim?"

"Uh-huh." He's got his head tipped back against the cracked plastic seat-back now, looking at the moon, an almost invisible horseshoe of silver. He stretches and the bottom of his T-shirt rides up to expose navy-blue boxers with little white anchor crests peeking out from his jeans.

He looks up after a moment, finds me staring, fixedly, at the elastic banding.

"Nice shorts," I offer.

"Hot, right?" He pulls the waistband farther out, snaps it. "Complete with the Ellery Prep motto: 'Live purely, seek righteousness.'"

I snicker and he grins at me, runs his hand over his face like earlier, yawns, then drapes his arm over my shoulder, warm fingers landing lightly near my elbow.

"There's an innovative move," I say.

"Again, a classic for a reason. Besides, we're on a Ferris wheel. It's like a reflex—practically Pavlovian."

"You simply can't help yourself," I say. "The motto on your shorts, no deterrent."

"Maybe you should take them off," Tim suggests. "Since they're obviously ineffective."

I elbow him.

The car rocks back and forth with a loud squawk, finally settling, tilted back in an unnatural position, so our legs are raised.

"I wish this wheel were running," Tim says. "Or we were at a drive-in movie. That would be a better atmosphere."

"Than this, which is kind of like being in a dentist chair?" I tilt back, close my eyes, his arm solid behind me, his index finger moving slowly up, down, around the bend of my elbow. Should be lulling, relaxing. But my skin's electrified. It's a cloudless night with a bite of chill in the air, sharp-sweet as an apple. The moon's just a slice and the stars look like a handful of glitter tossed across the black. I'm far away, floating in space, distant from everything and everyone except Tim.

His shoulders shift. His other hand reaches out, palm grazing across the back of my hand, fingers interlacing from above. Squeeze. Then nothing.

Just us.

His hand, my hand.

Should be innocent. Middle school moves.

But isn't.

Here in the dark where I can see clearer . . . if it isn't innocent, it *is* simple.

"The next move?" I say, a few minutes later. "I think it's this one." I pretend-shiver, press closer to his side. He makes a soft sound of surprise deep in his throat, then gathers me tighter.

I trace one finger lightly up and down his jeans, circle it around his kneecap, feel him shudder. He shuts his eyes, a wince, like it's the last thing he wants to do but he can't help it.

"Cold?"

"Anything but. You?"

Shake my head as he drops his hand, so his knuckles graze my side, up-down, past the side seam of my bra, trailing over my rib cage, slow, slow, slow.

There's a flash of light, sweeping past us, then back, pinning us both, a brusque voice. "Who is that? Who's there?"

Tim swears under his breath, is up and out of the car, tugging me along before I've even inhaled, then we're stumbling across the hilly grass, huddling behind a huge billboard advertising

Hyman Orchards, The Apple of Connecticut's Eye. I look back, see the flash of a white car with a blue stripe, lights twirling, turning the fairgrounds ruby-red, lightning-bright.

"The police?" I say incredulously. "No way."

"*Shhhh.*" Tim plants two fingers on my lips.

"There weren't any keep-out signs. We weren't even doing anything!"

"If we'd had five more minutes we could have been."

"Who the dickens is that?" bellows the voice, closer now.

"We can get arrested for this? Seriously?"

"*Shhh,*" he says again, holding up a hand. "Let's not find out. The Stony Bay po-po are bored out of their skulls. They leap on this kind of shit. Trust me."

"I know you're out there," the voice says implacably. "State your name and come out."

Still pulling my hand, Tim crouches down and runs from behind the billboard into a patch of bushes. The flashlight beam zooms around wildly. Fizz of a walkie-talkie. "ATL suspect and/or suspects for trespass. Copy."

Loud crackle of unintelligible response.

I start to stand up, brushing off my shirt, prepared to argue. Tim yanks me back to the scrubby grass.

"Let go. This is ridiculous." I'm struggling against him, wriggling away. "Who do these guys think they are?"

"Alice," he hisses. "Nothing else is going on here tonight, unless they need to rescue a cat in a tree. They will bring us in, for real. That would suck for Joel."

For that I fall silent, stop moving. My police academy brother.

More crackling from the walkie-talkie. "UTL, repeat, UTL. Over."

Slow loop of the light all around. I press my head to Tim's chest, wriggle up to ensure my feet aren't poking out of the bush like the dead Witch of the East's, and then freeze, listening.

The shaft of light moves slowly, outlining the side of the billboard, up across the top, back down the side. What does this guy expect—that we're scaling the Hyman Orchards sign? To do what? Hang from our knees and graffiti it upside down?

Crackle-crackle. "No sign of the perp. Repeat, negative as of this time. Over."

"Perp? We didn't perp anything!" I whisper. "There was no caution tape, there was no no-trespassing sign."

"Alice. Be. Quiet."

Finally, the crunch of footsteps moving away. I begin to slide off Tim and he traps my hips between his palms.

"Don't move."

"What? Is he still there? Is he trying to fake us out? Do you *know* this cop?"

"I know almost all of 'em. No, he's gone. Don't move. Except the wiggling. That was good." Lips drag along my ear, his voice lowers, close to a whisper. "Alice. Kiss me."

"Tim . . ."

"I'm right here."

Me too, no honest way to pretend I'm not.

I squirm as if to roll off, but I have his sleeve, pulling him over with me until his face is above mine, the sliver of moon behind it.

I move my hands up slowly, inching, brush one dark eyebrow,

then the other with the tip of my index finger. Along one high cheekbone, the dip in the middle of his top lip, the bottom line of the lower one.

See the gleam of his eyes in the dim light. Watching. His skin, warm in the cool night air.

I twist a little underneath the length of his body, look away.

Try to laugh but there's hardly any air to breathe, he's so firmly against me, so it comes out as a gasp. He smiles, lifts to plant his elbows on either side of my head, nudging my cheek lightly with the left one so I have to turn my own head, look him full in the face.

"Alice."

Close my eyes. "You're totally taking advantage of this situation."

"Hell, yeah. You're free to return the favor." The tone is light, but his eyes are serious.

His hand slides across my neck, up behind my ear, thumb moving to the hollow of my throat where my pulse is knocking hard. I expect his lips, but instead I get his cheek, so lightly rested, it's almost not touching.

Rise and fall of his chest against me, leg edging between mine. Then stillness.

For a breath.

One more.

When our mouths meet, there's a suspended instant when Tim freezes, total tension in his shoulder and neck muscles, but then he dives into me.

I hear myself make this noise in my throat, and I'm pulling him tighter against me, sinking into him. I'm shivering, actually shaking and making sounds...I don't know...they'd embarrass me if I could stop. But I can't.

We pull apart for a moment, breathing hard.

"This could be a big mistake." I slide my hands down to his hips and lock them closer, hard against my own.

"Nope. I've made mistakes. They don't feel like this."

"Gotcha," says a loud voice. We both jerk our heads up, blinded by a flashlight. Tim swears under his breath. I hold my hands up to shield my eyes. Tim flips over to the side, in front of me, blocking me from the light.

"Stand up slowly," calls a voice. "Palms to your sides. No sudden moves. Step apart."

"*Shhh*," Tim whispers, moving a foot away from me. "It'll be fine. Just don't say *anything*."

"This is ridiculous," I say. The two policemen are talking to each other, all low official tones, walkie-talkies still crackling away, so I don't think they'll hear, but one of them freezes, shields his eyes, and flicks his flashlight back up.

"Oh, hell. That's my sister."

TIM

In the end they have nothing to bring us in for, although Alice manages to make it a very close call.

"Since when have you been skulking around checking out bushes like the pervert security guard at SB High, Joel?"

"This is part of my ride-along, Al. Since when have *you* been rolling around in the bushes with random dudes?" Joel flicks his flashlight up. "Oh. Hi, Tim."

I raise one hand. "Uh—hey, man."

"What I do is none of your business," Alice hisses. "And he's not a random dude, so—"

"Okey-doke," says Joel's superior officer. "Save that for the playground, kids. Speaking of which, you two"—again with the flashlight flicking from Alice to me, in case he'll need to ID us later in a lineup—"not smart to be around all that heavy equipment when the fair's closed. Easy to get hurt. But we can't arrest you for bad judgment."

"Lucky for you, Alice."

"Shut up, Joel," Alice says. "You hardly know him."

"Compared to you, guess not. He's what, Jase's age? When I said to relax and kick back, I didn't mean by hooking up with Holden Caulfield."

I shrug. Meh. Could be worse.

Alice, though, I expect her to flush, move away, put some distance between us. But instead, she edges closer, takes my hand. Moves a little bit in front, partially blocking me from Joel's amused grin, my shield.

"You hardly know him," she says again.

She stays close on the drive home too, scootching far over in the seat and up against me like she's still making some kind of stand, a statement, even though there's no one here but us. After I pull the car into the driveway, park it, I don't know what to do with my hands.

The fairgrounds, what we did there came naturally. Now it's like some movie moment, the motionless car, the cool dark around us, the streetlight picking up the shine of her hair. I've *seen* this in movies. I'm looking at us from a distance—waiting for some sort of cue: *Here is where you brush the hair away from her face, then you bend close and she makes that little sound of hers, halfway between a gasp and a hum of satisfaction. Then you kiss her and—*

Yup, I'm thinking in the second person.

Alice is looking at me, head tilted. I wait for her to look annoyed or puzzled, but she doesn't. I wait for her to take charge, climb into my lap, face me square on, lift the decision out of my hands and into her own. She doesn't. She studies me for a second more, then drops her head onto my shoulder, rests it, breathes in sync with me, but not like she's trying to. Just that she is.

No impatience rising off her, no confusion. It's like this is all good, just as it's meant to be. For some reason, I remember standing in the shower, the water streaming down—but not the times I've conjured up Alice there. Of being under the spray with Cal, him sucking on my nose. Me thinking that right in that moment, I had everything he needed, and he was giving me everything I needed right back, simply by being there.

ALICE

Resting my head against his shoulder. Something I've done without a second thought with my brothers. But never with any other guy. Tim would have no way of knowing that. But I do. When he tucks me nearer to his side, wraps a few strands of my hair around his fingers, lets them go, wraps them again, as though he can't help but keep touching me once he starts, it's then that I let it in. I'm most likely in love with him.

"This is the first time I've ever done this," I say, a few minutes later.

Alice rests back against the door, her shoulders flat against the screen.

"This?"

She knows what I mean, but I say it anyway. "Walked someone to their door."

Alice left the porch light on, but the kitchen's dark. The house is quiet in a way the Garrett house is never quiet.

To my right there's the long fence that separates the Garretts' yard from what used to be the Reeds'.

Big maple tree, tossing boughs in the blowing air, with that *shhh* sound leaves start to make when they're beginning to dry out. Clouds coming across the moon, wind swept in from down by the river, smells like riverweeds, mud, leaves, and drying grass, the kickoff of fall.

It's all quieter than anything in my world has ever been.

Peaceful.

Almost don't know what to do with peaceful.

Alice lowers her head, looks up through her crazy-long lashes. I brace one hand on the door, to the side, well above her head.

"I should have won you a big-ass stuffed teddy bear and one of those huge lollipops."

"At the Coconut Shy? I'll take a rain check."

"What about Joel?"

"More a High Striker kind of guy—always loved swinging that mallet."

"You know what I mean, Alice."

"Is he going to come looking for your blood because you had your hand up my shirt? I'm not thirteen. He'll show *me* no mercy, though."

She smiles, shivers a little.

"You should get inside." My voice comes out husky halfway, then breaks on the last word. The whole sentence is the opposite of everything I want to say, but that's probably a pretty good guideline still.

I lean down just as she moves up, on her tiptoes, one hand flat against my chest.

Her lips just touch against my mouth, then the cleft of my chin, back to my lips.

"Good night, Tim."

My lips on her forehead.

"Good night, Alice."

I can't remember ever having something and not reaching for more.

But I back away from her, hands in my pockets.

Enough.

ALICE

"Are you with *him* now?" The kitchen's dark, but the tone of Brad's voice is darker, one I've never heard from him. "Is that what's going on?"

"Where are you?" I'm flicking on the kitchen lights, all of them, one after another, waiting for the answer. Cell phones, God. Andy's been known to call the kitchen from the living room on hers. But Brad calling me from inside my own house is way too babysitter-slasher-horror movie.

"I was driving by to give you a printout of that new warm-up. The one with the trunk rotations? Cyn at CrossFit swears it cut her time by a solid five minutes. And there you are, with that redheaded kid."

"Where are you?" I repeat, walking through the living room, opening the bathroom door, back to the kitchen, the basement door.

"You can't be with that guy." Brad's voice is louder through the phone, and I think it's because I've found him—he's lurking in the basement just exactly like the movies, but no, he's just talking louder. "You're with me."

"We broke up," I say, sitting down abruptly against the wall by the basement door. "I told you that, Brad. We're not together."

"Alice. You. Can't. Be. With. That. Guy," Brad repeats. "He's a druggie with a kid. C'mon."

"He's in recovery and the baby is tempor—" I start, then stop. I don't need to defend Tim to Brad. "This is none of your business."

"You were the one who ended our break, Alice."

"It wasn't a break, it was—" I refuse to have this argument with a cell phone. "Where are you?"

"Nearby."

Now I'm outright scared. "Stop it! We are not dating anymore. Or working out anymore after this. We're done, Brad. This is not okay."

"That's exactly what I'm saying," Brad says.

And hangs up.

Chapter Thirty-three

ALICE

It starts when I'm driving.

Just as I've always been afraid it would.

This car whips by, passing on the right, swerving around, too close to my side, too close in front. I smash down on my brakes, but I'm on the bridge over the river, high up, and there's a strong wind whistling up from the bay, making the bridge cables overhead bounce and shake. The Bug fishtails a little, but I know I can correct it, happens all the time, not a big deal.

Until it is. Until the black sedan's weaving through cars far ahead of me, long past posing any danger, the Bug once again driving straight, nearly to the exit, but I'm chasing after something I can't catch.

My breath.

I'm only exhaling, no air coming in; almost right away my hands are tingling and seizing up because that's what happens, that's what bodies do, to get oxygen where it most needs to be, shut down the things that aren't as vital.

Except that my hands *are* vital because I have to hit the turn signal and ease down the ramp or someone will bash into me from behind or I'll go spiraling into the guardrail or—

Going hot, then glacial under the sweat breaking out all over my skin.

Don't know how I make it off the highway, onto the smaller Route 7, then down a few miles, to the Stony Bay exit. Later, I won't even remember how I did that.

Exit.

Downhill.

Left turn.

Familiar enough to be automatic, but it's harder and harder to pull any air in at all, some trapdoor in my throat has slammed shut, sealed so tight I can't even swallow.

I should pull over.

Here, on the shoulder.

But the curve of the road near the roundabout at the top of Main Street *has* no shoulder, the street's too narrow, no side parking, so I keep going, trying to shake my fingers out so they work better. So they work at all. Flatten my tingling left hand on my thigh for a second, then my right. Drive too close to the roundabout, so that one back wheel bumps up over the raised base, then slams down. Some old lady about to cross at the crosswalk in front of the Dark and Stormy glares at me because I don't stop for her.

I can't stop for anything, just need to get home.

Now my toes are tingling, edging into numb as I shove down on the brake to switch gears, fourth, third, second. Into the driveway, thank God, right behind Tim's car. Roll the window down, but even though air pours in, it's not enough. I'm trying to pull burning sandpaper into my lungs and it sears my throat all the way down.

Snatch at the door handle but it's not opening; it's locked and for some reason that's just it, too much. Bury my forehead in the crook of my arm, shoulders shaking, all of me shaking.

Then there are hands tight on my upper arms and Tim saying, "Alice. Alice!"

TIM

If this were another movie, I'd haul her into my arms and up the garage steps, kick open the door with one heel, muscle her over to the couch, all without breathing hard.

As it is, small as Alice is, she's so tense that I can't even bend her, much less scoop her up, so I half drag her out onto the driveway, back over onto the lawn, land on my ass with her held tight against me, rigid as a surfboard. She's, like, quivering, and I'm scared out of my mind.

So we're both gasping for breath. "Tell me what's going on!" I try for a calm, neutral tone. My voice cracks twice in the short sentence.

"P-panic attack." She's flicking her hand toward her face, the harsh breaths coming a little less close together.

"Do you have a—"

Something to fix this? What? An inhaler? It's not asthma. Brown paper bag to breathe into? Not on me, no.

"You're okay," I say finally. "Just breathe. You're okay."

Stroke her back in slow circles, like she's Cal.

"You're safe. You're okay." Her eyes are so wide, frantic. My chest clutches like I'm not getting enough air either.

"'S okay," I repeat. Her hand shoots out and grabs on to my wrist, tight. All sweaty. I rub my other palm against the back of it. Despite the sweat, her hand is icy. "It's fine. You're fine. It's all good."

ALICE

It takes about ten minutes, longer than I ever remember it taking. By the end, I'm lying across Tim's legs, my head in his lap, staring up at the wedge of his chin, the pale blue sky, the scarlet leaves of our maple tree filtering the light.

It'sokayit'sokayit'sokay. He keeps saying it over and over and finally the air comes all the way into my lungs and hangs around long enough to fill them. Still I don't move, and he keeps on massaging his palm over my back, my neck, my upper arms.

In.

Out.

In.

Out.

No idea how long we stay like that.

"Are you back?" Tim asks in a hushed voice.

I nod. "I think so." My voice is squeaky and breathless but at least I can talk.

So, progress.

"Can you walk?"

I shake my head.

"Do you want water?"

Shake my head again.

"Does it help if I hold you? No funny business."

"Funny business?" I say.

"I have no idea where that came from. Please forget I said it. What happened here? Can you tell me?"

Shake my head. My breath starts to clutch up again.

• ◦ • ◦

Five minutes later I'm flopped back on Tim's couch and he's pacing around the kitchen, waiting for water to boil. He keeps checking on me.

"Still okay?"

"Stop asking that. Makes me tense."

He runs his hands through his hair, short, sharp nod. "Of course. Sorry."

In. Out. I'm tracing slow circles on my thigh, concentrating hard on that. When I first had these, back in middle school, that's what the school counselor, Mrs. Garafalo, had me do. Circle, bigger circle, bigger circle. She also had music—a CD she gave me—lutes or sitars or gongs or something slow and rhythmic with no words.

"Have any music? Just, like, instrumental?"

He looks around the room, his fingers scrubbing at his hair, then reaches down and scoops something out of the basket, twists something, and sets it next to me. It's a small lavender stuffed elephant, evidently with a music box inside, because it's playing a song that takes me a moment to identify.

"'I Am the Walrus'?"

"I know. And it's an elephant. Don't ask. Obviously a refugee from the Island of Misfit Toys. Just close your eyes and listen, Alice. Do the breathing thing."

I tip my head back against the couch, listen to him moving around the apartment. Then I feel him standing near me.

"It's happened before," Tim says. Not as a question.

I nod.

"A lot?"

My stupid throat is tightening again. "Years ago. When I was twelve."

"Ah. Before you 'flipped it.'"

"There were other things going on. But yeah. Not since then. Till a few weeks ago."

He shoves a hand into the breast pocket of his rumpled oxford shirt, in that "reaching for a cigarette" way, comes up empty, looks around helplessly for a moment, then scoops up a fireball from a bowl on the table. Pops it through the plastic coating directly into his mouth.

"What happened a few weeks ago?" The fireball's scrunched in his cheek, so his words come out funny.

I start telling him. Only a few halting sentences in, Tim jumps up and starts pacing back and forth like a caged coyote. All the way through, he keeps peppering me with questions:

"Did you go by the bank?"

"Did you talk to a lawyer?"

"Have you tried going through Samantha?"

"I've thought about it," I admit to him, "but I thought, first—"

"You know you have to talk to Gracie," he says, setting tea on the coffee table next to my feet. My hand goes toward my throat and he grabs it, holds on to it, squeezes. "I know Grace Reed, Alice. She backs down. She's gotta know she's in the wrong all over the place here."

"You think she cares? This is the woman who was going to pretend nothing happened when she smashed her car into my family's life, Tim."

"Until Samantha called her on it. And your brother. She's a coward, really. Bullies usually are."

"These bills are going to collection. I got nowhere at the bank," I repeat, not telling him who I spoke with there, because why make things harder.

"So you have nothing to lose," Tim says. "Drink your tea. Let's get there. I have to pick up Cal, but not until four—that gives us plenty of time."

"I don't need you to go with me."

"I'm driving you, in case you freeze up. I'll be in the car outside, in case shit gets weird. And I'll have my phone, in case you need me to go ninja and crash through the window or something."

"But—"

"*Shhh.*"

"Don't *shhhh* me!"

"Angry? Good. Now let's get you to Gracie."

Grace Reed is wearing overalls, but designer—definitely not Oshkosh—and holding a paint roller in one manicured hand. "Yes?"

She looks a lot like Samantha, except her hair is silvery blond and straight, while Sam's is tawny and wavy. But Samantha doesn't have anything close to her mother's smooth, expressionless face. Everything Sam thinks is right there, easy to read. If Grace had expressions, she might have wrinkles. Laugh lines, like Mom, who I'm pretty sure is younger.

Reaching into my backpack, I pull out the pile of envelopes secured with a rubber band. "These are for you."

She takes a step back, her eyes skating over the envelopes, back to me. Opens the door wider. "I think you'd better come in. You can leave your shoes right outside."

Swallowing hard, I slip off my sneakers. She drops the paint roller into a paint pan, wipes her hands on her pants, and leads the way into the living room.

White on white on white, with a few splashes of black—the pillows, the frames of the muted photographs of Samantha and her sister, Tracy. The only color is a huge painting over the mantel of the white brick fireplace. Grace at a piano, with a pre-school Tracy and toddler Sam at her feet, all of them wearing dark green dresses with pink satin sashes. Sam is all ringlets and big wide eyes. Tracy looks a tiny bit scornful—typical, from what I know.

Grace Reed points to the frost-white couch, looming like an iceberg off the snowy carpet. "Would you like some lemonade?"

Please. We are not making this into a social occasion. I shake my head. Hold out the envelopes again. Repeat, "These are yours."

"I think I'll have a glass of Pinot, myself," she says, giving me a conspiratorial smile. "I've always hired someone to do the work before. Never appreciated how tiring it is when you DIY!" She click-clicks her heeled sandals across the wooden floor into what I guess is the kitchen. The footsteps seem to go on forever. Huge, this place. High ceilings. So white. I'm small, hunched on this sofa, cushions so puffy, my feet barely reach the ground.

My chest cramps.

Deep calming breaths.

I fan the envelopes out on the coffee table. She returns with a large glass of white wine, sets it down on the table with a clink, crosses her ankles, and looks me, at last, in the eye.

"Which one are you?"

I'm torn between rolling my eyes—yeah, "those Garretts" are one big indistinguishable blob—and throwing the contents of her glass in her face. Does she even know *Jase's* name?

"Alice. Jase's older sister. I do the hospital bills." I tap the envelopes with a finger, settle back on the couch, lean forward to touch them again. Grace's brows edge together. "These are yours. They've gone to collection. That affects my parents' credit, since their names are on them. Your bank wrote and said you weren't paying anymore. When I spoke to them, they said those were your instructions."

Grace Reed used to be a politician, and that practiced poise shows in her face, if nothing else does. She gives me a pleasant, small smile, but her eyes trade nothing away. She takes a sip, waits for me to go on, looking, at best, mildly interested.

"You cover it. That was the deal," I say. "The one you made with my mother *and my father*." I pick up one bill, hold it up like show-and-tell. "Dad's had a bunch of tests recently, and a few specialists in because of—well, because he needed them. The total so far is seventeen thousand dollars. I'll accept a check."

"I had no idea it would be this expensive," she says, bending forward to set down the glass, thinking better of it and taking a quick sip. "Fortunately your father is relatively young. He should make a fine recovery. I'm sure the doctors have told you that." Her tone's still light. She sounds like someone I'd run into at the post office, like it all has nothing to do with her, like *Wish you the best, buh-bye.*

"If he gets good care, he will. But if the rehab has to toss him out on his ass because he can't pay the bills, what then?"

"I don't believe they can legally do that," she says, and takes another sip, leaving a touch of coral lipstick behind. "In fact, I supported a bill that—"

"You're not the state senator now. You're the person who caused all of this."

The hand that lifts the wineglass is just a bit shaky; some sloshes over onto the coffee table. Grace takes a measured sip, sets the glass down, reaches out and touches my knee, confidingly. "Listen now, I know this has been an ordeal for your family. Make no mistake, it's been one for mine. It's affected everything. My relationship with my daughters. My romantic connection. Up in smoke. It'll follow me for the rest of my life. I may never be able to serve the people of Connecticut in any official capacity again. This may even rebound on Tracy and Samantha. Don't you think we've been punished enough for a mistake anyone could have made?"

"My parents wouldn't have made this 'mistake.' My brothers and I—who never swore on a Bible to uphold the law—wouldn't have either. My four-year-old kid brother would know better."

"Alison, you need to understand my position. The bulk of my money comes from a family trust. I do get generous dividends every quarter. Generous for my purposes. But not when one adds in astronomical medical bills. After this latest round of your family's, I barely have enough to pay Tracy's fall fees at Middlebury."

"Senator Reed. I don't give a damn. Sell stock. Sell paintings. Sell your Manolos. Use whatever extra you've put away in your sock drawer or stuffed in your bra. Pay the bills so my father can get the care he needs and we don't have creditors after us."

I start toward the door and her voice stops me. "I'm not even able to come up with Samantha's semester fee for Hodges." She stands up. "We can see the main school building from here. How will Samantha feel if she can look at it but not attend anymore? It's her senior year. She stands a solid chance at any one of the Ivies she chooses. That's her future. Is your brother planning to go to college? Or straight into the workforce?"

Being outright rude to this woman will only make her think she's more right and I'm more wrong. But—

"Jase has been in the 'workforce' since he was fourteen— working at my dad's store. Like my brother Joel and me. And yes, he'll go to college. If he gets a scholarship. Or some loans. If we come through this without going bankrupt. My parents went to college. My brother Joel went to college. I'm at nursing school at Middlesex College in White Bay."

"I had a fund-raiser there. Lovely campus. So rural. Is that a community college? I can't remember."

As if community colleges and public schools are some inferior species—unless, of course, you need votes.

"Yes, it is. And—and—I applied to transfer to Nightingale Nursing School—in Manhattan—for this fall. I got in. Off the waiting list, at the end of the summer. But because of what happened to Dad, I deferred. I'm not sure I'll ever get there now."

I haven't told anyone but Joel about those two things. Not even my parents. They would have argued. Another thing to add into Grace Reed's tally. Turning us into a family of secret-keepers. Something we've never been. Something that makes me a little sick.

"That is truly unfortunate," Grace Reed says, her voice sincere. "That's a wonderful school. I'm a huge believer in the value of a good education."

Yes, I'm sure you've made a speech about it.

She looks me directly in the eye now, her voice going quieter. "You're protective of your family. I'm the same about mine. I'm a single mom, Alison, and I've had to fill the role of both parents since before Samantha was born. Hodges is the only school she's ever known—it's been stability for her, an extended family."

"Not my problem, Senator Reed."

"That's a pretty cold comment, Alison. How would your brother—"

The two-tone sound of the doorbell. She startles, and for a moment her eyes flick around the room, almost frantic, as though she's making sure no evidence—her fingerprints on the bills, a shattered headlight from her car—is in sight. But the only evidence is me, my red face, the angry tears building in my throat.

"Samantha must have forgotten her key. Again. Why don't you come with me and I can let you out when I let her in?"

There I am, trailing after her clacking heels down the long hallway. I haven't fixed a thing. The only thing that's changed is that I hate her more.

"Samantha, I've told you and told you to remember that I—"

"Yo, Gracie," Tim says cheerfully. "You're looking lovely as ever. Already whipping the house into shape."

Grace looks like she's trying to smile and frown at the same time, which even she can't pull off—she looks like someone's just goosed her. "Ah—um—"

"Tim," he says helpfully.

She laughs. "I wasn't expecting you, Timothy."

"You know me, I get around."

I'm glaring at him from behind Samantha's mom. He takes off a pair of sunglasses I've never seen him wear and polishes them on his shirttail, still smiling. "I'm still welcome, aren't I, Gracie?"

"Well...yes, though Samantha's not home yet, but—I thought you were her, actually, but—my guest was just—"

"Yes, I came for Alice. I'm her chauffeur today. One of my many jobs. I'm working for the Garretts now. In all kinds of ways."

Grace, like other women in Tim's life, obviously has no idea what to do with him. She settles for a faint "That's... enterprising."

"Isn't it? I try not to pass up any opportunity. Hey, speaking of that, Brendan, your campaign manager? I guess I should say 'former campaign manager'—he called me this week. On your behalf. Another volunteer opportunity."

She does that tilt of her chin, mildly interested thing.

Tim raises his eyebrows at her, smile broadening. "Thinking of throwing your hat in for treasurer?"

"Just a thought," Grace says. "Not a lot of opposition and—it's late in the game, so it's probably not likely, but—"

"But you like to gamble. Besides, it's been a couple of months since you retired. Practically a lifetime in politics."

Politics are not my thing. But I get the definite sense that more is being said here than has been spoken out loud.

"Yes, well . . ." Grace's gaze flits from Tim to me. All the discomfort I wanted for her? I see it on her face now.

"Ready, Alice?" He slips an arm around my shoulder, herds me out the door. "Sorry to cut things short. I know Alice will continue your conversation another time soon. And hey, thanks for giving Brendan the heads-up to call me. I'm glad all the stuff from your last campaign is behind you. Ancient history, right?"

She's still standing in the doorway as Tim the chauffeur ushers me across the well-tended lawn to his car.

Chapter Thirty-four

ALICE

"Classic Grace," Tim says in the car, after I finish my description of the hellish visit. "Could have scripted it all."

"Why'd you tell me to talk to her if it wouldn't do any good? If you knew she was going to do all that—cry poor, and act like I was a big meanie and not budge an inch? And what were you doing, anyway? What was with the 'Yo, Gracie,' smooth campaign talk?"

"Trust me, Alice. It did some good. She's sweating right now. Count on it. Or perspiring, because sweating would be tacky. If nobody calls her on shit, Grace thinks no one sees it. Now she knows different. Me? I was just using what I knew and fucking with her."

All the anger that got lost under the white rug in the Reeds' hygienic little bubble buzzes around me now.

"It's not a game, Tim!"

He turns to me, face hard suddenly. For an instant, I can see how he'll look when he's older, when the sharp lines of his bones and the smoothness of his cheeks all come together to make a man's face. "I thought we'd been through this. I am taking it seriously, Alice. I'm taking *everything* seriously. But, hey, thanks for the reminder that ultimately I'm a loser. Almost slipped my mind."

"No." I grab his sleeve as he reaches for the gearshift. "I don't look at you that way. At all. I—I—"

He puts a hand on my leg. "It's okay. You're okay. Breathe. Don't worry about it. But also, stop saying that shit to me. I don't care about Pop's naughty list, but hell if I'll be on yours. If this is going to work with us, I can't be auto-fuckup all the time."

His eyes widen, as though the words startle him as much as me. But then he adds, "I mean it."

This.

There's a "this" and an "us." And he's just laid that on the table.

"Unless it's just a hookup, Alice. Or not even that." His eyes search mine. When I don't say anything, his voice falters, drops lower. "Can you please talk?"

"No, it's not. And you're—"

My hands are around the back of his neck now, and I'm kissing him, kissing him, kissing him. His shoulders are vibrating because he's laughing now as I'm practically climbing into his lap.

"Whoa. We're in the Hodges school zone. If we get hauled in on public indecency charges, Joel will show no humanity this time."

He slides me off, carefully moving me almost to the far side of the seat as though I'm magnetic or flammable, flashes a wink at me and turns around, elbow on armrest, to back up and pull out of the cramped parking space. I study him, sleeves rolled back, shoulders surprisingly broad beneath the rumpled striped shirt.

"When did you develop all this self-control?"

"You kidding? I have no self-control whatsoever. None." He sounds as though I've accused him of something shameful. "None."

"Every time we've kissed, you've stopped us."

He ticks things off on his fingers. "That night at the garage apartment when you agreed to let me stay there—"

"We didn't kiss then."

"I would have gone for it—you were the one who backed away. Also you were with Brad. The beach—too public. Also—other insane stuff going on. The Ferris wheel—that was the long arm of the law, also known as your big brother."

"And the house was empty."

"Sure. We could have used Jase's room. That would have been awesome." He punches in the cigarette lighter, blasts on the air-conditioning, readjusts the rearview mirror, concentrates hard on pulling out into traffic.

"Your apartment was empty too."

"Yeah, well. Man, this traffic better lighten up. I'm s'posed to pick up Nano before I get Cal, and Hester always freaks out if I'm late. God, that guy just went right through the stoplight. You see that?"

"Tim, are you blushing?"

"No. I don't blush. Guys don't blush."

"I think you are."

"It's hot in here, Alice. Can you crack open your window?"

It is not, in fact, hot in here. It's actually sort of a chilly, cloudy fall afternoon. Plus, he has the air-conditioning cranked, which is completely unnecessary. I open my window anyway.

He rolls his down too, and sticks his head out when we get to a stoplight, cooling his face. Which is not blushing. Because guys don't blush.

Chapter Thirty-five

No matter where we do it—the store, Waldo's house, the garage, whatever, the Cal exchange has this weird, sketchy vibe. First off, Hester and I are so frickin' polite that you'd think we'd have to be speaking in code, because there are no conversations on earth so dull as this except the ones in introductory language courses. Instead of, "Where is the pen of my aunt?" we say, "They were all out of Huggies, so I bought blah blah blah," or, "He only slept four hours this morning, but he had a nap in the car." Plus which, you'd think that Hester was one badass spy because each time I get a different girl—sloppy sweats, jeans and T-shirt, dress. Cleavage, no cleavage, turtleneck. Sometimes she's all flustered and nervous, sometimes she's poised and composed. Sometimes she's got notes written out about when Cal did what, sometimes she looks startled when I ask and says, "He did all the usual things."

This afternoon is awkward times eight hundred billion because Nan's along for the ride. So she's running into both my one-night-stand and its byproduct at the same time.

We're at the damn park again, which Nan just cannot get over. "It's weird. Who does that?"

"Dunno, sis. All the *other* mothers of my bastard children meet me at the courthouse. Who cares?"

Now Hester (Model 2.0: jeans and a sweater, both clean-looking) holds out a hand, and Nan takes it, scanning her face. Hester just looks back like she's expected close scrutiny. Nan's eyes run from the tip of Hester's head to the toe of her Keds. Then she drops down on her knees to look at Cal.

"He's beautiful," she tells Hester, who stays impassive. "When did you say his birthday was?"

"July twenty-ninth. Tim, I'm almost out of formula. You'll have to pick up some to get him through the day. Sorry." She hands me a crumpled twenty-dollar bill.

I shove it back at her. What the fuck? She's never done that before. And indeed, Nan's looking at me with *you deadbeat dad* written all over her face.

I squat down to Cal's eye level, unbuckle him, remove his latest stupid hat, which has mouse ears, and ruffle his flyaway hair.

"Hey kid."

Hester says something about having to run because it's her day to do whatever at the place where she works. Once again I'm smacked by how little I know this girl. Do I owe her that, the way I owe it to Cal, before they're both gone? I'm having a harder time than usual listening because I'm so focused on Nan's reactions. Also, Cal's grabbed my hair and is trying to stuff some in his mouth. And part of me is with Alice, wondering if she's okay, if she's worrying about Grace, starting to panic—

Squeal from the kid, another sharp tug on my hair, pulling me back.

"Yow, Cal." I disentangle his hand and he immediately grabs my ear and tries the same maneuver.

"Remember, adoption agency, you signing the birth certificate, next Thursday at three o'clock," Hester calls as we walk away. "Wear a tie."

Christ. "Right, sure," I call back curtly over Cal's slurping on my ear.

Nan says nothing as she watches me strap him in, let him gnaw on the knuckle of my index finger while I rummage in my pocket for car keys. When I finally locate them, Nan's still looking.

"Sooo . . . whad'you think?" I wipe drool off on the side of my jeans.

"Hunhn," Nan says, unhelpfully.

"*Hunhn*, what? Don't you think he looks like me?"

But Nan just cocks her head at me, then Cal. "Sort of . . . maybe."

"Nans, *look* at him." I reach under his first chin to indicate the cleft, wave my hand at his leggy little body. "Come *on*."

"I thought maybe it would just be obvious. He'd have a completely identical birthmark or something. I guess, the thing is, Tim, I can't figure out what she's up to. Why keep quiet so long and then show up—*ta-da!*—with a baby. Why not put him up for adoption right from the delivery room?"

It's not like I don't get what Nan's saying. I've had that thought. If Hester had just, say, written me a letter with the facts and some papers to sign off on, if Cal had been abstract, would I have left it at that? So much easier than these uncomfortable swaps, and weird-ass waiting-for-Hester-to-get-the-kid-together conversations with Waldo. Last time, I asked where the bathroom was and he said, "The body tries to tell the truth." Not exactly directions to the john.

"*Raaaaah. Rah. Rrraaaaaaaah!*" Cal contributes at this point.

I locate the set of plastic keys Mrs. Garrett gave me and hand them to him.

"What, you think she's one of those crazy people who steals babies, and she decided to bring me into her little scam so she can get access to my millions?"

"Don't yell at me," Nan says, her calm voice cutting through my increasingly loud one. "Maybe she wants you . . . back?"

"That would imply that she *had* me, that we had a thing going, which we didn't. So in this scenario of yours, she wants me, she decides to present me with a baby, because hell knows nothing turns on a seventeen-year-old guy like a *child*."

Cal hits himself in the eye with the keys, drops them, and starts screaming, pissed as hell. I grin, unbuckle him again, pick him up. He nudges his face into my biceps, stops screaming, and gives a long, shuddery sigh.

Nan closes her eyes, tips her head back against the car. "I'm tired of worrying about you, Tim."

"We could always swing by Troy Rhodes's house so you could get something to calm your nerves."

Nan repeats, as she has every single time I've brought this up, "It's not how it looks."

"Just so ya know, that's one of the least convincing of all bullshit lines. That one never even worked for *me*. What gives, Nan?"

"As if it's that easy," she says. "I'm finally not terrified you'll die of alcohol poisoning or in a car crash."

"Strange, I thought we were talking about you. Quit worrying then. Back to—"

"You're finally turning your life around, and now you have to get into *this* situation."

"You know what? You sound exactly like Pop. Situation. Circumstance. Issue. Try 'baby.' He's your . . . your nephew." The word tastes strange in my mouth. My sister's an aunt. Pop and Ma are grandparents. Why those should be so much harder to wrap my head around than the fact that I'm a father, I don't know.

She's giving me that same old *Not Again, Tim* face. Anger swamps in like a hot red tide. I hate to even touch Cal when I'm like this. But he's chomping away on my shoulder, oblivious to whatever it is pulsing in my veins.

Nan, however, must sense it. She slides her back along the car, away from me, wary.

"See, here's what I don't get, sis. Maybe you can explain it to me. All the mistakes I've made, and you and Pop are still on my ass when I'm trying to do the *right* thing. Temporarily."

"That's just it, Tim. Temporarily." She indicates Cal, my hand on his back, his cheek against my shirt. "And here you are. Acting like a dad."

"I'm not really acting like a dad," I point out. "Just babysitting. What do you want from me, anyway, Nan? You want me to say I don't know what the fuck I'm doing? Consider it said."

"I'm not worried you don't know what you're doing, Tim. I'm worried you do. Look at you." She waves her hand at me and Cal. "*That's* what worries me."

Nan's phone and mine vibrate simultaneously as I pull onto

the curb in front of our house, and I snatch hers before she can get to it. WHAT WE TALKED ABOUT STILL A GO? GOT ALL THE SUPPLIES, SO YOU *ARE* SET! —T.

"I don't even get how you can come down on me, Nano, when you're the one getting 'supplies' from the candy man."

"You don't know what you're talking about," Nan says, all heated.

"I know *exactly* what I'm talking about. No one knows better. So don't even—"

I'm so busy arguing with my twin that I don't notice the car parked behind us. Don't take in a thing until I hear Nan say, "Uh-oh." And look back to see Ma's figure bent over the trunk of her car, hauling bags and bags onto the driveway.

"She can't be worse than Pop about this."

"You didn't hear him when he first found out," Nan offers grimly.

Ma turns around as I get out and wipes her forehead, squinting at the car. "Timothy?"

"Uh, yo, Ma." Nan's sunk down in her seat and put her head in her hands.

"Well!" Ma says. "I was beginning to wonder if we'd ever see you again! Goodness!"

I pick up a bag, then another. They're all from the Christmas Tree Shops, Ma's addiction.

"Nanette! What are you doing, lurking in the car? Come carry some of this in. I got the cutest rug for your room!"

Nan looks apprehensive as she climbs out. Christ knows what the "cutest" rug might be, but I'm betting it won't go with her new look. I'm guessing kittens in a basket. With hats.

"Look at this!" Ma says, pulling something out of a bag. "Can you stand it?"

It's a four-foot-tall stuffed elf, in an apron that says THE HELP YOURSELF ELF, holding a bowl labeled SWEET TREATS. Piss-awful, but suddenly there's this this wave of—I dunno, sympathy, pity, love, whatever, and I start to give Ma a hug just as I hear a shrill *"Raaaaaaaa!"* from the car.

"Uh-oh," Nan repeats.

"What's that?" Ma cranes to see around me. "What's that sound?"

"Here, I'll get those." Nan grabs about seven of the bags and bounds up the steps into the house.

"Timothy?"

"Oh, yeah . . . um, it's uh . . ."

"RAAAAAAAA!" Cal sounds both loud and alarmed.

I hurry to open the back door and reach in for him.

Geez, Dad. I had no idea where you were! Don't do that again! It's scary. It makes me hungry! Raaaaaaa!

Ma has her hand to her mouth. and her face, always rosy, is completely white.

"Timothy Joseph. How did this happen?"

Let's see. Possible answers:

Well, Ma, I had sex with a stranger. But don't worry, I don't remember a thing about it.

God, I have no idea. I knew I should've taken better notes in health class.

Well, it turns out they were wrong, and kissing does make babies.

I tell the truth. "Uh, accidentally, Ma."

She marches up to me. "Like everything else in your life,

Timothy! Oh, sweet Lord, I cannot believe this! What will your father say!"

I jiggle Cal a little and he settles, slightly, then turns his head, with the expression he always wears when he does that, as though it's taking an enormous amount of energy and concentration, and focuses his blue eyes on Ma.

She looks back at him and I notice that her eyes are that same intense blue. Her red hair is fading into gray, but it has the same wave as my own. And Cal's.

Her voice is low. "How could you? We raised you better than this."

You guys raised me better, Ma. This was all on me.

The Jaguar reels into the driveway, as always reserved only for Pop's car. He's on his phone. Ma clucks her tongue. "I just can't imagine what he'll say. I'm afraid you're in for it, laddie."

But when he gets out, Pop barely looks our way. He lowers the phone, shields it with his hand, and says, "I'll see you in the office in a bit, Tim. I've made some calls about your situation with the child."

The shock, incredulity, and devastation show on Ma's face, plainer than the wrinkles and the makeup she hides them behind.

"I guess this is old news to everyone but me, then." She turns and walks into the house, stumbles for a second on the first step, leaves a bunch of Christmas Tree Shops bags in her wake.

I start to go after her—to apologize, hug her, to do some freaking—God, I don't know, whatever—thing. But the door closes behind her with a click. I stand there, look down at Cal.

He gives me the calm face back, then the goofy grin, like he's all full of confidence that I'll figure this out.

And again, I'm looking for direction from an infant.

Bring the bags in one-handed, Cal propped in my other arm.

Inside, Ma's nowhere to be found. No Nan either. I'm about to knock on Pop's door when there's the familiar rhythm of footsteps on the stairs. Ma's face is blotchy, her eyes blue blue against pink, puffy skin, and it near about breaks me. Sure, we Masons cry easily, but I don't get the idea there was anything easy about these tears.

"Well, then," Ma says, all hold-it-together smile and straight back, "now you'll be filling me in on the episodes everyone else has already seen."

Alice's "so we're playing it like this?" hits me. Mason family mode—moving right along, nothing to see here, folks.

From there, the conversation rolls pretty much as you'd expect.

Me: And then, blah-blah-blah.

Ma: Oh my sainted aunt!

Me: So she blah-blah-blah.

Ma: Stars above! This cannot be good for your father's blood pressure!

Me: Then I blah-blah-blah.

Ma: Sweet Mary and all that's holy!

Cal, finally fed up with the swaddling and maybe the exclamations: *Raaaaaaaa!*

Except for this part:

"He looks just exactly like you did," Ma says. "More like your twin than Nan ever was. Goodness!"

"Goodness had nothing to do with it, Ma." Ha-ha. I'm unsnapping the sleeper thing, getting ready for a diaper change.

To my surprise, she smiles, sets a hand lightly on my shoulder. "Let me do that. You're making a mess of it. Just like a man!"

On cue, the man of the house emerges from his gray cave, looks at us, says, "I got in touch with Gretchen Crawley, who runs that Crawley Center for Adoption Services in West Haven."

Cal, freed from his blanket, kicks his feet at me, his eyes shining. I cup my hand around his face, rest my fingers in those red curls.

"Excuse me? What happened to 'I won't fix this for you,' Pop?"

"This is strictly big picture. Not your strong suit."

"Maybe not, but I thought the deal was that you were out of this particular picture. Like Ma was. Apparently."

"Tim," Ma interjects, "you don't need to—"

Without looking at her, Pop holds up a staying hand.

"So what happened to this 'changing nothing about December'?"

"What about December?" Ma asks, looking confused.

In the dark about that too, looks like.

"She'll be happy to meet with this girl to discuss placement."

I focus way harder than I need to on the task of diaper changing, something that's pretty automatic at this point, and I'm acting as if it requires incredible reflexes, split-second timing. Cal snags my fingers as I peel off the tape, yanks them to his mouth, watching me intently.

"And with me, right?"

What he says: "It's not necessary."

What I hear: "You're not necessary."

Why does it piss me off so much to be shoved out of a picture I don't even want to be in?

The meeting I flee to, right after this? It's a topic one—and the topic is "acceptance," which generally makes people either eloquent or pissed as hell. Vince, who lost a leg and an arm in Afghanistan, yells and throws his crutch across the room, "Accept this? Fuck no." This other guy talks about how his wife accepted him, despite all his drinking and cheating, for years, then when he finally got sober, she got lung cancer and died before he could "give her all those good memories to replace the bad ones."

I talk about Ma, and her unexpected acceptance of Cal, and about the Garretts and how acceptance is a given there . . . then a word or two about Pop.

Jake sits next to me at the top of the long steps to St. Jude, after the meeting. Tears a bag of root beer barrels open with his teeth, holds it out to me, saying nothing.

I take one, slide it to the side of my mouth, just sit there, legs splayed, hands hooked together between them.

"Giving up the cigarettes." Jake says. "Again. This time, I hope to hell it's for good. You're a power of example, kid. And that is the last thing I ever thought I'd say to you."

I glance at him, manage a smile, turn my eyes back to my hands.

"Thing is," he continues, "when my partner told his parents he was gay, they called their pediatrician hoping there was an immunization to fix it. My folks, they called him to ask what he wanted for dinner so they'd be sure to have it ready for him."

Jake looks at me sort of meaningfully. Then sighs, smiles. "Sometimes . . . if we're lucky . . . we can find family in unexpected places."

ALICE

"So this is what normal people do for fun, huh?" Tim asks, sticking his head out the passenger window of the Mustang as it jounces over the dirt road.

"Who knows?" Samantha gathers her hair in a messy bun. "It just seemed like the thing to do. It's been all work and no play for most of us lately."

"*Ooooo*," Cal contributes. He's in his seat between Sam and me, wide-awake at eleven o'clock at night, eyes shining, arms waving. I look at him, look at Tim. His dad.

His dad.

Roll that around my head for a little.

I'll get there.

"This on Joel's patrol route?" Tim asks, catching my eye in the rearview mirror.

I grin. He flashes the dimple back.

"I don't think Stony Bay's finest bother with the corn maze at Richardson's Farm," Jase says from the driver's seat. "Let's park here before the underbody gets destroyed."

Actually a bit spooky. Richardson's Farm has a huge amount of acreage right along the salt marshes off the coast of Seashell Island where the marshes run into the bay. Tonight it looks beautiful and desolate, completely abandoned except for us.

"If we don't see the Great Pumpkin, I want my money back," Sam says, clambering out of the backseat, throwing her arms around Jase, who's stretching, fingers laced, looking out at the water.

Automatically, I'm pulling Cal out, holding his wiggling body tightly to my chest, reaching for a blanket. Tim's buckling on the BabyBjörn, muttering "Don't start" in response to Jase's muffled laugh.

Then I'm tucking Cal into the front pack, adjusting his fiercely kicking legs, snapping him in. Tim's pulling Cal's fingers away from my ear, my upper lip, the front of my hoodie, all the things he's determined to grab. We're in sync in a surreal way that I've seen with my parents, anticipating each other, compensating, filling in.

Crazy.

I'm doing this. I'm with a boy who has a baby and I'm right here acting like a mom.

I stumble over a rock concealed in the high grass, whoosh of exhale loud in the still air.

Temporary. This is all temporary.

By this time next year—God, by springtime—Cal will be with another family, Tim's deadline will have come and gone, maybe I'll be in Manhattan.

I don't get the rush of comfort I expect. Instead, my breath snags harder, my lungs too small. My phone chooses that second to buzz and I don't even want to look at it.

Ally, please. I can't give up. I won't. Where are you? Out with that kid? Alice, we're not

"All good?" Tim asks, his hand on my elbow, looking into my face, glancing at my phone.

I nod, shoving the phone into my pocket. All good if I don't need to use any air to talk.

He stops on the path. "Alice."

Sam and Jase are farther down the hard-packed dirt trail, almost to the maze, arms looped around each other's waists.

"What is it?"

I remember this from that seventh-grade year—one thing gets to you and then the others come in like a football pile-on. The good—Tim. The bad—this with Brad. The ugly—Grace Reed. In this moment, they're all stealing my breath.

Stay in the moment, stay in the moment, stick with what's happening.

Deep breath.

"She's really getting back into politics? Grace?" I ask. "They actually called you?"

"I see the romantic atmosphere is getting to you, you softie. Yeah, kiss-ass Brendan did. Not much time to assemble a team—since it's already October and elections are less than six weeks away. Don't worry, I'm not working for her again. Though it would certainly make Pop stand up and cheer if I did. Or at least give a faint smile."

"He'd honestly want you to do that?" Dumb question. I saw Tim's father in action.

"*Baaa,*" from Cal. We've entered the maze now, with its high hay-bale walls closing us in, away from the sweep of field running down to the ocean.

"Shit. Forgot the pacifier thingie." Tim offers Cal his thumb, notes my expression, pulls his hand away. "You betcha Pop'd want that. He doesn't know the reasons Grace pulled out of the race. Hardly anyone does. Your family. Me. Samantha, who was there when it went down. And Grace's boytoy Clay Tucker, who has reasons of his own to keep his lip zipped. There's only one real witness."

And no notarized document. Grace Reed can, once again, get away with it all.

I swear under my breath.

"There's an answer. We'll find it. Grace has plenty of chinks in her armor."

"We?"

"We. You get my political savvy and my sleazy, manipulative mind along with all my other many irresistible charms."

Cal's started bumping his head against Tim's chest, rooting for food, whimpering a little. We make a left turn, then another. The wind is rising, the autumn chill deepening with the night. Another turn and we practically stumble over Jase and Sam, all wrapped up in each other against a prickly wall of straw.

"A roll in the hay is supposed to be a figure of speech, you two," Tim says, bumping his shoulder deliberately into them.

"Move on," Jase says, out of the corner of his mouth, barely taking his lips off Sam's.

Tim reaches for my hand, tight grip. Warm. Down a long corridor, past a few moth-eaten scarecrows pinned against the side, and a bedraggled Jack Sparrow propped against a wooden stake. Two more turns and he backs me into a corner, rests his long fingers on either side of my face. "You asked for a kiss?"

"I didn't ask!"

"You're right. It was more like a demand. You wanted me to lose all self-control."

I hear Samantha's laugh, not far away.

"Not the ideal moment for that, Tim."

"Sometimes you just have to take the one you've got."

We're kissing in a corn maze twenty feet from my younger brother, with a baby wriggling between us.

And I wanted things simple.

TIM

"I think about sex too much," I tell Dominic, who's walking on the beach with me, exercising Sarge, his massive German shepherd. God forbid Dominic not have a dog as macho as he is. I've got Cal in the pussy front pack.

"There's a limit?" Dom picks up a piece of driftwood and tosses it with a neat flick of his wrist. Sarge catches it, shakes it ferociously, and then drops it at Dom's feet in a *killed it, next challenge?* way.

"Every second. Sometimes twice a second." I'm an asshole, because it's not sex I'm thinking about, it's Alice. All of Alice.

"Huh." Dom shoves his hand into the pocket of his jacket, yanks out a tennis ball, and hurls it. "Sounds normal, Tim."

"Freakin' inconvenient. Not to mention scary as hell."

"Wanting sex—or wanting it with Cal's mom?"

"Nope. *God* no. Kinda general. Kinda specific. Just constant," I continue, picking up a flattish rock and winging it into the water. My skipped stones always sink like . . . uh . . . stones. "You know how they say you don't do anything when you're wasted that you wouldn't do sober?"

"Yeah, they say that. Think it's bullshit myself."

"Really?" I'm relieved. "Because my sister keeps telling me this is all some elaborate plot of Hester's. I get paranoid and

I think maybe Nan's right, because when I see Hester, I can't imagine, like, jonesing for her. Ever."

My voice is rising, and Cal squirms, twisting his neck as if to face check and make sure I'm cool.

"This while thinking about sex every second," Dom mutters. "Here. Can I hold him for a sec? It's been . . . a while since I held a kid."

"Sometimes twice a second. Yep."

I unsnap the harness thing and Dom moves his hands around in this awkward way, like he's trying to figure out where to pick up something hot so it won't burn him. Then he finally settles them under Cal's armpits and lifts him up, looking him in the eye. And Goddamnit, he's got tears in his own eyes.

I reach down for a stone, even though this one's not nearly flat enough, rub my thumb against the mica, focus on the little flakes that flicker in the sunlight, not the wetness on Dom's cheeks.

"So damn small. You just forget," he says finally, and wipes his face on the shoulder of his jacket. He clears his throat, once, twice, this hollow, hacking sound, looks out at the water, adjusts Cal's collar, swipes the back of his hand over his eyes again. Finally, "Why scary?" He reaches into his apparently bottomless pocket and places a flat stone in my hand. "It's all in the wrist."

"I dunno. Don't want anyone hurt."

"You want to bag that chance, stick to celibacy."

"Yeah, and just keep beating my dick like it owes me money."

"That's beautiful, man." Dom shakes his head. "So—sex but not specific, huh? That even possible?"

"What about, uh, someone I've known for a while?" I ask, in this fake casual voice.

"Like . . . ?" Dom says.

"No one in particular," I mutter.

He gives me a *yeah right* look, sighs heavily. "Take it easy, Tim. Work on self-control. You're just beginning to think straight."

Here's the thing, though . . .

I am, I *am* thinking straight—about Alice. For, like, the first time, about her, about anyone. But I'm . . .

"Skip the stone, man," Dom says. "That you can control."

"I'm no good at that."

"Do it anyway."

"I feel like the frickin' Karate Kid. Are you trying to give me some, like, lesson in letting go or something?"

"I'm Portugese—we like to keep busy. Wouldn't do you any harm either. So I'm trying to teach you to skip stones. It's a dying art, like whittling."

"No way am I learning to whittle."

"You're always saying you need stuff to do with your hands," he points out. "Aside from the one you're already doing. Unlike that, it's something you can teach your kids."

"He'll be someone else's kid by then."

"I didn't mean only Cal, Tim." He peers at my face. "How you doing with that? Him?" I'm kicking at the sand with one toe, holding the flat granite rock tightly enough that the sharp edge digs into my palm.

"Good. Fine. Whatever. I don't know."

"That's four different answers. Which one's the truth?"

I toss the stone, which sinks immediately.

"Do *you* feel like he's your son? Like he—belongs to you?"

Yes.

God, I do.

Um. Shit.

Blindsided, I bend over, hands on knees. I fuckin' care about this kid. Not just like I'm babysitting him and waiting for his goddamn parents to come home. Like he's home when he's with me. Or fuckin' scarier still, I'm home when I'm with him. And Alice. And that's the thing . . . you let people in . . . they're there. They're a goddamn part of you. Except that at any time—soon, in Cal's case—anytime, in Alice's—they could chip right off and float away.

"Tim?" Dom's voice floats in my head, a little distant. "Tim. Talk."

Okay, okay. That's okay that I do. Care about Cal. Good that I do. Less chance I'll screw up and leave him somewhere by accident. It's a good thing.

Right?

But, God, why bother with this? I had the dad who wasn't there. Now the kid who won't be there. Which makes me another dad who won't.

Dominic reaches over, puts a new stone in my hand, bending his elbow around my neck, giving me a whacking hard pat on the back.

"Is this the part where we hug?" I ask.

"Manly back-patting is plenty. Save the hugs for the kid and Ms. No One in Particular."

Chapter Thirty-six

TIM

Self-control. Alice called me on having it, using it too often, but pretty sure we both know that's not what's going on here.

Whatever it is, I'm so done using it with her.

I'm across the kitchen in two strides, too fast to even see what she's wearing or her expression or anything.

I reach out, very slowly, rub my thumb along Alice's soft deep-pink lower lip. No lipstick or that sticky gloss crap. Just her, just Alice. Her dark lashes lower and she takes a deep breath. My thumb trails to circle under her jawline, tilting it gently up as my head slopes down.

A calmer, more deliberate kiss than we've ever shared. Different from the times before when we locked together fast and hard as if drawn magnetically. This is intentional, like it's saying something. When her lips part, it's a declaration as much as an invitation.

When I inhale, I take in Alice, sunshine, salty-sweet, peppermint. Not losing myself. It's finding her.

Oh, Alice.

She makes her little hum in the back of her throat, curling in. I edge my hands down her back, to the tops of her thighs, pulling her closer, just as she does the reverse, slipping her palms up under my shirt to shove my shoulders down. She was standing in the light from the window. Her skin is sun-warm under my fingertips.

Our kisses are still calm, amazingly, since all of Alice is aligned against all of me. I fall back against the wall, scooping her even closer as my fingers move down her back, slide along the tops of her legs.

I should stop. I'll stop. I'll just take this last minute. And this one. And this next one and . . .

"Wow. *Mommy.* Alice and Tim are kissing in the kitchen."

Alice jerks back from me and both of us whirl to look at George, who's wearing an I MET SANTA ON THE ESSEX STEAM TRAIN shirt and for some reason, pink sweatpants. "You two were kissing," he tells us, in case we might have missed it the first time.

"George . . ." Alice waves her hand in a circle, looking like she's trying frantically to come up with an explanation.

"Kissinnnnnnng," George repeats as Mrs. Garrett comes in with some shopping bags, followed by Jase, Andy, Duff, Harry, and Patsy. What, no camera crew?

"Hi Tim." Mrs. Garrett sets her bags down on the kitchen table. "Are you hungry? We ran out of everything—it was Cheerios or nothing—but we're restocked now."

I look up and meet Jase's eyes. He gives me a quick, rueful smile, and then becomes preoccupied with emptying grocery bags. No chance in hell he didn't hear George.

ALICE

Not surprisingly, Tim does not stick around. He says, "Thanks, Mrs. G. Gotta head out, I have a—thing. Catch you later, Jase. And, um, you too Alice." And leaves.

"Why were you kissing Tim, Alice?" Beating around the bush is not in George's bag of tricks. He pulls on the hem of my shirt. "The longest kiss was fifty-eight hours. Do you think they did that without drinking water? Wouldn't they die, Alice? How'd they pee?"

"I'm sure they . . . I don't—I was just, um . . . Here, Mom, let me help you put those away."

Mom, because she's tactful or because she's trying to torture me, says nothing as we put things in cabinets. Jase, who usually helps, who *was* helping, has faded away. The others always vanish at chore time, so it's just me, Mom, George, and Patsy in the kitchen.

Patsy attaches herself to my leg like a limpet. "Where Hon?" she cries mournfully. "Why Hon go? I love on Hon."

I sneak a look at my mother, afraid she's going to ask exactly how much loving on Hon I've been doing, but she seems preoccupied with putting away the frozen food, jamming the extra-large Sam's Club containers into our crowded freezer.

I'm humming under my breath when Mom puts a hand on my arm, nods her head at the cabinet under the sink where I've just placed a container of ice cream, a jumbo package of pork chops, two cartons of eggs, and a can of shaving cream next to the dish soap and the glass cleaner.

"Um . . ."

In the end she must take pity on me, and tells me to go upstairs. I am a coward and do it, leaving her to unpack the last forty-five grocery bags alone, or with the dubious help of George, who just takes something out, says, "Oh good, we have Oreos," and opens up the package. And of Patsy, still mourning the disappearance of Tim. "Want my Hon . . ."

Oh Pats. Me too.

• ○ • ○

I'm sitting on my bed a few minutes later, trying to resist the urge to march over to Tim's, when the door opens and Jase comes in with his corn snake entwined around his forearm.

"You've brought Voldemort to attack me?" I ask. Jase has always loved animals. His bedroom is like Petco.

"Nah. He escaped and made a break for Mom's shoe rack again." He sits down on the edge of Andy's bed, incongruously masculine against her lavender-and-purple tie-dyed bedspread. I've had years to get used to the fact that my little brother is a hottie, but his looks still startle me sometimes. Jase takes a breath, puffs it out, resting back on his elbows, letting Voldemort the corn snake sashay slowly across his chest, kicks the rug with his shoe.

"Just say it."

He glides a finger along the length of Voldemort. "This is your business, Alice. Just . . ."

We Garretts are all about two or three years apart in age, and you'd think that we'd be equally close—but in real life, it doesn't work that way. Not all the time. Things shift. But Jase and I have been tight ever since Dad drove Joel and me to the hospital to pick up Mom and the newborn Jase for the first time. In an attempt to stave off jealousy, as the story goes, she put him in my arms and said, "Here's your baby."

I believed her.

I called him "my baby Jase" for the first three years of his life. I used to crawl into his crib and hold his hand at night, sure he'd sleep better, be safer if I were there.

Maybe he even *was*. Because that closeness never has left.

330

His green eyes meet mine, then shift downward. "Don't do your thing with him, Alice."

"My *thing?*"

Jase has never warned me off a guy. I've done it to him (with girls, obviously)—once when I heard rumors about his ex-girlfriend Lindy and again when he and Samantha were briefly broken up last summer. I caught him by the sleeve as he was headed out to try to talk to her, get her back, told him to give it up, have some pride. As it turned out, I was wrong to do that, and they got back together.

So he has every right to advise me . . .

I warned Jase off Samantha because he was in too deep with her almost before they'd even spoken. I'd seen Jase catch sight of her walking up her driveway or looking out of her window and lose track of what he was saying. I wanted no part of that.

But this . . . is nothing like that. Not the same at all.

I fold my arms over my stomach, hunch forward against the inevitable real.

It's just like that. I'm just different now.

"Your thing," he says. "Your date 'em, dominate 'em, ditch 'em thing. Tim . . ." Voldemort slithers off his lap and starts to glide down Andy's bedspread in search of our closet, our shoes. Jase scoops the snake back around his wrist. He chews his lower lip, sighs.

"Tim what?"

"He's got enough going on. He doesn't need anything else messing with his head right now."

"Shouldn't you be off punching him because he's dishonored me?"

"You're completely capable of doing that on your own. If it were any other guy, I'd leave you to it—" A shadow crosses Jase's downturned face. He looks up at me. "What's up with Brad anyway? I saw you two running last week."

"He's out. For keeps."

"He knows that for sure?" Jase asks carefully, looping Voldemort around his neck and catching him as he slithers down the front of his shirt.

"I'm not stringing anyone along, Jase. Or playing games. I've been up-front with him. He's not happy, but he's gone."

"Let me know if that changes." He stands up, wrapping the snake around his upper arm this time. "Or you need backup."

"J.?"

He pauses in the doorway.

"It's not my 'thing.' With Tim. Not anything I know. I don't *know* what I'm doing. But I'm not out to hurt him."

He nudges the corner of my rug up, then back down with the toe of his shoe. "Alice . . ."

"What?"

"Do better than that." He heads out of the room before I can answer or argue or defend. Or tell the truth.

Chapter Thirty-seven

ALICE

"I just happened to be . . ."

"In the neighborhood?" Tim shoves the door open wider. He props one arm against the doorframe, shoves his hair out of his eyes, his smile shifting from sweet to wicked as he looks down at me. "You decided not to sneak in while I was out, play Goldilocks again?"

"That turned dangerous last time. I'm being civilized."

"Damn. Back to professionalism and rule-making. I thought we busted through that."

"You mean when we got busted? Jase told me to stay away. Not to do my 'date 'em, dominate 'em, ditch 'em thing.'"

"Yeah, I got a dose of that too. But here you are."

"Here I am. Come with me. Outside," I say.

He trails me down the steps, across our dew-wet grass to the purple-dark backyard, no questions asked, although they're radiating off him. I lead him back behind the pool fence, near the playhouse Dad started to build this summer, which still smells like fresh-cut pine.

"We're camping out?" Tim surveys the saggy army-green canvas tent, flap open, electric lantern set on low, floor heaped with blankets, pillows, sleeping bags.

I shrug. "We don't have to . . . Duff was having a sleepover, but they got freaked out. They're asleep now. Everyone is. I thought . . ."

"Are we telling scary stories? Playing Truth or Dare?"

"This is as far as I got with the plan."

"Works for me." He drops to his hands and knees, ducks his way through the flaps, halts a moment, possibly sighting the box of condoms over on the side of the tent, on top of a stack of Duff's LEGO Mindstorm books. Then he keeps moving, readjusts two pillows so they're lined up close to each other, smooths out the dark green nylon sleeping bags, turns over onto his back, and folds his arms behind his head.

Ruffled dark red hair, watchful eyes, at last a slow smile, vivid in the muted light.

He moves one hand down now, carefully, until it lies, palm up, flat on the blanket. Silent appeal. Eyes locked on mine.

"Do I have to dare you?" he asks quietly.

His hand, resting there. For a moment I stare at it, my stomach giving a small, jolting flip. Calluses. A little cut on the pad of the thumb. No Band-Aid, of course.

Something so Tim about that hand.

"No," I say. "This is more truth than dare."

I stretch out by his side, slide my own hand into his; tighten my fingers on the fast-beating pulse in his wrist, know it picks up pace, although his face stays the same—thoughtful, focused, only the widening of his eyes showing any effect. My whole body is both loosening and tightening at the same time.

"Can I ask you something?" I rush on before he can say yes or no. "All the flirting you've done? Now when I'm—here—it's different. It's like you're holding back. What is that? It's not—about the chase, is it?"

His thumb swipes across my hand, bump-traces each knuckle. Then he slowly pulls it to his lips, kisses the back. Rests his mouth there for the space of one breath. Two.

Then he meets my eyes.

"*Hell* no. No. I guess . . . I . . . wanted . . . you to come to me. Be sure we're in this . . . uh . . . together?" His voice cracks a little on the last word, flush high on his cheekbones. "Besides, um . . ."

TIM

Say it.

"Ah, I've never . . ." My voice is hoarse again. Alice's eyes, fixed on me, pupils wide and dark in the pale light from the lantern. Circle of green, glints of gold. Steady.

Say it.

"I've never had sex sober. Never. I—might actually suck at it."

Her crooked smile dazzles me, then she looks away, face revealing nothing now, not soft and open the way it was only a minute ago.

"Not that that's necessarily what's happening here," I add quickly. "Just—you know—fair warning—"

She's staring down at our hands wrapped up together. When she speaks, it's like she's addressing them. "I've always had to be in control. I've never—"

She flings the words out quickly, like she's being defiant. But there's her face and I can read it well enough now.

Not defiance. Bravado. She's scared.

Yeah, me too.

ALICE

I repeat, "I've never . . ." Never told anyone this. Not my best friends. Not my mother. Not the diary I don't keep.

"Not even, um, on your own?"

"Not even."

He looks a little staggered. Why did I let him know? Just more pressure. But Tim doesn't seem freaked out. Only surprised and a little sad.

I stumble to reassure him, piling on more hard-to-speak truth. "You've already made me feel things I didn't think I could feel. So, if we—when we—"

"We don't have to—" he says immediately.

"I know. I'm not saying anything has to be right here right now. Just that there are, um, things I haven't done. So, I might not be able to. It's not a big deal, so don't—"

"Truth, Alice?"

"Um—" That was about all the truth in me. What more?

"You won't fake it. Promise me."

This boy. Eyes on my face again, little smile lurking, just barely parenthesizing the corners of his lips. He lifts his eyebrows, waiting. And willing to. However long. At the sight of it, there's an ache in my chest, a flash of near pain, knife-swift, something letting go, slipping free.

"I do promise." The words come out in a whisper.

His fingers find me now, move to cover my heart, as though he knows.

I swallow.

"Also? If you have any, uh, suggestions for improvement along the way, you'll—"

"God, Tim. Is there nothing you won't say?"

"One or two things."

Now he's grinning again, the smile that goes all the way to his eyes, his entire face glowing. I shrug off my sweater. He flips onto his side, pulls me near.

Then he strokes up and down my arm, and as warm as his palm is, goose bumps scatter behind it.

Hand behind my knee now, pressing, the heel of his hand suddenly urgent, although his voice is lazy, almost drowsy, sharp contrast to the intensity of his eyes. "One more promise, Alice."

"Are you always this chatty?" My own voice, octaves higher than usual, gives me away.

"*Chatty?*" He starts to laugh.

I wince, look down. His hand is beneath my chin, lifting my eyes back to his face. "Sorry," he says. "Fair warning again. I'm gonna move your leg, like this, up over my hip. Promise not to kick me."

"Are you going to narrate this whole thing?"

"*Shh.*" A kiss, pressed against the corner of my mouth, the next word only a breath of air. "No."

Now my leg is looped over his hip, the side of my knee pressed against his waist. He's barely touching me—his hand hovering just above my skin—so close—the almost-graze of his fingers, along my thigh, down over my calf, to my heel, the arch of my foot. There he does touch, thumb pushing hard, then lighter, then outlining the whole shape of my foot, back up my leg, the lightest possible skim. His head bent to my shoulder now, not quite on it, but close enough to feel the uneven rise and fall of his breath, the rapid pounding of his heart.

"I'm gonna need to get that box over there. Soon. But not yet, because I have to—"

"You *are* going to narrate this, aren't you?"

"Not narrating. Appreciating. You have to give me time to let this—you—sink in." He pulls gently at my tank top, shifting it up over my stomach, peeling the straps down. His rough knuckles brush my skin and I inhale sharply. He does too. Then he sets his hand flat on my stomach, eyes serious, face wearing a look of concentration and determination.

He looks at me so long that I squirm, and he presses lightly on my stomach. "Let me look. You're amazing, Alice." His thumb touches my belly ring.

His lashes lift and he studies my face again. "What's wrong?"

"I'm . . . I . . . I need to know what you're thinking." My own thoughts are scattered—firing off rapidly all over the place. The look in his eyes, the feel of him solid against me, the scrape of his voice, husky.

"I didn't think I'd be here. Have this . . . you. How did this actually happen? And . . . and . . . how beautiful you are. Mostly the last one."

I prop myself up on one elbow, yanking at my tank, which snags on my earring.

"Yow!" I clap a hand to my ear.

Suddenly exuberant, moving fast, he detangles the snag, tosses my top somewhere, kisses my ear, which tickles. I'm exposed, open to the cool air, to him, and he's still dressed. I start giggling, part nerves, part excitement, part a jumble of things I have no experience with and no name for.

Reaching forward, I catch my finger in the waistband of his jeans, the back of my hand skimming the skin just above.

I put my other hand on his shoulder to steady myself.

We're both shaking.

"Lights out? I vote no." Another dip of his thumb into my belly button, then a teasing nudge, before he gets to his feet.

"Yes. Please."

"As you wish, then. Stay there."

Tim snaps the light off, but not before swearing, evidence he burned his thumb on the heated metal. Then rustling sounds of him closing the tent flap, then hunting around for the box of condoms. I sweep my hand out, locate them before he does, wing them at him. "Suit up."

He chokes and starts laughing. "Suit up? Wha-at? So this is a professional sporting event?"

Now I'm too impatient even to be embarrassed. I laugh too.

"Forget I said that—just—hurry, okay?"

"Jesus, you're bossy. Hang on."

Sound of a zipper, Tim kicking away his jeans, more rustling.

"All right, I'm coming back. No ninja moves now either."

"Hurry," I say again as he falls down beside me, laughing so hard, I start laughing again too. Lips on my bare shoulder, then finding one breast, hand cupped beneath, bringing me closer— but only for an instant.

I hear myself make a sound in the back of my throat, unmistakable frustration.

"Hurry, huh? What's your rush?"

"We want what we want when I want it," I whisper.

"Ah, so you want something, Alice? A glass of water, maybe?"

His index finger glides down from my chin, down the center line of my body.

"Grape-Nuts?" His breath stirs the hair curled around my ear. His mouth shifts down again.

I jerk against him, feeling too fast too good.

"What is it you need? Ask me."

"Being—able to—breathe—would be good."

"Overrated." His mouth travels back to mine. "Close your eyes. Just feel, okay?"

Twenty minutes, hours, weeks later, I drop my head to the pillow. "Wow."

"I'll say." Tim touches his nose to mine. "The real thing, Alice? Don't lie. I know anyway." He sounds slightly triumphant, but that's okay.

"I . . ." I take a deep breath, then can't do more than exhale, overwhelmed. "That was . . ."

The real thing.

Wow.

TIM

Alice falls silent, and I am too. The hair at her temples, damp, sticks to her hot cheeks. Totally light-headed even though she was the one who . . . I'm almost afraid to exhale, shatter the spell, afraid even now that she'll stand up and walk away and I'll . . . I don't know what I'd do.

What she does is laugh, almost without making a sound,

because she's totally winded. Her bare stomach shakes against mine—and for a bad second I'm afraid she's crying, which would suck. But no, laughing. She lifts one long graceful arm, drapes it, boneless, over my waist. When she moves, it's only to get closer.

I try to shift my hips away, give her room, time to recover, but my body is having none of that shit.

Neither is Alice.

Thank God.

ALICE

I'm pressing on both his shoulders, one knee against his thigh so he'll move onto his back and then Tim's grinning up at me, just as I realize my cheeks are hurting because I'm smiling so much, so hard.

"Tim?" My fingers trail over his chest, then the muscles of his legs, the developing lines of his abs, moving back to cup his jaw and kiss him speechless again.

"*Mmmf.*"

"Want to cross off another 'I've never'?"

His hands are frozen in the air by my sides, hovering as though he can't decide what to do next. "Yeah. This one." An arm goes up to cover his eyes. Under my hands, tension ratchets up in his muscles. "I lo—"

"—ve you."

"Alice! You didn't let me finish saying it. And that was my first time."

"Mine too. Sorry. You needed to know. Or I had to tell you. Tim, I—"

"Love you," he says. "Let me say it. Geez."

"Okay. If you—insist."

"I absolutely do. This is me, insisting."

He flips us and braces himself over me, on his elbows.

"I love you, Alice."

"Prove it."

"If you insist."

TIM

Making love. I've cringed every time Hester used those words. So off and awkward and unrelated to what actually goes on between two bodies. You make breakfast, you make time, you make the team. Love? Not so much. But I get it now. Like making fire. Not rubbing two sticks together to pull something out of thin air. More like finally being able, knowing enough, to warm your hands at something you built, stick by stick.

Chapter Thirty-eight

ALICE

I'm whistling in the kitchen as I pour cereal for my brothers and Duff's herd of nerds, Ricky McArthur, Jacob Cohen, Max Oliviera—the leftovers from last night's sleepover.

Harry's grouchy because they kept him awake most of the night. I was awake most of the night too, but I am definitely not grouchy. Joel, who came in bearing a huge box of donuts, a police cliché, smirks at me.

"What?"

"I dunno, Al. There are practically bluebirds and fluffy chicks fluttering around your head. Just enjoying the view."

"Chicks don't fly. Not even chickens fly," George says through a mouthful of Gorilla Munch. "You're silly, Joel."

"I'm serious. It's nice to see you so cheery. You look much less feral."

"Shut up, Joel." But I say it mildly, pouring myself coffee, and managing to ignore a barrage of fart jokes from Duff and company, Patsy's outraged screech because Harry's grabbed her sippy cup and is holding it just out of her reach, and George's lengthy explanation of the difference between feral and just plain wild.

"Rainbows, unicorns, kittens," Joel continues, chuckling even more. "Awww, Al."

TIM

I'm with Hester at Breakfast Ahoy. The far table on the left is full of swim team guys from Hodges, who I only dimly recognize. They're all carbo-loading like maniacs, shoving one another, laying stupid bets, arguing about who picks up the tab, dissing each other's form and time and attitude at the last meet, hitting on the waitress, doing stupid shit. My team from four years ago—I'd have been right there with them. Now they're like some tribe I'm observing from far, far away.

From everything, really. Any thoughts I have are back in the tent with Alice, breathing her in, watching her face. We never looked away from each other unless we had to close our eyes for a little.

"Uh . . . What?"

No idea how long Hester's been talking.

". . . why I didn't bring Cal along. Figured it would be easier to focus. Geez, Tim." Snap of fingers in my face. God, that's annoying. "You're not high, are you?"

"Nope. Focus on what?"

Hester scrabbles around in this tie-dyed backpack she brought, pulls out a sheaf of papers, shoves them toward me. "This is the consent form for termination of your paternal rights—it's called relinquishment. All you have to do is sign right here." She taps the line with an X, then drops the pen on the paper in front of me.

The pen's dark brown, glossy, with copper trim and copper lettering stamped on it. I don't need to look any closer to know how it reads: WINSLOW S. MASON, BRANCH MANAGER, STONY BAY BUILDING AND LOAN, STONY BAY, CT.

"You met with my pop." No emotion in my voice at all. None in me anywhere, really. Guess I should be surprised, but I'm not. Big picture. "When?"

"Two days ago," she says without hesitation. "He came by in the evening and talked to me and Waldo. I figured you'd told him to come, take over, move things along faster."

My coma-calm recedes. "Did he order you around, Hes? Intimidate you?"

"No! He was friendly, really sure what to do." She gives a little laugh. "Not like you and me, without a single firm opinion between us. Besides, you know Grand—his advice is a little murky. Everything sounds like a Japanese koan." She smiles up at me and I find myself looking back, not sure what to do with my face. Pop, fuck, whatever. He does what he does. This is almost over. That's what counts, right?

"This is all I have to do?" I click the pen, flip over the paper, and scribble a few circles to get the ink flowing.

"Yes. He had it all drawn up. All you need to do is sign it, then your father gets it presented to a judge, and once we find adoptive parents, we submit more paperwork and they approve it all as a 'good cause' termination. But you need to go first, because you aren't on the birth certificate and it has to be obvious to the court that you're surrendering all rights permanently."

I've flipped the papers over. A waitress blows through the swinging door from the kitchen and it flaps a little, making a crackling noise like something going up in flames.

Click the pen closed. Open again. Closed. Scratch my neck.

Relinquishing.

Surrendering.

All of this over, all of it.

All of it?

My head hurts like a mother, and suddenly I'm spent. Exhausted.

The nights of no sleeping, the diapers of doom, the freak-out moments when I'm afraid he's stopped breathing or that the car on the side street will keep going and T-bone mine directly into the baby's side. Having to take the kid with me everywhere like a squirmy twelve-pound ball and chain.

The sweaty fingers clutching my shirt. The cries I can't interpret.

Even the ones I can, when he stops in the middle of wailing and just stares at me—like he's saying, *That's right, here's what I was looking for.* The way that one smile made him look like a completely different kid. Not just a baby. Like mine.

Once again, don't tune in to Hester till she's halfway through whatever she's saying.

". . . your father's going to come by my house to pick it up so he can be sure to file it first thing in the morning. After that's official, your job is basically done."

"So this is my resignation notice? Or am I being fired?"

She laughs. "I never thought you'd show up for it the way you have. You've been . . . great. We do this, and then we have some interviews with prospective parents, choose, and get back to normal life. Chapter closed." She flips her dark hair back from her face.

We aren't ordering Chinese takeout here. "We don't agree on anything, Hester. How are we going to pick his new parents together?"

Hester sighs. "In this case, we both have the same goal. And Waldo and your father will be there to mediate. Along with the adoption counselor, I guess. But your signing off is just a technicality, your father said. If the birth father does nothing, he automatically loses all rights when the adoption goes through. So you don't even have to be involved, if you don't want to."

This again. "I wish everyone would stop acting like my being 'involved' was some sort of choice. I mean, I—he's—I . . ." I push back my chair. "I need some air." Bump into the doorjamb, like I'm loaded, head out on the Breakfast Ahoy deck. The air's so thick with bacon grease and maple syrup that you could put it on a plate. There are seagulls diving and plunging around the Dumpster and the faint breeze from the river is sending up nothing but sludgy air. Brace my hands on the rail, but it's still like I'm falling.

Get it over with.

All of it.

Slide back into my seat. Hester's texting.

"Do you have any pictures of Cal on there?" I ask abruptly.

Her eyebrows lift. "No," she says carefully. "Do you have any on your phone?"

Nope, as a matter of fact. But I'm not much for taking pictures. Still, there's some point I'm making here, and I'm too slurry-headed to figure out exactly what it is. It has something to do with Cal's impersonal sleeping arrangement at Hester's house, something to do with the scratchy sock monkey with the chokeable beady eyes she gave him, something to do with how she scrubs up with antibacterial gel before she takes him from me and after she hands him back, like she's going to operate immediately. Like I have cooties. Or Cal does. Something about this new thing he does where he opens and closes his hands when I come close, like he just can't wait to grab on to me. How he yells "Bah!" when no one has paid attention to him for a while. Something to do with "chapter closed," like he's some old textbook from sophomore year that I never have to look at again.

But I can't figure out what shape that kaleidoscope is supposed to click into.

Hester looks down at my hands. "What are you doing?"

I've taken the pen apart without even knowing I was doing it, and it's on the table in front of me—the push button, the clip, the thrust tube, the ink cartridge, the spring, the ballpoint itself, all scattered in separate pieces like I've dissected the thing for science class.

"*Now* how are you going to sign this?" She's half laughing, but exasperated, rooting in the diaper bag again.

"I'm not."

"Here's one." She waves another bank pen triumphantly. Then her hand freezes. "What?"

"Look . . . look, can't we do the open thing, adoption-wise? The one where the parents send you updates and pictures and shit? I mean, why not, that way we can just, you know, check up on him, whatever. Make sure it all works out?"

"No. I don't want that. Let's just let him go. Completely."

"No," I say.

What?

"What?"

"No." A little voice in my head is screaming at me to shut

up, waving me away from my next words like they're a pileup on Route 95. "I'm not doing it. I—"

Nearly every time words I can't stop have changed my life, it's been because I was being an immature, insufferable ass. Not this time. "He's mine, Hester. I'm not letting him go."

"You can't be serious."

"I can be." I swallow. "I am."

Do I mean that?

Yes.

I bend over the table, holding on to the edge, breathing like I've been sucker-punched. Like Alice.

Jesus, Alice. What's she going to think if I—

"Tim?" Hester's voice floats in my head, distant. "What's going on?"

Okay, deep breaths. In. Out.

If I take Cal, if I have Cal, that's it for being seventeen. I will have to man up, be there, put myself second, take care of business, day care and school and, hell, I don't even know . . . for years and years and years. Till I'm, like, old. Thirty-six or more. God.

"Tim. *Think*. That's crazy. You're in no position to take on a baby. You're living above a *garage*."

Of all the reasons why I'm in no position to deal with a baby, this has gotta be one of the less important.

"Your point?" I snap, lungs suddenly functional. "You're the one who's always calling me to come get him, or take him for the night because you just can't deal."

"And I admit it. I don't want this. Him. Besides, sounds like you kind of resent me for all this responsibility," Hester bites out, "so I wonder why you'd want more of it."

She waves her hands. Our waitress mistakes this for a signal to pour more coffee. Hester waits until the cup is full and the waitress has retreated.

"You can't be serious about this. Calvin isn't even four months old! How are *you* going to take care of an infant? You're a high school dropout."

"I did *not* drop out. I got kicked out." Like it's so much better. "I don't know *how* I'll take care of him. I guess the same way I've been trying to since you showed up on my doorstep."

The waitress returns and sets down Hester's wheat toast and my scrambled eggs and home fries. Hester continues to stare incredulously at me before finally continuing. "You're crazy, Tim. Selfish. Cal could go to a family, a real family, with—parents who love each other and . . . and things . . . and security and good schools and . . . everything that matters. And you think he'd be better off with his seventeen-year-old dad who lives above a garage."

"Will you quit it with the frickin' garage? Don't try to make it out like I'm some blue-collar townie boy who got you pregnant, as if that even matters. But we were *both* at prep school when we did the deed, don't forget."

She glares. "*I* haven't forgotten a thing. What I'm saying is that Cal shouldn't suffer because he was a stupid mistake. I have plans."

"*You* planned every bit of this. I didn't plan a thing."

"Exactly," she says, pointing her butter knife at me. "Which doesn't give me much confidence in your ability to be a father. Not to mention the whole 'you're an alcoholic' thing."

"Recovering. Recovering alcoholic, Hester. And I *already am* a father."

I have, for once, no appetite, and watching Hester butter her toast pisses me off. She puts butter on one corner, takes a bite, puts it on another spot, takes another bite. Who eats like that? It's like she can't commit to an entire piece of toast. The waitress, who evidently finds angry, recovering alcoholic teenage fathers of illegitimate babies who live above garages a turn-on, squeezes my shoulder as she refills my coffee cup.

Hester sighs and says in an elaborately patient tone, "I don't want to be fighting with you. If what it takes for you to realize you're wrong is a little time, take the papers home. Look them over. We can talk about it rationally next time."

"I won't change my mind," I tell her.

She stands up and shoves the sheaf of papers over the table at me. "Then you've lost your mind. I'll see you Tuesday. I'll call you about where to pick up Cal." She reaches into the diaper bag and pulls out a crisp fifty. "Here, this should cover the meal."

"Keep it," I snap. Again with the fifty-dollar bill. What did Pop do, tip her?

"No. You keep it. You can put it toward Cal's college fund. Maybe he'll end up going, even though you never will." She tosses the bill on the table, turns, and marches away, her ponytail swinging behind her.

ALICE

"For keeps? I mean . . . from now on? Forever?"

Tim, hands jammed in pockets, is looking out at the ocean,

not at me. He's barely met my eyes since he caught me as I was stretching after this morning's run, and said, "We have to talk."

Alarm buzzer, sirens, whistles. That's my line. The warm-up to "this isn't working." But our *this* only just started. And it's working for me, more than working. I'm Brad now, blindsided in the driveway?

"Not here," he added as Patsy pressed her nose against the screen door, calling "Hon" imperiously.

Tim insisted we go to the beach. Then said we should walk out to the lighthouse. Went on ahead of me so I had to scramble over the jagged rocks to catch up with his rapid strides. When he finally turned to face me, his shoulders were hunched, his face closed-off, as though expecting anger or criticism. Then he told me what happened with Hester. What he wanted with Cal.

His voice shook, he stumbled a little when he started off, but got calmer and calmer, quietly resolved, as he kept going.

"It's the only thing that makes sense. He needs me. I need to do this. I mean, I did this. And I can't—just—act as if I didn't and move on. Here's my chance to fix things, to get something right."

"For you or for Cal?"

Tim's eyes are practically blazing with determination. "See, that's the thing, there's no separating us. I'm what he has. He's what I have."

The craggy rock we're standing on, still wet from the last high tide, with a few globs of sea lettuce snagged on outcroppings, is not made for pacing around. I do it anyway, trying to jam this new fact into the picture I had of my life now.

My . . . boyfriend. My . . . Tim—not just a dad as a footnote in his life, a season. For keeps. Cal's father, for good, with all that means. No hand-offs to Hester. The crib a permanent fixture in the bedroom—until Cal's old enough for a big-boy bed. Tim needing to find daycare if he graduates from high school and goes to college. (Will he? How can he?) If he gets another job. Needing babysitters if we want to go out together at night. Responsible for immunizations and introducing Cal to solid food and potty-training and all the steps I know so well, all the duties and chores and worries and things I thought were only part of my life for a little while longer—and simply because I was subbing for someone else.

Tim, a father by his eighteenth birthday.

Me.

And baby makes three. Ha.

I sit down abruptly on the rock, barely feeling the seawater seep slowly through the seat of my jeans.

He slides down near me, but not too close, his legs dangling over the edge, tracing the seam of his jeans.

"I know what you're thinking," he says, addressing his knee.

"I doubt that." Since I myself have no idea.

"I knew it as I was saying it—to Hester. It's too much. The last thing you need. Now what you signed on for—which was, of course, my striking good looks and massive amounts of testosterone, not the byproduct of those things. I get it. But, Alice—what else can I do?"

He's trying for a light tone, but it falls flat, and his eyes are shadowed.

I fold my legs up to my chest, wrap my arms around them, rest my chin there. Look at him.

The straight nose with a few freckles, his hair, slightly too long again, the dark eyelashes, downcast, the tall, rangy body . . . already older-looking than he was a month or two ago.

"I won't hold it against you—walking away. I hope we can stay—"

"Don't you dare give me the 'friends' speech, Tim Mason."

"We're not even that? Shit, Alice. Okay. Okay. I get it."

"You can't get it. Because I haven't gotten it yet. You have to give me a little sink-in time."

His eyes, startled, move to mine.

"Another new ballgame. It's a lot. Give me time to get used to this." Another wave, another changed landscape.

"I'll give you anything it takes," he says. "All I've got."

"I know," I say somberly. Give his shoulder a small shove. "You had to do it, didn't you? Get all responsible on me."

"No one has ever said, least of all me, that my timing doesn't completely suck."

It's after eleven: everyone's asleep. Except me and George. He had a nightmare about clowns, and I've been going around and around in circles about bills and banks and Grace Reed. So we're huddled under Great Aunt Alice's big crocheted bedspread in the living room, and I'm reading George my favorite fairy tale, The Snow Queen. Gerda, the best fairy tale heroine. No sitting around waiting to try on slippers—nope, off to the coldest place on earth to rescue the hero.

Georgie likes Gerda too, that she and Kai, the hero, live next door to one another. "Like Jase and Sam did." He cozies closer just as there's a muffled knock at the door and a rattle of the door-knob. It's got to be Tim—who else would show up at this hour?

But it's Samantha, bundled into a rumpled letter jacket I recognize as Jase's, her hair all windblown.

George throws his arms around her knees, tells her he loves her, and asks what she thinks of clowns. She doesn't even seem to hear him. She's red-faced and I can't tell if that's the cold or the wind until I look into her eyes, which are almost glimmering. Not with tears, though.

Anger.

George tugs on the bottom of her jacket. "Sailor Supergirl, Jase is sleeping. I checked on him because I had a bad dream but he wouldn't wake up. His mouth was a little open, but don't worry 'cause that thing that people tell you about how you swallow spiders when you sleep? That's made up. Like no bubblegum trees growing in your stomach if you swallow gum."

"George—that's good about the spiders. But I need to speak to Alice." She smiles at him but is talking so rapidly, her words run together as if she's out of breath. Her eyes focus on me.

My little brother agrees to go back to bed if I pinkie swear that he can watch two episodes of "Animal Odd Couples" tomorrow. And if I promise there will be no clowns involved. He backs upstairs slowly, adding new demands: "And ice cream after breakfast? No, *for* breakfast. Promise?"

The moment his footsteps fade away, Sam says, "My mom. I found out she's been filling out my college applications *herself*. All to colleges far, far away, of course."

Seems to me this newsflash could wait till morning, even though it just adds to the Ten Things I Hate About Grace Reed list.

"But that's not even it. It's another thing—she told me that you'd come over to talk about the bills, Alice. I checked with Tim and he said it was true, that she stonewalled, and I'm done letting that happen. It's not okay. I know what happened with your dad. I saw it. Well, I was asleep but I knew something was wrong—and I didn't—well, I came to say that I'll . . . go to the police or whatever. Whatever it takes."

Before she's halfway through this speech, I'm pacing around the kitchen table, putting my hands in my hair and pulling, picking up an abandoned paper towel and shredding it.

Sam watches me, suddenly amused. "You want a cigarette? You look exactly like Tim."

"Ha," I say.

"He says that one too."

"Sam, are you really willing to do that? This? The police, everything?"

"Yes," she says—no hesitation. "I've been thinking about it for weeks. Since the accident. It's . . . I can't stop thinking about it, Alice. And now this." She closes her eyes, takes a deep breath. "But Tim said that you guys should talk with her first. Because if . . . if things go bad, if there's a trial, big-time lawyer bills"—Sam winces, shakes her head—"your family bills will be put on the backburner. Maybe forever."

"Damn, he's good," I say.

Sam laughs, looking much more like herself. "He'd be the first to tell you that."

"Yeah, but the last to believe it," I say.

She tilts her head, serious again. "You get him, Alice. I'm glad."

• ◦ • ◦

Like Tim with Cal, I see no other way. There is no other way. But instead of doing something out of a warm and open heart, I'm doing this because I am the only one cold enough. And it has to be just me—he's got Cal and Hester to handle.

When she opens the door, I brush past her, down the white hallway. I don't take off my shoes.

This time she doesn't offer a refreshing drink, small talk.

Nothing but her gaze, level on mine, moving to the stack of bills I set, yet again, on the glass-topped table. "These are copies. There are more than there were last time."

"I see that."

"I've seen this." I take the *Stony Bay Bugle* clipping off the top of the stack and hold it out to her. "'Former State Senator Stirs Speculation About a Return to the Stage.'"

"Yes. I've been approached for that state treasurer position. I make a difference in politics, Alison. I help people. I don't believe it's right to turn my back on that." She walks over to the tall arched window that looks out on her green lawn, still emerald even though we're well into fall. Not a fallen leaf on it.

"I'm not asking you to understand. You're still very young. It takes more perspective than you have to see that the greater good—"

"Senator, I'm not here for a debate. Here are the bills. You want to be treasurer? This is the perfect place to start. I talked to Samantha. It turns out your daughter would feel worse about Jase's father not getting the care he needs than about her needing to change schools. So, she's fine with going to SBH."

Grace looks at me sharply. "Where my daughter goes to school is hardly your decision to make."

"I know. The decision is hers. So is the one to go to the police as a witness to the accident you were involved in that landed my dad in the hospital. She's fine with doing that too."

Grace Reed is already pale as the Snow Queen. You'd think she couldn't get any more parchment-white. But she manages.

"You had absolutely no right to get involved in this."

"I didn't?" I laugh. "You *stopped paying the bills.* If it wasn't me, it would be Jase himself. We're all involved. My whole family is. So I need your word, and, actually, more than that. I need your signature on a piece of paper that says you will pay these bills, and any more that come, as long as they come. If not, Samantha will be changing schools. It'll give her a lot more time with my brother."

The last was an impulse. I really am made of ice.

I have a check in my pocket, folded along with the paper with her signature, when she walks me to the door. As I turn to leave, she rests a hand on my shoulder, very briefly. To my horror, there is almost a look of admiration on her face.

"You'd make a good politician, Alison." She smiles at me, all charm. "You remind me of myself."

God forbid.

Chapter Thirty-nine

Waldo Connolly opens the door wearing a dress.

Not sure I can handle this.

On closer examination, it's like a really long shirt—goes past his knees, and is loose, with little mirrors around the neckline. Not a dress, but still.

"C'mon in. Hester should be back soon." He turns, shirt flapping behind him, exposing hairy-as-hell legs. If he weren't relatively tall, I'd think he really was a hobbit. I follow, lugging the car seat and Cal. Starting to feel like my left arm is longer than my right from carrying this thing.

Get used to it.

Alice isn't the only one who still needs sink-in time.

Pop will totally stroke out about this.

Nano is definitely getting my college fund.

I set the car seat down and flop into the puffy chair next to it. A cloud of dust rises up, motes whirling in the air coming in from the high window, as crazy in motion as my thoughts.

Waldo puts on a kettle, hauls something that looks like a palm frond out of the fridge, and picks up his trusty machete. *Chop. Chop.* "You want to serve as a father to this child."

"Yeah. Sir. I mean, I already am. But I mean—from now on. Yes. I just want a little time to know for sure."

Chop. "That sounds brave. Maybe it is brave. But how's it going to work? Are you going to open your world and rearrange it around this baby? Put Calvin between you and your horizon?" *Chop-chop.* "You ready to put your money where your love is?"

Could this guy sound a little less like a fortune cookie on acid?

My throat hurts. Also my stomach, which it pretty much has ever since I said no to Hester. And told Alice what's up. Maybe I'm getting an ulcer? Waldo sweeps the junk he's hacked up and puts it in the teakettle, turns the flame on with a quick twist of his wrist. Looks like lawn clippings.

"Look," I say. "I'm not exactly sure what you're saying here, but . . . you may think I just . . . do shit without thinking, but that's not it. Maybe Hester can move on and forget about it. But not me. I'm not that guy. Uh, now. I don't even need to see her. I'm only here to get the rest of Cal's stuff."

Waldo moves back against the counter and looks at me, his face impassive. He reaches behind his back with one hand, without taking his eyes off me. Is he going for the machete? But no, he's just got some kind of tea strainer thing.

"You've bonded with this baby."

"Haven't you? You're the one who told Hester to keep him for a while."

"I'm sixty-four, Tim. I've learned that those irrevocable decisions deserve time. Michelle, Hester's mother, wasn't married when she had Hester. She regretted a lot about her choices. Hester's too young to start racking up more should-have's." He turns, pouring steamy hot water and lawn clippings into two gray-blue pottery mugs. He offers me one, hoists it like he's toasting me. "To the truth of our hearts, which can chain us down."

He puts his mug on the table, rests his chin on his palms, and does that intent-stare thing from under his bristly eyebrows. I stare back. *He* can blink first.

"Have you and Hester talked about Alex Robinson?"

Who? Oh, right, Hester's old boyfriend who did the long-distance-dump routine. Favorite tool of dickheads and douchebags everywhere.

"Sorta."

"Maybe you should explore that cave with a stronger light." Waldo reaches for a jar of honey and twist-pours some into his tea with this weird wooden spoon.

He sounds serious, his tone the way people's voices get when they're breaking bad news. I don't know why, but coldness crawls over me, icy-sharp, though the kitchen air is heavy with lemony steam.

"Could we cut the crap here?" I ask. "What exactly are you saying?"

Waldo scrubs his hand through his thatch of graying hair. "Alex and Hester were together for a long time." Now he's dropped his hand, paying unnecessarily careful attention to stirring his tea. Silence, except this thumping noise.

So?

What does that . . .

"I didn't hear any talk of you until the baby was a few weeks old."

Again, so?

"Until then, Hester was very insistent on him being Alex's." He stirs his tea some more, spoon clinking against the side of the mug. "She didn't bring you up to me until Calvin's hair started coming in."

The thumping is my heart.

"That's it, though—he's got my hair and . . ."

Waldo says nothing, heaving himself away from the counter as though he's suddenly gained mass. He pads out of the room, coming back a few minutes later with a picture in his hand. He passes it to me.

"I'll give you that the baby looks a hell of a lot more like you. Still, this is Hester's dad. Mike Pearson."

I check out the picture. In it, Hester's mother, still looking like *Madonna: The Early Years*, is laughing, one dimple grooving deep in her cheek, cleft cut hard in her chin, her head with its teased, streaky brown-blond hair resting on the pale stomach of a guy with his shirt off. A guy with puffy hair nearly as long as hers. As red as my own.

"You want plain talk? A conversation needs to happen between you and Hester."

Got caught in a riptide once and this is just like that, if the water burned and clung like just-poured tar. Everything's hazy with heat.

He looks just like me.

His hair. His dimple. His chin.

Everyone says.

Everyone but Nan. But what does she know—she's probably high.

Waldo's taken his tea, gone upstairs, humming under his breath, like he hadn't just used that machete on me.

Fist my hands into my hair, pull hard, slump back in the chair, then jump back up and stare at the kid. Look and look and look some more. Watch this quick smile race across his face when I move one finger down his cheek, see how he curls closer, grabs tight to my thumb without waking—even though he's usually restless and quick to wake up—*like me, like me*—bending his head close to my forearm, so sure I'm there. Now I get it, the goddamn all of it, that he's mine, that I made him, that I love him.

Hell to the hell. I throw myself back on the chair, splay my legs onto this bookend thing next to it, not giving a damn that I knock over some weird-ass statue of a chick with too many arms.

Little click of the front door and Hester comes down the hall into the living room on her little cat feet, which I only hear because I'm listening for her and every sense is amped up.

She's sorting through some mail, she doesn't look up as I stalk toward her.

"We need to talk."

She jumps a little, does that hand-to-heart thing and the letters flutter to the ground.

"A-about the adoption? Have you changed your mind?"

"Let's start somewhere else," I suggest, in that cornering-with-a-whiplash voice I learned so well from Pop. "Say, oh, last fall. You're gonna have to help me out here."

Hester sits down on this footstool thing with a little jolt. She's staring at me with the Bambi eyes. Hasn't looked at Cal once.

"So . . . Alex Robinson. Did he happen to pay you a visit in, say, early November?"

Look baffled. Say you don't know why I'm asking.

But she doesn't look baffled. And she doesn't ask why.

"Calvin is yours. I think."

"You. Think."

Then a rush of words like a flood I'm drowning in, yes, Alex was home for a long weekend for Veterans Day, but he's conscientious, I thought it was his, *wanted* it to be his—of course—at first, but then the hair—

My stomach clasps hard and tight, like someone's punching it with a hot fist. "Did we ever have sex at all?"

"We did make love," she breathes. "I would never lie about that. You can ask my friend Michaela, and Jude, and Buck. I told all of them right after the party."

"That wasn't 'making love.' It was sperm meets egg. Or not. Tell. Me. The. Truth."

She grabs a floor pillow from the corner and hugs it to her, quivering with suppressed sobs. "The truth is I hope it's you. I thought . . . I thought all along it was Alex's. I mean, he and I had a relationship. So I wanted it to be his. But all he said when I told him was that he was sure I'd work it all out. Work it all out! Like it was a geometry problem or something. That whatever I did was fine. Fine! Nothing was fine, Tim. They wanted to kick me out of Ellery, did you know that? Waldo brought in his lawyer and told them they couldn't, but I had to go the rest of the year, through graduation, knowing that they all wanted me gone. Alex didn't need to do anything like that. You didn't need to do anything like that. All you had to do was screw me once."

I can actually feel my hands around her neck, gripping hard, tightening harder on pulse and tendon and skin. Jesus. Flex my fingers, tighten them, jam them against my thighs. "Yeah, well, now you've done it twice."

I'm backing away from her.

"Where are you going?"

"Someplace safe. I'm taking Cal."

"You don't have to." She's across the room, grabbing my arm.

"He's coming with me. I don't trust you."

She raises her chin, gives a little nod. "All right. I accept that. Maybe I deserve it. But I am his mother."

"Must be nice to know that for sure. Get away from me, Hester."

Chapter Forty

ALICE

Tim's lying on his back on the grass outside the garage apartment, smoke curling in the air above him, cigarette in one hand, staring at the sky.

When I sit down on the bottom step near him, he doesn't even turn his head. The cigarette's nearly smoked all the way down. As I watch, he pulls another one out of the pack of Marlboros, lights it from the tip, drops the first butt into a foam coffee cup, where it hisses.

"Your mom tell you what's up?" His voice is idle, uncurious, like it doesn't much matter either way.

"Just now. Cal's fine. George was doing 'Itsy-Bitsy Spider' for him. He's good. Where were you?"

Tim takes another drag. "Went to town. Out of diapers. And cigarettes."

"You probably shouldn't do that with the patch on."

He tips the foam cup at me. In the bottom, floating in an inch or so of coffee, along with six or seven cigarette butts, is the nicotine patch.

He blows a smoke ring.

Then, abruptly, he rolls over on his stomach, crushes out the cigarette, gray eyes sharp. "There are all these things, all these little pieces of him that are just like me. I keep telling myself that. But you probably have more medical—genetic—whatever—facts than I do."

Facts come easily to my lips, like I'm reading them off the whiteboard at school. "It's not all that straightforward with physical characteristics. They don't just get inherited as simply as dominant and recessive. So that cleft chin?"

He nods, his eyes still locked on mine.

"Maybe yes, maybe no. The red hair. Same story. There's more than one gene controlling each. Who knows? The dimple. That's rare."

"Hester's mom has that. So you're saying there's no real way to tell. What about a blood test?" He strips his shirt down to his elbow, like I can pull out a Vacutainer and do a venipuncture right here and now.

"That can only rule someone out, not in."

He digs the heels of his hands into his eye sockets, shakes his head, then drops his fists again. The look on his face. Lost, frightened, frustrated. Despite the stubble and the circles under his eyes, it reminds me of George's expression when I can't explain exactly, scientifically, why an asteroid won't hit the earth. Can't tell him that we know for certain there isn't one already headed straight for us.

Tim just keeps staring at me like he doesn't understand the instructions, or doesn't want to.

My cell sings out "Eye of the Tiger."

I start to mute it, but Tim's hand flashes out, yanks the phone away before my fingers close on it. "Back off," he snarls into it.

There's an angry rumble of sound.

"I *said* back the fuck off. Leave her the hell alone. . . . Yeah, I'll make you."

He's practically baring his teeth at the phone and in an instant all my worry coalesces into fury. "Quit it!"

"*He* needs to quit it."

I jerk the phone out of his hand. "Cut it out, Brad. You're better than this. If you keep it up I'm filing a restraining order. Enough already." I hang up, hit the keys to block his number, my thumbs flying, then toss the phone on the stairs.

"There. Solved. I've got this handled. I don't need you—" *To fix it* is what I mean to say, but before I can, Tim puts both hands out, palms facing me.

"Gotcha. Not needed here either. That's great, Alice. Thanks. It must be terrific to have it all handled. Know how to handle it all."

"You know better than that. Quit acting as if you're the only one who ever feels anything. We can figure this out. We'll—"

"Except it's not your problem to solve, Alice, is it? I don't want to be handled. Just another item on your list of people to rescue, things to fix? I'll pass. How am I supposed to handle this? My son may not—might not . . . shit . . . might not be my son."

His hand trembles as he grabs the lighter again, shakes more as he tries to flick it and the sparks won't ignite. I take it from him, flip it, hold the flame to the cigarette he's jammed between his lips.

I'm helping him hurt himself.

Then I do more.

"Lighting up won't help Cal, dad or no dad."

"Whoops, thanks. Forgot how much older and wiser you are.

You're probably even 'mature' enough to be relieved about this. No need for *sink-in time*"—he makes air quotes—"right? Bye bye baby."

"You're the one acting like a kid here, Tim."

He laughs. "Sure. Got it. Thanks for the light."

Still laughing, he plunges down the driveway into the Jetta, out onto the road.

Going, going, gone.

TIM

I'll be just like him.

If Cal isn't mine, if I can't keep him, I'll be another Mason man with no photographs of his son on the walls.

My heart is doing this racing thing—maybe tension, maybe too much nicotine because I blew through a few butts before I remembered to adios the patch. Still, I fire up another, even though I feel more like yacking.

All the rules I broke, and it hasn't occurred to me for years to enter Pop's sanctum when he wasn't here, much less make myself at home. Now I throw myself into his well-padded chair, spin it around, legs kicked out. Never even did this as a kid.

Another twist of the chair and back to the desk, which has a stack of his blue-lined pads on it, a silver pencil holder full of his brown-and-copper building and loan pens. Desk calendar with Nan's field hockey games penciled in. One note, near the end of the month: "Crawley Center for Adoption Services, 3:30 p.m. Bring health records, birth cert."

Only noise in the room is the gentle burbling of the fish tank. No fish in the tank, however. Pop likes aquatic snails.

There they are, sliding up the wall and bobbing around on the lettuce leaves he feeds them every five days or so. Don't require a lot of upkeep, those guys. Not much attention paid. Not even to the big picture.

Twirl in the chair again, and this time my legs strafe the wedding photo—Ma with puffy sleeves, Pop with a shiny silk vest—the pen holder, and Nan's middle school graduation picture, Hodges beret and all. They tumble off the desk, land—a perfect basket into the leather trash can, as unerring as one of Jase's newspaper throws.

And I wasn't even trying.

I think I hear a door slam, but then all's quiet.

The little silver bucket is lined up; a good little accomplice, right next to the Macallan and the cut-crystal highball glass. No need to wait to fill it with ice. We want what we want when we want it, right? Into the tumbler it goes. One finger, two fingers, three. It sloshes onto my hand and the desk calendar. Wipe my hand on my shirt, but the desk calendar can fend for itself.

You still might be his father.

Don't do anything you can't take back.

But Cal's not here right now, he's safe with the Garretts. Nothing to stop my hand from reaching for the glass, from picking it up, turning it around, and frowning into it.

A Pop habit.

Don't think there's quite enough scotch in this glass, since I spilled some and all. It smells like disinfectant or that red stuff Ma puts on cuts.

But I'm tipping the glass and parting my lips when the office door swings open.

Chapter Forty-one

TIM

"Oh, Tim."

Nan closes the door behind her, so gently that it barely makes a sound, not even the usual click of the latch. Then she stands against it, blinking at me in the sleepy, unfocused way she does when she first wakes up, waiting for the world to make sense.

Can't help her with that one.

"Cheers!"

Now she's standing next to me, fingertips pressed against her lips.

Another "Oh, Tim."

She doesn't even sound surprised.

The glass travels toward my mouth again. Now she's shaking her head, that look on her face, corners of her mouth turned down, spaniel eyes. *There you go again.*

I respond to the words she doesn't even need to say— they've been said so often in this very room that they're probably hovering in a cloud above us. But then I catch a whiff of what surrounds her like a burnt, grassy-sweet fog.

"Don't judge, Nano. You aren't exactly on the moral high ground here." I sniff in an exaggerated way.

She lifts her forearm and smells her pressed Hodges navy blue blazer. Her red eyebrows shoot up like she's shocked, *shocked*, at the scent. Then it's like she crumples, spaniel eyes even bigger, face a paler triangle. "It's not what you—"

I laugh. Harsh in the quiet room. She flushes. "You know what? Forget explaining to you. You're just trying to blow off what's really going on here. What the hell is that doing in your hand?"

"Taking *waaay* too long to get to my mouth."

Tip the glass again, still with it too far from my lips, so some sloshes onto my jeans. Whoops.

She reaches out and I think she's going for the glass, but instead she rests her hand on my shoulder, awkward. "That guy you were turning out to be? I liked him. I was proud of you. In two months, you've been ten times the father Dad was. Ever."

"Except I love my kid. I mean—that kid."

Now she takes the glass out of my hand, and I let her, my fingers going slack. She sets it on the desk calendar, centers it like she's gonna be judged on that, turns back to me.

"Probably he loves us. He just isn't good at it."

"It's not rocket science, Nan. You show someone they matter to you—do whatever it takes to show that."

She lowers the hand resting on my shoulder, slides it to my own, and pulls, so we're both sitting on the couch, hand in hand like lost kids in a fairy tale.

"Drunk Dad will definitely hammer that home for Cal."

And then it's out, all of it, blurt it all out, all over her—Hester, Alex Robinson, Alice.

"What is it about those Garretts?" Nan's short, sharp laugh

sounds like it was rabbit punched out of her. "First they get Samantha. Now you."

"What they get is how to show up. The stuff that you and me aren't so great at."

"*You* help," Nan says, unexpectedly. "You're good at it."

"Yeah, right."

She looks me in the eye. "I owe you my GPA. My good grades in English. That." She gestures at the framed newspaper photo of her at the Fourth of July parade.

I've waited fucking forever for her to say this, admit it, and now it's just some little nothing, one of those things you desperately want for Christmas that you've forgotten about by the time the wrapping's in the trash.

But she's looking at me, The Look, spaniel face, like she's dropped something at my feet and I owe it to her to say how special it is, how much it means that she brought it to me.

I sigh. "Sure, Nan. You plagiarized from my papers, and even when I knew, I didn't say a word. I'm a hero."

"You helped me, Tim. You let me keep on doing it, and you didn't tell anyone."

"Just like you didn't let on that I was full of more drugs than a Pfizer warehouse. Yay for us. I'll stand right next to you at the next Fourth of July parade. Masons rule."

I reach for the glass again and she smacks my knuckles like an old schoolteacher.

"You helped me," she repeats.

"Nan, me 'helping' that way? Made you think you were crap. Helped cost you Samantha, if I'm guessing right. Help isn't supposed to make you weaker and even more effing lost. I might as well have been old Troy, supplying you shit."

"Don't say that." Her voice rises, higher pitched.

Not sure who she's defending. Also if it matters. Close my eyes. I would reach for the scotch again, but it's impossibly far away. My head hurts.

"You helped me."

"Stop saying that. So fucking what, Nan. So maybe you'll get into Columbia. Maybe. Gonna be happy there? I wouldn't take a bet on that one."

Tears stream down her face now, big gaspy sobs. She sounds like Cal, lost and sad and sure there's no help in the world for that. I let go of her hand, put my arms around her, pat, pat, circle, circle. Do everything but burp her as the tears and the shuddering keep on and on and on, like she's waiting for the one magic word or gesture that I'm so not coming up with.

"You could have *asked*," I say finally. Total opposite of reassurance. "I would have, I dunno, coached you or something without you ripping off shit behind my back."

Nan sighs. "Back then? You wouldn't have handed me a drink of water in the Gobi Desert. You wouldn't have shoved me out of the path of a meteor. You were gone, Tim. Don't you remember?"

I squeeze her hand, tug her a little closer so she's resting her cheek on my shoulder. "Not the way you do. That was sort of the point."

She shakes a little, but this time with the tiniest of laughs. "Guess so. Job well done."

I pull back, look at her. Her hair all over the place, except the pieces that are plastered around with snot, her "edgy" mascara making her eyes into a creepy clown portrait that only needs a black velvet background. God, what a mess. My stupid, crazy sister. I love her so much.

"Kid . . . Nan . . . I . . . I didn't screw myself to screw you up. I know that happened anyway. I'm sorry. I'm so sorry."

Pull off my long-sleeved shirt, pass her one sleeve, use the other myself.

"One, two, three, blow," Nan says, muffled by the shirt.

Ma always said that.

For a few minutes, we sniff and breathe at the same time, twins for the first time ever, probably.

"You weren't the only one to screw me up, so you don't get to take all the credit or the blame. I did a super job all by myself, but . . . but Tim. You and Sam were my best friends. You left me behind one way. Then she left me behind another."

"Kiddo. You couldn't have rescued me from anything I did. But Samantha . . . she was just down the road. A phone call away, as they say. All you had to do was say I'm sorry."

"You don't even know what happened," Nan says, a trace of her old self-righteousness creeping back.

Hell with that.

"I do, though." I lean back so we're once again side by side. Her head on my shoulder, my hand on her hair. We could be posing for a really effed-up version of one of Ma's twin pictures. "She called you on your bullshit and you ditched her. It's not exactly an original story. I've starred in it a billion times."

"Samantha's not perfect . . ." Nan says, and then she yawns, like even she's too sick of this to go on.

"Despite that sandwich board she wears that says she is?"

Watery giggle. "I hate you."

"Yeah," I say, hauling myself to my feet, using her thin shoulder as leverage. She catches at my leg to stop me, until I reach for the scotch and her fingers let go, hover in the air. "I hate you right back, kid."

I pour the scotch into the snail tank.

Nan comes up next to me and we both stare down into the clear water with its bobbing lettuce leaves and their little black passengers. I feel guilty.

"Did you just wipe out a squadron of snails?"

"Maybe. That was cold-blooded of me. Ha."

Nan looks over at Pop's desk. "Well . . . you come by it naturally."

I toast her with the empty glass. "Touché. Keep it up and there won't be any pictures of you in here either."

Chapter Forty-two

TIM

Nan brushes at the wet scotch stains on me, wrinkling her nose. "Yeech. You reek."

"You're one to talk, Bob Marley. Since we're spilling our guts: What the hell are you pulling, Nan? Truth, this go-round."

In the time it takes to brew a pot of coffee, we're chowing down in Nan's room, having dumped her top desk drawer out on the bed. It's much better stocked with candy than Doane's, Stony Bay's biggest dentist's nightmare.

"I'm seeing him, Troy, not for drugs," she tells me, all in a rush.

"Weed, then, obviously. Pills?"

She shakes her head. "It was for pills initially. My reliable supplier went and got himself clean."

I laugh obediently, thinking she's joking. For all my sins, I never dealt to my twin. But one look at her face and she's obviously drop-dead serious.

No.

I ignored her, I needled her, I didn't show up for her, but I didn't, didn't, didn't mess up my own sister. Something I know for sure.

Or not. I couldn't have forgotten that too. Could I?

"Take that back," I say, like the goddamn school bully.

"It wasn't you! It wasn't your fault. Tim. This one's on me."
She shuts her eyes, opens them.

"Nan. In God's name, why? Or, never mind that, what? Oxy? Percocet? Vicodin? Please, God, not E."

"None of those, Timmy. Ritalin. Remember when you went to that doctor who said you had ADHD because you couldn't focus?"

"The one who also thought I was bipolar? Because I was always showing up for appointments altered by a different substance? Yep. He was a genius."

"You didn't fill the prescription, but I did. I thought it would work miracles with my focus. And it did, I guess. I definitely concentrated on different ways to get my schoolwork done without actually having to do it."

"Aw, Nan."

"But then the prescription ran out. So I went to Troy."

"That bastard is—"

"He wouldn't sell to me. Or give it for free. Or write my papers, though one of his brothers does that on the side. His family is even worse than ours. But he did"—she looks down, then up at me, reddening—"ask me out. No judging. That Alice is a million times more of a badass than Troy will ever be."

"That I'll give you."

"My brother's in lo-ove."

"I sure am. And, as always, I've got better taste than you-oo." There's a pounding on the door.

Nan jumps like an overbred Chihuahua.

Really got to knock it off with these dog comparisons.

"Bet that's your girl," Nan says, giving my shoulder a shove.

"Nan . . ." I look down at my scotch-y jeans, my black T-shirt that smells like cigarette smoke, my bitten nails. "The last time I saw her I was a total jackass."

More pounding on the door.

"Go down before she gets the battering ram." Nan opens the bedroom door, shooing me out.

But when I swing open the front door, with its wreath covered with smiling pumpkins, it isn't Alice after all.

It's Samantha, all flushed, hair messy, Hodges uniform with its little plaid skirt rumpled, beret caught in a tangle of her blond hair.

"Everyone said you wouldn't come here but I—oh, Tim. Alice told me. It'll be okay. Thank God you're all right."

She throws her arms around my neck, in what may be a hug but is more like a choke hold.

Then she steps back, holding my arms just above the elbows, scanning me over. "You *are* all right, aren't you? It's like everyone's gone crazy tonight. My mother's freaking out—"

"About me?"

"No, because I did what you said, told Alice to go nuclear—but Alice is panicking about you—"

"Is she okay?"

"She started to really stress out. But she calmed down. She's out looking for you. We all are. I mean, Jase, Alice, me, Andy and a squadron of her friends. Mom's home with Cal and the phone. George is drawing up missing posters. He's scared. But you're okay. Jeez, Tim."

"Great, *George* knows?"

"You're not someone who can disappear without people taking notice."

"Neither are you," says a small voice from behind me, and Samantha's arms loosen; she moves aside to look past me, toward my sister, hesitating on the stairs.

"Nan." Sam sounds apprehensive, and damn right since Nan still looks like Pogo the Evil Clown.

Nan holds up a hand, silent, waves it a little, like she's returning the half wave Samantha gave her back at Hodges, weeks ago.

Sam's phone blasts "Life on Mars."

"God, it's Mom. No matter what's going on, her drama always has to be the biggest one."

Nan sort of snorts, but not rudely. "Remember what your sister always said? 'Grace Reed: the bride at every wedding, the corpse at every wake.'"

"I'd totally forgotten that," Sam says.

"I remember a lot of things," Nan offers.

"Can you two, like, hug or whatever? I have to get to Alice."

ALICE

Halfway to the beach, there he is, loping along, hands in pockets, head down. I pull over, call his name. "Get in!"

Tim breaks into a smile when he sees me, but it leaves his face just as fast. He pulls at the collar of his sweatshirt, folds his arms.

"Are you okay?" I climb out of the car. He steps farther off, but I grab his sleeve. "Tim, talk. It's me. Everything all right?"

"Nope. Sorry I was such an asshole, Alice."

"No, I shouldn't have fallen back on facts and genetic explanations. I should have just done this." My hands are around his back, my face against his chest. There's a shuddering breath against my cheek, almost a sob. He bends down and I tip up, touch my lips to his, which open, warm and welcoming, tasting faintly of root beer. He rests one palm against the back of my head, the other skimming down to my waist.

It's only when I pull back for air that I detect it—this smoky, slightly medicinal odor—

I swallow hard.

Tim gives a rueful smile. "Yup. That's exactly what you think it is."

I absorb this, choke back anything I might say.

"I only applied it externally. You know what, though? I'm thinking it's not really the best signature scent for me. I need something more musky, with some notes of leather and saddle soap."

"You didn't drink."

"Got way closer than I had any business doing. But no."

TIM

I hesitate for a minute or two outside the church basement door. Not only do I reek of scotch, I no doubt look like a mess in every other way. I stand there, remembering how when I first started coming to meetings, back at the beginning with Mr. Garrett, I'd pause in the parking lot and straighten my shirt and comb my hair and shit, like my mom would have done if I really were heading to church. Like I had to look so pulled together outside because I was such a hot mess inside. After a couple viewings of this, Mr. Garrett laughed, took the comb out of my hands. "The official photographer isn't here today, Tim. AA is strictly come as you are."

Yeah, no judging here. As I told my ma—that's why I need the strangers.

Chapter Forty-three

TIM

The lights are all on in the Garrett house when I get home, and I can see Mrs. Garrett pacing back and forth in front of the kitchen window, baby in her arms. Cal. Joel's motorcycle slant-parked near the house. Jase's tall figure balancing a gallon of milk on his shoulder, moving through the room. Duff and Harry and George sitting on the steps with ice-cream sandwiches.

And there's Alice. Cross-legged outside my door, waiting, with this little red-and-blue box in her hands, flipping it up in the air, catching it.

Then she catches my eye, stands up, and comes down the steps.

I spread my hands, *here I am*, and she comes closer, takes one hand, folds my fingers around the box. E-Z-Gene at-home DNA testing.

"You don't have to do it," she says. "But it's one way to be sure. If you put a rush on it, it only takes two days."

"For our next anniversary, you can just get me a tie," I say, sitting down heavily on the steps and flipping over the box to read the instructions.

• ◦ • ◦

I mail the swabbed cell samples—scraped from the inside of my cheek, then Cal's, the next morning, expedited delivery, return receipt requested. Everything but accompanied by armed guards. After I hand it to the postal clerk, I have to fight every impulse I have not to snatch it back from him.

E-Z-Gene my ass. This is the hardest test I've ever taken.

ALICE

"Bright side," Tim says, saluting me with his coffee cup as I polish off the last of my vegan burrito, bright and early at Garrett's Hardware the next day. He snags my hand just as I'm about to lick the last bit of guacamole off my index finger, and does it himself, looking at me underneath his eyelashes. "You wanted sink-in time. We've both got forty-eight hours. At least."

"Look, about that sink-in stuff," I say. "I never thought—ever—good riddance or bye bye baby or anything like that"

"Forget I said that. You were right anyway. Fuck the self-pity. I was just being a—"

"Whatever happens, Tim . . . it just . . . happens. I'll deal. We'll deal. As long as you don't go charging off to bathe in scotch."

"Deal. As long as you don't go facing down Grace without backup again. When I asked Sam if she'd be your ace in the hole, I didn't think you'd be going there without me."

"It had to be between me and Grace. You would just have been a distraction. I think she sort of has a thing for you."

"Christ, no. She just recognizes a fellow amoral person. One of her tribe."

"You remind me of myself." God. There aren't enough showers to wash that off me.

"We need to talk about choices, Alice," Dad says.

I look up sharply from the floor, where I'm once again packing things—Dad's about to be dismissed from rehab.

His tone is serious. I know what this is all about. Mom walked into Garrett's during lunch, catching Tim and me kissing, yet again. She didn't say anything, just offered to take Cal because she was headed to the playground with Patsy and George. But there's no doubt Dad heard about it.

"Look. I know what I'm up against here—I'm not flying blind. He's got a long road ahead of him and a lot of growing up to do—he's draped in red flags—I know that—and if he starts drinking or whatever again, all bets are off. I'm not walking that road. Well, not hand in hand with him. I'll be there, of course, because he's—he's worth it, but I won't be moving into the garage apartment with a baby and a drunken teenage boy, if that's what you're afraid of. I can look out for myself, Dad, I do, first and foremost—you guys know that—"

"While reassuring, Alice, that's not what we need to talk about. We'll get to that later."

"Oh." *What else have I done?* "If it's about the—"

Dad holds up a hand. "About the what, Alice? The store? Your schoolwork? Taking care of your brothers and sisters? Holding the fort down? Going up against Grace Reed? All the battles you're fighting? On how many different fronts? That's without any personal life of your own, plus whatever is going on with—"

"The recovering alcoholic high school dropout teenage father I'm in love with?"

He smiles. "Let's just call him Tim. Yes, except for that and whatever comes or doesn't come of it—none of these battles are yours to fight."

I open my mouth to argue and he stares me down. "None of them," he repeats gently. "No exceptions."

"But that's ridiculous, Dad. I'm, I'm one of us—that's who I am. When something happens to my family—"

"Al—yes, you are. But that's not all you are. And it's time for you to be Alice, not the standard bearer for your family. You can give that job back to your mother and me."

I'm hovering on a tightrope, somewhere between a relief so great that my breath comes out in a whoosh, and a totally lost feeling. This has been my fight. This is my job. Looking at Dad's steady green eyes, calm as they've always been, I shake my head.

"Dad—I have to do this. I'm supposed to do this."

"No, Alice. You're not. You didn't choose to have a large family. Your mother and I did. But this isn't the eighteenth century. We didn't decide to have you to be our workforce on the farm, or at the store."

"You didn't decide to get hit by a car—"

"And you weren't driving that car. This"—he moves one hand slowly down from his eyes, past his ribs, down the length of his body—"is a setback, and a pain in the ass. But it's all temporary. I'm a jock. I understand recovery time, when to push myself, when not to. You can let go of that."

Tears are jabbing at my eyes now, prickles of heat. I blink, swallow. "I know. I mean, I'm not giving up my life forever and ever. Just until things are on an even keel at home."

"When will that be, honey? When I'm all better? When the new baby is born? When Jase goes to college? When George and Patsy do? When the new baby is doing the solar system project? There's never going to be an even keel. It's a matter of constant adjustment. And that's just fine. I wouldn't recognize it any other way."

"But Dad—"

He puts his hand on my arm, shakes his head. "Speaking of balance, give me those." He indicates the crutches, propped against the wheelchair with all the other apparatuses of injury— the walker, the reacher, the quad cane. One tucked under an arm, he swings to a stand, grabs the other, walks a few steps, pivots, slide-walks back to the bed, sits down, looks at me, raising one eyebrow. He's whiter than my nurse shoes and sweating more than Jase during practice. And he's walking.

"Dad," I say, that word that means everything.

"Nothing to it," he says, completely out of breath. "By the time the new baby is walking, I'll be running wind sprints—if not well before. Pass me that reacher thing, if Harry hasn't broken it again."

I hand it to him, resolutely ignoring the fact that he's gasping for air. He hooks it into the handle of the bedside table drawer. Pulls. It clatters to the ground. I hand it back to him. This time, he pulls the drawer slowly out, then, winded, holds up a hand, breathing hard for a moment. Flash of Tim running on the beach at the end of the summer.

"Get me what's on top, 'kay?"

What's on top are two packages, both wrapped in construction paper, art by George. I recognize the troop of Garrett stick figures on one, accompanied by various pets, some of which we don't actually own, like a centaur and a whale shark. "The little one first."

The little one is covered with drawings too—a bucket, a broom—

I look up. "I never saw myself as Cinderella slaving away, Dad. I've done all this gladly—"

"And dutifully, and resentfully, and impatiently, and lovingly, and many other ways, Alice. I know. Open the little package."

Crackle of paper, and the Kleenex-wrapped contents drop into my hand—a cardboard heart with a gold star in the center, hanging from a twist of dark yellow pipe cleaner. Dad reaches for it and holds it up. "George does good work. Lean over."

"It's a—"

He attaches it to the front of my shirt, only pricking me with the safety pin once. "Your purple heart, Alice. Well done. You're discharged."

Tears hot on my face, so many, they're dripping off my chin. I put my hand over the heart, then my arms around Dad, my wet cheek against his sweaty, stubbly face. "I'm almost afraid to look in the second box."

His big hand comes up, rubs the back of my neck. "Oh, that? It's Godiva chocolates. The closest we could get to bonbons. Now go, lie back and eat them while everyone else is at the game and the house is quiet. As close to an even keel as we're going to get."

TIM

For the next two days—forty-eight hours—Cal gets a taste of what it's like to be a Garrett.

Mr. Garrett gets released from Maplewood, the deal being that he'll do daily physical rehab at Live Oaks Center for Living, the best PT place around, according to Alice the research queen.

"Doesn't that place cost an arm and a leg?" Joel asked as he, Jase, Samantha, Alice, and I pounded the last nails into the hastily constructed ramp for the Garretts' front steps—a bitch to build, but everyone but me got all stubborn about it and insisted it was a DIY project and not a call-in-a-professional one. Even when Joel put his foot through one of the floorboards.

"Not Dad's, in this case," Alice answers with a Cheshire Cat smile.

"Worth every penny," Sam agrees, sucking on her thumbnail, which she kept whacking with the hammer until Jase pried it out of her hands. "Every pound of flesh."

So the afternoon we bring him home, we've raked up all the leaves in the Garretts' yard, and the younger kids jump into them and make sure all that sweaty work is shot to hell. Joel lights up the coals in one of those copper fire-pit things. Mr. Garrett whistles for the kids and tells them all to find sticks. Everyone abandons the leaves, and piles sticks on sticks on sticks, so the coals get smothered and have to be relit.

"Do the honors, Duff?" Mr. Garrett calls. "Use the extralong matches, you little firebug."

"He always gets to light the fire! I never do!" Harry groans.

"You're seven. You have years of pyromania ahead of you." Jase claps him on the back, pulling him farther away from the leaping flames.

Mrs. Garrett stretches out a blanket on the grass and Cal

kicks the air and grins while we grill hot dogs and burgers and Patsy climbs into my lap with extreme firmness, planting her butt like she's hoping to grow roots. Every time I look at Cal, she claps her hands on my cheeks and turns my face away. Afterward, I put on the pussy front pack—Cal can look outward in it now—while everyone plays freeze tag. All these games I would have thought were completely lame—aren't. Patsy, however, hates the kid in the front pack thing a lot.

"No!" she bellows at me, pointing her finger accusingly. "No no no, Hon. Off boy!" She hisses at Cal. A sharp crease in my heart for a moment. Deep breath, it's gone. Thirty-six hours left still. Don't have to think about it now. Not yet.

If life is fair, Cal will get this. To be close to something like this. "You're not toasting," Alice says, sitting down thigh-to-thigh with me and indicating the packs of marshmallows, graham crackers, and Hershey's bars Sam just donated to the cause.

"Go. 'Way. Bye-bye, you," Patsy tells her, not willing to compete further for my affections. "Mines."

"No." Alice fixes her with her fiercest glare. "Mines."

Patsy looks disconcerted and begins to suck on her knuckles.

"No marshmallows?" Alice repeats to me, taking a bite of one, chewing.

"*This* is the moment where I say something about you being sweet enough?"

"This is the moment when I tell you that moment doesn't actually exist."

I check around, on the lookout for disapproving stares. None. Barely any attention at all, except from Patsy, dividing her glare between Alice and Cal.

So I bring Alice closer, kissing the corner of her lips, then her eyebrows, then returning to her mouth, holding on tight, until Cal gives a furious (and breathless) squawk from between us. Pulling away, I look over Alice's shoulder, catch Mr. Garrett's eye, feel the blood rush to my face. Mrs. G. is one thing, but him? But all he does is give me a quick smile, then turn his attention back to the fire.

"No shotgun, I guess," I say.

Alice rolls her eyes. "Dad won't be building an extension to the house just for us, but no, no shotgun."

"Hey, no problem. We've got the luxury apartment. The tent can be our summer home."

That night, the second we're inside the apartment, the sky outside opens up and there are torrents of hard rain, the heavy-fall, near-nor'easter kind. The windows look like they're surrounded by gray curtains, the sheets of water are so thick. Thunder rumbles. Alice holds Cal against her shoulder while I slam windows shut.

"Looks as though I'm stuck here."

It's twenty feet to her house, but I agree, "It *is* coming down pretty hard."

She sits on the couch, kicking off her flats, pulling her knees up under the skirt of her dress, resting Cal against them.

The rain's like white noise in the background, occasional flashes of lightning and low growls of thunder.

"You never dated at all, Tim?" Alice asks, flexing her toes. She has a little silver ring on one, with a turquoise stone. I slide my own foot against it.

"Nope. That would have taken too much focus."

She shakes her head, looking at me. She's got a fireball in her mouth and one cheek is bulging like a chipmunk's with a nut. "Mmm-hhh." She takes the fireball back out, holding it delicately between thumb and forefinger. "How can you stand these? My mouth is on fire."

I edge closer, bumping her thigh with my knee. "I like to play with fire."

Alice casts her eyes to the ceiling but then tips her forehead to mine. She smells like heat and cinnamon.

"They're showing all three *Evil Dead* movies back-to-back. Want to hang out and watch 'em?"

Her face lights up. "I love *The Evil Dead*! Got popcorn?"

No, I do not, since I'm shopping impaired. So Alice runs through the rain back to the Garretts', coming back with a few bags of Paul Newman's Best shielded under a yellow slicker.

She comes in, slamming the door loudly, waking up the kid. He squawks and Alice apologizes, but it's fine. I feed him his bottle while Alice makes popcorn in the microwave.

He finally crashes, resting against the crease of the couch to one side of me, and Alice puts her head in my lap, kicking out to the other side. Only a little while ago, none of this would have happened to me. I would never have spent time with a girl, much less one I was into, without doing more than curling my fingers in her hair. I wouldn't have known to keep one hand on a baby so he wouldn't roll over and fall off the couch. I wouldn't have felt content just listening to the rain and being there. I didn't even know what content was.

Chapter Forty-four

TIM

The next day's a school day for most of the Garretts; Mr. and Mrs. G. head off to Live Oaks for the first sessions, George and Patsy along for the ride. Cal and I have already been out with Jase, tossing papers. Alice has class all day but comes up to say goodbye, stays so long she's almost late and has to scramble, rushing around the apartment trying to chug coffee, pull her sweater back on and rebrush her hair, which I've completely messed up. Cal belly-laughs at her from beneath his baby-gym thing, and she tosses the dead duck toy at my head while I do bent rows with Joel's weights.

It's all good until things get quiet. Too quiet.

That's when you hit a meeting, and I do, then get coffee with Jake and walk on the beach. But it's cold and windy there, the sky harsh gray, this edge of winter in the air, even though it's only October. Where will Cal have Christmas?

Plus, I'm supposed to have my freaking life solved by then, according to Pop's line in the sand . . . this huge abyss at first— but nothing compared to now, to what I'm about to find out "with just a few EZ clicks to access paternity results."

Make a list:

1. Deal with GED. I took the test last weekend, without taking a prep test online, but I figured the real thing would be a good warm-up. I think I'm still screwing up on the math portion, even though I've got language arts, science, and social studies nailed.

2. Check out local community colleges, course credits, and day care. Maybe I can transfer from two-year to four-year when he's a little older. If that's the way it goes.

3. Talk to Ben Christopher. Grace Reed's opponent in the state senate election is a good guy. A shoo-in for the November election since she dropped out. And I actually liked politics before I realized I had to sell my soul if I was on board with Grace.

Oh, screw them and all the numbers that follow. It's too quiet, except for the noise in my head.

Even if he's not mine . . . maybe I could adopt him?

Yeah, because I look fantastic on paper.

Maybe my parents could . . .

Right. Give Cal a shot at being No One with the Nowhere Man. Not going to happen.

Maybe the Garretts could . . .

Then I'd get to see him all the time but have a safety net against screwing up.

Like they need a tenth kid.

Lunchtime at Hodges. Maybe she'll have her phone on.

"Nan. Come over? I can't be alone."

"I only have PE this afternoon. I can skip it."

"Spoken like a good delinquent. Thanks."

"I'm trying to own it." My twin's voice is so loud in my ear, it's like she's already in the room. "Besides, I have something for you to take a look at."

"Something" turns out to be the *Ellery Apogee*, last year's yearbook, which Nan somehow unearthed from my room. Alex Robinson must have known someone on the staff and worked the connection, because he's freakin' everywhere, but mostly as another little, white, prepped-out face in an interchangeable crowd. In his best close-up, in the Ellery newspaper office, settling back in a chair, all chiseled jaw and incisive stare, Hester's standing next to him like she's his secretary or office page or something.

"I don't know," Nan says slowly, holding up the yearbook close to Cal's face.

"He's so little, Timmy. His features are so . . . soft. He could be anyone's baby. Yours, Alex's, Leonardo DiCaprio's . . ."

"I think we can safely eliminate the King of the World.."

Cal makes one of his little spastic jerky movements with his hands, clenching and unclenching his fists, but staying asleep. "Can I hold him?" Nan whispers.

She drops the *Ellery Apogee* and curls the baby into her lap awkwardly. I hover my hand nearby to fix the way she's holding him, then let it drop to my side. Not going to be one of those control-freak dads.

If I am a dad.

Nan whispers, "Dad won't help with Cal, you know. He just won't. Unless you do go for adoption. Mom . . . maybe. She said she might come by later. But, Tim? My heart hurts every time I think what you'll need to do to keep this baby. I know I couldn't do it. Wouldn't even *want* to."

"You'd feel different if he was yours," I say. Then get that twist, stab, burn in my stomach. Because who knows.

"Hellooo. Hell-ooo-oo," calls a voice.

No knock, still, for Ma. "Everyone decent?"

An odd question since I'm here with my twin sister, but trying to figure Ma out is like trying to read fortunes at the bottom of a beer can. "Door's open," I call. Ma bustles in with a cardboard box of stuff and several bags from the Christmas Tree Shops. Oh help. "Here, let me get that." I take the box from her. It's got tons of baby stuff in it—books and stuffed animals and this seat with elastic attached at each side. It's pink.

"I could only find Nan's bouncy swing," Ma tells me. "Now that I remember, I think you wrecked yours somehow. But I found some of your old things and washed them all—except the books, of course."

She reaches into the box and pulls out the bouncy thing, glancing around. "It has to hang in a doorway." She walks over to the bedroom door and reaches for the frame, bending apart this clamp to try to attach it. But she's way too short to reach, so I go over and take it from her.

"You have to latch it around the wood and make it really secure," she instructs. After a few minutes of wrestling, I get the clamp attached securely. Ma immediately grabs Cal and sits him in it. He looks stunned and instantly face-plants on the little tray in front.

"Ma, maybe he's a little young for that. And you know he might not be staying long."

Like the kid's a hotel guest with an undetermined check-out date.

"No, he's holding his head up fine now, aren't you?" she says in a high-pitched voice. His forehead scrunches up like he's trying to figure Ma out. Good luck with that, kid. Then he pushes his feet against the floor. The chair bobs up and down. He does it again and beams at us.

Ma smiles back at him. I wonder if she was like this with me and Nan when we were babies. She looks . . . relaxed. Calm, almost. Happy?

Because Dad's got the adoption under control and this is all short-term?

"Ma, I might not have him for much longer . . ." I say again. Less than twenty-four now.

"We shall see what we shall see," she says enigmatically. "Look what else I brought. This was your favorite book when you were little. *Busy Timmy*." She hands me a little yellow book with a redheaded kid on the cover. Since he's, like, three or something, I can only hope Timmy wasn't busy with the sorts of things I got busy with in later years.

Nan starts giggling. Cal's now actually bouncing, pushing his legs down and bobbing in the air higher and higher.

"I bought him some clothes too," Ma tells me. "Yours were pretty much all stained, so I don't have many hand-me-downs from you."

Yup, there's a theme here. I trashed my bouncy swing and my wardrobe. Soon she'll tell me I wrecked hotel rooms and smashed toy guitars.

"You could even coordinate your outfits."

Uh, hell no. "Thanks, Ma. This was . . . this was awesome of you to do."

She blinks at me for a second, her face startled, then says briskly, "Well . . . naturally. He's just a baby. He can't help how he got here, can you, Calvin?" She has that singsong voice. Cal's into it, though. He pauses in his bouncing and gives her his smile, then goes back to hopping up and down and up and down.

"He pretty much got here the usual way, Mommy," calls Nan from the kitchen.

"Nanette Bridget! We don't need to discuss that sort of thing. You both know what I mean. The sins of the fathers shouldn't be visited on the innocent."

As it turns out, Ma has also brought food, some big sticky-roll-type things. They have about eight cups of sugar in a single bite, but they taste good with the coffee Nan's made. Cal bounces and beams at us, and we eat. It feels like we're a family. Surreal.

Chapter Forty-five

TIM

Hester being Hester, she doesn't leave me be in my bubble-world with Cal and the good stuff. She texts:

NOT COMFORTABLE WITH THE WAY WE LEFT THINGS.

UNDERSTAND THAT YOU'RE ANGRY BUT THERE ARE TWO SIDES TO THIS.

WANT TO HAVE A CONVERSATION LIKE ADULTS.

After the last one, I text back, totally misspelling because I'm furious. Is that what we air? Not seenin huge materity level going on here.

The phone immediately rings as Alice is coming in the door with Chinese food.

"I am his mother," Hester says in a low, trembling voice. "You don't have the right to act like you have all the power here. Maybe you don't have any at all."

I slam the phone down.

Call Hester back. Apologize. Alienating her is stupid.

Twelve hours or so left, if there wasn't some lab disaster or it didn't get lost in the mail on the way.

• ○ • ○

Go to three meetings on Tuesday and that takes up four hours, when you factor in travel time to and from (which I do).

Take Mr. Garrett to physical therapy and a meeting afterward. Five hours.

Alice catches me checking my computer and drags me into the shower. Don't know how much time that takes up, because it's not long enough, even though the hot water comes to an end long before we do. We use up two bars of soap, though.

"You don't actually have to do this, you know. No one's making you," Nan offers. We're chowing down on ice cream at Doane's, downtown in Stony Bay. Nan's got some god-awfully large banana-split-type thing, and I'm all about the chocolate and coffee double scoop.

"Good thing, right? If someone was trying to make me, I definitely wouldn't do it." I position Cal, who's slumped on my lap, away from Doane's biggest draw, Vargas, the candy-corn-attacking robot-chicken. He gave me nightmares when I was little, worse ones when I was tripping. Cal keeps peeping around my shoulder, letting loose a blood-curdling yell, hiding, then peeping again.

Nan points with her spoon. "Seriously, no court is ordering a test. If you wind up keeping him, if you don't have to prove parentage for some adoption deal, what does it matter?"

"*Raaah!*"

"*Shh.* Just don't look, Cal. You were the freaking snake in the Garden of Eden about this, Nano. All 'he could be any-one's baby'. . . Now I'm not supposed to find out? Besides, it's too late. They'll send an e-mail tonight. Or tomorrow."

She stirs her ice cream, reducing it to a mud-colored soup. "You could delete it. Without reading it."

But the thing is? I couldn't. The voices that have told me to make things easier on myself or avoid the truth—they've always lied to me.

Congratulations! It's that E-Z! Double click on the link and follow our instructions to get the facts on your paternity relationship!!

Two exclamation points, seriously? They're awfully cheery about this.

My mouse hovers over the link.

Then I push it away, off my mouse pad. Turn off the monitor.

I'm alone in the apartment, except for Cal, who's crashed at the moment.

Jase is at school. Nan too. I could text and ask either of them to ditch—but that seems like bad karma.

I could take it over to the Garretts', sit down with Mr. and Mrs. G.

I could even call Hester, since this involves her just as much as me. Maybe a whole lot more.

Meh. Or maybe not.

I move the mouse into position again. Move it down the screen. Click. Click again.

ALICE

The apartment's dark and cold when I get in, at almost eleven o'clock at night. "Tim?"

No answer.

He's fast asleep, curled on his side, Cal tucked against him. Tim doesn't stir, but Cal's eyes open and he stares at me. I rest my hand on his red curls.

"Good news," Tim says, his voice thick with sleep. "He's yours."

I laugh quietly. "And?"

"Don't know yet." His hand catches mine. "I thought I might need a shoulder and his is not quite up to the job."

"Very broad shoulders here," I offer, sitting down on the bed beside him. "Freakishly, really. Joel used to tell me I'd make a great linebacker."

"But I *am* officially a high school graduate. Passed the GED test . . . so there's that."

I'm kissing him and saying it's great—and it is—and he stops me, fingers on my lips. "I need to just do it, don't I, Alice?"

I nod.

"Just do this," he repeats, slides up to a sitting position next to me, pulling Cal with him, standing up, moving to the computer. "One click. Simple. E-Z."

He settles in the chair, shakes the mouse so the blue screen lights up.

His hands slide under the baby's armpits. Cal strains toward him. Tim rests his forehead against the baby's. Takes a breath. Hands Cal to me.

"Want me to do it? You can hold him and I'll—"

He shakes his head, clicks on the line, reads out loud: "E-Z Gene, the finest and least expensive OTC paternity kit offers you blah, blah, blah . . . the analysis seeks matches of the allele number values between the alleged father and child . . . you can be included as father with as few as one allele match . . . exclusion involves . . . Jesus Christ, where's the link?"

He clicks, shuts his eyes, opens them.

I close my own.

Silence.

"Did you look?"

Silence.

"Tim?"

Chapter Forty-six

It's not babysitting if it's your own child.

"I guess—" Swallow once. Again. "I was babysitting. After all."

I'm reaching for Cal, and Alice's eyes are all shiny with tears. Beautiful colors in those eyes. I'm wiping at them with the edge of Cal's blanket. He's grabbing at the other edge and trying to stick it in his mouth.

"*Raaah?*" Now he's reaching for my nose.

That little wrinkle between his eyebrows, those worried lines, just like mine.

But obviously not mine.

I put my thumb against them anyway, smooth them out.

"*Shhh,* Cal. You're good. I'm here."

More tears running down Alice's face, but at least she's not sobbing out loud. I keep mopping at them with the corner of this navy blanket, one of the few things I bought for him, along with the dead duck toy, to replace Hester's many modes of sock monkeys.

If Hester keeps Cal—which she has a right to do and I . . . I . . . don't—I won't be able to protect him from the stupid monkeys anymore. I won't be able to protect him from anything.

Alice hands me the baby, turns away for a minute, wiping

her eyes. Cal wiggles closer and I hold him, maybe too firmly, judging by the angry squeak.

Then somehow I'm on the bed with Alice facing me, the kid in between, and her arms around both of us and it would be good to throw up or cry or do something now, but nothing's coming.

Grateful for Alice's silence. Glad she isn't saying she's sorry. That her arms around me are enough. Almost everyone I know would say something. I can hear all the voices.

Nan: Oh, Timmy. I knew there was something not right about this. But you don't have to tell anyone . . .

Jake: You find your family in unexpected places.

Ma: This little one can't help how he got here.

Pop: You're well out of that disaster. You couldn't have handled it anyway.

Jase, Samantha, Mr. and Mrs. Garrett: We're here.

Dominic: C'mon over. I'll teach you how to take apart the engine of a Harley and put it back together again. That you can control.

Waldo: Blowing in the wind through the long strange trip it's been.

Hester: I had no choice. Now we can both move on.

"So," I say.

Alice takes a deep breath, but stays quiet, tightening her arms around us.

"I can cross both 'Most likely to never graduate from high school' and 'Most likely to be a teen father' off the list. Efficient, right?"

"Leave room to write in 'Most likely to get it right in the end,'" Alice says.

So *that's* when the goddamn tears kick in.

Chapter Forty-seven

TIM

Time, which was dragging its ass like hell when I waited for E-Z-Gene to come through, is now on fast-forward.

So, no, Hester's not going to keep the baby. Cal. Who I guess is Calvin from now on. Or whatever name his new parents come up with. Waldo, and this adoption lady Pop found, and Pop—who is no longer technically in a position of authority here but who never lets that slow him down—big picture—are meeting in Waldo's living room, and Hester and I are ordered to get snacks or make tea or just stay out from underfoot. After all the "be a man" stuff, we're supposed to be good kids and do as we're told.

Old Alex Robinson has to sign off on the "Affidavit of Paternity" now that he's done his own E-Z test and found out all his alleles are where they should be in order to claim Cal as his kid. Which he has to do so he can go through more legal stuff to "Renounce Paternity" once the adoption is under way. Is it me or is this effed up? Like marrying someone so you can divorce them.

But Alex has no problem with all this, except that he has some exams coming up and needs to get his wisdom teeth removed, so he's doing it all long-distance, since that works out better for his schedule.

Better for his health too, really.

Dick.

"I wish it had been you—if that helps," Hester says now.

I nod, say thanks, although it actually doesn't make much difference one way or another what she thinks or wishes or wants.

To the last, "I just don't get you," will be Hester's and my theme song.

Kind of like me and Pop.

As we were walking into Hester's this morning, he pulled me aside for a second. "Er . . . Tim."

Then, of course, the requisite cell phone check, looking-off-into-the-distance thing. Finally. "It's . . . good that you have the ability to admit that this is not your mess to clean up and to walk away. That shows maturity."

He looked me in the eye then, with this expression I don't think I've ever seen on his face, like he was actually waiting to hear what I had to say.

The weird thing? Got nothin'.

I've thought, all this time, that it would mean a lot if he could say he was proud of me. This was as close to that as it's probably going to get. But—it's like getting a prize in a contest you didn't enter. Because actually, Pop, what showed maturity was my *not* walking away.

"If I'd known what I know now," Hester says, "I would have had you with me in the delivery room."

There's an opportunity missed.

"I'm sorry you ended up getting hurt," she adds. "I never meant to do that. Even though having you around in this made me feel much less . . . alone, if I had it to do over again, I wouldn't have gotten you involved."

"I wouldn't want that," I say.

She's concentrating on making coffee, measuring out the grounds in this methodical, scientific way, but when I say this, she looks up, studies my face. "You really wouldn't, would you? If I could go back in time, I couldn't say the same."

My automatic Hester-fury, that anger that comes out with her so damn easily, hovers, then recedes. For the first time, I think it's a damn good thing Cal is going to be adopted. Neither his mother nor his real father wants him. He'll never have to know that.

"So strange," she adds. "There were moments in this whole thing when I thought . . . it would make things better if you and I were a couple. That it wouldn't be this embarrassing 'teen mom' story if that happened. But you didn't fall in love with me. You fell in love with Cal. You really were . . . are . . . his father. In all the ways that mattered."

Here's where I should probably—hug her or something. "Yeah, um, thanks. Hester. I know this—all of this—sucked ass for you. I'm—"

Sorry? That sticks in my throat. Fuckin' Alex Robinson should be the one spitting that out.

She's looking up at me with those big question-mark eyes, just like Cal's—she's *his* mother—and I lick my lips, swallow, find the words. "I wish things had gone the way you planned. I hope they do from now on."

For a second, my hands hover at her shoulders—my old problem: what do I do with my hands? A question I didn't have to ask when they were full of Cal.

I didn't know what I was doing when I first got him. I didn't understand how he worked at all. By the time I handed him back, I knew. I knew what cry was hungry, angry, tired, lonely. I knew when he needed something to hold in his hand or to put in his mouth. I knew when to hold him and when to put him down. Maybe it isn't that Pop didn't try those things with me— maybe I was just always at some frequency he couldn't turn his dial to. Not his fault, and not my own. I'm lucky that wasn't me and Cal. I would have missed a lot. And I'll take missing him, for a long time or even forever, over having missed that.

"Hester, we need you in here," that Mrs. Crawley calls, poking her head into the kitchen. "Hello, Timothy. You're still here? We're all set—you're free to go."

Back to my normally scheduled life.

Epilogue

ALICE

"Yours to command. Where's this mysterious place you wanted us to go?" Tim asks, rubbing his hands together because, of course, no gloves. The car heat's on, but the window's open, and he has to raise his voice to be heard over the swish of the tires.

"Would it be mysterious if I told you? Just go left when I say and right when I say."

"As you wish."

I planned this—rehearsed it—the way I used to do with my "It's been great fun but we're done" kiss-offs. But still. For most of the drive to McNair Beach, I look down at my gloves, pull them off, push at my cuticles, unzip and rezip my coat, fiddle with the heat. When I start drumming my fingers on my leg, Tim puts his hand over them. "Alice, what's going on?"

I swallow.

"Do I have to dare you? Say it."

I squint over at him, then back down at our hands, the knob of his wrist bone, his slightly chapped knuckles. Finally: "I deferred Nightingale Nursing again. Take this right, here."

Tim glances at me, frowning. "But, but—you accepted. You were in, you were set—"

For the first time since I made the call, a stall, hitch of my breath.

But . . . Yes. Because now I have a choice, my own choice, instead of just doing what I *have* to do. Even if it looks like the same thing.

"Still set. I just told them I'd see them next fall."

"Are . . . are you doing this . . . Who are you doing this for, Alice?"

"For me. Look, it just makes sense. They can't promise housing, and that's a huge deal when it's New York City—and they can't positively guarantee my student loan anymore—and this way I'll have another semester at Middlesex Community to get more experience on the floor, I'll be around for the new baby, and Dad's great but, you know, he has a ways to go, and Garrett's isn't going to run itself, so it's simply—"

"Was I a factor in this decision?"

"You were in there."

"I was *in* there? Was it good for you too?"

"Gah, Tim."

They've cordoned off the parking lot at McNair Beach, so we park in what's basically a snowdrift right outside. You can see a sliver of ocean—barely—through the path between two high dunes, snow piled on sand, looming like the Pyramids against the pewter sky. The low-hanging clouds, snowfall over, are lifting, giving way to muted light slanting through.

We sit there. Tim's hand still around mine. He smoothes his thumb from my knuckle down to my wrist, head ducked, ginger hair flopping onto his forehead, curling a little at the back. His lips are slightly pursed, like he's about to whistle. But, silence, doubly quiet in the winter-still hush. Just the brush of his thumb. The crinkle of his parka as he shifts a little toward me. I lean back, smile, get an answering grin, dimple deep.

"You know we have to hit the beach," I say at last.

"We do, huh? You win the race to the breakwater. I'm forfeiting."

But he climbs out of the car anyway, comes round to open my door, which takes some doing—snowdrifts and all. The snow gets into the top of my boots as we trudge along, it's higher than my knees in some places, and the wind starts rising again, whipping our hair back. Tim holds up his hand—stop—then struggles through the drifts until he's standing in front of me, bends down, pats his shoulders with the palms of his—*still* ungloved, of course—hands. I wrap my arms around his neck—"No choosing this moment to throttle me, Alice"—my legs wrap around his waist, he scooches me up onto his back, and we head toward the bay.

For a few minutes all I hear is the rustle of our parkas, Tim breathing a little hard (I loosen my grip), but then as we get farther up the path, the roar of waves, loud in my ears. High tide. But so different from the sparkling green-blue of the summer sea. We reach the top of the bluff, the angry ocean in front of us, waves beating hard, foam churning, deeper gray than the sky, pounding against the packed sand, then the *shhh* of water drawing out to sea, dragging stones, surging forward again.

I slip off his back, take a few steps forward, and Tim snags the hood of my parka and turns me around, flush up against his coat, wet with blown snow. I expect a kiss, but instead he puts his freezing cold palms against my face and says, "I haven't been here since I was here with you. That was a good day."

"It was." I search his face. His eyes are set on me, the same intense slate color of the sky today. I smile. "It was also exactly two and a half months ago. Give or take."

"Riiiiight . . . ?" He drags the word out. Shuts his eyes for a moment. Then says, "Um. Can you cut the mystery now? Historically, girls telling me about timing like this . . . makes me . . . nervous."

"No! Not that. God, Tim. We didn't have sex on the beach that day, for God's sake."

"Well, no, but—"

"Geez, it's not that. It's just, kinda, our anniversary. Sort of."

He starts to laugh, eyebrows raised. Then his face goes serious. "I think you're pushing it, date-wise, but I know what a sentimental fool you are. Pussycat." His face cracks into another smile, lighting the whole damn sky.

"Cut it out. Here."

I slide my hands up his arms, press the back of his neck, warm over the chill of his coat, until he leans down, exhaling a sigh against my cheek, my lips catching his, his mouth drawing away for an instant, then a sharp tang, tart and sweet; his tongue tastes like lemon drops, his latest sugar fix.

"So . . ." I whisper, catching my breath.

"Yeah. So. You know I'm not patient." His hands tighten on my back, then slip down, low on my back, lifting me higher so our faces are level and our mouths align perfectly.

"So far, I've given you a nicotine patch, some sneakers, and a paternity test. You suggested a tie for our anniversary, but I . . . I figured I owed you something more romantic."

"Alice . . . I kind of thought the whole deferring thing was, like, all the gifts for all the Christmases forever. That was plenty. But I'll . . . um . . . cherish this. Whatever it is."

I pull away from him, step back, my boots crunching on a shell beneath the snow. "I've been back here since that day we were here. Once. A few weeks ago. Thinking. I walked all the way." I point far up the beach, to where the spit of land curves.

"Impressive."

"Anyway." I unzip my parka, ignoring his lifted eyebrows, take out the contents of the inside pocket, curl my fingers around it. It's warm from my body heat. "Anyway. I found this." I drop it into his hands, a reddish slate stone, ocean-worn, shaped roughly like a heart. "It's got this little hollow, see, and you can rub it—kind of a calming thing—when you . . . need something to do with your hands. You say you still don't always know what to do with them. And I know you're definitely *not* taking up whittling."

I finally look at his face. His lips are a little parted—also faintly chapped—his eyes as calm and . . . tender . . . as I've ever seen them.

"Thank you," he says quietly, and puts it into his pocket at the same time he leans forward for another kiss, this one just a touch of lips, potential promised, bargain sealed.

"Although I notice you didn't wrap it."

"I'm too cheap to buy wrapping paper. Besides, why hide it and make you work for it? It's coy "

TIM

Hard to believe, but true: I actually marked it on my calendar. More what Alice would do than me, but yeah, X marks the spot in December when Pop's deadline is officially up.

X for expiration date.

Which would be today.

When I made those lines on the calendar, with the only pen

I could find—running out of ink, all kinds of symbolic—that's what it was: The day the ticking stopped and the bomb went off.

Standing here now, towel on, fresh out of the shower, I do this body-check thing—part of Alice's new skills for staving off panic attacks. No wetness from my eyes, though I've been pretty much a wuss lately. No strangling tangle of barbed wire in my throat. No bomb fragments tearing through me, cluster-exploding through tissue and bone. I feel those things, sure, but not like before, not usually—not anything Grape-Nuts and having had Alice in the shower with me wouldn't help. And except for the X, this space on the calendar looks just like the others.

Just another day.

Well, except it is Christmas Eve, so there's that.

And my first visit to Cal in his new digs, so there's also that.

I guess as adoption processes go, this one went fast. Didn't seem like it to me, or to anyone probably, except Alex Robinson. I knew right away that the choice of prospective parents was right, but Hester was . . . indecisive, Waldo a little inscrutable with his advice, and Pop, who had his fingerprints all over the thing when the ball started rolling, extricated himself when my "job was done."

The more things change . . . right?

After the day I handed Cal over—which I don't want to think about, thanks—I tried to give the new family of three time to settle in so they could bond and get comfortable together and be, you know . . . family.

Lasted three spaces on the calendar—or two and a half days if I'm being completely honest. So, I'm still working on the patience thing. But, as Dominic would remind me, aren't we all?

Visiting Cal someplace that isn't the garage apartment with people who aren't me in charge of him?

Yeah.

Well.

I change my shirt three times. Seriously. Like I'm going to a fucking job interview. This is a kid who's gotten just about every body fluid there is on my shirts—even blood, 'cause as I was suiting him up on Turnover Day, he bashed his nose hard into my collarbone and got this nosebleed and this tiny bruise—so I handed the kid over looking like a prizefighter who'd lost a round.

After the shirt dilemma, I actually make a goddamn list, partly because my brain keeps doing this blank-out thing. Maybe there is a little shrapnel in there from deadline day.

1. Drop off Christmas presents to Ma, Pop, Nan. This is the first year in who-the-hell-knows that I've actually done the present thing, so I figure whatever I give is a bonus. Picture of Cal in Santa outfit for Ma. Picture of Cal and me snapped in front of Vargas the candy-corn-attacking chicken for my sister—Cal's screaming and Nan's laughing nervously. Picture of Cal, Nan, and Ma for Pop, with card telling him to put it in his office. Because I'm still an asshole.

2. Go to a meeting. Which I'll need after this visit to my parents' house.

3. See Cal at Jake and Nate's house. It'll be fine. I've been there before, for Chrissake.

4. Then home. Christmas Eve at the Garretts'. I don't know what that even means. With luck, Alice for a sleepover? That may be pushing it, the night before Christmas, but hey.

5. Then the next few squares of the calendar, then the next calendar, which will not be the babes on bikes one Joel left behind.

ALICE

I'm sort of getting a rhythm going with the whole Christmas cookie production. Okay, we're out of some things—the semi-sweet chocolate chips I bought yesterday, for example, but flexibility is key and all that.

I'm working on it.

Harry comes up behind me, grabs the spoon out of the cookie batter, and slurp-licks it all over.

"Knock it off!" is barely out of my mouth before he's rushed to the sink, spat out the batter, and started spraying water from the sink nozzle over his tongue.

"It's not that bad. That's what you get for eating raw batter!"

"Oh barf. A hundred times barf," Harry gasps out, wiping his tongue on a dishcloth.

"I'm sure it's not that bad," Mom says from her seat at the kitchen table, where she's trying to sew cotton balls onto a flesh-colored leotard, size 2T, because Patsy's a sheep in this year's church Nativity play. We had them all glued on, but Pats kept finding the costume and plucking the balls off.

"Shorn Sheep Patsy," Dad said cheerfully, when Mom unexpectedly lost her cool about this. "It'll work."

Mom wiped her eyes with the heel of her hand. "We're just lucky if she's not Rabid Coyote Patsy."

"Grrr," Patsy contributed.

Now she's butting her head against my leg saying, "Hon where?" and my cell phone is ringing (Brad—not picking up), and Duff's tried the batter and is saying, "Is this chocolate . . . or is it *excrement?*" and Jase and Joel are coming in from some sort of brother-bonding workout session with that eau de sweaty boy with a splash of coffee and an undertone of bacon.

Joel picks up one of my early cookie attempts and tosses it Frisbee-style at Jase. "Think fast."

But Jase is checking his phone and it hits him in the chest and bounces off.

"Penalty! Now you have to eat it." That's Duff, singsong.

"Hysterical, all of you," I say. "I'm going for a run. Make your own damn cookies."

TIM

At Ma and Pop's front door, ever festively decked out for Christmas with a herd of stuffed reindeer heads. Just the heads, mind you, mounted on the door, with these shiny black eyes and stuffed white antlers. Like Rudolph's revenge: The Christmas all of the other reindeer finally got what was coming to them. Crack my knuckles, knock, only a second before I'm swept in by Hurricane Ma.

"Goodness! Don't be shivering out there—but for heaven's sake use the mat and don't tramp snow all over the good carpet."

Awkward doesn't begin to cover the five minutes I'm there, in this room with its shiny-mirror lake, open-mouthed Christmas Chorus Dolls that actually look as though they're screaming, not singing. And more pinned all over the tree.

Ma shouts, "Nanette!" and Nan comes on in—with Troy—from the kitchen, where they were, apparently, baking brownies, because why the hell not.

"For non-pharmaceutical use only, man."

Shoulders braced, fire pit back in my stomach, waiting for Ma, for Nan, to ask, or say, anything about Cal or his new parents. But they don't. Nan's hug is a little on the Heimlich maneuver side, and Ma pretty much has an aneurysm about a rip on the shoulder of my parka, but other than that, no dramarama and I'm nearly out the friggin' door and—

"Your father wants you in his study."

Fuck.

The thing is, I can just . . . not go. *You can choose where your feet take you, man.* That's Dominic again, who's like my own little Jiminy Cricket, Portuguese fisherman style.

But I go. Because, whatever.

The more things change . . .

Pictures restored to the desk, no snails in tank though (!), Pop doing a cell-phone check. It's like that stopwatch he clicked on back in August, ticking to D-day, cryogenically froze the whole exhibit.

"Yo, Pop," I say, not sitting down on the couch. "Merry Christmas."

He puts down the phone, lowers his palm, the "sit" gesture for dogs.

Do I get a treat if I do? Can already feel Bastard Tim creeping in, running through my bloodstream.

For the first time, I notice that the size of his chair positions him automatically higher than anyone on the couch. Plant myself there anyway, arms outspread along the top, ankle crossed over knee.

Fine. Pop can win the Great and Powerful contest.

He clears his throat.

I clear mine. Run my finger around the inside of my collar.

Neither of us says a thing for a sec. He picks up a pen, initials something, then drums the end of the pen against the chair arm.

Tap. Tap tap tap. Tap.

"You've done what you needed to do," he says after the requisite eon.

Pop has to be the one to mention Cal?

"The college fund stays in your name. I'll keep paying your health and car insurance. The allowance ends, because you're eighteen now, but the others are yours. To keep. Merry Christmas."

I'm rising before he's even finished, right when he says "ends," and step up close to the chair. A flash in his eyes—alarm, maybe.

"Thanks," I say.

That earns me a swivel of the chair to put the phone down.

"But, I'm set. Nano can have my share to help with Columbia, if she gets in. 'Roar, Lion, Roar.' Merry Christmas."

"I thought you were done making rash decisions, Tim."

Now I'm out the office door and he's trailing me, even after I call bye to Ma and Nan—and Troy—and hit the front steps.

Snow coming down, again, the wet kind that clings to your clothes and hardens, there's this whisk of wind, and flakes blow down my collar. The trees shake, and glops of snow splat onto the street. The piles on the sides of the road are already that dirty-brown-sugar shade.

I turn to face Pop just as he skids on a patch of ice. Grab his hand to balance him. His fingers splay out, like he's still falling instead of holding on. He gets his balance back, reaches into his blazer pocket. For the cell phone? Fifty bucks? But his hand comes out empty, and he looks at it for a second, while I slide into the car, buckle up.

"Buy Nan a college education, Pop. Buy Ma a milkshake."

So, yeah, we're being given our privacy, even though no one calls it that. Jake has to stir something on the stove and his partner, Nate, is on call and must return a message or two. So it's Cal and me, me and Cal, in the living room with the big-ass Christmas tree and the menorah and glass-fronted case in the corner full of worn baseballs and old-style gloves.

As Jake leaves the room, he glances at me, then puts Cal into this saucer-type thing instead of into my arms. Maybe giving Cal back after being on the other side of the hand-off is also hard. Already hard.

Cal fists and unfists his hands, arms out, his "pick me up" thing, says, "Bob!"

"Already forgotten my name, huh?"

His nose looks better, bruise still there. He's wearing this new outfit, like jeans and a button-down shirt, which has this big drool-oval on it. No socks, though. They're lying like road-kill near the couch. Still likes to get as naked as possible, this kid.

Sure enough, now he's trying to stuff the collar of his shirt into his mouth. I pull it out and he clamps down on my thumb with his two sharp bottom teeth. When I pull it away, he goes for my nose, chomps. "*Yow*, Cal."

"Bob," he says, muffled, because his mouth is full of nose.

Maybe that's his new name.

None of my business.

Right?

I fucking hated the name Calvin from the get-go. Now I want to tattoo it on the kid's arm so it will stay, stay, stay.

Time to go.

So I call to Jake and he comes out of the kitchen looking disheveled and pissed off.

I automatically apologize for whatever the hell I've done. He shakes his head, smiling at the floor, then at me. "What, you think I'll make you run ten times around the track the way I did when you were a mouthy middle-schooler?"

That would be easier.

Turns out he's all bent out of shape because Nate baby-proofed the burners and Jake can't figure out how to turn them on.

I kiss Cal on top of his red, fluffy head, do a swift chin-swipe drool-off with the bottom of my shirt, and hand him over like Hester used to, all speedy like he's scorching my hands, and beat it out the door with Jake trailing behind like Pop, but not.

Say the Merry Christmas thing, thank-you-for-letting-me-visit, and don't ask what they're planning to call the kid.

And then Jake asks me that very question.

"I'm, uh, fine with Calvin. Actually."

Weird look from Jake, and it turns out that the question was what do I want Cal to call me.

"Uncle Tim? Just plain Tim?" he offers.

"Whatever works, as long as it's not Bad Example Don't-Be-Like-Tim."

"As long as it's not Wait, Who's Tim?" Jake corrects, and pulls me in for a half hug, and I let him.

"Waiting for someone?" I ask around a grape Tootsie Pop—my latest addiction.

Alice flushes, sweaty at the temples, hot as hell in black ski-type pants. "Just"—*pant*—"shoveling." Halfway up one side of the driveway, she's left a cleared path, although the Bug is a hump of snow, and the van has all its scrapes and dings frosted away.

She bites the thumb of her mitten, pulling it off, wades through the snow and takes me around the elbows, looking me in the eye.

"So? Cal? You? Jake and Nate? How'd it go?"

Just shoveling, my ass.

I wonder how long she's been out here. Her eyelashes are frosted, her lips look chapped, and she's already cleared the path to the garage steps.

Oh, Alice.

I pop the pop out of my mouth. "Well, you know. It was

touching. Poignant. We all wept. Cal had made me a home-made present, since Christmas was coming. It was a used dia-per, but you know, it's the thought that counts. Jake and Nate and I all gathered around the booze-free Wassail Bowl and sang 'What Child is This?' or, no, '*Whose* Child is This?' And then—"

She puts two cold fingers over my lips. "Tim. C'mon."

I shrug. It's snowing kinda hard again, and snow's piling up on her white knit hat and the shoulders of her bright red parka, her nose a little pink. Alice in Wonderland, winter style. We should go inside and warm up—something to look for-ward to—but instead I shove my hands into my pockets, stamp snow off my boots, then try to wrestle her for the shovel—

"Tim!"

"Yeah, Cal has this awesome room—huge—and Jake and Nate are all jazzed, and there are eight million presents under the tree, and since the last stuffed animal I bought for the kid turned out to be a dog toy, he's coming out way the hell ahead. The whole house is already kid-proofed and shit, and all's well that ends well or whatever." I bend, shovel some snow, manage to toss a few loads of it to the side before Alice puts one foot on it and slides her re-mittened hand up my shoulder to where my pulse jumps in my neck.

"That all sounds great. Can I have the no-bullshit translation now? Or do I need to get the talking stick?"

"Same moral. He's in a good place. It's the Right Thing."

"And?"

"And it's going to suck. For a while. I'll live. Got a lot to live for, Hot Alice."

• ◦ • ◦

At some point, I'll need to tell Alice more. About the college money, and that I'm basically broke now. But of all the "challenges" we face, I don't think there being no chance of my being her sugar daddy is going to be one of them.

So, yeah, I trail after her toward the Garretts' house. I can see Patsy at the door, her breath making this little circle on the glass, her hands—bigger starfish than Cal's—plastered against it.

Christmas Eve at the Garretts'. Like I said, I don't know what that means.

Not Ma's special whiskey-spiked eggnog, dinner at the club, that weird a cappela group that always sings there, Nan's tense white face, some chick in green velvet that I run into and try to charm out of her pants on my way to the punchbowl or the head.

And an evening I mostly don't remember.

Things will be different tonight.

Because of the previews I've already had this winter, I know about some things—the fire, well-built because Jase built it and he's like a freaking architect with the logs. That popping sound when sparks fly out. Hot cocoa and cider. Alice in blue pajamas and this fuzzy robe that manages to be just . . . lovely on her. Harry and Duff, who have gone around with their faces red and white and sticky for the last week, candy cane junkies on a bender. That wet-dog mitten smell from wool stuff drying in front of the fire. Mr. Garrett reading these stories and doing all the voices, even if he skips huge parts that might possibly scare George.

Those other times I've sat in front of the fire at the Garretts', I've had Cal, and spent most of my time negotiating lap space with Patsy, and trying to make sure the kid didn't eat a popcorn kernel or get too close to the fire. It'll be different tonight.

They have to have a double row of stockings to fit everyone. There's one for me too. One for Cal. We weren't sure the adoption would come off before Christmas.

But I have a feeling there would have been one there for him anyway.

Yeah, so—nothing gets lost. Cal isn't, and not just because he'll still be a little part of my life. I get to carry him with me, the way you do all your memories and mistakes. He started out a mistake I had no memory of, and he wound up being, well, my kid.

Maybe thinking any one person can show up and give you all you need is as much of a delusion as thinking you can find truth in a bottle. Maybe you can just find what you need in little pieces, in people who show up for one crucial moment— or a whole chain of them—even if they can't solve it all. Maybe this is the secret of big families, like the Garretts . . . and like AA. People's strengths can take their turn. There can be more of us than there is trouble.

ACKNOWLEDGMENTS

Every day I find more people to thank in this writing life of mine. Every letter I get from a reader, notice from a blogger, comment or question from a librarian—my gratitude is boundless. There is no way I would be here, and enjoying it so much, without the time and effort and kindness of all of you.

All of you—starting with my erudite, extraordinary editor, Jessica Dandino Garrison, who always knows what I, or my characters, love scenes, and books themselves, need before I do, and stands ready with adjectives, plot ideas, exclamations, questions—and cupcakes. Her contributions go far beyond the call of duty—she's invaluable.

And Penguin Random House in general, a mighty army at my back—Lauri Hornik, Namrata Tripathi, Dana Chidiac, Jasmin Rubero, Maya Tatsukawa, Lily Malcom, Kristen Tozzo, the awesome Tara Shanahan, and truly everyone in Sales, Marketing, Design, Managing Editorial, Production, and Sub Rights who has a hand in the life of these books. The careful, cautious, and kind Regina Castillo. The talented Theresa Evangelista. So many magicians behind the scene.

Christina Hogrebe—my agent/miracle worker/thoughtful critic/judicious story and business advisor and friend of the bosom to both me and the books. You have been, from the start, one of the best and brightest and most amazing of all my lucky breaks. Thanks are inadequate. Gratitude = endless.

The rest of the JRA team—most especially Andrea Cirillo, Meg Ruley, Rebecca Sherer, Jessica Errera, and Jane Berkey.

A huge shout-out to all the friends of Tim, who believed in this story and this boy from the get-go—my peerless Plot-monkeys: Shaunee Cole, Jennifer Iszkiewicz, Karen Pinco, and Kristan Higgins. Yes, the fabulous KH, as remarkable a friend as she is a writer—generous beyond words with her time and kindness, ever willing to crawl into the trenches with me, Tim, and Alice, and drag the good stuff out.

Heartfelt and hearty thanks to Deb Caletti, Trish Doller, Jennifer Echols, and (again) Kristan Higgins for their kind, kind comments about this book.

Friends near and far who read, listened, and supplied car suggestions, medical details, "guy" translations—particularly Alicia Thomas, whose cut-to-the core critiques made this a better book. Huge thanks to Kim and Mark Smith, Paula and Roy Kuphal, the mighty awesome Apocalypsies, and the FTHRWA critique group, particularly Ana Morgan, Amy Villalba, and the late Ginny Lester.

Of course, always, my father, my brother Ted, Leslie and Grace Funsten. Colette Corry—who spent endless hours with me and Tim. Tina Squire, friend of a lifetime.

Brian Ford—once my teacher, now my friend and fellow writer, funny, acerbic, generous and wise with his comments, critiques, and questions—who never failed to say "show it to me" when I struggled over a scene, and spent almost as much time in that tent as the characters and I.

Finally, the ones who fill my every day with laughter, love, laundry, and flat-out joy, my husband, John, and K, A, R, J, d, and bookworm C—you're everything to me.

Keep reading for a teaser of
MY LIFE NEXT DOOR.

A BOY. A SECRET. A CHOICE.

MY LIFE NEXT DOOR

Huntley Fitzpatrick

Chapter One

The Garretts were forbidden from the start.

But that's not why they were important.

We were standing in our yard that day ten years ago when their battered sedan pulled up to the low-slung shingled house next door, close behind the moving van.

"Oh no," Mom sighed, arms falling to her sides. "I hoped we could have avoided this."

"This—what?" my big sister called from down the drive-way. She was eight and already restless with Mom's chore of the day, planting jonquil bulbs in our front garden. Walking quickly to the picket fence that divided our house from the one next door, she perched on her tiptoes to peer at the new neighbors. I pressed my face to the gap in the slats, watching in amazement as two parents and five children spilled from the sedan, like a clown car at the circus.

"This kind of thing." Mom gestured toward the car with the trowel, twisting her silvery blond hair into a coil with the other hand. "There's one in every neighborhood. The family that never mows their lawn. Has toys scattered everywhere. The ones who never plant flowers, or do and let them die. The messy family who lowers real estate values. Here they are. Right next door. You've got that bulb wrong side up, Samantha."

I switched the bulb around, scooting my knees in the dirt to get closer to the fence, my eyes never leaving the father as he swung a baby from a car seat while a curly-haired toddler climbed his back. "They look nice," I said.

I remember there was a silence then, and I looked up at my mother.

She was shaking her head at me, a strange expression on her face. "Nice isn't the point here, Samantha. You're seven years old. You need to understand what's important. *Five* children. Good God. Just like your father's family. Insanity." She shook her head again, rolling her eyes heavenward.

I moved closer to Tracy and edged a fleck of white paint off the fence with my thumbnail. My sister looked at me with the same warning face she used when she was watching TV and I walked up to ask her a question.

"*He's* cute," she said, squinting over the fence again. I looked over to see an older boy unfold himself from the back of the car, baseball mitt in hand, reaching back to haul out a cardboard box full of sports gear.

Even then, Tracy liked to deflect, to forget how hard our mother found being a parent. Our dad had walked away without even a good-bye, leaving Mom with a one-year-old, a baby on the way, a lot of disillusionment, and, luckily, her trust fund from her parents.

As the years proved, our new neighbors, the Garretts, were exactly what Mom predicted. Their lawn got mowed sporadically at best. Their Christmas lights stayed hung till Easter.

Their backyard was a hodgepodge of an in-ground pool and a trampoline and a swing set and monkey bars. Periodically, Mrs. Garrett would make an effort to plant something seasonal, chrysanthemums in September, impatiens in June, only to leave it to gasp and wither away as she tended to something more important, like her five children. They became eight children over the years. All approximately three years apart.

"My unsafe zone," I overheard Mrs. Garrett explain one day at the supermarket when Mrs. Mason commented on her burgeoning belly, "is twenty-two months. That's when they suddenly aren't babies anymore. I love babies so much."

Mrs. Mason had raised her eyebrows and smiled, then turned away with compressed lips and a baffled shake of her head.

But Mrs. Garrett seemed to ignore it, happy in herself and content with her chaotic family. Five boys and three girls by the time I turned seventeen.

Joel, Alice, Jase, Andy, Duff, Harry, George, and Patsy.

In the ten years since the Garretts moved next door, Mom hardly ever looked out the side windows of our house without huffing an impatient breath. Too many kids on the trampoline. Bikes abandoned on the lawn. Another pink or blue balloon tied to the mailbox, waving haphazardly in the breeze. Loud basketball games. Music blaring while Alice and her friends tanned. The bigger boys washing cars and spraying each other with hoses. If not those, it was Mrs. Garrett, calmly breast-feeding on the front steps, or sitting there on Mr. Garrett's lap, for all the world to see.

"It's indecent," Mom would say, watching.

"It's legal," Tracy, future lawyer, always countered, flipping back her platinum hair. She'd station herself next to Mom, inspecting the Garretts out the big side window of the kitchen. "The courts have made it absolutely legal to breast-feed wherever you want. Her own front steps are definitely fair game."

"But why? Why do it at all when there are bottles and formula? And if you *must*, why not inside?"

"She's watching the other kids, Mom. It's what she's supposed to do," I'd sometimes point out, making my stand next to Tracy.

Mom would sigh, shake her head, and extract the vacuum cleaner from the closet as if it were a Valium. The lullaby of my childhood was my mom running the vacuum cleaner, making perfectly symmetrical lines in our beige living room carpet. The lines somehow seemed important to her, so essential that she'd turn on the machine as Tracy and I were eating breakfast, then slowly follow us to the door as we pulled on our coats and backpacks. Then she'd back up, eliminating our trail of footprints, and her own, until we were outside. Finally, she'd rest the vacuum cleaner carefully behind one of our porch columns only to drag it back in that night when she got home from work.

It was clear from the start that we were *not to play with the Garretts*. After bringing over the obligatory "welcome to the neighborhood" lasagna, my mother did her best to be very unwelcoming. She responded to Mrs. Garrett's smiling greetings with cool nods. She rebuffed Mr. Garrett's offers to mow, sweep up leaves, or shovel snow with a terse "We have a service, thanks all the same."

Finally, the Garretts stopped trying.

Though they lived right next door and one kid or another might pedal past me as I watered Mom's flowers, it was easy not to run into them. Their kids went to the local public schools. Tracy and I attended Hodges, the only private school in our small Connecticut town.

One thing my mother never knew, and would disapprove of most of all, was that I watched the Garretts. All the time.

Outside my bedroom window, there's a small flat section of the roof with a tiny fence around it. Not really a balcony, more like a ledge. It's in between two peaked gables, shielded from both the front and backyard, and it faces the right side of the Garretts' house. Even before they came, it was my place to sit and think. But afterward, it was my place to dream.

I'd climb out after bedtime, look through the lit windows, and see Mrs. Garrett doing the dishes, one of the younger kids sitting on the counter next to her. Or Mr. Garrett wrestling with the older boys in the living room. Or the lights going on where the baby must sleep, the figure of Mr. or Mrs. Garrett pacing back and forth, rubbing a tiny back. It was like watching a silent movie, one so different from the life I lived.

Over the years, I got more daring. I'd sometimes watch during the day, after school, hunched back against the side of the rough gable, trying to figure out which Garrett matched each name I heard called out the screen door. It was tricky because they all had wavy brown hair, olive skin, and sinewy builds, like a breed all their own.

Joel was the easiest to identify—the oldest and the most athletic. His picture often appeared in local papers for various sports accomplishments—I knew it in black and white. Alice, next in line, dyed her hair outlandish colors and wore clothes that provoked commentary from Mrs. Garrett, so I had her down as well. George and Patsy were the littlest ones. The middle three boys, Jase, Duff, and Harry . . . I couldn't get them straight. I was pretty sure that Jase was the oldest of the three, but did that mean he was the tallest? Duff was supposed to be the smart one, competing in various chess competitions and spelling bees, but he didn't wear glasses or give off any obvious brainiac signals. Harry was constantly in trouble—"Harry! How could you?" was the refrain. And Andy, the middle girl, always seemed to be missing, her name called longest to come to the dinner table or pile into the car: "Annnnnnnnndeeeeeeeeee!"

From my hidden perch, I'd peer out at the yard, trying to locate Andy, figure out Harry's latest escapade, or see what outrageous outfit Alice was wearing. The Garretts were my bedtime story, long before I ever thought I'd be part of the story myself.

Continue reading for an exclusive bonus scene starring Jase and Samantha!

⁓

"This is the single most awkward moment of my life," Jase's sister Andy says, as he wheels his Mustang into the sweeping driveway of Hodges.

"I'm sure it's not!" Okay—not helpful. Catching sight of Andy's pained expression in the rearview mirror, I add, "I mean, this is not even awkward. It's just different. That can seem awkward. Which this isn't."

Jase ducks his head to hide a smile, reaches out and squeezes my knee—part thank-you, part quit-while-you're-ahead.

"I mean"—I twist around to face her—"it's the Freshman-Sophomore Annual Costume Ball. It's supposed to be awkward. You've seen every teen movie ever made, right?"

"Now I wish I hadn't." Andy sounds muffled. She's sunk so far down in the cramped backseat that her knees are in front of her mouth.

"That him? Your date?" Jase asks, as we pull up to the fake fortress that is my prep school. This year the Costume Ball theme is . . . Sherwood Forest. Hodges is massively overdecorated, firepits blazing and teachers with fake battle-axes guarding the portcullis.

Yeah, my high school has a portcullis. We won't even get into the moat—where tonight, there are actual swans.

"Jesus," Jase says, scanning the premises. I realize with a jolt that he's never been here before. After our whole long hot summer, together as much as we could be, we're just barely getting used to the separateness of fall.

"Oh my God. That's him. Over there by the— Oh God," Andy says. "This is the wrong costume. This is the wrong move. This is the wrong school. Why did you let me wear this, Samantha?"

"He's wearing green tights," Jase offers.

"You look terrific," I say, twisting around again for one last check. "Don't forget your bow and arrow. Check out all those cookie-cutter Maid Marians. You're Will Scarlett. Nailed it."

"If he tries anything—" Jase starts. "You have your cell, Ands, right?"

"Jase! Don't even," Andy says.

"God knows I don't want to, but—"

"Or you could just pour boiling oil on him." I squint up at the school towers—where there do seem to be large, menacing cauldrons poised. Hodges lives for realism.

Andy's date is tapping on the side window. Not only tights but a jaunty red feather in his hat.

Jase gives me a quick almost eye-roll.

"Points for authenticity," I say.

"Any final words of advice?" Andy leans forward to peer into the mirror, edging a pinkie under her left eye to remove a smudge of mascara, then scrubbing a finger over her teeth to make sure there's no lipstick stuck there. Outside the car, her date shuffles awkwardly from one foot to the other.

"Don't accept any drink from the punch bowl," Jase says.

"Duh, Jase. What about you, Samantha? Brothers are so useless."

"Someday this will all be funny."

"I can't even tell you how not promising that is." Andy pushes the lever to flip the bucket seat forward, nearly hurtling me through the windshield.

"Slow and steady, Ands," Jase says. "Jesus." He rubs his fingers across my forehead, even though it didn't hit anything, his thumb brushing over one eyebrow, then the other. Then, gliding it down, he gives my chin a slight nudge, as though angling me for a quick kiss.

"At least wait until I'm out of the car!" Andy says, with a long-suffering sigh.

She opens the door, and the guy—what's his name again? Wait, isn't that Kyle from last summer? Post-it-note Kyle? Reigning champ of how to break a girl's heart with office supplies? I thought . . . But he reaches in and takes her hand, pulling her up onto the stone-paved walkway.

"Make good decisions!" I call. Then to Jase: "I feel like we should have taken pictures."

"There's only so far I'm willing to go with the 'now we're role models' scenario," Jase says. He leans across me, though, one last look out the window at his little sister. But Andy's already joined a group of couples, all similarly decked out in outfits that will embarrass them later, if not right now.

Jase settles back, shifting into first gear, then gunning the car unusually fast. I scoot closer, to the edge of my bucket seat, slide my palm up over his shoulder to the nape of his neck.

Wow. Tense much? His neck muscles are rigid.

I glance behind us. "God. Junior prom last year. I went with Michael—Kristoff. I told you about him. He got all emo halfway through, started talking about the sickening entitlement of the privileged class, and insisted we leave and go back to his McMansion and make out because he was stressed."

Jase laughs, easing into a stop at a red light. "I'm so glad it's now, not then. Top down?"

"Absolutely," I say, and he cranks something on the side, lowering the windows with a slow, jerky motion, then more of the same as the convertible hood folds back into the well of the car. We both tip our heads back, breathing in the clean nearly night air, a little smoky with some early fall barbecue.

"Did you go to your junior prom?"

He seems to be exhaling, more relaxed the farther we get from Hodges. The place has that effect on people.

"I did," he says. We turn onto the main road, passing a carful of what appear to be court jesters. Including hats with bells.

"With . . . ? The theme was . . . ? You had a great time . . . ? You've blocked the whole thing out?"

"With Lindy."

Ah, yes. The only girlfriend of Jase's I've heard about. But there have to have been more. I mean, come on. The last of the sunlight is picking out the summer blond streaks in his brown hair. He's got that little furrow between his eyebrows he gets when thinking or concentrating . . . or remembering.

I wait.

"And the theme was . . . " He squints. "Um—Rock and Roll Is Here to Stay? Lindy wore this, uh . . . big skirt thing."

"Like a poodle skirt?"

"Yeah!" he says, as if shocked that I guessed. "It had a dog on it. Also a security tag. That should have tipped me off, but I was too busy being embarrassed about the hair gel. Mine. But she insisted. I mean, she put it in."

Right. Shoplifting Lindy.

"I'm so glad it's now, not then . . ." I say, my index finger finding that crinkle between his brows, pressing it away. He shivers, flashes a smile, then back to eyes on the road.

"Plus, she insisted I bring along my guitar."

"The guitar you have yet to serenade me on."

"That's the one," he says cheerfully. "So, your prom—theme?"

"American Gothic."

Sharp burst of laughter. "Overalls? On the guys?"

"And pitchforks!"

"Authentic!" he says, "Good time had by all?" He cocks an eyebrow at me.

Flashback to Michael whispering in his darkened room that I'd be happier if I took my apron off and got comfortable.

"Nope, not me."

I've been so busy just enjoying being with Jase, in the car, the breeze rushing by us. I've barely noticed that we've headed through town, past Main Street, off Route 3 into the older, more peaceful part of Stony Bay, where the scattering of small split-level houses are set way back from the narrow road, shielded by trees. Now we're bumping along the hilly, pitted dirt lane that leads to Aspen Lake.

Word at Hodges has always been that this is the "hook-up hangout" for the public school kids. But once again, just like the last time we were here, the parking lot, the lake itself . . . all ours. We both climb out of the car. Jase reaches out his hand, takes mine with a quick squeeze. The wind rises, ruffling his hair, flicking goosebumps down my arms and legs.

"Want to?" he asks, nodding his head toward the water, rippling silver-black in the gathering dark. The huskiness of his voice skates over me, then pools deep, igniting a whole different kind of shiver.

"I don't . . . have my suit." In contrast to his low tones, my voice is unnaturally high. I'm not nervous. It's just . . . just . . .

"The water's warmer than the air," he assures me, pulling me in, tight and hard, and I laugh.

"It's possible there may be a few other heat sources," I say.

"There could be." He steps back, shrugging off his shirt, stepping out of his jeans, kicking them away. He grins, cheerfully unselfconscious, and here I am, slowly unbuttoning my own shirt. Which would be a whole lot sexier if it weren't my Hodges white oxford with the crest on the pocket. At least I'm not still wearing the beret.

My hair catches on the back of my bra, tangling in the hooks. Jase leans forward, his fingers slow and sure across my back, unhooks it while bending his lips to my shoulder.

Oh. Wow.

He's standing close to me, so much taller, when my kilt comes off. Ridiculously, I start to fold the clothes—look up at him, see his eyes locked on me. Then I smile, toss my clothes randomly into the darkness.

If you're breaking the rules, he told me the first time we swam together, it might as well feel like it.

Now, like then, it feels both dangerous and the safest thing in the world.

"One last swim!" Jase calls, going for a straight run into the lake, then a shallow dive. He bobs back up, flicking his hair back, treading water, droplets splashing silver-bright off his arms.

"You know that's what they always say right before the grisly death in horror movies," I shout after him. But I wade knee-, then hip-deep.

"Meet you at the float!" His crawl slices a path through the dark water. For an inhale, an exhale, I stand, watching, digging my toes into the silty sand.

Then I dive too.

The jolt of cold yanks my breath away. I thrust up to the surface. The icy shock of water cuts against the still September heat. Swim team competitiveness kicks in then, and I duck under, propel myself fast, faster until I reach out to touch his elbow, glide my fingers over his back. But before I can he's already standing on the raft, shadowed against the sky. The straight line of his shoulders, the solid tension of his stomach . . . I climb out and lean up against him, pressing against his wet skin. He pulls me even tighter so I'm sealed against him.

"Our first date," he says into my wet hair. "It was this. Here. Remember?"

"Technically, our first date was on my balcony."

"Okay, technically—but not officially," Jase says, shifting to look at me, gaze moving slowly from my face to my toes, then back up. After a moment, he shakes his head, takes a few paces back, as if he needs just a little space. The float slopes under him. I sit down at the edge, feet dangling, and after a minute, he joins me, tangling his toes with mine. "The balcony—that was curiosity. Testing the waters. "

"Or your climbing skills. And the sturdiness of the trellis outside my window."

"Or those. Nothing whatsoever to do with the girl I was climbing toward. Nope. Nothing." He leans back, flat against the old wooden float, laces his hands behind his head, closes his eyes.

The raft rocks gently. "I've wondered . . . why that night?" I ask. "I mean, why right then? We'd been neighbors for years. You'd seen me before—"

"You mean I'd watched you before."

"Okay, creepy."

Jase rolls over on his side, smiling. "For ages."

"Yeah, not helping." I prod him with my knee.

"I'd wondered why you were out on those particular nights—but not others. What was happening inside your house. Or what you were looking for. That night, I guess I was done speculating." He shakes his head, his dark waves already drying. "I'm not sure I can really . . . I don't know if I have the right words for it."

"Those'll do," I say. He reaches out, tracing the outline of my forehead with his index finger, looking at me, eyes intent, seeing everything I can't say.

"I hate that we're selling my house—that I'll be on the other side of town." The words are out before I'm done thinking them.

"Samantha," Jase says, still looking at me, "dinky-small Stony Bay? That's nothing. Six miles. I've run it. Easily."

"Right, right. Faster than a speeding locomotive, no doubt."

"You could swim it. Just as easily. If the roads were rivers."

One of those abrupt New England breezes shushes past us, fluttering and shaking the aspen trees on the sides of the lake. They rustle, drier than a few weeks ago. I move closer, breathing in the sweet, peaty smell of the water, the lingering whiff of shampoo and sunscreen coming off Jase's skin. "What about next year?"

"It's next year. We don't need to figure it out yet."

Last week, my mom left a stack of college catalogs on my dresser. None for schools here in Connecticut. Most were West Coast—California,

Oregon, Washington. One in London. One, actually, in China. Good God.

I love that Jase thinks next September is far away. But, truth, it isn't.

Pressing further forward, I slip one leg in between his, nudging his thighs apart easily, lake water still damp on my skin. And his own. He presses his knees closer together, capturing me.

"So when's the actual move?" His voice has this relaxed, fake-casual sound to it that I recognize. It goes with what our friend Tim calls Jase's "Who me? I'm just a dumb jock" Jase Bland Face. He does get it, then— the tick-tock toward next fall and everything after. But Jase will always believe in the happy ending.

"The move? Apparently yesterday." Then I tell him everything— Mom picked me up at school and drove to our new place, this insanely sterile condo on the hill that overlooks Stony Bay, with no more explanation than "Here we are!"

I'd known it was coming—SALE to SALE PENDING to SOLD on the sign outside our house—but suddenly it was a done deal. New paintings, all new furniture. "It's like she vacuumed away our old life, just ordered a fresh one from Pottery Barn."

"Jesus," he says, tightening his legs even harder around my own. "Good thing I've got a firm hold on you."

"Notice I'm making no move to get away. Whatsoever."

Jase shifts closer, nudges my chin up with his. His lips both playful and intense, coaxing, inciting, at the corner of my mouth. "Sam," he says. I feel the warmth of his breath, the heat of him against my cold skin. Shiver again, head to toe, low in my stomach.

"You have to kiss me now," I tell him, and feel his smile as his mouth finds mine.

"Have to," he whispers back. "Want to. Need to."

There are so many things I can think of that I need and want. Someday. Some way. But, in this moment, all the most important ones are here and now.